Against the Empire

The conflict between the Galactic Empire and the planet Accord's tiny, uppity Ecolitan Institute has been chronicled in *The Ecologic Envoy* and *The Ecolitan Operation*.

Now that conflict explodes into the battles and triumphs of *The Ecologic Secession*. At this pivotal moment, under the leadership of Jimjoy Whaler—former agent of the Galactic Empire, now head of the Ecolitan Rebellion—the final war breaks out.

A story of heroism and historic change, *The Ecologic Secession* brings to a hard-hitting climax one of the finest hard-SF adventures in years.

Tor books by L. E. Modesitt, Jr.

In this series:
The Ecologic Envoy
The Ecolitan Operation
The Ecologic Secession

The Forever Hero
Dawn for a Distant Earth
Silent Warrior
In Endless Twilight

L.E. MODESITT, JR.

The culmination of the Ecolitan Trilogy.

THE ECOLOGIC SECESSION

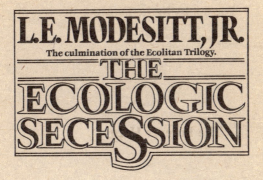

A TOM DOHERTY ASSOCIATES BOOK
NEW YORK

This book is a work of fiction. All the characters and events portrayed in it are fictional, and any resemblance to real people or incidents is purely coincidental.

THE ECOLOGIC SECESSION

A Tor Book
Published by Tom Doherty Associates, Inc.
49 West 24th Street
New York, N.Y. 10010

Cover art by Wayne Barlowe

ISBN: 0-812-50348-1

First edition: July 1990

Printed in the United States of America

0 9 8 7 6 5 4 3 2 1

To Kristen Linnea,
for her determination,
her love,
and her desire to
do life right.

... I ...

"You really think he's the answer to all our problems, don't you?" The bronzed woman with the long silver hair stared at the Prime Ecolitan. Her face and figure were youthful under the unadorned forest-green uniform. The intensity of her green eyes and the faintest tracery of fine lines edging from the corners of those eyes contradicted the impression of youth.

"No. I never said that." Sam Hall glanced from the tall woman seated across the wooden desk-table from him. "He has talents and a unique outlook that we need."

"He's a sociopathic killer with a few stray ideals, and he turned to us to save him from his former colleagues."

"Major Wright—"

"Soon to be Ecolitan Professor Whaler, I understand."

"—understands the business of survival. He also has a deeply developed sense of ethics."

"Just about personal survival." The green eyes flicked from the floor to the half-open window. "Sam, I don't understand you. You've devoted your entire life to your ideals and to building the Institute into a force for the good of ecology. We've worked hard to avoid the usual problems of Imperial colonies, to prepare the way for a peaceful transition to independent status. Now . . . along comes Major Wright, the most bloody-handed of Imperial Special Operatives, and you order us to make sure he doesn't get killed on our turf. Given Imperial politics, that's understandable. But then you ordered me to ensure he knew everything about Accord—about the Institute—when that knowledge could bring an Imperial reeducation team down on us faster than a jumpshift. Not only that, but you want him to report that information to the Intelligence Service. So . . . we work with him and get him back where he came from, again possibly revealing capabilities we've spent decades building in secret.''

She brushed back a strand of the long silver hair, looking from the darkening western horizon to the Prime. ''Then, when he's safely out of our jurisdiction, he destroys half a planet. With most of the human Galaxy looking for him, he comes running, and again you order me to take him in. If the man had learned *anything* from us . . . but he's the same old killer. He's close to the ultimate weapon—that much I admit. He can probably destroy anything ever conceived of by civilization. We can't hide that kind of weapon.''

Whhhssttt . . . A gust of wind reminded both Ecolitans of the coming rain.

Sam Hall nodded, not agreeing, but acknowledging that he had heard her complaints. ''Who will know he's here after he returns from Timor II? Especially after Dr. Hyrsa finishes with him?'' The white-haired Prime briefly placed a square-fingered hand on the small stack of papers that threatened to lift from the polished wood.

''Sam, he's so hardheaded that even a complete cosmetic surgery won't hide him for long—not without a complete personality change. And that won't happen. Major Jimjoy Earle Wright has more blood on his hands than half the villains we scare our students with.''

The Prime Ecolitan smiled softly, looking out into the late afternoon at the thunderclouds gathering over the hills to the west of the Institute. The line of gray that heralded rain appeared as though it would arrive before the twilight—but not by much. He said nothing, steepling his fingers.

''Sam, won't you at least tell me why?''

The white-haired man straightened in the all-wooden chair, letting his hands rest on the smooth natural wood of the table. ''Times have changed. They always do, you know. The Empire's politicians respect only force—force they can see. Force they can measure in their own limited and conventional perceptions. Our biologics mean nothing to them. Does a salamander understand a jaymar's flight or stoop? Only the Imperial Intelligence Service understands the danger we pose, and, for political reasons, they refuse to tell either the High Command or the Senate.

''We lack anyone who can project force so effectively as can Major Wright. Yet that is precisely what we need. Once he establishes that Accord, through the Institute, possesses a credible military force—''

''We don't have any real space force, let alone a credible one,'' interrupted the woman. Her long bronzed fingers, with their short, square-trimmed nails, whitened as she gripped the arms of the wooden chair where she sat.

''You are forgetting Major Wright's considerable talents, Thelina.''

''Talents!'' The word burst from the Ecolitan's lips. ''You act as though he could build and command a space force single-handedly.''

Sam Hall waited, gentle smile unchanged.

''Sam, he's nothing but a hired killer. He'll never be more than that.''

''Just like another hired killer would never be more than a cold-blooded Hand of the Mother . . . ?''

Thelina pursed her lips, but the Prime Ecolitan let his words trail off.

Thrummmmmm . . .

The light in the room dimmed as the thunderclouds and rain approached. A gust of wind riffled the handful of papers on the table that served as the Prime's desk. Sam stretched his left hand and gently held them down. ''You have taken a rather strong dislike to the man. Do you know why?'' His words were gentle, almost abstract.

Thelina shrugged. ''Do you want a catalog? He acts as though nothing but death could stop him, and maybe not even that. He murdered more than fifty thousand innocents on Halston. He destroyed an entire Imperial outpost to escape—and then thought that we'd be impressed because he rescued two of the rebels the Empire was trying to kill. He still doesn't seem to understand that Accord is an Imperial colony, and that we have to watch every orbit we break. Worst of all, he takes apparent pride in being a one-man killing machine.''

The Prime nodded. ''Did you know that he's from White Mountain? Or that he had one of the highest recorded Service entrance-exam scores ever? Or that he's had his calligraphy exhibited? Or that he could have supported himself as a professional musician?''

Thrummmmm . . . thrummmm . . .

Thelina frowned simultaneously with the thunder. ''I'm supposed to be impressed?''

Sam sighed softly. "No. I just thought you might consider that there is more to Major Wright than meets the eye."

"There may be, Sam. There may be. He certainly doesn't show it. Or any of those finer qualities. And all your persuasive words aren't likely to change my mind."

The older man laughed. "Words never do. Perhaps his actions will, once he returns."

The younger woman shook her head slowly. "After he fakes his own death to get the Empire off his trail. Will it work?"

"It should. The bodies will show a complete DNA match, and that's what the Special Operatives base death verifications on. The courier is equipped exactly as when he commandeered it. All that should prove his death."

"Until his oh-so-submissive personality reexerts itself and screams to the Galaxy that Major Wright is back in business destroying real estate and killing innocent bystanders."

"Why don't you help the Major change, then, Thelina?"

She shook her head more deliberately. "A man like that?"

"Will you give him a chance?"

"Only because you ask it. Only because of you, Sam, and what I owe you."

Thrummmmmm . . . thrummmmmm . . . whhhhsssstttt . . .

The papers began to lift from the table, and Thelina swept out of the chair to close the sliding window to a crack.

For a long moment she looked out through the rain at the Institute, at the low buildings housing the laboratories, the classrooms, and the physical-training facilities. Under the low and grass-covered hills beyond the classrooms and the formal gardens were the underground hangars for the flitters—and for the other equipment the Empire did not know about, equipment no colony was allowed to have. That the Institute had developed and controlled such resources was only a legal technicality that would not have amused the Imperial Senate, much less the Imperial Intelligence Service.

The Prime Ecolitan watched her, a faint smile playing across his lips.

Thrummmmmm . . . thrummmmmm . . . The thunder rolled eastward from the mountains, and the rain dropped in sheets onto the thick green turf and the precise formal gardens.

In time, a tall woman walked down an empty corridor, still shaking her head, leaving the lean and tanned Prime looking into the darkness of the storm alone.

. . . II . . .

Cling.

"Time to jump. Point five. Time to jump. Point five."

The pilot, wearing unmarked greens, glanced over at the silent figure beside him. The other, a woman wearing the uniform of a lieutenant in the Imperial Space Force, remained facing the screens, saying nothing.

The control room flashed black at the instant of jump, that subjectively infinite blackness that ended so quickly it could not be measured.

Cling.

"Jump complete. Jump complete," the console speakers announced impersonally. "Insert course tape."

The pilot touched the console again. "Manual approach."

"Control returned to pilot."

The pilot began entering figures and inputs. A representational plot appeared in the lower right-hand corner of the main screen.

"Two plus to target. Not bad," the pilot noted to himself.

The figure in the copilot's couch said nothing. The representational screen showed the system entry corridor as clean—the only moving symbol the single red dot of the courier itself. The target—a mineral-poor planet too warm for comfortable human existence, though technically habitable—glimmered a dull silver-blue on the screen.

The remote observation station was the only other red on the screen, a technicality, since the station was in a stand-down

condition and would remain so unless triggered by certain activities or by a distress call.

The pilot checked the controls, the readouts, and then locked
the control settings. He stood up, wrinkling his nose at the faint
remainder of decanting liquor, a lingering acridity mixed with
sweetness.

With a brief head-shake, he glanced back at the screens, then
headed down the narrow corridor to the crew quarters. He carried the pouch of tools he had retrieved from the small storage
space behind the control couch.

Three meters aft of the control room bulkhead, he stopped
and slid open a cover set into the side bulkhead, toggling the
switch inside. A hatch set into the deck irised open.

After easing himself down the ladder in the low gee of the
courier, the pilot began to work.

"Power flow meter . . . check . . .

"Compensator . . ."

Clink . . .

In time he came to a black cube, which he did not touch, but
which he carefully checked, noting the model number and the
other features. He nodded.

". . . hours since power-up . . ."

Then he shook his head. ". . . stupid . . ." He stood up from
his kneeling position in the cramped power room and went back
up the ladder to the control room.

The figure in the copilot's seat had not moved. The pilot ignored the still form as he reseated himself to manipulate the
ship's data system once again.

"Time to programmed deceleration is point five," announced
the console's measured voice.

The pilot looked at the representational screen, then called up
the forward navigation screen. His fingers continued to skip
across the keyboard. Then he tapped a last key and straightened,
stretching in place and unconsciously brushing a short strand of
black hair off his forehead.

He glanced at the copilot's seat and shivered, looking away in
spite of himself before he stood and walked back down the
narrow corridor to reenter the power room.

Once on the deck below, he made several last-minute adjustments before gathering his tools and climbing back up the ladder. Then he triggered the lock switch and resealed the hatch.

His steps back to the control room were quick, his motions precise as he replaced the tools in their storage space.

"Point one until programmed deceleration."

With a sigh, he strapped himself back before the controls, not that such a low level of deceleration would affect the interior gravity of the courier. Only a slight *humm* and a barely perceptible jerk marked the beginning of the deceleration. The pilot watched until he was certain that the courier was maintaining the appropriate low-power approach to Timor II.

Then he unstrapped again. His destination was the forward crew stateroom—scarcely more than two bunks and the accompanying lockers. There a still form lay cocooned in each bunk, fully webbed in place. He repressed another shudder and closed the hatch.

Three steps away was the wardroom-common-room-galley, where he opened a package of dried rations and sipped a glass of metallic-tasting water. Methodical mouthful by methodical mouthful, he chewed the rations.

After rinsing the empty glass and replacing it in the rack, he headed forward.

Nothing had changed in the control room except the screen readouts showing the courier's progress and diminishing power reserves. The pilot sat down and waited, half alert, half resting.

"Programmed deceleration ending in point one. Programmed deceleration ending in point one."

The man stretched before calling up more detailed readouts from the courier's data banks. The readouts confirmed the accuracy of his piloting and of the data supplied by the Institute.

Cling.

"Programmed deceleration terminated. In-system closure rate is beyond normal docking parameters," the console announced mindlessly.

"Of course it is," mumbled the pilot. He pulled the estimated approach time from the system. Less than point three. "Anytime now . . . anytime now."

"This is Timor control. This is Timor control. Please declare your status. Please declare your status."

"Timor control, this is Dauntless two. Dauntless two. We have system power failure. System power failure."

"Dauntless two, declare your status. Are you disabled or operational? If possible, state your status in Imperial priority codes . . ."

The pilot waited for the computer-generated message to end.

"Timor control. Code Delta Amber slash Omega Red. Delta Amber slash Omega Red. Ship control number is IC dash one five nine. IC dash one five nine."

"Dauntless two, you are cleared to lock one. Lock one. Lock one is illuminated and marked by rad beacon."

"Stet, Timor control. Approaching lock one this time."

The pilot split the main screen, the left half for visual approach, the right upper quarter for a local representational screen, and the right lower quarter for a system-wide representational view. After that, he began to enter the manual approach profile, continuing to check the representational screens as he did so.

"Dauntless two, approach speed is above recommended closure."

"Stet. Will reduce approach speed."

"Dauntless two, approach speed is above recommended closure."

"Hades . . ." mumbled the pilot, his fingers on the controls. A flare of gold showed on the close-in representational screen as the last of usable power reserves flowed forth.

"Dauntless two, closure is acceptable. Closure is acceptable."

"Many, many thanks, you mindless machine." The pilot did not transmit his words as he continued to make what adjustments he could with the remaining power.

A single line of green flashed on the close-in screen, indicating a tiny vessel departing the station at extraordinary speed—a message torp. He noted the time absently, estimating that he had a minimum of roughly twenty standard hours to complete the conversion and disable certain station functions. Even as he mentally filed the information, his fingers initiated another minor correction.

In one moment of respite, he wiped his damp forehead with the back of his sleeve before the sweat ran into his eyes. Despite the chill of a control room where his breath nearly stood out as condensed vapor, he was hot.

Clunk . . . clung . . . cling . . .

"Locking complete," announced the courier's console. "Receiving aux power from lock."

"Dauntless two, interrogative medical assistance. Interrogative medical assistance."

"Timor control, negative. Negative."

The pilot made an inquiry through the direct data link.

The message screen responded. "Input Imperial power usage code."

The pilot frowned, then shrugged, tapping in an active code, though one which did not match the ship.

"Power transfer beginning," the screen responded.

Nodding, the pilot watched the power reserve indicator as the bar inched upward.

"Power transfer complete. Further transfer would limit station requirements."

The indicator bar rested at sixty percent, more than enough for the next phase of the mission.

The pilot stood, letting the harness retract, massaging the muscles in his temples with the fingers of his left hand, trying to relax. Finally, he retracted the control console into the standby position.

Kneading the tight muscles between his shoulders with his right hand, he walked back down the narrow corridor to the second crew compartment. There a single cocooned figure rested within the crash webbing.

The pilot surveyed the crewroom, not looking at the face of the courier's fourth still form, then bent and released the harness. He took a deep breath, then eased the figure out of the bunk and over his broad left shoulder, straightening as he did so. Wrinkling his nose at the acridness of decanting solution, he cleared his throat once, twice . . .

. . . *cccaaaCHEWWW!!! . . . CHEWWWW!!!*

He brushed the other bunk with his shoulder before regaining his balance and shifting his footing to free his right arm.

. . . *cccaccCCHEEWW . . .*

Ready as he was, the second series of sneezes did not unbalance him, but he was forced to wipe his nose on the back of his right sleeve. The soft coarseness of the open-weave green fabric relieved some of the itching.

Despite the courier's low internal gravity, he moved slowly and deliberately back to the control section.

Still avoiding looking at the face of the man who wore an Imperial flight suit and a major's insignia, the pilot strapped him into position.

As he straightened, his eyes instinctively went to the face of the silent form before the controls. The pilot in greens shud-

dered, in spite of himself, before retrieving his tools and heading
back to the lock that would lead him into the observation station.
"Jimjoy, old man, looking at your own dead face is enough to
unnerve anyone."

Once in the courier's lock, he pulled on the heavy-duty vac
suit that did not belong there and attached several tools to the
equipment belt. The others went in the suit's thigh pouch. He
had left the crew suits in their assigned lockers.

With a last check of the courier's lock, he adjusted the helmet
and tapped the plate.

Hhssssttt . . .

As he had suspected, the station pressure was lower than the
ship standard. Within the three steps he took into the maintenance lock, his suit was creating a trail of fog before the remaining condensate disappeared.

Two hatches marked the smooth gray metal of the far lock
wall. A green light shone above the right-hand one. The left-
hand hatch was dark.

He extracted a tool from the belt as he walked toward the
left-hand hatch, trying to recall the details of the standard ob-
servation/rescue stations.

In less time than it had taken him to cross the maintenance
lock, itself large enough to house the courier docked to it, he
had manipulated the fields behind the hatch controls. The heavy
door swung inward.

DANGER! INERT ATMOSPHERE. DO NOT ENTER. That was
what the plaque over the inner door read.

He ignored the warning just as he had ignored the lock on the
outer door. Shortly the second locked hatch yielded to his touch.

"This is a prohibited area. Unauthorized personnel are not
allowed. Failure to leave the prohibited area could result in extreme danger or death. Failure to leave the prohibited area immediately could result in extreme danger or death."

The man did not acknowledge the words as he toggled the
lighting controls beside the inner hatch. Less than nineteen standard hours before an Imperial response.

His steps vibrated through the heavy suit as he followed the
corridor toward the station's maintenance section. In passing, he
noted a section where planetary survival equipment was neatly
racked. After he had made the necessary alterations to the courier, he would need to remove enough equipment for four people. Remove it and store it in the courier's small hold.

He hated to spend the time, but he would not have ignored the equipment if he intended to use it, not when he was so desperately wanted by the Imperials, not when he needed them to believe his life was at stake. With a deep breath, he continued down the corridor to his destination.

The clearly marked hatchway—"Maintenance"—was also locked, although it provided even less of a challenge than had the outside locks.

Inside, he studied the arrayed equipment, mentally organizing what he would need before beginning. After a time, he lifted a rodlike device and the accompanying power line reel and strode quickly back toward the courier. The station gravity—roughly one-third gee—was enough for him to carry the equipment comfortably.

Soon a stack of equipment stood by the unopened outer lock that would gain him access to the station's hull—and the courier's as well.

"Next . . ."

He removed two items from the pile and returned to the inner area of the station, where destruction of certain monitoring and record-keeping equipment was necessary. That destruction triggered the launch of yet another message torpedo, noted and ignored by the suited man.

On his return, he forced the lock on the survival storage area and began the first of several loads of assorted material. Unlike the maintenance equipment, the survival equipment went into the courier's hold—the forward one.

When he had stowed the last survival suit, he stopped in the courier's mess, slumping into an anchored plastic chair for another tumbler full of metallic water and another set of tasteless rations. As he swallowed the last neutral crumb, he checked the time. Sixteen hours yet.

That was followed by a partial desuiting, the use of certain sanitary facilities, and a sigh of momentary relief.

With a second sigh, not of relief, he began to resuit.

In less than a quarter of a standard hour, the man in greens and the heavy vac suit stood inside the outspace lock from the maintenance space, locking the power reel connections in place, first on the rod-shaped device, then to the special receptacle inside the open lock.

He touched the rod. The indicators on the cutting laser flared red.

L. E. Modesitt, Jr.

The pilot tugged on the safety line again, making sure that the lock lines were secure before easing his way through the open hatch.

Supposedly, what he was about to do would work, according to the more obscure survival manuals that no one ever read, but he was not aware that it had ever been tried.

Inside the helmet, he smiled. In fact, the emergency conversion didn't have to work. He only had to do it well enough so that the majority of the courier reached planetside on Timor II.

His momentum carried him to the end of the line, where he steadied himself with a gauntleted hand. The dark bulk of the observation station shielded him from the direct light of Timor as he triggered the laser.

Fifteen hours to modify the courier, drop it planetside, make a rendezvous, and disappear. When the Empire eventually got around to investigating, the Service would find the bodies of the four people who had ravaged Missou Base and New Kansaw orbit control. Finish to one Major Jimjoy Earle Wright. Except that was just the beginning.

. . . III . . .

"Transmission from the observation station off Timor II, sir."

"Timor II? And . . . ?"

"The remotes indicate that Dauntless two—that's the *D'Armetier* . . . the courier taken from New Kansaw—has locked in there."

The Admiral straightened in his chair. "How good is the data?"

"Good enough that Special Ops analysis insists it's a real courier."

Frowning, the senior officer sat back in the padded chair. "That's a class four planet, isn't it?"

"Yes, sir. Marginally habitable."

"Do Service catalogs show the station as unmanned?"

"Yes, sir. But with limited repair capability."

". . . makes sense . . . Wright could gut the station with his abilities . . . refuel and be off . . . before we get there . . ."

"Sir . . . ?"

"Send a corvette. Just one."

"Just one, sir?"

"One way or another, he'll be gone before the ship gets there, if he was even there to begin with."

"You think it's a setup?"

"Given Major Wright? I doubt it. That man works for no one but Major Wright. There's no sense in taking chances. Warn the corvette crew. It could be an ambush, probably set up inside the station. Have them take their time. I'd like to see if there's any indication whether anyone else is involved."

"You really don't think so, do you?"

"No. But he's outguessed us all so far."

"What do you really expect?"

"I don't know. The time delay bothers me. He's been somewhere, and that's the real question. I doubt we'll find out that."

"But we have to try?"

The Admiral shrugged. "Have any better ideas?"

"No, sir."

"Send the corvette."

. . . IV . . .

Jimjoy shifted his weight from one side of the chair to the other. "You didn't mention psych treatments."

The silver-haired woman who stood at the other side of the small office met his eyes without challenge, but without flinching. "You didn't ask. And as I recall, you weren't exactly in a position to ask for too many conditions, Mr. tentative Professor Whaler."

He sighed. "Why? So you can ensure I don't upset the proverbial quince wagon?" His jaw hurt, and they hadn't even really started in on the real work.

"Apple cart," she corrected him, picking up a thick file from the desk beside her. She thrust the bound stack toward him. "Because you are, to put it bluntly, a borderline sociopath, with no recognizable form of unified ethics and no conscience." The Ecolitan looked at the man who sat in the hospital chair, his bandaged face so covered as to be unrecognizable.

"Strong words . . ." His headache was beginning to return.

"Do you want an accounting? A listing of the names, a categorization of the millions of liters of blood you have spilled, frozen, or cremated? It's all here, unless there's even more than the Institute could uncover."

"Ecolitan Andruz . . . I admitted I was scarcely perfect. But if you insist on turning my psyche inside out, you'll have less than nothing." He wanted to know why she was pushing the issue even before the major surgery had begun. "And why are you insisting on all this now?" A flash of pain scorched up his jawline, needling into his skull.

"You are already resisting. If you don't change psychologically, at least to some degree, the Empire will pick you up from your old profile within months. Is that what you want?"

"Do you want some lily-livered professor? With skills and no way to apply them? Is that what *you* want? No challenge to your expertise and authority? My so-called imbalance is certainly part of what I have to offer." He tried to lean back and ease the tension in his body, but the combination of the pain and the muscle relaxants made conscious control difficult—one reason that he had always avoided drugs.

"That is doubtless true, and for that you should be grateful. We still think we can improve some of your underlying attitudes without crippling your ability to act. That means knowing more about how you work. Whether you know it or not, you are paying a price for what you have done."

"So? I paid it. Not gladly, but I did." The dull pounding in his temples had become a heavy continuous hammering. He eased himself forward in the chair again, trying to concentrate on the woman.

"You really don't understand exactly how heavy a price . . ."

"You don't know everything, Ecolitan Andruz." His voice sharpened. "What do you want? True confessions of a confessed mass murderer? Tales of tragic triumphs in service of the mad Empire?"

"If you want to tell those tales . . . but frankly, I could care less. I'd rather see you stew in your own poisons." She deposited the heavy folder back on the desktop. "What you do is your choice, not mine."

"Then why . . ."

"Because the Prime Ecolitan insists you're worth saving. I agree with Sam's sentiments, but question the reality."

"Aren't *you* optimistic?" He didn't bother to disguise the sarcasm. Not only did his head ache, but he was getting dizzy.

"You wanted my thoughts. Your possibilities are only limited by the greatest pigheadedness I've ever seen."

He sighed, leaning forward and holding his head in both hands at the top of his forehead, where there were no bandages.

"Are you all right?"

"No. Does it make any difference?"

"You . . ." This time she was the one who sighed with heavy exasperation. "We'll talk about it later. I didn't mean to push."

"Don't bother."

"You're refusing?"

"No. Pigheaded, but not stupid. Accepting. I don't have to like it . . ." Lifting his head, he sighed again, softly, aware that sudden movements triggered the heavier throbbing. "When does this all start?"

"When you feel better." She touched the console, then waited. A tall and thin woman entered the room. "This is Dr. Militro. Doctor, this is . . . Professor . . . Whaler. I wanted you to meet each other now . . ."

Jimjoy stood, aware of the rubbery feeling in his legs, but determined to make the effort. "Not exactly pleased, Doctor, but . . . appreciative."

"Please sit down, Professor."

Jimjoy sank back into the chair, watching Thelina Andruz rather than the doctor.

"Professor . . . Doctor . . . I need to be going . . ." Her piercing green eyes rested first on Jimjoy, then upon the black-haired doctor.

Jimjoy only nodded.

"Thank you, Ecolitan Andruz," the doctor noted politely, turning again toward Jimjoy, but waiting until the heavy wooden door had closed. "Professor . . ."

"Call me Jimjoy."

"Very well. This is not a time for heavy analysis or deep thought. I would like an accurate summary of your background, beginning from when you can remember. You do not have to use names. We are talking patterns. First, though . . . how do you feel?"

"Honestly?"

"Honestly."

"Like hades."

"What if I meet you in your room when you feel better?"

"I'd like to start now . . . before I think too much . . ."

The doctor smiled. "Believe it or not, it won't be that bad."

"Not for me, Doctor, but for you . . . it will be hard to remain objective." Jimjoy grinned brittlely under the bandages, recalling the incidents on New Kansaw, on Halston, on *IFoundIt!*—just for starters. Maybe Thelina was right. He shrugged, then winced as the pain ran up his jawline again. "At the beginning . . . I was born on White Mountain, the

Hampshire system. That's right at the edge of the habitable zone, lots of lakes, and rocks, and ice. Short summers. My mother was the Regional Administrator. Women run most things there, except for the heavy equipment and the asteroid mining . . .''

The doctor nodded without taking her eyes off him.

...V...

19 Novem 3645
Demetris

Dear Blaine,

You've already gotten the official report on old zipless. Evaluation was stretched to the limit to list the *Halley* as operable. Even at one hundred percent, we'd be outmatched by the Fuards. I preferred the Halstanis, thank you. But their new Matriarchy seems more economically oriented. Not the guys on Tinhorn, though. Once a Fuard, always a Fuard.

Rumor has it that the Fuards have some new wrinkles in the works. Right now it's close. Our training's better, at least. Tactics, too.

Understand the great and glorious Imperial Senate turned hands down on the Fast Corvette. Reports from the faxers here don't put it that bluntly. More like: "In view of the escalated costs associated with building the FC, the Senate rejected the Emperor's request to build two hundred FCs, and instead voted for a feasibility study."

A nerdy study! Out here on the perimeter, I need another study like I need a light sloop. Seriously, what's the scoop on getting something better than old zipless? And before my kids are in Service? Not that the *Halley* wasn't a fine ship in her day, but her frames were plated before I was old enough to read about the Academy, much less go.

Helen and Jock send their best. Cindi's not old enough to, but she would if she could. Even out here, they're both a joy. Two probably is too many for someone who's "high-risk," as Helen puts it. With old zipless, she doesn't know how high.

Let me know.

Mort

. . . VI . . .

CRACK!!!

A single bolt of lightning jabbed from the towering thunderstorm that straddled the center of the lake.

WHHHHsssttttttt . . . The first dark funnel dipped toward the skimmer as he guided it between the three-meter waves raised by the storm. By the time that funnel had brushed the wave crests to the west of him and folded itself back into the thunderdark clouds, another funnel was snaking toward his skimmer, this time from the south, as the storm beat its way northeast.

Jimjoy could feel the whiteness of his knuckles on the tiller of the light lake craft, as much as he tried to relax and avoid overcontrolling.

CRRRACCKKK! Another bolt flared, even closer.

WHHHSTTTT . . .

CRACK!!

He glanced to his right, trying to catch sight of Clarissa's skimmer. Once again she had dared him, older experienced sister to younger brother, and once again he had fallen for it, going deeper into the storm pattern than was wise, just to prove he could do her one better.

HSSSSSSSTTTT . . . CRACK! CRACK! CRACKKKK!

The last flare of the lightning lashed less than a quarter kay from him, almost outside the main storm flow.

"NOOOO!" The hellish energy had not struck in the storm, where he tossed, fighting his way through and around waves he should have been able to avoid if he had only gauged the storm track correctly, but right through the blue skimmer that had almost dashed past the curtain winds and into Barabou Notch.

"NOOOOOO!!!" Not Clarissa. Not again.

"Noooo . . ." groaned the man in the hospital bed.

No one answered his groan, and Jimjoy slowly opened his eyes. The monitoring equipment focusing on him reported the change in his awareness.

"Hades . . . same dream . . . again . . ." He wanted to shake his head. Instead, he lay there for a time. The ceiling overhead was green, a pale green that reminded him of the way his stomach currently felt. Turning his eyes to the side without moving his head, he could see that the heavy wooden door was ajar. No one passed by outside.

Clarissa—how many years back? Hadn't he gotten over that? Lerra—not mother, don't call me mother—had never said one word about it. She had just gone and had Anita. Was Anita the Regional Administrator now? No, not yet; Anita was still too young. She couldn't have finished all the requirements. Besides, could she be Regional Administrator if Kaylin were the System Administrator? That was what Lerra had wanted.

He blinked slowly, feeling the wetness in the corners of his eyes, wishing it would go away before anyone came in. Dr. Militro would certainly be interested in the dream. He tried not to shiver, to push away the feelings he had felt on a slow skim back into Barabou Harbor all too many years earlier.

He slowly eased his head away from the direction of the door, wincing at the tingling in his scalp and the increased intensity of the headache he felt with the movement. The softness of the light outside indicated twilight at the Institute.

Funny, until he was actually in it, he had never realized that the Ecolitans had quietly maintained a complete hospital. Even in his previous months as a "guest" instructor, he had not noticed the facility. They hadn't so much hidden it as simply placed it within the central research complex.

Deciding to sit up, he slowly—very slowly—used the bed controls to ease himself more upright. Just as slowly, he reached for a tissue. He put it down, afraid that poking around the bandages might result in scars.

Then he noticed the stack of tapes and materials on the hospital's bedside stand. On top of them was an envelope.

He reached for it, ignoring the twinges in his head and the residual soreness in his shoulders and ribs.

A single note card was inside, and he slipped it out.

> These are the materials I mentioned. If you want to qualify as an instructor, you will need to pass an examination, both in theory and in practice, on the ecological materials.
>
> The Prime has waived, in light of your extensive experience, similar requirements in your specialties and granted you status in piloting, navigation, hand-to-hand combat, and military operations. You'll probably also receive status in electronics—practical and theoretical—and in contemporary political science, and perhaps one or two other areas. That will be enough to justify granting you the status of Ecolitan Professor . . . if you can master journeyman status material in the ecological disciplines.
>
> These tapes and the introductory manual are the beginning.
>
> The doctors tell me that the headaches will continue for several days, but represent no impairment of mental faculties and should not affect your learning, especially with your mastery of relaxation and combat meditation skills.
>
> T. Andruz

"You're all heart, Thelina. All heart." Just like Lerra. He did not even bother to sigh as he studied the pile of material. Finally he lifted the thin manual that was supposed to provide an overview.

Click . . . tap . . . tap . . . tap . . .

He ignored the footsteps.

"Well, I see you're awake even earlier than Dr. Hyrsa had anticipated. We'll be taking off the pressure bandages on your face tomorrow, I think, and we'll all get to see what you look like, Professor Whaler."

"Not really a professor . . . uccouughh . . ." The cough was almost painful, both in his shoulders and in his face. Like the nurse, he had to wonder exactly what he would look like. While he had seen the profiles and sketches, there was a big difference between art and your own flesh.

Dr. Hyrsa had been careful to point out the limitations of what she, or any surgeon, could do, given his insistence on not having his muscular abilities and coordination impaired.

"We can alter the fingerprints, retinal prints, eye color, and facial bone structure . . . improve the chin. Fix the hitch in your shoulder. It will start giving you trouble before long anyway. We can extend your legs about five centimeters with the bone we've cloned from you, but that will mean at least three months of therapy and supervised physical redevelopment . . ."

"Isn't that a risk?" he'd asked, worried about the operation failing and losing his legs or their complete use.

"Any surgery is a risk, but the leg extension is relatively simple as these things go, and our unqualified success rate is above ninety-eight percent. Broadening your shoulders is a slightly high risk, but there we have an incipient problem to correct anyway . . ."

The other problem had been the cosmetologist.

"Permanent color? Not sure I like that . . ."

"There is a slight risk, less than one case in one hundred thousand, according to the risk assessments, of triggering simple skin cancers—not melanoma. The identity chart matrices show that without a complexion alteration the other changes will not be sufficient . . ."

He had shrugged, wondering what he had let himself in for.

Now he knew. He ached all over. He had been in the hades-fired hospital for more than six weeks, and now he had headaches. He had never had headaches.

"They all say it's just a formality, Professor Whaler," added the nurse. She was white-haired and professionally grandmotherly. "And the way those Institute folks look up to you, I'm sure that you're just being modest.

"Now let's take a look at you . . ."

He put down the thin manual. It could wait a few minutes. But that was about all, from the amount of the materials Thelina had left.

His scalp half itched, half hurt. They'd warned him about that too. "And don't scratch!" Thelina had added. As if she had ever had to go through what he was undergoing. Fat chance.

". . . uuummmm . . ."

"That shouldn't hurt, Professor . . ."

"Doesn't . . . except when I cough . . ."

"Coughing's good for you. Just hold a pillow against your diaphragm if it's too much."

Damned if he'd use the pillow. Of course, Dr. Militro would point out that stoicism that served no purpose was mere masochism. He let his breath out gently and reached for the pillow laid next to Thelina's materials.

Outside, the twilight was sliding into dusk, the green of the upper hills he could see from the window fading into gray. The nurse switched on the room lights and twitched his covers back into place.

"Monitors show you're doing better than expected, and they had projected a quick recovery. Haven't had one this special for several years."

"Do you have many cases . . . like . . ."

"Like you, you mean? Distinguished scholars who want to start all over . . . not many. One every year or so. There was— but I really shouldn't discuss it, they say. They never tell us who you were, only who you are. That's better. Always look to the future. That's where we'll have to live.

"Is there anything else you need?"

"Something to drink?"

"You can have just a little bit of this." She went out into the corridor and returned with a paper cup. The cup was the first disposable thing he had seen at the Institute, either this time or in his earlier visit. For the hospital, it made sense.

"Now just sip this slowly. If it stays down, and it certainly should, you can have some clear liquids for dinner. You should be back on solid food by tomorrow. That's really just a precaution until Dr. Hyrsa is sure everything has stabilized."

He almost shivered. Stabilize? What was there to stabilize?

"Don't worry. If the doctors here can't do something, they don't. It's just that simple." She checked the nonintrusive monitors again. "I'll be back with some more to drink later."

He looked out at the twilight on the eastern hills, picked out a single star winking in the gray-purple sky, then tried to identify buildings from their outlines. He had been brought in quietly, through an underground tunnel that he had never suspected even existed, directly into the hospital area. He had not seen the Institute itself this time. The outlines looked as he had remembered them, although some of the trees were now bare in the local winter.

So far as he knew, only Thelina, the cosmetologist, and the doctor had actually seen his unchanged visage. None of them, himself included, had seen what he looked like now, or would look like once he healed and the various swellings and stiffnesses subsided.

But the dream . . . he had not thought about Clarissa's death since . . . since at least pilot training . . . perhaps longer. He started to shake his head and stopped in mid-shake as both scalp and headache warned him.

With a sigh, he retrieved the manual. Studying and learning were less dangerous than remembering. He'd understood that for a long time.

. . . VII . . .

Jimjoy sat on the edge of the hospital bed, letting his bare feet touch the warm tile floor. As the nurse stripped the last of the pressure bandages from his face, he tried to keep his shoulders relaxed. They began to ache every time he tensed up, and he wondered if they always would.

"Just a moment, Professor Whaler, and we'll have these off. Then you can see how you look." Her voice contained the professional brightness he had always associated with nurses. He didn't know which was worse, the false booming heartiness of the men or the blithe cheerfulness of the women.

"What I look like," corrected Jimjoy.

"Dr. Hyrsa is very good, Professor. You look fine. A few small bruises, but that's all. Those heal quickly. No more than a week or two at most."

Thud. The wadded-up bandages echoed in the container set by his feet.

"Bruises?"

"Not exactly. They look like bruises, but they're not."

Thud. More bandages clunked into the container.

How many kilos of dressings had he been wearing on his face alone? The shoulder dressings had been disposed of several days earlier.

"You hair is coming in nicely."

Scrttchhh.

"Ooooohh . . ."

"That was a little sticky, but that was the last one . . . and

Dr. Hyrsa did a nice job—as usual. I'll even bet you'll be pleased with the results."

Jimjoy did not look at the proffered hand mirror, instead running his fingers across his face, tracing his cheekbones and his chin line. Under his fingertips he could feel the usual stubble of unshaven beard. He was supposed to have higher cheekbones, green eyes . . .

"Are you ready to look in the mirror, Professor?"

He sighed and took the lightweight mirror from the red-haired nurse, who held it practically in his face. He held the mirror without lifting it.

With another drawn-out breath, he brought up the mirror. The face was that of a stranger. Not even a near relative, but a total stranger.

He gripped the mirror tighter to keep his hand from trembling as he studied the reflected image. The face frowned at him. *His* face frowned at him.

His nose was sharper, finer, and more aquiline than his original nose. The cheekbones were clearly higher, and his chin was a touch more pointed, not nearly as squared off as he recalled. His eyes were a piercing green, much like he remembered Thelina's. But he had only a colorless stubble for eyebrows and eyelashes, and his scalp was a hairless bronze . . . or was it graying before his time? Bronze? His entire face was somehow bronzed.

Despite the itching of his scalp, he did not scratch it, but pressed the skin gently to try to relieve the sensation. He could feel the stubble of regrowing hair under his fingertips. Then he studied his hands before lifting his eyes to the mirror again. He was bronzed indeed, bronzed over every millimeter of his body.

"Are you all right, Professor?"

"Just thinking . . ."

He held the mirror closer to his eyebrows, angling it to catch their color.

"Silver . . ." His hair and eyebrows were going to be silver. Dr. Hyrsa had only told him that his hair would be lighter, much lighter. She had smiled when he had said he wouldn't mind being a blond, but she had not agreed with him.

"Silver . . . be an old man before my time."

"I doubt that. With all your improvements, you'll outlive

us all. Besides, you were in excellent shape to begin with.''

Despite her soft voice, her words and not just the professional tone in which they were delivered somehow bothered him. He ignored the red-haired nurse and turned the mirror up toward his scalp. Silver.

Hades! While he didn't look anything like he had, he'd certainly stand out in a crowd now. Taller, with bronze skin and silver hair . . . how could he ever do what he'd done before?

He put down the mirror on the rumpled sheet beside him. Thelina had silver hair, the same light bronze complexion, and could still disappear as effectively as any Special Operative.

Thelina? The pieces snapped together inside his skull. ''Nurse—did you ever work with Ecolitan Andruz?''

''Professor, I couldn't rightly say which Ecolitans I've worked with.''

''Andruz. Silver-haired. Bronzed, with green eyes, a sharp tongue . . .''

''Now, Professor, no woman would like to be characterized by her tongue . . .''

Jimjoy waited. ''Silver hair,'' he finally prompted, trying to catch the nurse's eye as she bent to pick up the container holding the used bandages.

''You must think we have a fixation on silver hair. We deal with all kinds of hair color—brown, red, black, gray. Some have been women, perhaps with silver hair. I could be wrong. I don't remember names.''

''Here,'' he said tiredly, picking the mirror up and handing it back.

''You don't like how you look?''

''I guess I liked the way I used to look more than I thought.''

She took the mirror. ''Could I get you anything to drink?''

''No. No . . .'' He looked down at the alternating ceramic triangular floor tiles of black, green, and gold. What else had the Ecolitan surgeon done? What other ''improvements'' had he blithely agreed to?

''*Whffffuuuugh* . . .'' His sigh dragged out. Even his stomach muscles still ached. And the ache in his shoulders was threatening to return at any moment.

"You need to rest, Professor Whaler."

"All I've done is lie around."

"Just swing your feet up and think about it."

"Ooohhh . . ." The involuntary exclamation as he twisted drew a quickly suppressed grin from the nurse. Although stretching out was scarcely painless, the rest of his movements were silent.

In time, so was the hospital room, except for the sound of breathing.

. . . VIII . . .

Jimjoy looked around the hospital room. One compact kit bag containing all of his current worldly possessions rested on the single chair. No flowers, no cards to take with him. Just the good wishes of Cerrol—the white-haired nurse—Verea, and Dr. Hyrsa.

Although Jimjoy had hoped that a silver-haired Ecolitan would visit him, Thelina had not shown up after she had introduced Dr. Militro. Instead, she had sent two heavy packages of instructional materials with cryptic notes implying that he learn virtually every word and concept before he would be truly fit to be classified as an Ecolitan.

Since the Institute did not provide personal fax terminals, he had not even been able to fax her. Nor did he know how or where to send a note, assuming he had been foolish enough to write down anything.

With a sigh, he picked up the kit bag. It was light enough not to strain his rebuilt shoulders, even before the weeks of rehab scheduled for him, and the weeks of conditioning necessary after that.

The room was ready for its next patient.

"Good luck, Professor," called Verea from her console.

"Thanks, Verea."

The junior medical tech with the coppery hair waved briefly.

Jimjoy pushed open the wide wooden door and stepped out into the open staircase, avoiding the elevators—the only ones he had seen on Accord.

His steps were easy. He was in terrible shape, and it would

be months before he was back in the condition necessary for the events to come. But his muscles were still there, out of condition as they were.

Stepping through the doors at the foot of the stairs, he saw two people—a young man in tans at the hospital information/admissions/guard desk and a young woman in Ecolitan field greens by the front doorway. He had met the young woman—Mera—once before, in what he was coming to think of as his second life, his service as an Imperial Special Operative. She had been his driver.

Would she recognize him in this third life?

"Professor Whaler?" asked the black-haired woman.

"The same," acknowledged Jimjoy. "And you are?"

"Mera Lilkovie, student third class."

He inclined his head to her. "Appreciate your help, Mera."

"That's what we're here for, Professor."

He forced a laugh. "Not really. You're here to learn, not to transport partly disabled staff, but I appreciate it." While he could hear the deeper timbre of his voice, would the change in pitch, combined with the physical and cosmetic differences, be sufficient to pass her scrutiny? Then again, she had only driven him once, and that had been well over a standard year earlier.

"The car is outside. Do you have anything else?" Her eyes flickered to his short silvery hair that was well beyond a stubble, but still too short for all but the strictest military organizations.

"No."

"That makes it easy, then."

She showed no sign of recognition, unless she had been instructed not to. He doubted that. She turned and held the door.

Jimjoy stepped out into the hazy noontime sunshine, still amazed at the informality of his departure. That morning, Gavin Thorson, Sam Hall's Deputy Prime, and the Ecolitan in charge of all staffing arrangements at the Institute, had appeared in his room and announced that Jimjoy had been assigned permanent senior staff quarters—at least as permanent as any such quarters were—and that he would be discharged for background briefings and rehabilitation. A car would pick him up at 1100 hours local and take him to his quarters, where a minimum of linens and furniture had been supplied. And a full set of Institute uniforms, plus a few items of leisure clothing.

Jimjoy could either eat in any one of the Institute dining

facilities or, once he familiarized himself with the Institute's supply procedures, cook his own meals.

Thorson had then handed Jimjoy his I.D., credit number, current account balance, and a folder containing his résumé, complete personal history, projected teaching load for the following quarter, his briefing schedule, and an accelerated follow-up course in ecologic and personal ethics for one James Joyson Whaler II. The material duplicated what Thelina had already provided.

James Joyson Whaler II—that was the first time he'd seen his new name in print. But why had the Institute delayed in identity conditioning?

Thorson had waited for him to absorb it. "Not that much of this should be a surprise to you, you understand, but we're asking a lot of you. Even so, the Prime and I welcome you back, Professor Whaler," Thorson had said.

"Jimjoy, please."

"Jimjoy it is."

That had been it. Now he was walking toward a groundcar to begin a new life for real—for the third time. He almost shook his head. That was another mannerism he would have to eliminate—or limit. He tried pulling at his chin. In time, perhaps he could replace the one gesture with the other.

He also had to learn his own new personal history—cold—before he really appeared in public.

"Professor, our car is the one on the right."

"Thank you." Jimjoy angled his steps toward the pale green electrocar. After opening the rear door himself, he tossed the small kit bag onto the far side of the seat and eased in. The twinge in his shoulders as he bent forward reminded him that he had been in the hospital for a reason.

Clunk. Mera shut the door behind him.

"You have not seen your quarters?"

"No, young lady, I have not. They were arranged while I was incapacitated."

"You will be pleasantly surprised." The car moved forward smoothly and turned to the right at the end of the semicircular drive. "All the new staff members are."

He looked back, noticing that the building where he had stayed bore no indication it was a hospital. It was not the same building into which he had once carried an injured student less than two years earlier. Of that he was sure.

That led to other concerns, such as exactly how many medical facilities existed on the grounds of the Institute, and how little he knew about the people to whom he had entrusted his life. Not that he had had many options.

"Exactly where are the staff quarters?" He paused, wondering how much he was supposed to know. "I've studied the maps, but . . ."

"It's not quite the same thing?"

"Right." Jimjoy nodded.

"Have you visited the Institute before, Professor?" Mera asked.

"Not in this particular life, at least." He forced a short laugh.

"You know, you must be very special. The Institute doesn't grant many full fellowships or professor's chairs."

"Especially not to former outsiders?" he asked.

"No. I think Professor Firion is one, and they said one of the senior field trainers was an outsider, but that's rumor."

"I'm probably asking a stupid question, young lady, but could you enlighten me on the differences in meaning here at the Institute between professors, fellows, and Ecolitans?"

The electrocar purred up a narrow road and by a stone wall. Jimjoy kept his face impassive, although he recognized the orchard. He had wondered where the road led, and it appeared he was about to find out.

"Well . . . anyone who has graduated from the Institute or passed the equivalency tests and been accepted by the Prime or the examining Board as proficient in all the required skills is an Ecolitan. Most Ecolitans are Institute graduates, but you don't have to be.

"Fellow actually means Senior Fellow of the Institute, and that takes longer. Professors are Senior Fellows with specific responsibilities. That's what makes you unique."

While Mera was practically begging for an explanation, Jimjoy let the not-quite-asked question pass him by. "And the quarters?" he prompted.

"Oh, just up the road here. You can actually take the footpath between the hills and along the brook and walk to the main grounds faster than going by car. That was to discourage groundcars when the last Institute plan was developed."

"And did it? Discourage the use of groundcars?" he asked with a smile.

"Not really. No one used them anyway."

The car swept between two massive pinelike trees flanking the narrow roadway, slowing to nearly a crawl as the pavement ended in a narrow stone-paved lot. The entire parking area was less than twenty meters long and not more than five meters wide. A vacant green groundcar was parked at the far end.

Terraced stone walkways paralleled the parking area and continued up the sloping terrain toward individual wooden structures set roughly ten meters apart. Each was two stories, with wide front and rear wooden decks, a sharply pitched roof, and large windows.

"You get the end unit, Professor." Mera pointed as she brought the electrocar to a purring halt beside the empty green car.

"New kid on the block?" asked Jimjoy. He looked at his quarters-to-be again. Perhaps a shade narrower than those farther uphill, but still two stories, with both decks, and the same detailed workmanship and contrasting dark and light woods—all in all, quarters probably better than those offered to all but command-class officers in the Empire. "All to myself?"

"Unless there's someone I don't know about. You certainly can invite anyone to share your hospitality." Mera turned and grinned at him. It was not quite an invitation.

"That tired of Institute quarters?" He grinned back.

"Not yet, Professor. But try in a year."

He started to shake his head, then remembered and pulled at his chin. "Remind me of that, would you?"

"I just might, Professor. I just might." She bounced from her seat.

Jimjoy moved more carefully, still not quite certain which movements triggered which pains. As he stepped out, he surveyed the area, from the neatly groomed bushes and short grass to the rows of low silver blooms growing beside the slate gray of the stone walks and steps.

Click . . . clunk . . .

"Ready?" asked the student.

"I can take that!" protested Jimjoy, realizing she had retrieved his bag.

"No problem, Professor. Suares would have my head if she learned I'd let you carry anything."

He cut his shrug short as his shoulders protested and followed her up the wooden steps. A cold breeze carried the scent of firs and the promise of rain. Overhead, the haze had thickened into light clouds. Toward the west, behind the lower clouds, lurked a darker presence.

Thrummmmmm . . . The thunder, faint as a half-played beat on a child's drum, whispered through the afternoon.

Stopping at the doorway that Mera had opened but not stepped through, Jimjoy followed her eyes. Beside the blond wooden squared arches of the front doorway was a plaque. *J. J. Whaler, S.F.I.*

"You first, Professor."

Jimjoy stepped into a small foyer, floored in narrow planks of close-grained golden wood. The walls—all the walls—were wooden. Well finished and satin-lacquered. Although the wood had been refinished for him, a few dents and rounded edges showed that there had been previous occupants.

Past the foyer, with its narrow closet for coats, cloaks, or whatever, and through another squared arch, this one without doors, Jimjoy stood in a single long room running from one side of the dwelling to the other—perhaps eight to nine meters. The center of the room was open to the beamed ceiling. The entire southwest wall was comprised of wood and glass with just enough wood to hold the glass. Each window on the upper level could swivel open, and sliding glass doors framed in wood ran in multiple tracks the width of the room.

To his right, a railed but open staircase rose to the second story, where it opened onto a loft. From what he could see, the loft joined two rooms, one at each side of the house.

He walked left, toward the open kitchen area and the dark bronze wooden table and wooden chairs—the only dark objects in the entire room. On the table was an oblong white card.

He forced himself to pick it up slowly. The message was neatly inscribed on the stiff card with a green triangle in the upper left corner: "Welcome home, Professor. Sam."

Home? That remained to be seen. White Mountain had been home once, too. And so had Alphane. Neither had been, though he had thought of each that way.

He set the card back on the table.

"Don't you want to see the rest?" Mera was smiling, bouncing slightly on the balls of her feet, still holding his single kit bag in her left hand.

Jimjoy repressed a frown. "Of course."

"Besides the deck, there's the upstairs."

Jimjoy took the staircase, his steps heavy on the carpeted runner.

"Your room is the one at the far end."

"My room?"

"The main suite?"

"Suite?"

"Well . . . maybe not a suite, but . . . you'll see."

He did. The room, with an oversized bed, a dresser, a bedside table with a lamp, and a table desk with a console and matching chair, had enough open floor space to look uncrowded. All the furniture was a light bronzed wood. The only fabrics in evidence were the forest blue of the quilt, the matching curtains on the two windows that flanked the bed, and the two throw pillows—cream—on the bed. Above the sliding glass door that opened onto the upper deck was a wood-slat shade that rolled down for darkness or privacy, or both. A spacious fresher/bathroom was visible to his left through an open archway.

His eyes strayed back to the forest-blue quilt. He swallowed. Once, twice.

"Like it?" Mera had set the kit bag next to the closet door.

"It's very . . . very coordinated."

"The Prime thought you would like the color."

"You picked out the furniture?"

"I had some help from Kirsten—she was my second-year roommate. We worked with the woodcrafters to get it right. The downstairs was left here, but the Prime thought this should be new for you."

Jimjoy did shake his head. How had Sam Hall known about the forest blue of White Mountain? A lucky guess? Not likely. The room was more to his taste than he dared to admit.

"It's . . . I like it," he finally admitted.

"Thank you. We hoped you would. Kirsten and I, I mean."

"You did a very nice job."

"I know, but it's more important that you like it. We wanted you to feel at home." She shifted her weight from one foot to the other.

"Thank you. Really don't know what else to say . . ."

"You don't have to. You're pleased . . . but I think it brings back old memories."

"It does," he admitted, "but that's not necessarily bad. I still think I'm going to like living here very much."

"We hope so."

"So do I. So do I."

"If you need anything else . . ."

"No . . . I'll be fine."

"There's a package on the counter downstairs. It has directions to everywhere and the times everything is open. Just ask anyone around."

Jimjoy followed her down the railed and open stairs, watching from the open door until the pale green of the electrocar had purred from sight.

Then he sank onto the couch, staring out at the gathering thunderclouds, listening to the winds of his own thoughts.

. . . IX . . .

27 Janus 3646
New Augusta

Dear Mort:

I'm sorry about my slowness in getting back to you, but for some reason, I just got your screen. Deeptrans is backed up again.

You're probably back out on-station now, but I'll torp this off anyway while I've got a moment. I managed to win an argument with Tech and pull new drives away from a station-keep in Sector Five and get them routed to you. The Rift hasn't been a problem, and nothing's happened in Five for a couple of decades, but robbing Peter to pay Paul will catch up with us all someday.

You guessed right on the study thing. When the cost of the FC came in, Senator N'Trosia blew quarks, and they weren't charmed, either. He yelled about two hundred years of peace and cooperation, and about how we had managed to keep the peace through diplomacy, and how there was no need for a Fast Corvette when the Attack Corvettes were still perfectly functional. Politics!

So we got a study. In the meantime, the Admiral—do you remember Hewitt Graylin, the guy who was a dec up on us, the one that set the flic records that are still standing? He's the new Fleet Admiral for Development, and he just briefed us on the Fuards' new destroyer. Why they call them destroyers and we call them corvettes escapes me. The mission's the same. Except they're more honest in their nomenclature, and their new ones are really something. Supposedly, they have instantaneous post-jump acceleration, and the ability to rejump without repositioning, plus a few other things best not gone into here. We've discussed the possibilities, so you know what I mean.

We'll keep pitching, and you try to keep the old *Halley* together. Congratulations on the not-so-recent new arrival! Don't know how I missed her or how you managed it, but that's a touch of envy. We (I) failed the gene screen. Guess that's another price for being on Old Earth. Looks like adoption if we want another. I don't know. Sandy has to think it over.

Blaine

. . . X . . .

"Professor, according to Kashin, *Theories of Warfare,* a government fully backed by a people with an ideology has an advantage over a pragmatic system. What you said seems to contradict that." The youngster with the barely concealed smile waited.

Jimjoy quirked his lips before replying. "Mr. Frenzill, Kashin included a number of qualifying statements. Do you, perhaps, remember them?"

"All other political conditions being equal . . . including real and not apparent resources . . ." Student third class Frenzill's smile had vanished.

Jimjoy studied the class. All twenty looked awake. Roughly one-third appeared to understand the argument.

"Before we go on, for the benefit of Ms. Vaerolt, Mr. Yusseff, and the remainder of the third row, I'd like to repeat the point to which he has taken polite exception. *Ideology does not win wars or battles.* Fanatics or even true believers have won wars, and they have lost an even greater number." Jimjoy paused. Three other heads showed mild interest, although Gero Yusseff was still asleep with his eyes open.

"Mr. Frenzill, what caused the fall of the Halstani Military detente?"

"The rise of the Matriarchy, ser."

"Wrong, Mr. Frenzill. That is a tautology, a definition, if you will. The Matriarchy, despite the Hands of the Mother and a strong ideological hold on the populace of Halston, had been unsuccessful for more than a generation in even gathering seats in the popular assembly.'' Jimjoy surveyed the faces.

''Ms. Jarl?''

''Wasn't the Matriarchy successful after the Bles disaster?''

''What was the Bles disaster, exactly?''

''Professor . . . everyone knows that. It was news for weeks.''

''Humor me, Ms. Jarl. Tell me what it was.''

The blonde squirmed slightly in her seat, licking her lips. ''Well . . . the fusion power station malfunctioned . . . and most of the military command was celebrating nearby . . . so no one was left to stop the Matriarchy . . .''

''Very convenient, wasn't it.'' Jimjoy watched the students shifting their weight, realizing that he was leading somewhere. ''Now, does anyone want to speculate on the probability of only the *second* power plant accident of this magnitude in recorded history occurring at a time when it would wipe out not only an entire planetary government but also the majority of the military High Command? Or the fact that the government which took over had been unable to do so through conventional means?''

''Are you suggesting . . . it was deliberate?''

''I'm not a great believer in coincidences. Are you? Would you stake your life on them, Ms. Jarl?''

''Professor?'' asked student third class Frenzill.

''Yes, Mr. Frenzill? You were about to observe that I had said ideology did not win wars, and here is a case where the popular ideology won?''

''Yes, ser . . .''

''There is a significant difference between causality and apparent results. The cause of the Bles disaster is still unknown. What gained the Matriarchy power was not its popular ideology, but the annihilation of its opposition. To the degree ideology allows you to mobilize superior resources, tactics, or commitment, it will win battles or wars. But . . . the distinction is important . . . *ideology does not win wars*. Any comments? Questions?''

There were still too many blank faces. He sighed. ''All right. Your assignment, due five days from now, is a short essay. No more than one thousand words. Take a position. Give me a logical proof of why ideology wins wars or why it doesn't. Any essay which does not support one position or the other will be failed. Any essay which repeats my argument blindly will also

be failed." Another look around the class, and he could see that
at least three students glared at Frenzill.

"Is that clear?"

"Yes, Professor."

"Now . . . beyond the question of ideology is the main point
of today's lesson. Mr. Yusseff? MR. YUSSEFF. Thank you."
He waited momentarily for the groggy Yusseff to realize he was
the focus of attention. "Mr. Yusseff, you may get the assignment
from either Ms. Jarl or Mr. Frenzill later. Since we are attempting to analyze the basis of military power, my question to you
is: Do you agree with Kashin's theorem of pragmatic causality?
Explain why or why not."

More squirms around the classroom, Jimjoy noted. Despite
the openness of the Institute, sometimes he wondered how much
intellectual challenge the students actually got. Repressing a sigh,
he waited. He liked the hand-to-hand better, but Sam had insisted on Jimjoy's undertaking the warfare course. Jimjoy suspected a lot of others could have taught it better, but he owed
everything to Sam . . . so . . . all he could do was his best.

... XI ...

The nameplate read:

Thelina X. Andruz, S.F.I.
Meryl G. Laubon, S.F.I.

With a shrug, he stepped up to the doorway.

Tap . . . tap . . . The knocks on the heavy and dark-stained wooden door were even, almost precise. Jimjoy shifted his weight from one foot to the other. He wished he weren't standing at the doorway, but Thelina had continued to avoid him, time after time. When she couldn't, she was so politely professional that the planetary poles were warmer than the atmosphere surrounding her.

The door opened silently. Jimjoy tried to keep his mouth shut. Thelina's silver hair was cut short, barely longer than his own, which, although he was overdue for a haircut, was scarcely more than five centimeters long. "Come on in, Professor." Thelina shrugged as she stepped back from the half-open doorway. Wearing pale green shorts and a short-sleeved blouse, she was barefoot.

"Professor?"

"I'm happier with titles right now."

Jimjoy followed her through a single long room with kitchen facilities at one end, including a glass-topped table in a dark wood frame, and a sitting area with chairs, two low tables with matching lamps, and a couch arrayed around a small stove at the other end. Open and railed stairs rose from the right side of

the entry door to the second level. The far wall was comprised
of two floor-to-ceiling windows and a set of French doors in
between. Jimjoy followed her out to the timbered rear deck.
Three wooden chairs were spaced around a heavily varnished
dark oak table. A single half-full mug sat on the table, and a
book—*Field Tactics*—lay closed beside it.

He glanced overhead, but, despite the mugginess and the over-
hanging clouds, he could see no rain to the west.

"Have a seat. Would you like some cafe?"

"No, thank you. A glass of water?" He took the chair opposite hers.

"No problem." Thelina slipped back through the louvered
door.

As he waited, he surveyed the deck. The pattern seemed similar to the house he had just been assigned, but he'd never been
in any of the other senior staff homes before. His quarters—or
Thelina's and her colleagues' quarters—seemed incredibly spacious for fellows of the Institute. He shook his head.

"Your water, Professor." Thelina placed a heavily tinted tumbler—no ice—on the table before him. He caught a scent of
something, perhaps trilia, before she efficiently sat down at the
other side of the table.

"How about 'Jimjoy'?"

"It lacks distinction and the stature reflecting your deep and
valuable experience, Professor Whaler."

He sighed. "What about . . . 'I'm sorry'?"

"That wouldn't be a bad start, Professor—if you really meant
it."

"I might. If I could figure out what I said that was so offensive."

"After rewriting history? You really mean that, don't you?"
She took a sip from the dark green mug. "You are even denser
than . . . there isn't an apt comparison . . ." She kept shaking
her head intermittently.

Rewriting history? Jimjoy sipped the water, trying to keep
from frowning. Rewriting history . . . she couldn't mean that.
Even if he had said something wrong or misleading in his warfare class, she had been cool to him before that. Cooler than the
water in front of him. He took another sip.

Thelina touched the book, turned it over, but left it on the
table, saying nothing, not even looking his way.

He took a third sip, concentrating on the taste of the water, a

coolness he hadn't thought about in a long time. Even without
ice it was cold. Cold and fresh. Like a lake called Newfound,
where he had stood beneath the firs sighing in the winds and
listened to the steady lap, lap of the water.

That had been a life, before . . . there, once, he had been
happy. She had been as clear and beautiful and unspoiled as the
lake itself. Christina—he wondered what might have been if he
had accepted the life he had been born to instead of trying to
escape. Yet here he was, trying for still another life . . .

"Professor?"

"Oh, sorry."

"Professor Whaler, I do believe you were kays away."

"I probably was, Ecolitan Andruz. I probably was."

"Probably?"

"All right, Senior Fellow of the Institute, Ecolitan Andruz.
You are, as usual, one hundred percent correct. My thoughts
were elsewhere."

This time Thelina was the one to sigh. "Just about the time
you start to act human, you revert to the standard Imperial pro-
tocols."

Jimjoy caught her green eyes and stared directly at her. "We're
too old for games, Thelina. And too much rides on us to have
time for games."

She returned the gaze, so directly that he finally blinked.
"Professor, that attitude is exactly what is wrong with the Empire and your thinking. First, we all die in the end. All we have
is the trip through life. Without games, without spice, and without meaning and love along the way, life doesn't offer much. It
doesn't help when you distort what really happened along the
way. And second, no one is indispensable. Not me. Not you."

. . . *thurummmm* . . . Jimjoy looked over his shoulder, toward
the west. The darkening clouds and the mist lines below the
clouds spelled an oncoming storm.

Whhhipppp . . . A gust of wind, with the scent of rain, flipped
open the back cover of the book Thelina had turned over.

"Do you want to wait for hard evidence, Professor Whaler,
or shall we retire to the living room?"

"I bow to your superior knowledge, Ecolitan Andruz." Jimjoy
picked up his tumbler and stood. "What about the chairs?"

"They'll be fine. They're oylwood." Thelina closed the book,
picked it up, and reached for her now-empty mug. She did not
look back.

Jimjoy closed the louvered door, nearly bumping into Thelina. "Excuse me." He stepped back quickly, pushing away the thought triggered by her standing so close. Why, he still didn't understand, not with her continual hostility.

Halting, he turned and watched the clouds darkening and tumbling upward even as the rain began to spatter on the deck outside. A single shaft of sunlight played upon a tree-covered mountainside kays westward. As Thelina ran water in the small kitchen, he watched the line of sunlight disappear.

"How about an amendment to my last statement?"

"No apologies this time?" She had replaced the mug with a tumbler of water. She set it on the table and eased into the chair, tucking one leg under her.

"Thelina, I am what I am. I probably should change some of that, but to apologize for what I am is hypocrisy." He sat down in the chair opposite hers and sipped from the glass he still carried. "You are right about life being a journey. That was what I was thinking about when I drifted off. But . . ."

"Surely you aren't going to claim that you are indispensable?"

"Not indispensable . . . not exactly. The universe, or most of the people in it, could care less whether you or I exist, or about what we do. The universe could also care less whether we enjoy life and the journey it represents.

"Now, I can't claim to know history the way old Sergel Firion and his staff do. But there have been times in human and alien histories when individuals have made a difference. There have been discoveries that no one else besides a single scientist has even understood for decades. There have been political actions taken, battles won, and conquests made that have changed history because of a single and unique individual." He paused and took another sip from the glass, grateful that Thelina was still at least seeming to listen.

"Likewise, some discoveries could have been made by dozens of individuals, and some battles and political actions were taken by possibly the worst of all possible candidates.

"As far as Accord is concerned, only a handful of individuals understands more than a fraction of the structural and political problems involved. You and I happen to be in that handful. Denying that is like denying"—he glanced out at the wet deck— "that it's raining outside. If we don't act, someone else will have to. Someone besides an ex-Imperial Special Operative and a former Hand of the Mothers.'' He grinned at her and waited.

Thelina met his grin blankly. ''What else have you figured out, Professor? Besides the obvious? That just makes what you did worse.''

''If you please, what did I do that was so inexcusable? And what is this rewriting of history?''

''Your whole warfare class is talking about it. How you pointed out how convenient it was for the Matriarchy—''

Jimjoy's stomach turned upside down.

Thelina stopped talking as she saw his face. ''How can you be so perceptive and so dense? You didn't even realize . . .''

''No. It was used only as an example of how ideology by itself cannot gain control, of why force is required to obtain control.''

Thelina looked at the woodstove in the corner.

He took a deep swallow and finished the water, looking for somewhere to put the tumbler besides on the finished wood of the table.

''You destroyed Military Central.''

''You gave up.''

''No price too high for you, Professor . . . no burden too great?''

''There might . . .'' He looked at her face and stood up. ''You're angry because what I've said threatens your tight little conception of the universe. Because I've put my neck on the line and think you might have to also, if you believe what you say you do.''

''How can you even suggest that?''

''Because all you do is poke holes in what I've said and done. That's easy. Lord knows I've said and done a lot wrong. But you won't accept the fundamental truth of what I've said. You didn't like it when I told you in that cell in your mining station that first principles are first. I'll admit you're right. There is more to life than the end. But the Empire doesn't think that way, as you have so clearly pointed out. If you want to preserve the idea that the journey is more important than the destination, it means putting your sweet little ass on the line. Not once, but time after time. And I still don't like games. Games are different from love, and sunsets and sunrises.'' Surprisingly, he had managed to keep his voice even.

Thelina's face was still expressionless, although her eyes looked cold.

"I'll think about what you said," he finished. "Then . . . someday when you're in the mood . . . let me know."

Thelina remained immobile in the chair, and started to open her mouth.

"Don't bother with another flip or sarcastic answer. Good day, Ecolitan Andruz." Jimjoy walked straight to the front door, not looking back, and closed it quietly behind him.

As he walked down the wooden steps, he started to shake his head, then remembered and pulled at his chin instead. The dampness and splatter of the rain were welcome, despite the dull ache in his muscles from his ongoing efforts to regain his conditioning. All he'd wanted to do was apologize, to get a warm word or two, and now he'd made it ten times worse.

He began to run, heading out around the lake and hoping that his muscles would hurt even more by the time he reached home.

. . . XII . . .

"I'd prefer your permission," stated the tall, silver-haired man.

"You have *my* permission and support, but not the Institute's. Right now the Board wouldn't support such an action."

"Why not?"

"The Governor's on the Board."

Jimjoy pulled at his chin. Nothing was straightforward. He paced around the end of the table, then back again. "That's the choke point. With the Haversol System Control gone, it would take the better part of six months to mount an attack. So long as it stays, they can have a squadron here in days."

"They couldn't otherwise?"

"Oh, they could. But with no guarantee of power reserves . . . with no clear support trail . . . blocked by the Rift . . . there's not an admiral in the Service who would want to do that. Not with the Fuards looking for any weakness. Not with the Halstanis ready to use any Imperial military action as a lever to gain trade concessions from the other independents."

"*If* what you say is right, what would keep the Empire from immediately associating the action with us?"

"We might have the best motive, but the 'accident' would be staged not to have Accord's fingerprints. The Fuards would be as likely a set of suspects as anyone." Jimjoy licked his lips, pursed them together, then waited.

"All the way out here?" The other's voice was amused.

"Right now they're everywhere."

"That takes care of the military aspect, for a little while. But why won't they replace the station immediately?"

"Immediately means six or seven weeks—five tendays—"

"I understand both weeks and tendays."

"—at the earliest. If nothing is happening elsewhere in Sector Five, and if they have a spare fusactor. That's what they need."

"They couldn't just lift one from in-system?"

"No. Civilian systems aren't compatible without rework. It could be done, but it would probably take more time than bringing one halfway across the Empire." The former Imperial Special Operative cleared his throat. "Then, if we could take out the five system control stations inward from there . . ."

". . . you've effectively buffered us. Which is fine, except that there's limited political support."

"I've been working on that, too."

"The manifestos?"

"Some of them. Someone else seems to be publishing their own . . . and there's that new Freedom Now Party. They're so radical that mere independence seems conservative."

The other man laughed softly.

"I thought so," noted Jimjoy. "Is there anyone else?"

"No, but a number of us are using several other avenues."

"Not enough people."

"Not enough we can trust—at least until you take out orbit control. I assume that's the second step."

"I need a team for that. Destruction's easy. Capture isn't. We need orbit control. Need it to act as if it were still Imperial under our control."

"Buying time."

"Exactly."

"I can provide you with what you probably cannot obtain alone—for the first step. You may be on your own after that."

Jimjoy looked into the shadowed eyes of the older man.

"You're telling me that if I act, you become the target."

"Since you asked . . . yes."

"After all you've done, I'm supposed to go ahead?"

"Do we have any choice? Really?"

Jimjoy stopped pacing. "What about Thelina? Can't she help?"

"She won't approve anything you do. Not now. Not anything that threatens me, even if it's for the long-term good. She has the resources to block you. She would. By the time you convinced her, we'd have a reeducation team here. She hates what you stand for, and you don't have time to change that.''

"I suppose not.''

"Gavin will get you what you need. Don't let anyone else know. You're having additional medical treatment.'' His eyes twinkled.

Jimjoy nodded slowly. "Are you sure?''

"No. Are you?'

"No. I don't see any other alternative that will protect Accord.''

"Neither do I. Neither do I.''

. . . XIII . . .

"Captain Erlin Wheile, Technical Specialist," Jimjoy announced to the Imperial Marine at the military lock.

"Your orders, sir?"

Jimjoy handed over the folder to the Marine technician, along with the databloc that contained far more information than the folder. The folder was for people, the databloc for his ostensible destination's personnel control system—in more ways than officially intended.

"Have a seat over there, Captain." The Marine handed back the orders and the cube and pointed to the black plastic seats through the gate to his left.

Buzz. The gate opened to allow Jimjoy to enter.

"You're lucky," added the Marine. "The next shuttle to SysCon will be locking in less than a standard hour."

Jimjoy nodded politely. "Needed some luck after the transshipping . . ."

"Getting here isn't always easy."

"Not from Demetris." Once through the gate with his ship bag, Jimjoy hesitated briefly.

"You got all the luck, Captain."

"Right."

Jimjoy carried his baggage into the nearly empty waiting area. Both an older woman wearing the insignia of a medical tech and a young man in a general technician's uniform looked up. The medical tech immediately dropped her eyes from the chunky and aging junior officer to her portable console. The technician studied Jimjoy until Jimjoy caught his eyes and held them.

After a moment, the young tech looked away.

In turn, Jimjoy eased himself into one of the unyielding black plastic chairs, setting his ship bag at his feet.

The Council was going to be upset, very upset, when they discovered what he was doing, if they discovered. They hadn't seen an Imperial reeducation team. As for Thelina—he didn't want to think about that. She might not speak to him again, assuming he escaped from the mess he was about to create.

He shifted his weight on the hard seat, glancing over at the older technician, who was engaged in some activity with a pocket console—chess, redloc, or something more esoteric. She did not react to his scrutiny, but continued to touch the tiny keys with precise movements, far too quickly for chess, standard games, or data manipulation. If she were playing redloc at that speed, even against a pocket console's memory, she was good, very good.

The technician apprentice kept looking first at Jimjoy, then at the senior technician, and then down at the scuffed plastiles. His black hair barely covered his pale scalp, and the gray of his coverall, which retained its original creases, was still a distinct and recognizable color.

Jimjoy stretched and began to consider how he might have to modify his plans once on board the system control station. The theory was simple enough. The Empire would find it difficult, if not impossible, to maintain easy access to the systems leading to the Rift without at least some functioning system control stations for repowering and replenishment.

Since jump drives and functioning fusactors did not coexist—for more than milliseconds—system control stations became essential tools for conquest or control. They had the fusactors, the long-range lasers, and the overall fleet support ability. Removing the system control stations made invasions problematical and conquest impossibly expensive. Of course, removing an orbit control station wouldn't stop a cruiser with a sunburster or a planetbuster—just make it difficult. Besides, most of the time, destroying real estate eliminated the resources you needed to control in the first place.

He pulled at his chin, looking up as another Imperial technician, female and only a shade older than the recruit, plopped herself into one of the hard plastic seats midway between the two men.

". . . friggin' screen jockey . . . cruddy bitch . . ."

Jimjoy took in the clear complexion and the angelic face with the less-than-heavenly language and stifled a grin, noting how the initially disgusted expression on the recruit's face was followed by a speculative look. The woman ignored both glances and bent down to yank her kit bag closer to her feet.

"SysCon shuttle now docking," announced the overhead speakers.

Only the recruit stiffened. Jimjoy and the two women knew the delay before the process was completed, especially if cargo and equipment were involved.

Clunk.

Wsssshhhhtttt. The familiar sounds of docking and off-loading continued for a time.

". . . glad to see some new faces . . ."

"Not like Vandagilt, you mean? . . ."

". . . I could have *died* when I saw her there . . ."

Jimjoy smiled at the chatter of the two young Marines first off the shuttle. Behind them trooped a handful of technicians, most carrying full kits.

Cling.

"Shuttle for SysCon now ready for boarding."

Jimjoy straightened, but the young recruit was quicker, making it to the lock door even before the barrier had dropped away. The senior medical technician stowed her pocket screen and shook her head as she watched the youngster's haste. The physically attractive junior technician awkwardly hauled a bulging bag over her shoulder and followed Jimjoy.

No one else entered the shuttle.

Jimjoy looked around the windowless cabin with twenty utilitarian couches and strapped his kit into the locker under a couch.

"Prepare for departure for SysCon. Please strap in. Regulations require all passengers remain in their couches during the shuttle run. We anticipate locking at SysCon in less than two stans. Thank you."

Jimjoy strapped in, then stretched out for whatever sleep he could get. He would be getting precious little of that after he reached SysCon. His eyes closed even before the shuttle had unlocked from Haversol orbit control.

"Approaching SysCon."

He blinked, trying to reorient himself. Had he really slept almost two standard hours?

The medical technician was yawning as he looked her way.

The recruit merely looked tired, and the other technician was still mumbling obscenities.

Clunk.

"Locking complete."

Jimjoy began to unstrap, thinking about his next steps.

To make an Empire work required standardization, and standardized equipment and installations led to standardized responses by standardized personnel. All of which made destruction easier. The technology, the patterns, and the weak points were always the same. Every SysCon station had the same in-depth defenses, with outlying sensors, remote lasers, and off-station patrol craft. All controls were centralized in the operations center.

Theoretically, the way to destroy a station's capability was to destroy the operations center. Unless you used planetbusters, or their equivalent, destroying the ops center meant suicide. Since he had decided against suicide on general principles, and since he had no planetbusters in his kit bag, he had developed an equivalent.

Cling.

"Personnel may use the forward lock. Please exit in single file."

Jimjoy retrieved his bag, letting the efficient-looking medical technician and the technician apprentice lead the way. The beautiful, if candid-tongued, technician rummaged through her oversized kit, looking for some last-minute item—like her orders or personnel databloc.

Swsssshhh. The inner lock door irised open. Over the shoulders of the recruit and the medical technician, Jimjoy could see that the station lock was already open.

"Step up, please."

Jimjoy eased forward as the medical technician dropped her kit back in front of the console and handed over her orders and databloc.

"Technician Meirosol?"

"Yes, Technician?"

"You're cleared to return to SysCon."

"Thank you."

"Next."

Jimjoy waited while the sentry processed the recruit.

"Next."

Jimjoy handed his orders and databloc to the sentry, a bored-looking woman seated behind a half-shielded console. Behind her, encased within a set of screens, sat a professionally intent Imperial Marine with a laser.

Jimjoy almost shook his head. The screens prevented use of projectile weapons, and the theory was that no one could get a laser power pack through the locks without triggering alarms. All true enough. But the kinetic velocity of an old-fashioned hand-thrown knife was below the threshold of the screens, and there was nothing to prevent an intruder from wearing ablative reflection thins under makeup to give himself the instants needed to disable both guards.

While there were plastic knives in his belt, he did not intend to use them, not unless the false nature of his orders was detected.

"Captain Wheile?"

"Yes, Technician?"

"You are cleared to Inprocessing. Have you been on Haversol SysCon before?"

"No."

"Take the corridor to the right. First hatch on the left. . . . Next."

Jimjoy picked up his orders and databloc, then his bag, and followed the directions he had been given, not that he needed them.

He took a deep breath as he started toward the designated hatch. As always, but particularly after his time outdoors at the Institute, the air smelled more mechanical and oily than ever.

Snnniffff . . . His nose was beginning to run, letting him know that it was displeased with the general atmosphere inside the system control station.

Ummmmmm . . . Clearing his throat didn't help. In any case, one way or another, he wouldn't be on board terribly long. After another deep breath, he stepped into the personnel section.

"Yes, Captain?"

The personnel technician looked vaguely interested, in a polite way, in the overweight officer.

"Wheile, Erlin, Technical Specialist, reporting as ordered." He handed her the orders and the databloc.

A puzzled look crossed her face as she looked at the orders, then back at him, then at the databloc. "Don't recall any inposting on you, Captain."

Jimjoy sighed. "I certainly didn't ask to be shuttled from Demetris."

"Demetris?"

"Yes, Demetris." Jimjoy's voice took on a slightly irritated tone. "Back-to-back tours like this, after all these years . . ."

"I understand, Captain, but . . . there's no advance on you. Let me check."

"The databloc should show my posting."

The technician looked at the heavyset officer, then at the databloc, and shrugged. "That doesn't—"

"At least check it—make sure I'm real."

The woman smiled faintly as she took the databloc and inserted it into the scanner. She waited.

Jimjoy could see the green light flick on from its reflection on her badge.

"It says you're real, Captain, but that still doesn't tell us what we're supposed to do with you."

"Wonderful. So what do I do? Get back on the shuttle? Return to Demetris and tell the Admiral it was all a mistake? Or will they say there's no place for me there, either?"

The technician looked apologetic. "These things do happen, Captain. Much as we try to avoid them, sometimes personnel on Alphane fouls up."

"So what do I do now?"

"I'll book you into the transient officers' quarters for the moment. We'll process what we can and request your inposting. Have a good meal and some sleep, and check back in tomorrow morning."

Jimjoy shrugged. "Anything else I can do?"

"Not really, Captain."

"So . . . point me in the right direction . . . would you?"

"Third level north, second spoke. We're on the mid-level, just inside the first spoke . . ."

Arcane as the directions sounded, Jimjoy understood them. He nodded.

"Here's your temporary badge, Captain. It's good for everywhere except comm and ops." The technician handed him the coded square bearing the resemblance of his present appearance. "It's coded to your stateroom . . . number three delta."

"The proverbial closet, I take it?"

"A bit larger, sir."

Jimjoy clipped the badge to his tunic, then hoisted his bag.

"Thank you." He turned away, then turned back. "What time tomorrow?"

"Around 0900. There's no reason to get here earlier."

He turned back toward the hatch and started for the transient officers' quarters, trying to bring a hint of a waddle into his walk.

"Technician Smerglia . . . ?"

Since he had managed to get the databloc read by the station personnel system, he had less than two standard hours to get ready. The bag over his shoulder, he continued toward the access shaft that would lead to the north, or upper, side of the station. Even with his waddle walk, it didn't take him more than five standard minutes to arrive at his temporary quarters.

Three delta made a closet look spacious, reflected the Ecolitan. Just a bunk with a reading light, a narrow hanging closet, and a locker under the bunk. He shook his head as he slid the doorway shut behind him.

Clunk . . . He shook his head again as he edged the bag inside the sliding door it had not cleared. "Not even enough space to get the kit inside."

With a sigh louder than he felt, he slid the doorway shut and levered the bag onto the bunk, looking around the closet stateroom. Despite the standardization of the system control stations, some provided small consoles for visiting officers. He had not been provided with one, which meant a little more work in finding a vacant console where no one would complain.

In quick motions, he shoveled out the uniforms and clothing and placed them in the open locker—except for a standard shipsuit, which he draped over a hook in the narrow closet. The two belts he laid aside, as well as the toiletries kit and the spare pair of boots.

The bag empty, he flexed its fabric side, half twisting, until the seam opened. Removing the plastic stiffeners one at a time, he stacked them on the bunk. Then he repeated the process with the bottom. The stiffeners on the bottom were noticeably thicker and went into a second pile.

Off came his boots and the undress travel uniform. The uniform went into the locker, and on went the shipsuit. He placed the stiffeners in the pockets where they temporarily belonged. Next he reclaimed the small plastic-composite tools from the bootheels, before separating out a dozen centimeter-square cubes from the remainder of the heels. One he set aside. The rest and the tools went into the shipsuit's belt pouch. Finally, he put on the real boots and transferred insignia and badges from the travel uniform.

After a last look around the cubicle, he picked up the small black cube and placed it within the pile of clothes he had never worn, nor intended to. Although he could have worn them, doing so would have been mentally and physically uncomfortable, especially around stray voltages or eddy currents.

He opened the sliding door and stepped into the corridor, closing the door behind him. A junior officer had just passed, heading back toward the shafts leading up or down station.

He followed the woman, since the station library was usually somewhere off the main deck. No one gave him even a passing glance during the transit of three decks and a quarter spoke.

The library was empty, except for one duty technician.

"New here," he explained to the young technician, who looked blankly at him. "Arrived before all of the inposting materials. So . . . personnel suggested I come here and spend some time learning about the station. Is there a standard information package?"

"Sure, Captain, but you don't need to—oh—"

Jimjoy nodded. "Right. The woman I'm replacing hasn't left yet. So I'm stuck in one of the TOQ closets. No console, no access . . ."

The technician shook his head sympathetically, then ran his hand over short, stubbly red hair. "We don't have much privacy, sir. Just the three terminals there." He pointed to three utilitarian gray consoles on the wall.

"No problem. Better than my present closet." Jimjoy offered his badge.

"Don't need that, sir. Those are open access, the control is right here."

"Oh . . . fine . . ." The Ecolitan tried to sound bored. "Any special codes to call up the briefing package?"

"No, sir. We're all plain language here, not like the older stations. Just ask what you need."

"Thank you." He waddled toward the group of consoles.

"Take either of those on the left, sir. The keys stick on the right one."

"Thanks," grunted Jimjoy as he sat before the console, studying the setup and waiting for the technician to unblock access.

He almost nodded when he saw the standard databloc access

port. Although it wasn't needed here, the Empire hated to make differing console models. He could have inputted his commands from memory, but that would have taken longer, and there was always the chance that he would key something wrong.

The screen swirled, and the face of a pleasant-looking woman appeared. "I'm LISA—Library Information System Applications. What would you like to know? You may use the menu or request other information directly by using the keyboard."

Jimjoy tapped the keys, adjusting the volume downward and calling up the standard systems orientation.

"This is Haversol System Control Station. Located three point eight standard A.U. from Haversol primary, it has been in operation in its present configuration for thirty-five standard years . . ."

The screen displayed a three-dimensional cutaway of the station.

As it did so, Jimjoy palmed a databloc from his thigh pouch and slipped it into the almost dusty scanner slot.

". . . powered by a fusactor class three, with class two screen capabilities . . . including a full aquatic exercise facility on the main deck . . ."

Now that the technician was back into whatever clandestine viewing he had interrupted to help Jimjoy, the Ecolitan smiled ruefully and touched the keys, calling up the second screen momentarily.

"Read data A . . . enscore . . . delay twenty sm . . . exscore . . ."

"Accepted."

Then he flicked back to the briefing, using the time to locate and reconfirm the locations of his next targets. Whether or not he made it through, he'd left behind, where Thelina and Mardian would find it, an outline of the strategy he'd employed. He hadn't liked leaving a data trail, but he owed her that much, since he hadn't dared to brief them, and they probably wouldn't be all that happy about his "borrowing" the beefed-up needleboat.

He checked the time, then forced himself to wait through another series of briefing bits until he was certain that his departure wouldn't be viewed as too abrupt. He left the databloc in the scanner. It would take care of itself in another standard hour or so, or sooner if anyone tried to remove it.

Finally, he stood up.

"That's about all I can take for now."

"Huhh?" The technician looked up so guiltily that Jimjoy had a hard time smothering a smile.

"That's about all I can take for now," he repeated.

"Pretty boring, sir?"

"I've seen supply manuals more interesting," admitted the pseudo-supply technical specialist.

The technician nodded.

"But I'll probably be back later to see the rest."

"All right, sir."

"Thank you."

But the technician had already returned to whatever he had called up on his own screen.

Jimjoy waddled back to his closet, aware that he was right on schedule, as if he were heading back just before the first mess, when transients were expected in the wardroom. The door to his stateroom/closet opened to his badge, more easily this time.

Once inside, he stripped to the waist and pulled out the bottle of "fragrance." Off came the spare tire around the middle, which he then let resume its prearranged shape as a small datacase. The flat stiffener cards from his kit bag went into the equipment belt.

He reached over and nicked the corner of the black cube in the pile of clothes that were not clothes, and then stepped into the corridor carrying the datacase.

Three corridors, five salutes, and two changes of directions later, he placed the datacase into the proper fire control recess next to a heavily armored conduit. After checking the cubic detonator, he twisted the corner. Too bad he couldn't place the charge exactly where he wanted, but when the time came, it would create a large enough hole along one set of command/control axes to compound the confusion, not to mention the loss of atmosphere.

Jimjoy continued onward, glancing at the corridor lights—still glowing steadily. The ventilators pumped forth in their regular rhythm the same oily air that he had disliked for years, recirculating it through the kays of vents and filters and scrubbers.

With almost a sigh, he extended a card toward the air-lock access scanner.

Click . . .

The lock opened nearly in his face.

"You're not—"

Jimjoy's hands flashed, and the technician crumpled into meat and cloth. Jimjoy grabbed the dead man's badge from his tunic and, taking advantage of the opportunity presented, placed the badge into the scanner, tapping in a series of maintenance codes.

"Cleared for exterior maintenance," flashed the minute screen above the scanner.

Even as the screen finished, the Ecolitan dragged the dead figure into the lock with him. Although he might have wished for marauder-type space armor, the old general-purpose baggy would have to do. It did have the belt for his tools and the flat plastic squares. And, initially, he would be less conspicuous.

Once the helmet was in place, he slipped the first prepared card into the lock scanner. The light winked green. Jimjoy retrieved the card and tabbed the outer lock release, holding himself in place while the air puffed from the lock. Then he slapped the flat plastic against the thinner bulkhead membrane beside the hatch framing, breaking the seal on the thumb-sized detonator. He repeated the process on the outer wall. One down, and a minimum of twenty more to go.

The broomstick came out of its brackets without even a hitch. Fuel? Three-quarters—enough for the moment.

The interior lock lights, dim red for vision adjustment purposes, continued to provide steady illumination. The Ecolitan shook his head, wondering how effectively the virus would be able to infect the SysCon operations net. A gentle push-off with his booted feet carried him and the broomstick away from the station's hull, but toward the northern end. The air lock's outer door winked shut as the automatics triggered.

A silent burst from the front squirter slowed the stick to a slow walk as Jimjoy aimed himself toward the next lock and its lights.

"ExOps, this is OpCon. Interrogative maintenance from alpha center. Interrogative maintenance from alpha center."

Jimjoy winced inside the suit, taking in the approaching lock lights. They shed an unblinking light.

"OpCon, ExOps. Negative on scheduled maintenance this time. Negative on scheduled maintenance this time. Interrogative your last."

Clunk . . . The vibration as the stick grazed the station hull translated into sound inside his helmet. He triggered the lock and waited until the outer hatch irised open. Inside, he slapped another plastic square in place and triggered the detonator. After repeating the process on the outer bulkhead, he pushed off again. Two down.

"ExOps, OpCon. Lock sequencing indicates external operations ongoing this time. Interrogative source."

"OpCon, will check master log."

"Stet, ExOps."

The lock lights continued unblinking. Jimjoy passed the next lock without stopping, angling across to the second spoke. He'd hoped for a bit less time before the virus struck, and a more lethargic reaction from the station crew.

Clunk . . .

The third air lock was an emergency lock, as were most of the spoke locks, and Jimjoy had to practice contortions to place the charges. Another push-off, and he was headed back inward toward an equipment lock on the main frame between spokes two and three, northside.

"ExOps, we have a lock entry spaceside on lock epsilon three gamma."

"Stet, OpCon. We are sending a recon team."

"ExOps, transfer Sigma Charlie. Transfer Sigma Charlie." The comm frequency turned into a flat hiss.

Scrambled communications meant someone was beginning to take things seriously. Jimjoy glanced around, calculating where the recon team would appear. ExOps was southside, about spoke four. And the damned lights still burned steadily.

Clunk . . .

No one was near the big equipment lock, even after the double-sized hatch irised open. This time Jimjoy slapped three separate charges into place—on both exterior and interior bulkheads—before kicking free.

The broomstick crept around the edge of the main hull, within an arm's length of the composite plating. Now that the station was at least partly alerted, the last thing he needed was a radar or EDI reading.

A glint of light off armaglass caught his attention, up near the southern tip of the station. Jimjoy calculated, then angled his broomstick more directly southside.

Clunk . . .

The secondary supply lock was vacant—as it always was except in emergencies. The Ecolitan slapped six more charges in place—three interior and three exterior—and triggered them.

"OpCon, snowman on delta—"

Jimjoy smiled at the broken transmission as he pushed away. Someone had touched the wrong control, then caught on.

He angled past the heat transfer plates marking mid-station and onto the southern side, still less than an arm's length away from the exterior plating. Balancing on the broomstick, he retrieved another charge from the almost depleted supply in the pouch. With a quick motion, he pressed it against the station plates, then used the squirter to keep him close to the hull.

The idea had been to create enough chaos so that his entry into first the fusactor and then, if possible, the weapons storage bays in the armory would not be noticed. Once the security system was immobilized, or at least so erratic that no one in operations could believe it, and with the two dozen major leaks and half-dozen jammed air locks, the maintenance crews would have their hands full. Except that nothing had happened yet.

"Blowout! Section two delta! Blowout in two delta!"

Jimjoy eased the broomstick even closer to the hull in reaction to a pair riding their own sticks a quarter diameter away. They passed behind a stub spoke, number four, apparently without seeing him.

"Blowout! Section three. Lock jammed . . ."

The Ecolitan nodded, wishing that the main power system bugs had taken hold. He glanced over his shoulder.

"Hades . . ."

A single broomstick bore down on him from behind, less than twenty meters away. How had he missed it?

The heavy knife came out of the equipment belt, as did the small can of spray. Then he stopped the stick, flipped it, squirted once to kill his relative speed, and triggered the can.

The polymer spread into a glistening shield just as the laser triggered, and collapsed as rapidly as it had formed.

The knife left his hand, heading through the dissipating silver haze.

The broomstick rider tried to dodge the heavy razor-edged plastic weapon, but his accumulated momentum was too great, and his air spilled from a suit split from shoulder to hip.

Jimjoy swallowed hard, forcing the bile back into his throat, and nudged the squirter to avoid the still-flailing figure that cartwheeled past him.

With another swallow, he edged the broomstick toward the fat-looking nodule connected by the umbilical to the south end of the station. Another look at the scattered lights of the station.

Still nothing. He was running out of time. But he couldn't even begin the next phase unless the virus had been successful in penetrating the SysCon operating codes.

Again Jimjoy studied the lights framing the nearest lock.

Was there a flicker? Definitely, a pulse to the lights. Once, twice . . .

He began to toggle through all the SysCon frequencies. The helmet receiver hummed, and he halted the cycle to listen.

". . . control . . . intermittent power . . . interrogative . . ."

"OpCon, interrogative status. Interrogative . . ."

". . . lost slush on tank one . . . lost slush . . . strains . . . three epsilon . . ."

Jimjoy smiled faintly and goosed up the broomstick another notch, heading toward the fusactor module. Now, within minutes, no one would have standard commlinks, thanks to his efforts in the library. And the maintenance crews would have their hands more than full.

". . . MAYDAY . . . DAY . . . spoke five . . ."

". . . spoke six . . . uncontrolled lock cycles . . ."

Still scooting along in the shadows within an arm span of the hull, he could see assorted vapor puffs and flashing lights. Ahead, the umbilical to the fusactor grew larger.

"Raider six, OpCon . . . omega black . . . black . . ."

Jimjoy shivered at the last broken transmission. Although the power cycles had disrupted the scramblers, the operations center had clearly decided they wanted him very dead. They didn't know who he was, or where—yet.

He glanced around again. So far, so good. In a few moments he would have to leave the shadows and cross the open gap paralleling the umbilical.

Crump . . . whhhstttt . . . The sounds of destruction filtered through the headset momentarily. He shook his head, thinking, idiotically, that he should be trying to pull at his chin.

Even in the sunlight no one pursued him, as the puffs of vapor continued to spill into the void.

Clunk . . . The impact nearly flattened him against the plates surrounding the fusactor assembly. Surprisingly, the broomstick had not bent. He checked the squirters. Less than fifty percent.

He inserted the I.D. code card into the scanner slot. For several moments, nothing happened. Then the access light winked green and the codeboard lit.

With a sigh, Jimjoy tapped out a code, altered but based on an older, valid entry code, and waited with a small probe.

The entry light flickered amber, and Jimjoy pressed the tip of the probe against the edge of the I.D. slot, triggering the modified pulse current. The light turned red, then green, and the hatch irised half open.

With the opening just wide enough for Jimjoy to scramble through, he barely got his left boot clear of the edge before the lock slid shut. The inner door was unguarded, opening at his touch as he floated in null-gee. The grav-fields had been shut down by the power fluctuations, but the power sections were engineered to work without grav-fields, since they provided the power for and had to precede the fields.

Inside, he pulled himself hand over hand around toward the section he wanted. Once there, he withdrew several tools from his pouch, taking off his gauntlets but leaving his helmet in place.

The adjustments were minor, and their immediate effect would scarcely be noticed amidst the power surges already racking the station. He hoped to be clear of the station before the final impact.

After replacing the panels he had removed for access, as well as his gauntlets, the Ecolitan pulled himself back to the lock, where he made two more adjustments, ensuring the outer lock would open once, and only once—to let him out, along with the extra broomstick he had unlatched from the lock wall.

It did, closing quickly enough that, again, he almost lost a foot.

"Charlie three, leak on delta five. Class three."

"Stet. Delta five with a four patch."

"Blowout in supply two . . ."

"Hades . . . get that sucker . . ."

Overhead, in his present orientation, the SysCon station presented an array of flashing lights, some hints of what appeared to be mist, and a handful of space-armored figures.

Jimjoy checked his orientation again, slowly swinging the first broomstick about. The second was tethered to him. Then he lined up the pocket EDI, trying not to think about the next step.

"If . . . if . . ."

He pressed the squirter control, letting the broomstick carry him out toward the station-keeping area. According to the postings, two couriers, a scout, and three corvettes stood off-station. The corvettes were useless.

The EDI needle seemed to match his vector.

He took a deep breath, then another, then held it and listened, as he chin-toggled from frequency to frequency.

". . . section four beta . . . secure . . ."

". . . blowout uncontained in supply two . . ."

". . . kill the frigger . . . whole section . . ."

". . . ExOps . . . no sign of intruder . . ."

With a last deep breath, he touched the squirter controls. The broomstick carried him into the shadows and toward the station-keeping area, directly toward the dimmest of the EDI readings.

He forced himself to let up on the squirter. He'd need all the power he could muster at the other end, and he had more air than power.

Turning his head, he watched the SysCon slowly recede, its gray-and-silver bulk blotting out less and less of the stars, lock lights still flashing intermittently, puffs of vacated atmosphere still jerking forth.

How many had died? He tried not to think about it. Maybe Thelina was right—that he was nothing better than a cold-blooded killer who justified his actions with simplistic principles. Had the young library tech deserved to die? He certainly had had nothing to do with wanting to crush Accord. Nor had the medical tech absorbed in her redloc game.

". . . slush two frozen . . . tank three . . . whole system's shot . . ."

". . . blowout . . . four epsilon . . ."

". . . power pulses from fusactor . . ."

He shivered and turned to watch the blackness before him, straining for the glint of metal or the dullness of composite plates, continuing to check the EDI for the slightest twitch. The broomstick carried him onward into the darkness, outward toward where he hoped to find escape—one way or another.

. . . XIV . . .

Was there a glimmer ahead? Just off the left of the broom-stick's heading? With all Imperial hulls designed as nonreflective, the dim sunlight from Haversol had not proved much help in locating the off-station ships.

Jimjoy checked the EDI, uncertain whether the needle leaned off-center.

Buzzzzzzz . . .

The alarm sounded, and the EDI display vanished simultaneously.

"Hades . . ." muttered Jimjoy, careful not to trigger the suit's transceiver. Without turning, he began to pull in the spare broomstick that had trailed behind him until he held the narrow frame in his hands, his knees still holding him on the exhausted composite-metal structure. As quickly as carefully possible, he positioned the unused broomstick next to the one he had ridden and eased from the one to the other. Only after he was in place did he release the tether and transfer it to the spent vehicle.

The mass of the used stick, however insignificant, might be necessary, and since it currently had the same momentum as he did, there was no point in letting it go . . . yet.

Then he touched the activator stud, watching the EDI display light up. The needle was definitely moving leftward, toward the glint he had seen, or thought he had seen.

The problem was his limited fuel. If he ended up heading toward a corvette, he was as good as dead. He needed a courier or scout, preferably a courier, and ideally one in a stand-down status.

". . . blowout patch gone . . . four delta . . ."
". . . power surges . . . continuing . . . non-SysCon origin . . ."
". . . frigging designs! Clamp . . ."

A vague outline appeared ahead to the left, visible as a dark patch against the stars. To the right was the darkness of the Rift, against which no hull shadow would be visible until he was nearly upon it.

He glanced down at the EDI as the broomstick coasted outward. The outline looked too solid for the kind of ship he needed, but if he didn't have some other hint before long . . . He shivered inside the suit, although he was not cold.

Twitch. The EDI needle shivered, but remained fixed. Jimjoy watched as the needle and the shadow edged ten degrees leftward off his heading. Then he studied the area to the right more intently as the EDI shivered again. Was that a small fuzzy black patch?

He almost shrugged as he touched the squirter controls, beginning a gentle curve away from the corvette and toward what seemed to be a smaller spacecraft.

". . . damned power surges . . . fusactor . . . interrogative . . . umbilical . . ."
". . . OpCon . . . negative . . . negative . . . work party . . . for fusactor . . ."

Jimjoy swallowed. His timing was finer that he would have liked, and he hadn't been able to modify any of the ship or station tacheads. So EMP detonations were going to be minimal.

The EDI needle suddenly flicked rightward. Jimjoy couldn't help smiling as the needle centered on the darkness ahead.

". . . OpCon . . . access blocked . . . lock inoperative . . ."
"ExOps, OpCon, imperative immediate access to fusactor . . . umbilical . . . interrogative release . . ."
". . . sabotage . . . interrogative . . . say again, ExOps . . ."

Jimjoy peered ahead at the darkness within the darkness, then triggered the squirters for a short burst. The EDI remained locked on the ship ahead, whose shadow loomed larger.

He keyed in the squirters for full forward thrust, trying to kill off his outbound momentum before he either flattened himself against the hull plates or went flying by and into an orbit which might be of interest to astronomers or future archaeologists, but would cease to be of much urgency to one Jimjoy Whaler. Even now the name sounded foreign.

". . . cutting laser . . . op immediate . . . laser . . . ExOps . . . do you read me . . ."

Jimjoy pursed his lips at the frantic sounds of the transmissions from behind him, even as he concentrated on guiding the broomstick to the courier ahead. He had too much velocity, careful as he had thought he had been, for the squirters to kill. He had to hit the courier—squarely—and hope the collapsible frame would function as designed.

". . . frig . . . regs . . . need that cutter . . . NOW!!!"

Whhhssssssstttt . . . The vibration of the final squirter thrust killing the broomstick's velocity fed back through the framework and into his suit.

Clunnnnk . . . Jimjoy winced at the sound. Anybody awake and on board the courier certainly wouldn't have missed his arrival.

As the broomstick absorbed the shock, he reached out and planted the sticky lock loop on a hull plate before any recoil could separate him. Even so, as he clicked the safety tether fast to the loop, he and the courier began to separate.

"Ummmffff . . ." The jolt of hitting the end of the safety line caused the involuntary exclamation.

After dragging himself back to the hull, hand over hand, he eased the first broomstick out of the tether loop and left it floating beside the courier hull. Then he began a careful scramble toward the main lock. Along the way, he checked to ensure his remaining knife was still available for use. While the stunner might be more useful, it was what any crew would be concentrating upon.

Finally, he floated outside the crew lock.

"Well. . . ." With a deep breath, he touched the access stud, waiting to see if he needed to use his tools.

The red panel winked on as the outer door slid open.

Moistening his lips and swallowing, Jimjoy pulled himself inside, upright, to anticipate returning to ship gravity. His feet touched the deck, and he stepped fully inside, tapping the stud to close the lock.

"WHO . . . UNIDENTIFIED VISITOR, PLEASE IDENTIFY YOURSELF!"

Jimjoy winced at the volume of the inquiry.

"IDENTIFY YOURSELF!"

"Wheile, Erlin, Captain, I.S.S., Technical Specialist."

"Likely story . . ." The metallic sound of the suit speaker still conveyed the skepticism of whoever was inside the courier.

"May I come aboard?"

"You already are, without invitation." The speaker's tone was all too reminiscent of a passed-over courier skipper.

"May I come aboard?"

"Everything else is crazy—why not? Keep your hands in plain sight."

Jimjoy released his breath and keyed the lock controls for the inner door, waiting for the release inside. Finally the panel blinked, then turned steady green. The inner door irised open, and he stepped through.

A baggy-suited figure stood two meters from him, a laser aimed straight at his midsection. "Again, who are you? How did you get here? Why?"

"Erlin Wheile, Captain, I.S.S., Technical Specialist."

"Supposed to believe that?'

"Check with ExOps," suggested Jimjoy. "Had an intruder. Hit me with a stunner from about a meter away. Suit helped, but I was headed outbound, without enough fuel to get back. Only hope was an off-station ship. Bent the hades out of the broomstick."

"Likely story."

The lock closed behind Jimjoy.

"Fine. Check your screens. Is there anything around here? You think anyone is crazy enough to deliberately take a broomstick ride in the middle of nowhere in hopes of finding a ship?"

"Point, but not much of one." The speaker's voice was still muffled. "Take off the helmet—slowly. Keep your gauntlets on, and your hands in full view."

Jimjoy almost sighed. Clearly an officer with some understanding of suits. He carefully loosened the maintenance-type helmet, following the other officer's directions. As he cracked the seals, he could hear only the ventilators hissing. At least there was but a single crewman aboard.

He began to lift off the helmet, watching the other's gun-hand gauntlet.

"Bast—"

Clang . . . clunk . . . The helmet clanked off the Imperial's upper arm.

Whhsssttttt.

Thud.

"Hades." Jimjoy managed to steady himself against the bulkhead, forcing himself to breathe, despite the fire in his right shoulder, as he looked at the fallen figure in the narrow passageway. The officer lay facedown, motionless. Although he could not see it, Jimjoy knew a heavy knife protruded from the chest of the woman. Sooner or later, it had to have happened.

Some gesture, some look, despite the disguise, had betrayed him. But Ladonna had always said she would recognize him anywhere. Especially after the *IFoundIt!* mission, when he had gotten Sashiel cashiered for incompetence.

Well, she had recognized him, or what he represented. It didn't matter which. And she was dead. And he wasn't in exactly wonderful condition. Despite the protection from the suit, his right arm didn't work. His nose protested the smell of burned flesh.

He took a deeper breath, ignoring the fire shooting across his chest, and concentrated on calling up the pain blocs, focusing on the bland but stale metallic odor of the recycled air. The effort it took made it clear he didn't have much time.

The controls were only five steps away. He took one step, then stopped. Another long step, and he crossed Ladonna's body. Step and rest, step and rest, step and rest. In more than the one-third gee of the ship, he would not have made it. Step and rest . . . all for a mere five meters in low grav.

". . . don't relax . . . don't relax . . ." Jimjoy did not realize he was vocalizing his thoughts until he recognized the voice as his own.

His right arm dangled, but his left swung the fingertip control pad—normally used for high-gee, outside-the-envelope maneuvering—into position.

Ignoring the checklist, he brought the board to life, checked the power, and began to preprogram the outsystem course, the jump sequence, and the inboard course to Thalos. If he collapsed, the pre-programming might get him close enough to be rescued. Otherwise, he would modify the course as the ship neared each decision point.

"AlCom, this is Haversol SysCon. Haversol . . . all units . . . imperative . . . stand . . . SysCon . . ."

"AlCom . . . negative . . . negative . . ."

". . . Radian Throne . . . request . . . imperative . . ."

Jimjoy ignored the conflicting transmissions for SysCon evacuation and alternatively for station-ships to stand off, slowly completing his power-up and waiting for the board to wink green.

"Ready for departure," announced the console.

Jimjoy did not wait for the completion of the courier's announcement before stabbing the stud to trigger the drive controls.

"Speedline four, interrogative action. Interrogative action."

Jimjoy sighed. "Negative action. Negative action. Maintaining station."

"Radian Throne, this is Courage three. Interrogative status SysCon."

"Courage three, Radian Throne. Stand by. Clear this frequency.

"Speedline four, Radian Throne. Imperative you hold station this time."

"Radian Throne, Speedline four," rasped Jimjoy. "Interrogative your last. Interrogative your last."

"Radian Throne, Hawkstrike one, standing off this time. Standing off this time."

"Hawkstrike one, negative. Negative standoff. Hold your station . . ."

"Frig you . . ." muttered Jimjoy almost under his breath, but deliberately keying his transmitter.

"Interrogative last transmission. Interrogative last transmission."

Jimjoy ignored the request from the station-keeping commander and edged up his drive velocity. Even the motion in his fingers sent twinges through his other shoulder. The laser should have cauterized the arm enough so that the blood loss was minimal, but there was no way to tell what internal bleeding might be occurring. He didn't want to think about the nerve damage.

". . . standing by not advisable . . . AlCom . . . interrogative . . ."

". . . OpCon . . . power . . . surges . . ."

"Speedline four, return to station. Return to station."

"Stet. Returning to station," Jimjoy answered, knowing that the courier needed every instant of acceleration possible, since he could not personally survive a high-gee run.

"Hawkstrike four, return to station. Return to station."

"Negative, Radian Throne. That is negative this time. ImpOrd three point five beta forbids hazard of vessel in noncombat situation."

"Hawkstrike four, I say again. Return to station."

"Departing station this time."

WHHHHHHHEEEEEEEEEEEeeeeeeeeeeeeeeeeeeeeeeeeeeeeeee-eeeeee . . .

The scream of white noise—that and the EDI pegging off the register—told Jimjoy that Haversol SysCon was no longer a threat to Accord.

He could sense the control area turning gray around him, and wondered if he would be able to rouse himself for the jump . . . if he should try . . . but, damned if he wanted to give Thelina the satisfaction . . .

. . . *cling* . . . *cling* . . .

As if from a distance, he could hear the chiming, the distant sounds of the morning bells on White Mountain, rebounding over fresh white snow . . . or was it the sounds of evening bells from the meeting house on Harmony . . . ?

He pried one eye open, reached—and was rewarded with a searing line of pain down his right arm.

Haversol, Ladonna, the laser wound, and now the jump.

With an effort he used his left hand.

"Jump parameters outside acceptable envelope."

He squinted at the readout. Once, twice. On the third try, he could read the numbers. The dust density was above acceptable levels.

His left hand tapped out the query.

"Probability of successful jump is ninety-eight point five."

His fingers slashed the jump command stub, and instantaneous endless blackness flashed up around him. For that instant, the pain in his shoulder became a kind of pleasure, but only for that instant.

Back in real-space the searing continued, with each instant adding yet another needled blast.

Jimjoy took a breath and concentrated on rebuilding the pain blocs. After a while, the searing receded, and he could see the board clearly enough to realize he needed to reconfigure the small remaining jump. He did, one finger at a time, one calculation at a time, and touched the jump button.

Again the blackness relieved the pressure of the blocked pain, but even in null-time, Jimjoy did not relax the blocs, just waited.

"Jump complete."

With another effort, he began to reprogram the entry curve to Thalos, that airless moon off Permana, the Accord system's fourth planet, trying to ensure that the final deceleration would occur with Permana's bulk between the courier and Accord orbit control.

As a last effort, he also programmed the Mayday message for transmission on the Institute's scrambled frequency—but only after deceleration halted.

His fingers touched the controls, and the ship began its inward curve, a curve that he hoped would bring him back. He'd done what he promised to Sam; and Thelina would never talk to him again. Why did he worry?

From that point, events took on a gauzy texture . . .

. . . did he actually adjust the curve to compensate for dust . . . ?

. . . or boost the decel power to cut closer to the Institute base . . . ?

. . . or tell the needleboat standing off the courier to just go ahead and wait until he was dead . . . ?

. . . or did the grayness roll in over him at the moment the courier entered the system?

. . . XV . . .

The Admiral took a deep breath, then glanced up at the holo view portraying New Augusta from the air. His fingers drummed on the bare wood as he pursed his lips.

After a time, he looked back at the hidden screen, recessed into the wooden table and displaying its message only to someone sitting in the Admiral's chair.

"Haversol SysCon — Status Report.

"Facility: OMEGA

"Survivors: 87 known (10.1 percent of estimated POB/E)

"Ships: HMS PIKE (cc) — OMEGA
          HMS DEGAULLE (lc) — OMEGA
          HMS NKRUMAH (lc) — DELTA
          HMS LEGROS (ft) — OMEGA . . ."

He skipped to the analysis, picking out phrases.

". . . simultaneous use of ANT (accelerated nerve toxin), fusactor bottle effect, tachead explosions, and wide-scale EMP effects point to a well-orchestrated military operation, rather than an accident or a terrorist attack . . ."

"Brilliant, just brilliant," muttered the Admiral. "Of course it was military. But whose military?"

". . . the Haversol SysCon 'incident' bears no identifiable modus operandi associated with past or present efforts of either the Halstani or the Fuard Special Operations teams . . ."

". . . knew that . . ." The Admiral rubbed his forehead and returned his study to the screen.

". . . the statistical comparator found the greatest similarity between the Haversol SysCon 'incident' and Imperial Special Operative techniques . . . correlation level of fifty percent plus . . .''

The Admiral shook his head before touching several recessed keys in quick succession. The screen displayed a second document.

"JIMJOY EARLE WRIGHT III
DECEASED . . ."

He skimmed through the file, again mentally noting key elements.

". . . use of EMP as a detonating mechanism during HUMBLEPIE (see Halston 'accident') . . .

". . . ability to infiltrate and destroy installation warned against him was highlighted by his presumed destruction of the New Kansaw facility through the use of the Masada safeguards . . .

". . . piracy of HMS *D'Armetier* was attributed to Major Wright, after diversion of a planetary shuttle into the New Kansaw orbit control . . ."

The Admiral frowned, again all too aware of the pounding in his temples. He jabbed at the controls.

"Profile of Major Wright (DECEASED) achieves 78.4 percent correlation with assumed and reconstructed modus operandi for destruction of Haversol SysCon."

The senior officer glanced at the holo view of the capital once more before touching the console controls and rereading the words displayed on the screen for at least the fourth time.

". . . wreckage of the HMS *D'Armetier* discovered on the surface of Timor II (see catalog Red 3-C). Remains of four bodies were on board. Two were positively identified by physical remnants, Imperial tag trace, and absolute DNA match. Two were tentatively identified as New Kansaw rebels—one male and one female.

"The two positive identifications were:

Jimjoy Earle Wright III
Major, I.S.S./S.O./B-941 366
Helgran Forste Mittre
Lieutenant, I.S.S./ A-371 741.''

Finally, the Admiral blanked the screen.

"The only one, and he's dead." He reached for the hypnospray, hoping that this time the medicine would relieve the headache.

. . . XVI . . .

Overhead was gray. Swirling, spinning gray. He could not move, his chest bound by an invisible band that made each breath an effort. Fire gnawed at his right shoulder, but he could see no flames, feel no heat on his face.

Closing his eyes replaced the gray with featureless black, but his eyelids wanted to remain closed.

"Acchhh . . ." His cough sounded strangled in his own ears as he forced his eyes back open.

The gray overhead was gray—solid gray rock. The fire in his shoulder ebbed, until he tried to shift his weight off his aching buttocks. Then it seared all the way down his arm and back through his chest. Down his arm?

Jimjoy wanted to shake his head, but knew he should pull at his chin. He couldn't, not with the padded cuffs around his wrists. Where was he? Not on Accord, not with the dark rock overhead. Thalos, where he had ended up after his first escape from the Empire?

". . . thought you were awake, but you really shouldn't be, Professor Whaler." The woman's voice was low but pleasant.

"Accccchhhhaaa . . ." Clearing his throat didn't make breathing any easier, but the dryness subsided. "Where . . . ?"

"Thalos," answered the green-clad woman as she adjusted something in the apparatus behind his right shoulder. The fires in his arm and shoulder eased. "You've been under for a while. That's hard on your lungs, but the first stages are critical, and any jerky motions damp retakes."

"Gibberish," he mumbled, because none of what she said made any sense.

"You really overstressed your system, but we've got it all under control. I'm going to put you back under for a little bit. We need another day to ensure everything takes, but you're doing just fine. Just fine.

"Now, try to relax. . . ."

Even as she spoke, he could feel his muscles begin to loosen.

". . . any . . . choice . . . ?"

"No, Professor, you don't. We can talk about the reasons later."

As the grayness dissolved into black, he understood she was talking to keep him calm while whatever she pumped into his system took effect.

When his eyes blinked open again, the overhead gray was clearer. The gumminess around his eyelids remained. His right shoulder and upper arm throbbed with a dull ache, and the padded cuffs were still in place around his wrists. A fractionally deeper breath indicated that the invisible band still encircled his chest.

He'd clearly been rescued, if rescue were the correct term, by the Institute. In what light his return was regarded remained another question. That all depended on Sam; on what he had been able to do. The dimness of the lights signaled local night, or the equivalent.

Shifting his weight did not bring the agony he recalled from his previous awakening, only a slight intensification of the throbbing in his arm.

"How do you feel?" asked the low-voiced woman from behind his shoulder.

"Better . . ." His throat was dry and he swallowed once, twice, in an effort to moisten it.

"I'd like you to try and rest quietly. I'm going to loosen the cuff on the left arm, but you'll still have to stay on your back. I know it's sore, but regrowth doesn't take in null-gee, and trying to handle partial field generation isn't possible within a field."

"Regrowth . . ." he croaked.

"Partial regrowth," she corrected. "The bone cells were mainly all right, but you lost all the nerves along the upper arm and most of the musculature. That's why the pain was so great, why you've been under sedation for so long. But don't worry. The arm regrowth took just fine. It's going to be painful sometimes, especially since the nerve confusion will take time to settle out.

"You've got some fluids in your lungs, but they're within limits. Tomorrow we'll move you into postural drainage for a bit, before letting you sit up."

"How . . . about . . . arm . . ."

"Your arm will be fine. You will need a great deal of therapy before it's normal again. How fast is up to you." She frowned as she bent over to loosen the cuff. "No, you can't start now. You'll need another few days in solution at least."

He managed to turn his head to see the molded tank attached to his shoulder and in which his right arm lay.

"I'll be back in a moment. You can wiggle your fingers on the good arm and move it *gently.* Don't touch anything on your right side."

"All . . . right."

He focused on the overhead. Would they take all this trouble if he were destined for disaster? He did not shake his head, although he felt like it.

Another set of footsteps echoed on the stone.

He glanced toward the doorway, taking in the blond-haired new arrival. The second woman eased over to his bed. Why was Meryl here? At least he thought it was Thelina's quarter mate.

"Are you awake?"

"Barely." He tried to force a smile.

"Thelina will be here in a few minutes. She's angry. Don't let her blame you." Meryl's lips pursed. "Just remember. She's mad. She needs someone to blame. Besides herself."

Jimjoy squinted up at her, trying to hold her fading image in view, at the words that seemed to come from so far away. "Angry . . . because . . . Haversol . . . ?" Each of his words took a separate breath against the invisible band encircling his chest.

"No. Because—My God! You don't even know. How could you? They called it an accident. It wasn't—"

"Ecolitan," intruded a second voice. "He's not to have visitors yet."

"Just a moment. He needs to know." Meryl bent closer to Jimjoy. Her face was damp, pale, and a wisp of hair brushed his cheek. "The Empire—Special Operations—someone—murdered the Prime. Sam and Gavin Thorson. An accident, but we know better. Thelina wants to blame you. Don't let her."

Her hand squeezed the fingertips of his left hand, the one that he still seemed to have, and he blinked.

When his eyes reopened, she was gone. Another slow blink, and a woman in green was adjusting the apparatus attached to his right shoulder.

"You're doing fine, Professor. Just fine."

Another blink, and she was gone. Just the gray overhead above him. Solid gray. Solid, unlike the swirling gray of winter on White Mountain. Solid, unlike the black-and-gray bolts of the storms of Accord. Solid dull gray.

He could hear the footsteps on the polished rock floor.

Tap . . . tap . . . tap . . .

"Hello, Thelina." He managed to keep his throat from rasping.

"Hello, Professor." Her voice was low, almost ragged.

"Sorry . . . to keep meeting you like this . . ."

She edged up to the left side of the bed, looking down at him. Even in the dim light he could see her eyes were bloodshot. She looked from one end of the bed to the other, slowly shaking her head.

"That bad?"

"Always a flip comment, Professor?"

He sighed—almost. His breath caught with the pain in his chest.

"No . . . you bring out . . . the best . . . in me."

She studied him for a long time, not speaking.

He lay there, unwilling to say anything.

"Meryl was here."

"Yes."

"She told you about Sam."

"A little . . . an accident . . . not an accident . . . killed Sam and Gavin Thorson. That . . . was it. Said you were upset. Said you might blame me . . ."

"I found your package."

"And . . ."

"You're a bastard—a cold, unfeeling bastard. You're effective. Sam knew it. He knew we needed you. He knew you might be his death. He's the hero."

Jimjoy waited, watching the tears stream down her cheeks, understanding, he hoped, at least a small fraction of what she felt, knowing that the only man who had supported him and believed in him was dead.

". . . know . . . you even feel it . . . a little . . ."

Jimjoy nodded, not wanting to speak.

For a time, the room was silent, except for the background hiss of ventilators and two sets of ragged breathing.

"I need to go . . ."

"I know . . ."

Did her hand touch his, ever so lightly, as she stepped away? Or had he imagined it?

"Take care, Professor . . ."

"You . . . too . . . Ecolitan Andruz . . ."

His cheeks felt damp. But it had to be from his gummy eyes. It had to be.

. . . XVII . . .

Dear Blaine:

Should have faxed you earlier. Hadn't realized how time has gone, but with the buildup out here, the increased tours, didn't seem to have a minute. If it's not one Fuard thing, it's another.

Torp trash says they blew out Haversol SysCon. That true? If you can't say, don't. But I couldn't figure anyone else who could.

Halley's down again. Converter fused solid after overjump. Managed to coast in-system here. Hell of a thing not even being able to lock by yourself, and halfway across the sector so I can't even see Helen, Jock, and little Cindi. She's a doll, but sometimes these days I think I scarcely know them. They don't know me either.

What's new on the FC? Rumor has it the Senate passed a resolution declaring it obsolete before it would be ready. Serious???

Had a near miss last month with one of the new Fuard destroyers. Couldn't believe it. Damned thing came out of jump going sideways. Ran circles around us.

Way it looks now, I guess I'll be out here longer. New I.S.S. personnel directive—extending command tours another two standard years, except for promotions. Won't be in the zone for another two. So it's two more years with the old *Halley*—if either of us lasts that long.

My best to you and Sandy.

Mort

. . . XVIII . . .

"Whereas Imperial technology, equipment, and expertise have been provided to colony planets at substantial risk to the provider and represent the contribution through sacrifice by honest citizenry interested solely in benefiting their fellow beings;

"Whereas said equipment and technology have been provided to endow colonists and their successors with the ability to survive and prosper;

"Whereas the peaceful use of knowledge and technology is the right and heritage of all thinking beings;

"Whereas the abuse of Imperial technology has led to great loss of human life, human suffering, and substantial loss of capital resources by the law-abiding citizens of law-abiding planets;

"Whereas the inability of colony planets to prevent the misuse and malappropriation of technology and the continued failure of these selfsame colony planets to bring to justice those responsible for such great loss of life and irreplaceable resources have become evident;

"THEREFORE, be it resolved by the Senate, in accord with the Charter, and under the powers invested in this Body, that:

"The presence or use of offensive weapons upon any aerial or off-planet self-powered craft or fixed emplacement, other than those operated directly by duly constituted Imperial Forces, is hereby forbidden;

"An additional ad valorem tax of five per centum on the as-

sessed value of all production or sale of raw materials, semifin-
ished or full finished goods shall be paid to the Revenue
Collection Service, excepting those goods produced within any
planetary system which has accepted full voting membership in
the Council of Systems;

"The revenue raised from such ad valorem tax shall be devoted in total to the maintenance and enhancement of Imperial
interstellar capabilities in the areas of colonization, exploration,
and colonial protection, including, but not limited to, shipbuild-
ing, research, development, and training of personnel;

"The results of all research efforts funded directly or indi-
rectly, or arising from an Imperial colonization effort, shall also
be made available to the Consortium of Advanced Studies;

"And, finally, the enforcement of these provisions shall be
the duty and obligation of His Imperial Majesty, as delegated
under the Charter and set forth herein, modified as necessary
with the further consent of the Senate for full implementa-
tion."

"Debate is now open on the measure," intoned the clerk in
black.

By the lowered benches behind the rostrum, two individuals
nodded to each other.

"So we spent all this money, and the little buggers aren't
grateful. They want to do things their way? What else could
you expect, Stentor?" His voice was nearly a whisper, designed not to be heard above the formal debate taking place
behind them.

"Are we speaking candidly?"

"Don't we always?"

"Nothing. I expect nothing from the colonists. They are not
the issue at all. The armed forces, the Service in particular, and
the Fuards are . . ."

"You think a display of resolution by the great and glorious
Imperial Senate will pacify the eagles and the Fuards?"

"I'm not really that ambitious. I merely wish to raise the
issue early, to preempt the firestorm it will become later. To
provide a focus so that something more extreme is not
adopted."

"You think that this is the most moderate of approaches possible, then?"

"It may be still too moderate. Admiral KeRiker has proposed

militarizing all orbital and space travel facilities serving colony planets, even those with locally elected governments and independently and locally supported off-planet facilities. As for the Fuards . . . nothing will pacify them.''

"You may be too late.''

"I may. But may I count on your voice?''

"My voice? By all means. But my vote is the will of the people's.''

"I understand . . .''

. . . XIX . . .

Jimjoy frowned at the console. Doing was so much easier than planning, especially when he had relied so much upon instinct, rather than trying to chart out all the possible variables.

Chrrrupppp . . . Outside, another of the local birds called out a greeting.

Letting his hands rest below the keyboard, he looked out at the bare limbs of the T-type maple. Through the branches he could see the native grayoak, not properly an oak at all, which did not shed leaves seasonally but throughout the year, although the leaves looked like gray leather in the cold of winter and early spring.

On the maple's top branch roosted a purplish jaymar, one of the few Accord avians he recognized. Not that recognition was difficult. Jaymars had a call more raucous than a crow's, manners less acceptable than a pigeon's, and an appetite less discriminating than a sea gull's. Only their striking purpled-black feathers were pleasing—and, according to the ecological purists, their singular ability to remove carrion and/or wastes.

Chuuurrrrpppppp . . .

With a drawn-out breath, he flexed his right hand, trying to loosen the stiffness of skin and muscles. Now the pain in his shoulder had diminished, using the console was no longer a chore. Returning to teaching *Theories of Warfare* had been almost a relief—except for Yusseff's sleeping in class.

Because Ecolitans had the odd habit of disappearing and reappearing—injured and otherwise—no one had asked him about the bulky regen dressing. But they had sighed at the return of his logical argument papers and his insistence on questioning fundamental assumptions. Several Ecolitans had covered for him, including Thelina, who had left him notes—most impersonal— on the two sessions she had taught on tactics under the military dictatorship of Halston—pre-Matriarchy.

Mardian, the other tactics professor, had handled the majority of the classes and had left a note. "Too bad you didn't opt for teaching years ago!"

Jimjoy stroked his chin at the thought. Without the mistakes he had made . . . but that wouldn't help him with the next phase. He needed an entire set of manuals for the crew he had yet to assemble.

"Datablocs," he mumbled. "Use of coding . . . access to Imperial datanets . . ." All of the loopholes and techniques he had developed needed to be reduced to simplified procedures for others without the benefit of his experience. At times, he was amazed at how much he had learned.

"Right . . . good for the ego . . ." He almost grinned.

Chrrrupppp . . . churuppppp . . . With a double raspberry, the jaymar flicked its tail and launched itself into the late fall drizzle.

A wisp of woodsmoke swirled above the bare branches, and Jimjoy sniffed for the welcome acridness. The closed door blocked any scent, and he turned back to the screen.

". . . system access codes . . . classified by type of system . . ."

He leaned back and tried to catalog mentally the types of systems, finally pulling at his chin before listing each one that came to mind, following each with a brief description and the probable types of access codes. By the time he finished his rough listings, the hardness of the wooden chair had numbed his buttocks, in spite of the pillow he had placed on the seat.

". . . someone's going to buy it . . ." He addressed the closed sliding door that would have been open to the upper deck of his bedroom on a warmer day. "How can you tell them everything . . . ?"

Even as he tried to outline what he knew in detail, he was beginning to gain a healthy admiration for Sam Hall. For some reason, that admiration did not extend to his former superiors in Special Operations.

Why? Because Imperial Special Operations only told you the minimum necessary, on a need-to-know basis. Why he had survived so long—besides being near suicidally fatalistic, or worse, according to Thelina—was because he had tried to learn more. As much as possible, whenever possible.

He touched the console and flipped back to the beginning of the latest document, adding a caveat on the fact that the information presented did not represent everything necessary, only what was available.

"Even that's cheating." He sighed again, looking out the wide sliding glass door. The wooden decking was now thoroughly wet, and the raindrops were splashing up against the glass.

Chhhurrrppppp . . . The jaymar sat on the railing, looking directly at him, as if to ask where the scraps were.

After making sure his latest changes were incorporated into the document, Jimjoy stood up from the console, stretching gingerly, but leaving the equipment running. Then he headed downstairs.

A faint odor of woodsmoke had drifted in, probably through the thin crack he had left in the kitchen window.

The main floor was gloomy, dampish, and he stopped by the cold woodstove. Finally he slipped the kindling in place and lit it, waiting to make sure that the pencil wood had caught before adding the wood he had split months earlier. Had it been last fall?

After closing the stove, he walked over and opened the pantry shelf. As he had recalled, there was indeed a box of stale crackers, from which he extracted a handful. He glanced at the woodstove, where a glow flickered through the mica-glass. The shrouded flames made the long room seem warmer already.

Crackers in hand, his right hand, he walked to the sliding glass door onto the main deck. "Ummhhhh . . ." He managed to get the recalcitrant slider open enough to toss the crackers to the far side of the deck.

Chhurrrppppp . . .

Even before he had closed the glass, the jaymar was swooping down.

Jimjoy smiled. Some brashness ought to be rewarded.

He retrieved a pearapple from the fruit bowl. Fruit wasn't his favorite, but eating the starch and sugars he naturally preferred would have left him with the rotund profile of the gray ceramic woodstove.

Chhhurrruuupppp . . .

"No, you don't get more . . . shouldn't have given you that."

Chhurrupppp . . . With another flick of the tail, the jaymar disappeared.

Standing by the kitchen counter—dustier than he liked, but not enough to encourage him to clean quite yet—Jimjoy took small and slow bites from the pearapple. Later in the afternoon he needed to walk to the physical-training center for another round of exercise and therapy. Exercise and therapy—he hadn't expected nearly so much of either.

Thrapp! Thrapp!

With a frown and a last bite, he straightened, tossing the fruit core into the composter slot.

"Coming!"

A blocky man with the muscles of a powerlifter stood on the front deck. Rain glistened on the dull green waterproof he wore.

"Professor . . ."

"Geoff. Come on in." He stepped back from the door.

Geoff Aspan stopped on the tiles and shut the door behind him, glancing toward the stove. "See you've got a fire going."

"No so much for the heat—just wanted to get rid of the damp. Right now I'm a little stiff . . . let me take that." Jimjoy took the jacket and hung it in the otherwise empty closet. "Can I get you anything? Have some redberry juice, a couple of bottles of Hspall . . ."

"Actually, even though I'm not begging, the Hspall sounds good. Can't stay too long. I promised Carill I'd be back before the kids came home. She's taking the late shift with the field team."

Jimjoy had not even considered whether Geoff was contracted—or had children—even though the other Ecolitan had helped him occasionally by suggesting additional exercise or therapy for particular problems after the laser damage.

Jimjoy pulled the bottle from the back shelf of the keeper. Cold—but it should have been. It had been a housewarming gift.

Had it been from Mera and her friend? So it had been there for close to a year.

"It's cold." He laughed as he opened it. "Glass or bottle?"

"Bottle's fine." Geoff had turned one of the straight-backed wooden chairs around, sitting on it with one forearm resting on the low back and looking out at the rain.

Churrrppppp . . .

"You got one of those pests."

"Made the mistake of letting him, maybe it's a her, have some scraps." He extended the bottle to Geoff.

"Sort of like them," mused the dark-haired man as he took the ale. "Thanks."

Jimjoy eased onto the other straight-backed wooden chair. "I like their brashness."

"I suspected you would . . . Major . . ."

Jimjoy nodded. He wondered how long before the handful of Ecolitans with whom he had worked would recognize him. "How many of you . . . ? Think it's going to be a problem?"

"Kerin and I figured it out right after you started exercising when you first came back. None of the students, except maybe Jerrite, would recognize you from techniques. Your posture is a bit different, you're physically bigger, your voice is lower, and your entire complexion is different."

"Techniques?"

"Right. You're too good to be anyone else. The problem is that Dorfman has been asking questions about where you came from. He's close to Harlinn, and he's under Temmilan's thumb."

"Temmilan . . . had worried about that."

"So did Sam. That's why he had her posted to Parundia. Her tour is up in about two tendays, and Harlinn's sweet on her."

"I've got trouble." Jimjoy pulled on his chin and looked out the window. "More than I already thought. What's Kerin think?"

"If you weren't hooked on Thelina, it wouldn't matter what she thought." Geoff snorted. "It doesn't matter anyway. She says body postures don't lie, and you're honest. Don't know that I believe the posture bit, but I agree with her." He shifted his own posture as he took a quick swig from the bottle.

Jimjoy wished he were holding a bottle, or something. "Sometimes—hades, lots of times—I wish I weren't." He wondered why he was telling a near stranger. "She's attracted— Thelina, I mean—but she has no intention of ever letting me know that."

"Have you told her how you feel?"

Have you told her how you feel? The question echoed in his thoughts, and he glanced outside, where the rain was pelting heavily again, puddling on the deck and splashing against the glass. Jimjoy pursed his lips, swallowed. "No. I've thought about it, but every time I get close, she picks a fight."

"Hmmm . . . makes it hard . . . glad Carill's more relaxed."

"She from Accord—originally?"

"We both are. Sometimes she works under Thelina. You know, Thelina's only been here four, five years . . . and she's almost as good as Kerin . . . better than me . . . on the hand-to-hand . . ."

Jimjoy, trying to keep from frowning, got up and pulled another stove log from the short stack by the stove. He slipped on the insulated leather glove, opened the stove, and dropped in the log. The three split pieces he had used to start the stove were mainly glowing ashes.

Clunk. The stove lid dropped back into place.

"Any suggestions, Geoff?"

"*Not* telling her hasn't worked, has it?"

"No." He didn't quite have to force the short laugh.

"So tell her." The training expert took another swallow from the half-empty Hspall bottle.

"That why you came over?"

"Partly . . . but mostly to let you know about Temmilan."

"Thanks." Jimjoy looked out the window, where the rain continued to lash the deck. "A lot to do, and not much time."

Geoff stood up. "That's the definition of life, Professor."

"Jimjoy. Please, just Jimjoy."

"Fair enough. I need to get back. Shera and Jorje will be home any instant, but I appreciate the Hspall."

Jimjoy walked to the front closet, pulling the other's jacket out. "Here you go. Still damp, I'm afraid."

"No problem. Let me know if I can help."

"I will. I will."

Jimjoy watched from the open doorway as the blocky man threaded his way off the deck and dashed uphill through the near-torrential rain. Finally he shut the door.

Have you told her how you feel? Why not?

"Because she'll cut you to ribbons . . ."

Shaking his head, he collected the empty Hspall bottle, rinsed it out, and set it with the rest of the glass remnants. Manual recycling was still not a habit.

Upstairs, the console waited for him to finish the training manuals no one but Sam Hall wanted. And Sam wasn't around to appreciate them.

He took a deep breath, dried his hands on the rough towel, and started toward the stairs.

... XX ...

15 Trius 3646
New Augusta

Dear Mort:

Once again, I'll have to apologize for being late in back-
faxing. What with one thing and another, somehow I put it off.

I don't know whether to envy you or worry about your being
out there where you can do something. You were right. N'trosia's
the new Chairman of the Defense Committee. They changed the
name, too, from Military Affairs to Defense. We don't want the
Galaxy to think we're warmongers, do we? Anyway, the distinguished Senator has another study in hand to show that even if
we started plating the frames today, the FC wouldn't be ready
for fleet action for five years, and the full force of one hundred
couldn't be deployed for ten. By that time, according to his study,
the FC would be obsolete. So why bother to spend trillions of
credits for a corvette that would be outdated before it spaced?
So help me, not a single senator asked how outdated the ACs
would be by then.

Then the Haversol thing came up, and N'trosia even twisted
that. He claimed that the FC wouldn't do a thing against sabotage and that we needed more for Special Operations, not for
ships that couldn't prevent such disasters. Not that the two are
related, of course.

Looks like the Committee is buying N'trosia's argument, and
if they do, so will the entire Senate.

I passed on your account of your encounter with the Fuard to

Admiral Graylin. He's had several reports like yours. His theory is that they're testing us in every way they can. Last week we had a briefing on another new development. Pardon me if I'm sketchy, but you'll have to fill in the details, and I'm sure you understand why.

Rumor has it that the other fellows have come up with a way to use high-speed jump exits with a hull twice the size of their current destroyer hulls. Figure out what that means if they can build cruisers with the speed of corvettes, excuse me, destroyers. Enough said. Maybe too much said.

The gene thing led from one thing to another, and Sandy and I decided it wasn't going to work out. I understand she and Marie are on Haldane now.

Keep in touch. I'll try to be more regular in responding.

Blaine

. . . XXI . . .

Since, based on past experience, he didn't have much time before Thelina cut him off or he stalked out unable to contain himself, he didn't bother to sit down—in either the comfortable chair or one of the hard wooden ones. How the Accordans found those wooden chairs comfortable he still didn't know.

"You're the head of Security."

"Since when?" She stood a meter away, her left hand on the handle of the sliding door. That close, he recalled how tall she was. Graceful and well proportioned, she didn't seem large except next to someone else.

Outside, the night wind whistled through the wooden railings whose outlines were concealed by the reflection of the room in the glass sheet of the door.

"Since before I first showed up, maybe since you left—"

"Leave it at that, please. We try to avoid bringing up your past. Grant me the same courtesy." Thelina gave a half shrug and turned to face him.

He nodded. "No discourtesy meant. But I have a problem."

"You do have a few." She continued to look him straight in the eye. Her direct study reminded him of Clarissa; why, he wasn't certain.

"Yes, Thelina, I do. Shall I start with the first?"

"Start wherever you like."

The faintest tinge of trilia reached him, and he wanted to step forward and to back away, both at the same time. "Fine. My first problem is that—"—he swallowed—"that I love you, and you do your—"

"You can't love me. You don't know me. Loving someone who isn't even in their real body means nothing. You're infatuated with Dr. Hyrsa's creation. I'm just a body to you."

He couldn't stop the sigh. "I know more about you than you think . . . but I don't want to fight about it. I've told you how I feel. You want to dismiss it—fine. You want to continue to pick fights—fine. Just think about it."

"I'll think about if—if you think about—about something else."

"Something else?"

"I shouldn't have put it that way." She gave an exasperated sigh. "I'll just ask directly. Why do you have to prove yourself to every woman?"

"I don't."

"You don't? What about your sister? Your mother? The Empire?"

"What about them? They're dead."

"That makes it worse. Now you can never prove to them that you, a mere male, deserved their approval."

Jimjoy looked away from her steady green eyes, over her shoulder, out into the darkness through the reflected scene in the glass, trying to determine whether the fast-moving clouds from the west had yet arrived overhead.

"You don't even want to face it, do you?" Her voice was so low he almost missed the words.

"Face what?"

She shook her head slowly.

"And where does the Empire fit in?"

"Empires are women . . ."

He didn't know whether to laugh or frown. "You can't be serious."

"I'm very serious, and you know I am. You just don't want to hear."

He took a long, deep breath. Then he took a second one. "I'm confused. I tell you I care for you." He looked down and finally met her level glance. "That I love you . . . and you tell me that, first, I can't possibly love you, and second, that I'm a slave to approval from women . . . and the Empire. I've opened myself up, and you use the opportunity to chop me up."

"Professor . . ."

"And can't you just call me Jimjoy?"

"No. That would make me a substitute for your mother, or your sister."

"A substitute?" Jimjoy blinked, feeling like a man walking the edge of an unseen cliff.

"I'm just the last in a long series."

"You think that my whole life is just trying to get approval? That nothing I have done is because it was worth doing?"

"You've tried to do the impossible. Time after time they tried to let you kill yourself. But you kept succeeding; you kept doing the impossible. They wouldn't give you that approval. That's why you left. I think that if they'd given you a great big medal with 'Galactic Hero' printed on it, you would have allowed yourself to be shot quietly. They wouldn't. They kept insisting that you didn't exist. So you're going to force them to admit you do.

"Why did you insist on keeping your nickname? You keep telling everyone to use it, almost like advertising. Are you trying to commit suicide? The psyprofile indicated we had to let you keep the name, unless we wanted to try to rebuild your whole personality. If we did that, we'd have a nice, useless, well-muscled, and well-adjusted nothing.

"You used the same mission profile on Haversol. You just kept pressing to get more approval. Each time you push for recognition, you also are saying, 'Go ahead and find me. Shoot me, if that's what it takes.' Don't you understand?"

"Understand what?" He wanted to wipe his forehead, but then, that was the way he felt with Thelina about half the time.

"Women are approval mechanisms. I'm attractive, bright, and as close to your physical-ability level as any woman is likely to be. I'm smarter than you are, and I have the ability to reward you. That's why you want me. If I love you, then I become the ultimate approval for you. And I won't do it. I won't." Her voice was ragged.

He swallowed. His mouth was dry, and the swallow did not help much. "Because I want you to approve of me, you won't . . . even . . . consider . . ."

"I didn't say that. I said I won't be your approval mechanism. You have to love me for what I am, not the image I fit in your twisted value scheme."

"But I do."

"You might . . . but you don't. You don't even try to learn who I am . . . as a person . . . what I like . . . what activities I enjoy . . ."

He stood there forever—that was how it seemed—balanced on that unseen cliff edge, teetering there between the unreal world reflected in the glass and the unreal world where he stood.

"I . . . never . . . thought of it . . . quite that way . . ."

"I know . . . that's why I told you." Her voice went from the gentle tone back to professional Ecolitan. "Your next problem . . . Professor?"

He wondered if he should have walked out then, but he was having trouble not shaking where he stood. So he put both hands behind his back, near parade-rest style, and took a slow, long breath. "Temmilan Danaan. She's an Impie plant, and Dorfman's her tool. He's just about figured out who I am. Kerin Sommerlee and Geoff already know."

"And since Harlinn's close to the Dorfman clan and thinks we can wait out the Empire—based on his theory of historical inevitability—you think you'll be targeted once she returns?" Thelina looked over his shoulder toward the front door, then back at him.

He ignored the look, concentrating on her. He had heard nothing. "No. I *am* targeted. You know that. Except I'm dead. Temmilan will reveal I'm not, and that the Institute has more abilities than the Empire realizes. She doesn't understand that just uncovering me will get the Empire to act immediately."

"Why do you think so?"

"Simple. Once I'm found alive, Special Ops statistics will show that Accord engineered the suspected Fuard destruction of Haversol SysCon, that other agents have been gathered by Accord, and that Accord biotech is good enough to infiltrate anywhere in the Empire. That enough for starters?"

She nodded. "There's more, I presume."

"Third, I had started the manifesto operation—"

"You?"

"Yes, me. I started writing the things to stir up some popular support, but outside of a handful of people, it wasn't generating enough support. At first Sam didn't know it was me. He used the manifestos to build the Freedom Now Party. Except he's dead, and I don't know who followed up. Someone has—and I would have guessed you—except it didn't quite fit . . ."

Thelina tilted her head, then turned toward the shining black of the closed sliding glass door. The door shivered from the wind. Reflecting the lights in the room against the darkness outside, the image of the room moved once, twice, before settling, and revealing a figure by the stairs.

Jimjoy said nothing about the newcomer who waited behind him, although he could feel his shoulders wanting to tense.

"Occasionally, Professor—occasionally—you surprise me. Some of your manifestos are surprisingly well written."

Determined not to rise to her baiting, Jimjoy swallowed. "Thank you."

"Your reasoning is close. Meryl is the one who worked with Sam."

Jimjoy nodded. "So that was why she came to the hospital."

Thelina frowned; then her face cleared. "After Haversol, you mean."

"After Haversol, yes." He cleared his throat. "We need to increase the pressure."

"We? Exactly what do you mean?" asked a new voice, as cool as Thelina's.

Jimjoy turned toward Meryl. "Does the average person here really care? I doubt it. Most people just want to live their lives in peace. They fight when there's no choice, and sometimes not even then. From what you've said, people here are different, but I haven't seen that much difference. I'm not counting the Institute and the leadership here.

"Take your capital—Harmony doesn't feel that different from a dozen other semi-independent colonies or dependencies. You've been so successful in developing your way of life that most people truly don't understand how antithetical it is to the Empire. Or how much the Empire might come to fear Accord."

"What sort of pressure did you have in mind?" Meryl had walked over to one of the wooden chairs beside Thelina.

"A few follow-up stories on Imperial reeducation teams. Like the story they refused to cast or print on Luren . . ."

"Why would they print it now?"

"They won't, not for several tendays. Then the situation will have changed."

"You realize, Professor, that your confidence verges on total arrogance?" asked Thelina.

"There's my last problem," Jimjoy said.

"Well, don't spare us that one, either."

Meryl winced at the tone in which Thelina's response was delivered.

Jimjoy took another deep breath. "How and where do I train a team to take over orbit control?"

Meryl nodded. Thelina shook her head, not in negation, but not in approval. Outside, the wind whistled through the railing of the deck.

Finally Meryl looked at Thelina, then back at Jimjoy. "Carefully, and without the knowledge and approval of the Institute."

"I take it there's more than one Temmilan."

"Your brilliance continues to astound me." Thelina's tone was dry.

Meryl almost winced—again.

Jimjoy ignored both. "How do I get a group of Ecolitans together under the imprimatur of the Institute without the Institute's support?"

Meryl looked at Thelina, who looked back at Meryl.

"The same way we always do."

Jimjoy grinned wryly. "More explanation, please."

The two exchanged glances. "We ask for volunteers."

"Look, I'm talking about training a group that will eventually be the Accord variety of Special Operative."

"You can't call it that," observed Thelina mildly.

"I know. They ought to be more broadly trained." He cleared his throat.

Both women waited politely.

"How about calling it something like 'applied ecologic management'?"

"You also have a way with euphemisms."

"Any better ideas, Ecolitan Andruz? Like how we get the Institute to allow us to develop an accepted new discipline with apprentice and journeyman status?"

"That part's easy. We just make it a sub-branch of the field training. You're already listed as a qualified master in field training, and with the approval of the majority of Senior Fellows in a major discipline, any master can develop a more specialized sub-branch."

"I take it security, or whatever euphemism you use, is also a sub-branch."

Both women nodded solemnly, a solemnity that could have concealed laughter.

Jimjoy wanted to shake his head, instead remembered to pull

at his chin. "And nobody says *anything*? What about budgets? Supplies?"

"If it goes beyond the department's budget, you have to get the Prime's approval, except for security, and that budget is approved as a whole a year in advance, with the ability to commit up to fifty percent more. But you have to answer for the overrun personally to the Prime."

Jimjoy took a deep breath. "When do you want the plan?"

"Tomorrow at the latest. You don't have much time."

"We don't have much time," added Meryl.

"Tomorrow," he agreed, looking out into the darkness. "Tomorrow."

. . . XXII . . .

tomorrow of the shuttle. You can chase time a little—"

"We don't have much time," added Mary.

"Tomorrow," he agreed, looking out into the darkness. "To-morrow . . ."

24 Quintus 3646
Demetris

Dear Blaine:

Just received your latest. Arrived here at home rather than station catch. Too bad we can't receive torps, but they'd never know where to send them.

Sorry to hear about you and Sandy, but keep the stars, keep the stars. Wish I could say more, but what is there? Helen and I both care, wish you the best.

Some ways, I wish I hadn't heard the latest rumors. Now there's another one—about the courier that disappeared, a year ago, I guess. Was it the *D'Armetier*? Anyway, torp tissues said it showed up on a T-form planet where no one expected it and with a cargo of bodies—and no one can account for the missing time. That sort of thing doesn't play well with the crews. Any way I can refute it?

Then there's the continual battle against obsolescence. With old zipless cracking around the frames every other jump, the thought of being chased by something twice as big and twice as fast, with even better jump accuracy and exit speed, doesn't exactly improve my outlook. Talked about it with Helen, and she's asked me to consider putting in my papers after this tour.

Can you do anything? Sure, the FC isn't *the* answer. But *Halley*'s older than half my crew. It's still the latest we've got. Any hope of new development, like the CX concept? Understand you've put it out for costing and tech evaluation. That true?

New exec arrived. Querrat—Francie Querrat's cousin, graduated six years behind me. Seems as sharp as Francie—miss her, and that's another one I hold against Tinhorn—and he'll work out. No-nonsense, but the crew respects him from the start.

Not much else new. Cindi's growing like a sunplume, and Jock's learning differentials. Demetris is nice enough, but it's not home. Miss the winters. Once a Sierran, always a Sierran, I guess.

Mort

. . . XXIII . . .

The woman in the faded blue trousers and gray sweater turned over the cream-colored oblong as she closed the door behind her.

"Thelina Andruz, S.F.I." was written in old-fashioned black ink on the envelope. The envelope itself was lightly sealed. How long the envelope had been there she did not know, although the heavy paper was still crisp, and there had been a light rain the night before. The ink was unmarred.

Her lips pursed, and in the dimmer light of the wood-paneled foyer she squinted at the precise handwriting, almost a bold and thick-lined calligraphy.

Cocking her head to the side, ignoring some blond wisps of uncombed hair that framed her face, she grinned. Then she cleared her throat softly. Finally she called upstairs. "Thelina. You have an invitation."

Silence.

"It's impeccably correct," she called again.

"I have a what?" Wearing a heavy terry-cloth robe and a towel over her hair, turban fashion, Thelina stood at the top of the stairs.

"I'd say it was an invitation of some sort . . . very formal . . . linen paper and black ink—like something that the Council—"

"Oh, Meryl, just open it."

"I couldn't do that. It's sealed and addressed to you. Personally."

"Is this a joke?"

Meryl turned the envelope over, holding it up so the calligraphy faced Thelina. "It doesn't appear to be."

"All right." With a sigh, the taller woman made her way down the stairs, quickly yet precisely.

"Here you are, honored lady." Meryl grinned.

"You know."

"I know nothing, but I'm a pretty good guesser."

"So?"

"Let's see."

Thelina shook her head, then flicked the flap of the envelope open with a short and well-trimmed thumbnail. "A second envelope . . . very formal indeed."

"How is it addressed? Just 'Thelina,' right?"

"You know." Thelina glared at her housemate. "Is this some sort of game?"

"No. But it figures."

"You aren't saying."

"I might be wrong."

"Never mind." The taller Ecolitan eased open the inner envelope, scanning the heavy linen card she held by the lower right corner. She read it once, then again.

Watching her friend, Meryl began to grin even more widely.

"This . . . he . . . this is impossible!"

"The good Professor Whaler?"

"You've seen his handwriting before?"

"No. How else could he address your charges? You claimed he knew nothing about the real you. You really asked for a formal courtship. He took you at your word."

"I never said . . ."

"Not in words."

"You're impossible . . . you're both impossible . . ."

Meryl held out her hand for the card.

Thelina handed it over brusquely. "*You* go."

"No. You go."

"I despise him." Thelina tucked the inside envelope against the outside one, then placed the card under both flaps.

Meryl arched her left eyebrow, holding Thelina's eyes.

"What should I wear?"

After grinning again, Meryl shrugged. "Something suitable and casually formal, in keeping with the tone of the invitation."

Shaking her head slowly, Thelina handed the two envelopes and the card to Meryl. "Men."

"Agreed." Meryl read the card, with the letters written so precisely that they almost appeared typeset.

> The honor of your presence is requested at an outdoor luncheon for two at 1315 H.S.T. on the fourteenth of Septem at the lookout on Quayle Point. Refreshments will be provided . . . suitable attire is suggested. . . .
>
> James Joyson Whaler II,
> S.F.I.

The sandy-haired Ecolitan laid the card and envelopes on the small foyer table and followed her friend upstairs. Suitable attire, indeed, would be necessary. Especially if it looked like snow. But an outdoor luncheon?

. . . XXIV . . .

The tall man, bearded and bent and wearing a faded brown
greatcoat, hobbled from the library's public section, pausing frequently on the staircase. His breath puffed around him irregu-
larly in the chill early morning air.

As he reached the top step, resting against the railing to catch
his breath again, a younger man emerged, black-haired, with the
collar of an advocate's tunic peering above and out of a quilted
winter jacket that was unfastened.

The advocate who was not an advocate looked up, ignoring
both the old man and the middle-aged redheaded woman coming
down, took the middle of the staircase, and bounded up the steps
to street level two at a time. The steam of his breath was as
enthusiastic as his pace. In his right hand he carried an envelope
the size of a thin folder of standard paper.

The older man limped in the same general direction as the
pseudo-advocate, somehow not quite losing sight of the young
man as both made their way uphill, away from Government
Square and toward the outworld commercial section.

By the time the white-haired man had crossed Carson Boulevard, the morning sunlight had lifted the frost from the still-
green grass everywhere its rays had struck. Those few who
walked in the early Tenday sunlight no longer saw their breath,
and the frost only lingered in the shadows.

By the time the tall man had crossed Korasalov Road, he had
unbuttoned the top button of the greatcoat and watched the
younger man enter a low two-story building. His limp increased
as he plodded after the other, mumbling through his beard,

loudly enough for a passing runner to veer away with a look of annoyance.

In time he approached the locked door of the building, where he fumbled at the lock momentarily, staggered against the doorframe, as if for support, before stumbling, then tumbling inside as the heavy carved door swung open. A second runner, observing the scene, just shook his head and concentrated on keeping his pace.

Down the dimly lit interior hallway limped the oldster, stopping at last by the door he sought, where he listened quietly for a time.

Thump . . . thump . . .

The gaunt man rapped on the door, the sound of his knuckles muffled by the heaviness of the wood and of the metal beneath it. "Marissa! Open up! I know you're here . . ." He ignored the brass plate on the door's center panel.

CentraCast Business Publications
Harmony Information Center

. . . thump . . . thump . . . thump . . .

"Marissa . . . you let your father in." His voice cracked, not quite in hysteria. "I know you're in there."

The other doorways on the short hallway remained closed. All were news-related businesses, not surprisingly, since the two-story building was the Business and News Center. Nor was the lack of response surprising, not on Tenday, when most Accord businesses were shut down.

. . . thump . . . thump . . . thump . . .

"Marissa! Open this door!"

He paused and took a deep breath, waiting as if to regain his strength. After a time, he leaned toward the door.

Thump . . . thump . . . thump . . .

"Marissa, you listen to your father . . ."

The hallway remained silent.

Thump . . . thump . . . thump . . .

"Marissa . . . worthless girl . . . just like your mother . . . open this door . . ."

As he leaned back, the door opened full. The black-haired young man stood in the doorway, a stunner leveled at the disheveled oldster.

"You . . . you're not Marissa. What have you done with her?"

''There is no Marissa here. You're disturbing everyone. Please leave or I'll call the—''

Thrum.

The young man toppled forward, without even a surprised look on his face, only to be caught by the ancient's too-well-muscled arms.

Clunk. The stunner echoed dully on the scuffed wooden planks.

The tall man stepped inside the office, scanned the front room. Two consoles with battered but matching chairs, a short, squarish green upholstered love seat, two wooden armchairs, and a table, around which the armchairs and the love seat were clustered, constituted the furniture. A single curtained window joined the rear wall and the right wall, providing the room's only light. In the middle of the left wall a door opened into an even dimmer room.

In the front room one console was turned on, a pale green square.

As he completed his near-instantaneous survey, the man in the greatcoat lowered the unconscious man. He recovered the stunner and closed the door.

With quick motions, he set the young man in a wooden armchair, the type favored by all Ecolitans, and balanced him in place, letting the arms dangle. The folder lay on top of an envelope on the operational console. The older man in the greatcoat noted its presence as he polished the fingerprints off the stunner with a cloth retrieved from an inside pocket of the worn coat. With the thin transparent gloves on his own hands, he had no worry about leaving his own prints. He levered the setting up to the maximum level before placing it in the limp hand of the unconscious man in the chair.

With quick steps he moved into the small equipment room that lay through the open door in the left wall. Two locked cube cases sat against the back wall, and several cases of fax equipment were stacked carelessly around. All but one were covered with dust.

A muffled *click* caught his ear, and he slipped from the equipment room back into the front room, standing behind the wooden chair facing the closed door.

After waiting about the length of time it would have taken someone to walk from the side building door to the CentraCast door, he lifted his own stunner.

Click.
Thrum.
Crummmppp.

A dark-haired woman slumped through the door and onto the unscuffed planks inside the office. A large envelope slipped from her hands and skidded across the wood until it rested against the throw rug on which the low table sat.

He dragged the woman inside. After extracting the key from the door, he closed it with a *click* and set her in the chair opposite the unconscious young man. He slipped the key, on its plain steel ring, into her right jacket pocket and struggled with the closures on the jacket, opening them all, but leaving the jacket on her.

His gloved hands deftly opened her belt pouch, subtracting one or two items and replacing them with several others. His nose wrinkled at the scent of melloran that enveloped her as he continued his search-and-replace efforts.

In time he shifted his attention to the younger man, adding several items to his person.

Then he replaced the contents of the envelope carried by the woman with another set of documents, and placed the envelope on the table in front of her. In turn, he lifted the several sheets of copied public records from the envelope by the still-humming console and replaced them with other copied public records.

Taking a deep breath, he looked around the room again. His eyes moved to the stunner lying in the lap of the unconscious man, and he bent down and checked the charge indicator. It would be sufficient.

Retrieving his own stunner, he set the charge as low as possible and aimed the weapon at the woman's head from a meter away.

Thrum . . . thrum . . . thrum . . . thrum . . .

Her body twitched after each shot, and by the last shot her face was slack, her chest barely moving.

The tall man took the slack hand of the unconscious man, the hand holding the stunner. He positioned the man so that he held the stunner against his own temple.

TTHHHHRRRUMMMM . . .

Clank. The body twitched once. The stunner struck the floor, where the tall man left it on his way out of the office.

. . . XXV . . .

(ANS) Harmony [14 Septem 3646]   Local authorities are still investigating a mysterious suicide/attempted murder which took place in the CentraCast offices over the enddays. Local sources indicate the dead man was a junior Ecolitan attached to the Institute for Ecologic Studies, but his name has not been released. The woman, a Senior Fellow at the Institute whose name has also been withheld, suffered severe brain damage from a stunner bolt. The man apparently then turned the stunner on himself.

Items found on the two and in the office indicated that the woman had attempted to break off a love affair. Well-placed sources indicate that the two had often been seen together.

Other sources indicated that the woman had just returned from a temporary assignment on the Parundian Peninsula. Such assignments are frequently used as a disciplinary tool. Further comment could not be obtained from the Institute, since the official who assigned the wounded Ecolitan died several months ago in an equally unusual flash fire in a training vehicle.

Diagrams of the same type of training vehicle were found in a folder at the CentraCast office, but local authorities refused to speculate on any connections between the two incidents.

. . . XXVI . . .

Jimjoy set the second basket beside the table, checking again to see that the green linen cloth would remain in place against the light breeze from the east. With the chill of the wind came the scent of fallen leaves.

On the table were two large crystal goblets rimmed in thin bands of gold and green, two smaller goblets with the same pattern, two sets of gold-plated dinner utensils, two green linen napkins, two butter plates, two salad plates, and two luncheon plates. All the plates were of pale green china with a single golden rim. An armless chair sat behind each setting.

In the unopened basket were the various courses he had arranged for the luncheon, as well as the small bottle of Sparsa and the thermos of ice water.

He stood and surveyed the lookout. The stained wooden railings, smoothed to the finish of glass, still guarded the drop-off. Behind him, the saplar forest covered the crest of the hill from which Quayle Point projected.

With a wry smile, he recalled the first time he had climbed the hill, right through the forest. The sap secretions had ruined that set of greens. Then, like now, there hadn't been the small buckets attached to the trees, since the Institute tapped the sap only during the spring. Even upwind from the trees, he could occasionally smell their mint-resin odor.

He and Thelina had watched the sunrise, and she hadn't spoken to him then, either, even though they had walked back to the Institute together.

From where he had placed the table, the center of the Institute was visible, although the outlying training areas were not. Nor were the underground facilities. Even now he doubted that he knew of more than half the hidden emplacements—if that. The Institute was like an old Terran onion, pungent and with layer hidden behind layer.

The sun warmed his back, even as the wind from the east cooled his chest. He wore only a set of heavy formal greens. Still, the breeze was nothing more than a fall zephyr to a man born and raised on White Mountain, although those years had been two lifetimes ago.

A shadow made its way up from the Institute and across the forest as, overhead, a scattered handful of puffy white clouds swam toward the west, along the southern mountains to his right.

After a glance at the flat strip on his wrist, he reached down and pulled the thermos from the provisions basket. The dark organic-based plastic felt smooth against his fingers. 1314 Harmony Standard Time. Even though he pursed his lips, his hands were sure in filling the two large goblets three-quarters full with the spring water.

There was always the possibility she wouldn't come. He hadn't asked for an RSVP, probably a grievous breach of etiquette in itself. 1315 Harmony Standard Time. With a frown, he stared at the Institute, wondering . . . hoping.

Crunnchhhh . . . The footstep on the path was so faint, almost fainter than the susurrus of the wind, that he almost missed the sound.

Stepping away from the table, he waited.

Like him, Thelina wore formal greens. Her short silver hair glittered in the sunlight as she walked from the path and across the grass. Her eyes widened slightly at the formal setting of the table.

"You did mean formal, didn't you?"

He bowed at the waist, slightly. "The setting is formal, the locale informal, and the repast, alas, probably not up to either, or to the guest."

She inclined her head. "The speech is also rather formal."

"It's been suggested that one should know someone, their likes and dislikes, before attempting informality." He stepped forward and gestured, pulling out the chair for her.

"I think I'd better help with this." Thelina helped guide the chair she was taking into place. "Chairs don't slide on grass very well."

"I'll talk to the plant biology department about improving that characteristic." He reached for the basket. "Please pardon some informality. Do you like Sparsa?"

She nodded, her eyes traveling toward the lookout, and to the Institute beyond and below.

Thwupppp . . . Jimjoy uncorked the green-tinted bottle, then eased the sparkling wine into the smaller goblet before Thelina. He filled his own goblet and sat down across from her.

"If I might ask," she began, "where did you get such a co-ordinated setting?"

"In Harmony. Thought I might have some use for it in the future. At least I could dine in style. The setting would make up for my cooking."

"You do cook?"

"I'm from White Mountain. That's a long time back, but how could I be male and not cook? Certainly I'm not up to my father's standards, but . . ." Jimjoy shrugged, and waited for Thelina to taste the Sparsa.

She caught the flick of his eyes from her face to her goblet. Her hand reached for the goblet and lifted it, holding the crystal for a long instant before carrying it to her lips for a small sip.

Jimjoy followed her sample, although his was a short swallow, rather than just a sip.

"Grand Sparsa in crystal. Perhaps the second time in my life."

"You like it?" he asked, wishing as he did so that he hadn't.

Her lips quirked. "How could I not? What did this set you back?"

He smiled faintly. "If I told you, would you enjoy it more or less? Please enjoy it." He took a second, smaller sip, letting the taste linger.

"Are you—"

"No." He cut off her question, knowing where it might be leading. "I only asked you for luncheon, and I selected the lookout as a place to enjoy the best I could provide. That's all."

Her smile was part annoyance, part amusement. "Do you always answer questions before they're asked?"

"Usually not. I apologize. You wanted to ask . . . ?"

"I'll phrase it a bit more delicately. Aren't you concerned I might not fully appreciate what could be considered more than a little ostentatious?"

"That is a possibility. I had hoped that you would wait until after the luncheon to make a final judgment."

She took another sip of the Sparsa as the breeze fluttered her silver hair. "That's a fair request."

He eased his chair back, careful to avoid snagging the legs on the grass, stood, and bent to open the basket again. From the insulated plastic came the two rolls and the butter. From the bowl, after he unsealed it, came the salad. With the tongs, he deftly laid each piece of mixed greenery on the salad plates. From another small container came the nut garnish. Then he removed the clinging seal from a small pitcher, again of the same gold-rimmed green china, and placed the pitcher in the middle of the table.

Without another word, he replaced the basket and reseated himself, retrieving the linen napkin from the grass next to his chair, where it had been carried by a brief gust.

He nodded. Thelina nibbled at the warm roll, leaving the butter untouched. Then she set the remaining half roll back on its plate, picked up her fork, put it down, and reached for the pitcher. She raised her eyebrows.

"Oh, nothing special. Call it a house dressing. As close to my father's as I could make it."

Thelina poured a thin line of the amber, spice-tinged liquid over the greenery. She extended the pitcher to Jimjoy.

"Thank you."

"Thank you," she answered. Her tone was gentle. She waited until he had added the dressing to his salad before lifting her fork. "Very good."

He acknowledged the compliment with a nod and a soft "Thank you," and followed her lead in addressing the greenery. The first taste told him that, this time, he hadn't overdone the lemon, and the dressing had just the touch of tang he had wanted.

After another measured mouthful, he set down his fork along the edge of the salad plate, watching Thelina finish her salad, enjoying the relish with which she ate.

Another shadow from the fluffy overhead clouds crossed the table, and the wind ruffled the green linen.

"A little chilly when you lose the sun."

"It does make a difference," he agreed.

"You look . . . comfortable. Are you wearing just your greens?"

A touch of a smile crossed his face. "Just my greens. I'd hoped it would be a little warmer—the way the long-range forecast had predicted."

"You're not cold?"

"No. Are you?" His voice carried a touch of concern.

"No. But I took certain precautions, like thermals." She smiled. "Would this really be considered a warm day on White Mountain?"

"Not a summer day, but certainly a pleasant fall day. What about where you're from?"

She tilted her head. "Call it a crisp fall day or a warm winter day."

He stood and returned to the basket, pulling forth two insulated, self-heating containers. From the first he eased the contents onto Thelina's plate—thin white slices of meat, covered with a golden sauce containing dark morsels; split green beans sprinkled with a mist of nutmeats; and a circlet of black rice. He repeated the process with his own plate, replaced the empty containers in the basket, and reseated himself.

Although the cloud had passed and the fall sunlight bathed the table, thin wisps of vapor still rose from the plates.

"If I could, I would have managed hot plates, but that just wasn't practical."

Her eyebrows rose again as she picked up her dinner fork. "You actually cooked this yourself?"

He nodded.

"Every bit of it?"

He nodded, then grinned. "I'm out of practice. I tried each course twice over the past week. This was the first time they all worked out together, and I wasn't sure they would." He inclined his head. "Go ahead. It's better warm, and it won't stay that way very long."

Thelina took both knife and fork and the invitation. Jimjoy followed, although eating more slowly, tasting the sauce critically, noting that it had almost separated again, although he'd gotten the taste right.

"You really did this?"

"Yes."

"It's marvelous."

He nodded, knowing that it was good, although not as good as he had secretly hoped.

She stopped and looked at him, putting her utensils down. "It's not as good as you wanted, is it?"

He sighed. "It's good, perhaps even a bit better. I'd really hoped it would be spectacular."

"I'm flattered." She paused. "I really mean that. I am flattered. No one has ever done something like this for me. Especially not with their own hands."

Jimjoy couldn't help smiling. "I'm glad. Shouldn't say that, but I am." He took another bite, hoping Thelina would still enjoy the remainder of her meal after his confession that it had not reached his standards.

She did, finishing everything on her plate, and even using the remainder of her roll to catch the last of the sauce. She took another sip of the Sparsa, emptying her goblet.

He stood, refilled it, and removed all the plates, stacking them neatly in the basket.

"Could we just talk for a bit?"

He closed the basket and sat down, his forearms on the table, leaning slightly, but only slightly, toward her, noticing how her hair sparkled in the afternoon light, how graceful she looked sitting there.

"No matter how much you protest, you listen, don't you?"

Nodding, he waited.

"You don't like to ask questions, and you wait for people to talk. Sometimes, though, people won't talk unless they're asked."

"Sometimes," he responded, "people don't know what questions to ask, or when."

"You don't like women very much. You can love them, but you don't like them."

He pulled at his chin, conscious of the wind riffling the linen tablecloth and his hair, conscious that he was squinting to see as he faced the slowly lowering sun. "You may be right. And you? Do you feel that way about men?"

"Does it show that much?"

"I'm not sure anything shows, except I seem to bring out stronger feelings in people. Something, maybe a lot of something, hits you wrong. And I . . . anyway . . ."

She ignored his unfinished statement, looking out beyond the lookout. "I don't trust men. The men you trust are the ones who hurt you the most."

He took a deep breath, slowly. "You may be right about that, too. Except I'd say that whoever you trust can hurt you the most. It doesn't mean they will. They can, though. Could you trust your father?" Even as he asked the question, he wondered whether he should have.

"I don't know. He died when I was twelve. And he was too sick to care before that."

Jimjoy frowned, wondering how anyone on any civilized planet would be condemned to a lingering death.

"He was on the proscribed list."

Jimjoy kept his mouth in place. The proscribed list—there had been rumors of the device, how the Matriarchy had used it to punish its opponents long before the Military Directorate of Halston had fallen. He pursed his lips, then looked at Thelina, and guessed. "Didn't they keep their word? Or was it too late?"

She met his eyes. "When he found out, he committed suicide."

"And you kept your part of the bargain?"

"Yes."

"Do you want to tell me about it?"

"No. But I will . . . if you'll tell me how you got from White Mountain to the I.S.S."

"All right." Even in the sunlight he could see the tenseness that might have been caused by the cold. "I have liftea or cafe. And dessert. Would you like either?"

"I'll wait on the dessert. The liftea would be nice."

He took almost the last items out of the basket—the china cups and saucers and another thermos, from which he poured.

"Thank you." Thelina immediately took a sip of the liftea, without the sugar Jimjoy was placing in the center of the table.

He added sugar to his, waiting for her to begin.

"We lived on an out-continent in one of the ring systems. That's where the Matriarchy has always been the strongest. They controlled the health network. My father was a magistrate, and he ordered the doctors, and they were mostly women, to abide by the Spousal Consent Laws . . ."

Jimjoy shuddered. Those few systems that had given spouses the right to insist on offspring observed the practice mainly in the breach—except for the now-deposed Militarists in the Halston systems and the Fuards.

". . . and somehow he came down with Ruthemnian Fever. No one would treat him, and none of the other magistrates or enforcers would insist. They might be next. I watched my mother begin to die in her own way. She pleaded, I think. It did no good." Thelina took another sip of the liftea.

Jimjoy's eyes flicked past Thelina to the jaymar climbing away from a ferrahawk. The nuisance bird avoided a stoop from the predator by darting into a saplar stand below the lookout. The ferrahawk recovered and began a circling climb away from the saplars and to regain altitude for future hunting with less troublesome prey.

"So I went to the Temple. I wasn't even twelve. My father's dying was killing my mother, and I loved her. What else could a girl do?

"They came the next day and took him to the hospital. Less than a tenday later, he was home, cured. The day after that he stepped off the Malyn Bridge. He left a note, but I never understood it. I still don't. My mother died the next spring, I'm told, after I entered training."

Jimjoy could feel his hands tightening against the green linen tablecloth, wanting to strike out. He forced his muscles to relax and took a sip of his rapidly cooling liftea.

His eyes caught hers for an instant, then dropped from the darkness he saw there.

"Did what the note say matter? Or that he killed your mother?"

"I remember enough . . ."

Jimjoy took another sip of his tea.

". . . the part . . . he wrote something like 'I cannot be bound to be enslaved and forever beholden.' And he said that I had made my bargains for myself, not for him."

"They wouldn't release you?"

"I didn't ask. What was left? No sisters, no cousins. My brother left before I could remember him."

Jimjoy drained his cup with a sudden swallow. "Feel . . . I don't know . . . compared to you, I had no reasons." He looked toward the west, over Thelina's shoulder, squinting slightly as the sun eased downward. "You know my mother was a regional administrator. Her mother had been the sector chief. Two older sisters to begin with. Kaylin and Clarissa. Clarissa was the golden girl. Tops in her class, beautiful. She could sing, she could sail, she could paint, and everyone loved her. So did I. I wanted to do everything she did. Better, if I could. The singing—actually put together a band. Male bands were a real novelty, and we did all right, but my mother was smart. She left me alone, just put pressure on the parents of the three others. Pretty soon I had no one to sing with. I couldn't paint that well, but I tried calligraphy, and Clarissa couldn't do that. She pushed me, but it wasn't nasty."

He looked down at the green linen.

Thelina said nothing.

"Kaylin came back from Cirque, the university. Selected as the Diplomate, and, of course, the Regional Administrator had a party, honoring the number-one graduate student in all of White Mountain. My father outdid himself with that banquet.

"I'd graduated from Selque, the local pre-university, number one, first man in a generation. Also won the open skimmer title that week—we used the week system there, just like on Old Earth. Plus a few other honors here and there. Not only didn't I get even a small dinner, I was gently reminded to make a tactful appearance at Kaylin's festivities and then disappear.

"Three weeks later Clarissa was killed on the lake, after I'd taken her dare. I beached the boat in our harbor and walked all the way to the Imperial Shuttleport, took the tests for a Reserve commission, and passed. They sent me to Malestra."

"Just passed?"

He laughed softly. "With a perfect score . . . for all the good it did me. I never got a letter, a fax, or anything."

"A perfect score. Did you tell anyone? Even where you went?"

"There was Christina . . . but her family had already shipped her off to Cirque, just like Kaylin. She never returned my faxes, but I really don't know that she ever got them. I was too independent, unpredictable, for her family. Maybe that's just my wanting to be that way. I faxed Kaylin once. She cut me off. I sent two hard-copy faxes. Both were refused."

Thelina pursed her lips. "Did you tell any of this to Dr. Militro?"

"Some. Not all. Not about Kaylin's party. Not about Anita."

"Anita?"

"After Clarissa's death, Lerra—she wouldn't let me call her mother—decided to have another child. That was Anita. What she probably had to live up to . . ."

Another set of clouds, grayer, thicker, passed over the sun, and a colder wind whipped the linens. Jimjoy stood up and reached for the basket, bringing out the last items, setting one before Thelina and one at his place. "Crème D'mont. Try it before we both freeze." He seated himself.

He wasn't freezing, but even with the thermals under her greens Thelina was drawing into herself.

She took a small bite, then another. "How many times for this?"

"Actually . . . none. I fix it for myself on and off." He took a bite twice the size of hers. "Just not too often."

"If this is any sample of how you cook, you're a far better cook than I am. Or than Meryl."

Her eyes met his, and their green, for once, seemed less piercing, not as if he were facing another challenge.

Even so, he wanted to look away. Instead, he answered. "This is about the best I've done. Too lazy most of the time."

"Too lazy?" Her voice sounded puzzled, and as if her teeth were about to chatter.

He reached for the thermos and refilled her cup. "Finish that while I pack this up. If I make you stay here any longer, you'll turn into a block of ice." He eased back his chair and began to replace the remaining utensils in the first basket. "Lazy?" he reflected as he removed his dessert plate. "By the time I'm in my quarters, fixing anything feels like a chore. Then again, some days everything feels like a chore."

"That doesn't sound like the Special Operative who ran himself almost to death on at least two occasions."

He smiled wryly, briefly, as he finished packing up everything except the cloth and her cup and saucer. "Suppose not. Would you believe that I'm also a coward at heart?"

"No. Not a coward. A man who could never afford to show fear, I think." She emptied the cup and set it down.

Jimjoy retrieved her cup and saucer and packed them, along with the green linen that flapped in the stiffening breeze. "Knew that anyone who wasn't afraid was a damned fool, but I couldn't ever believe it." He glanced up. Except for the far west, the entire sky was cloudy, hours ahead of the forecast. "I'm afraid I'll have to reveal some of my secrets, since we're going to have to cut this short. The weather didn't follow the forecast."

"It doesn't, not on Accord." She stood up. "What can I do?"

"If you wouldn't mind . . . there's a pack stashed behind that boulder—" He gestured to a point behind her left shoulder. While she hurried toward the rock, he began to break down the chairs, then the table. By the time she had returned, he was tying three bundles of wood together.

"You asked me to get that just so I wouldn't see how you took those apart." Her tone was mock accusing. She handed him the pack and watched as he fitted the two baskets and the bundles together. "Ingenious."

"It is. Not my idea, but I remembered it from New Avalon. They like elegant picnics there, I'm told. Waltar's made it for me. I guessed some on the design, but Geoff helped me out."

Thelina shook her head as he slipped the pack on. "Are you sure I couldn't carry something?"

"No. It all fits together. Bulky, but it's not even as heavy as a standard field pack, especially now. Shall we go?"

Thelina opened her mouth, then closed it for a moment, before finally nodding.

Jimjoy, conscious of her walking beside him, forced himself to concentrate on the path. The wind tugged at his tunic, and he could sense the chill in the coming storm. Snow—or freezing rain—but not for a few hours, he guessed.

"You've made things even more complicated now," she said as they passed the curve in the path below the saplar forest. Ahead lay the Institute.

"Suppose so. Nothing's ever turned out simple. But how do you mean it?" He could sense her shrug.

"You're no longer just the cold and efficient Special Operative or the brilliant Professor Whaler who leaves his students' preconceptions in tatters. You're not just a soulless killer."

"So what am I?"

The silence was punctuated only by two sets of steps, one heavy, one light, and underscored by the whistling of the wind.

"I don't know. I don't think you do, either."

He had to shrug, though the gesture was restrained by the picnic pack. "You're right. I don't. Once I thought I did." He took several more long steps, which she matched, as she had all along, before he added, "I've thought so more than once. I was always wrong."

The path branched in front of them, and they took the left-hand branch, the narrower one that led to the cluster of housing where Thelina lived.

"I almost didn't come."

"I worried whether you would."

"I know. I saw you checking the time. Twice."

Her tone said she was smiling, but he wasn't sure whether he should look. Finally, after an instant that seemed like eternity, he did. She was.

He couldn't help grinning, and she smiled even more knowingly.

"You're blushing" she observed, still smiling.

". . . know . . . can't help it . . ." He stopped at the steps up to her front deck.

Thelina turned to face him.

Jimjoy realized he hadn't said what he really wanted to say. Yet he had said all he could. Finally, after holding her eyes, as the wind whistled around them, as he could see her repress a shiver, he moistened his suddenly very dry lips. "Thank you."

"You won't—no, you're right . . ." For just an instant, she looked as bewildered as he felt. Then she was back in control. "I had a wonderful time, and I won't try to spoil it by trying to drag it out. Thank you."

"So did I."

"Next time will be my treat." She put one foot on the first wooden step, her eyes still on him.

He nodded. There would be a next time, at least. "Go get warm."

"I will. Thank you. I mean it. Freezing or not, I enjoyed every minute."

He didn't know what to say, except "So did I" again. So he just looked, waiting for her to go up the four steps to the deck.

She took the steps deliberately, then stopped and turned at the top. "Thank you."

Her voice was soft, slightly more than a whisper, but each word lingered in his ears.

He watched the door close before he turned to carry the picnic pack back. He had some cleaning up to do, and then some. Not that he minded, not at all. Not at all.

. . . XXVII . . .

Jimjoy straightened the quilted martial arts jacket and brushed his short hair back. Why he bothered he didn't know, since the next set of exercises would only disarrange both.

". . . two, three . . . uhhh . . . two, three . . ." The improvements in his shoulders and the slight addition to his height, even with Dr. Hyrsa's work on his muscles, hadn't improved the overall muscular tightness he'd inherited, or diminished his need for stretching exercises.

He took a deep breath, ignoring the subdued scents of sweat, steam, and pine resin that seemed to characterize every exercise facility on Accord.

"Watching you makes me glad my parents were relaxed." Geoff Aspan grinned at the taller Ecolitan.

"Relaxed, hades. If they were *that* relaxed, you wouldn't be here." Jimjoy took a deep breath and went back to work.

Geoff grinned, then wiped the smile from his face.

". . . two, three . . . unhhhh . . . two, three . . ."

"We've got problems."

Jimjoy, catching the seriousness in the other's voice, stopped and looked up from his stretched-out position on the mat. "Why?"

"Here comes Kerin, and she's ready to kill."

"Your problem, Geoff. I only work here part-time." Jimjoy was grinning as he kept working on stretching out his back and leg muscles.

"This look's for both of us."

"How do you know?"

"You obviously haven't been contracted or married. All women have that look, and you'd better learn to recognize it. Worse yet, there's enough time before my next group."

"Mmm . . ." Jimjoy kept stretching. Thelina had such a look, except that she still didn't feel he was worth wasting it on.

"We've got troubles." Kerin Sommerlee's voice was low, but at the tone, Jimjoy got up, straightened his jacket. She turned and walked back toward the staff office.

Geoff looked at Jimjoy, who returned the look.

"We've got problems," repeated Geoff.

Jimjoy just nodded as the two of them followed her.

Kerin just stood inside the office, empty except for the three of them. "Two Impie agents, snoops, not Special Ops, hit orbit control on the way down. Same pair that were here and left right before Sam's murder."

"Accident, you mean?" asked Geoff.

"Murder."

"Thought so," muttered Geoff.

"How did you find out?" inquired Jimjoy. "About the Impies?"

"Thelina stopped by. Said she didn't know whether you were a charming liar, a lying charmer, guilty by association, or just guilty. She isn't holding her breath, but she does suggest you take the next shuttle to Thalos—the long way. She'll worry about the rest of the budget and the students. Oh, hades!"

Kerin turned to Geoff. "Here comes the entire second class. Can you get out there and keep them directed or misdirected?"

"Sure, but—"

"Thanks, Geoff."

As he left, Geoff gave Jimjoy a look. The look said: You're in for it.

"I don't know what you did, if you did, or why, but she's gone so far out on the proverbial limb for you she'll never get back. I hope—never mind." Kerin Sommerlee shook her head. "Just putting you two on the same planet together . . . we didn't even ask for you . . . Sam thought—"

"Out on a limb? Why? Supporting my training idea?"

Kerin turned from looking at the incoming group to Jimjoy, black eyes drilling into him. "Training idea? Do you really think she'll be able to conceal the fact that you plan to develop a team of killer commandos that will eventually match or exceed the

Imperial Special Operatives? Do you think the Fuards would let you? Or the Matriarchy?''

"Who would believe it?"

"If it were *anyone* but you, no one."

Jimjoy sighed. "Kerin, they don't know it's me."

"Not yet. But how many more people will be the victims of trumped-up murder-suicides, or accidents? Why can't the Empire just leave us alone? Why can't you and Thelina leave us alone? Why can't my girls just grow up without living through this war you seem determined to start?''

Jimjoy looked back at her, sadly. "They can. You can. Just welcome the Imperial reeducation teams, the fifty percent income levies, and the security guards on every corner in Harmony for as long as it takes for you to become dutiful little Imperial citizens.''

"That's fine for you. You haven't already lost your lover. You don't have two little girls you have to leave every time you go into the field. You don't have to wonder if you'll come back. Or if they'll remember you when you don't. Or who will take care of them when the cause has taken their mother and their father.

"What will you say to Carill when Geoff doesn't return? Or to Shera and Jorje? You'll return. We won't. The gods of war aren't merciful to those of us who don't glory in it.''

"I didn't know . . ." Jimjoy's voice trailed off momentarily. "And I didn't ask you to go. I asked for volunteers. I didn't ask Geoff.''

"No. You didn't know about us. But you didn't ask, either." Kerin looked at the polished stone floor. "Sam did, and now I can't even argue. He left hostages behind. So I want to blame someone . . . and you're that someone.''

Jimjoy took a deep breath, absently noting that the pine-resin smell was stronger in the office. "Sorry. Still think it has to be done—if your daughters are to have a chance for what you want for them.''

"You're an easy man to respect"—she looked back at him—"but a hard man to like. And probably harder to love. Thelina's my friend." She paused and caught his eye. "I don't like to lose friends, either. Or see them hurt.''

Jimjoy looked away this time, swallowing. What he didn't know about people . . . what he hadn't wanted to know? He shook his head slowly.

Kerin shook her head even as he did.

For some reason, he wanted to hold her, to tell her things would be all right, to lie about the future. Instead, he forced himself to look back at her. She was staring at him, and there was darkness in both their eyes.

They stood there in the dimly lit office, neither speaking.

"You'd better get moving."

Jimjoy nodded, then reached out and squeezed her shoulder. "Thank you."

"For what?"

"For reminding me." As he slipped toward the back of the office, toward the door leading to the staff dressing room, he swallowed again, thinking about Kerin's two girls, wondering if they looked like their mother, and about Geoff's Shera and Jorje.

As a Special Operative, he hadn't had to worry about the incidentals—except they weren't incidentals. Not any longer. He moistened his lips as he began to strip off the jacket even before reaching his locker.

No, not incidentals. . . .

. . . XXVIII . . .

Jimjoy swallowed once, moistened his lips, and took the wooden stairs evenly.

Around him swirled the gray mist that was a combination of frozen rain and fog, lending an unreal atmosphere to the late afternoon.

Thelina should have been back from the field training staff meeting. But "shoulds" didn't always translate into reality. Especially where she was concerned. And her message had been clear. Get to Thalos. But he couldn't leave without saying what he had to say.

Chuurrruppp . . .

The raucous call of a jaymar echoed from one of the bare branches hidden in the mist.

Jimjoy grinned fleetingly as he stepped up to the door, pleased at the scavenger's call of support. At least he felt it was support of some sort.

Thrapp. Thrapp.

He waited, hearing the muffled sound of feet on the wooden floor inside, wondering whether Thelina or Meryl would open the door.

A sliver of golden light, followed by a breath of warm air—trilia- and cinnamon-scented—spilled onto the porch where he stood as the door opened.

"Oh. . . ." Other than offering momentary surprise, Thelina's face was unreadable.

"Sorry. I'd just like a moment, if I could."

"Come on in." Thelina still wore a set of field greens, muddy beneath the knees, and a set of heavy greenish socks. "I just got back—literally." Her left hand flipped toward her legs. "As you can see." A smudge of dirt or mud on her left cheek almost appeared like a bruise, and her short hair was damply plastered against her scalp. She stepped back.

Jimjoy closed the door and glanced into the main room. Even from the foyer he could feel the warmth of the fired-up wooden stove. "Too cold to get cleaned up yet?"

Thelina nodded as she gingerly eased herself into one of the straight-backed wooden armchairs closest to the stove. "I'm also too tired. Sit down. You had something in mind?"

Jimjoy took the other wooden armchair, sitting on it at an angle to face her. He looked at her face, catching the almost classical lines as she closed her eyes momentarily. The warm light of the lamps and the flicker of orange from behind the mica of the stove lent a hint of softness to the cleanness of her features, to eyes and a nose perhaps a touch too strong in full sunlight.

What had she been like before?

"You had something in mind?" she repeated.

"Sorry . . . just thinking." He straightened up in the chair. "You put yourself directly on the line for me. Why?"

"I didn't do it for you. I did it because your program is the only chance Accord or the Institute has—and because I promised Sam I would, no matter how I felt about you."

"Hades . . . Sam could have ensured a successor . . . couldn't he?"

"Yes."

Jimjoy turned in the chair, glancing through the glass of the sliding door at the mist outside. Beyond the far deck railing he could see only vague outlines cloaked in gray.

"Either he didn't want a successor, or . . ."

"Or?"

"Nothing." He understood, he thought. All of the first-class strategic brains at the Institute were women. And Accord was not the Matriarchy, but an Imperial colony.

"Nothing? You came over here in the rain to bother an exhausted woman for nothing?"

He sighed. "No. I came to thank you. I came to tell you that I still care for you, and I came to admit that you were right. I was attracted to a facade at first. I admit it. But I've seen enough to know that the facade isn't a facade, that it reflects you. And I wish Sam simply could have named you his successor.''

"Me?" Thelina sat up, looking surprised for the first time he had known her.

"Seems clear to me. For the most part, once you leave Sam and Gavin Thorson out, the sharpest of the Senior Fellows are women. You, Meryl, Kerin, Analitta . . .''

"What about you?" Her voice was softly curious.

"Me?" He felt like an echo. "I'm too new, too unknown. Too much of a lone wolf. I could do something about as big as my training group.'' He broke off. "That was why I came—to tell you how much your support meant, especially when you don't care that much for me.'' He stood up and faced the window, where the twilight had begin to darken the mist and reduce the visibility further.

"Anyway . . .''

"That's not quite what I said." Her correction was also soft, though her voice did not sound tired.

Jimjoy shrugged without looking back at her. "I don't know that I'll see you again for a while." If ever, he thought, the way things are going now. "And I wanted you to know"—he swallowed—"that you were right . . . and that I still care for you. Didn't want to leave without telling you." He turned and looked at Thelina.

She had left the chair and taken a step toward the door, not exactly toward him, but not avoiding him, either. She stepped to the glass beside him.

For a time, nearly shoulder to shoulder, they watched the mist swirl around the deck and the trees beyond, slowly darkening with the twilight. As they watched, he realized again how tall she was, something hard for him to believe for all her grace. Finally, his right hand found her left, and his fingers slipped into hers.

"Why do we fight so much?" he asked softly.

"Because I don't trust men, and you don't trust women.''

"Could we try?" His fingers tightened around hers, but he did not dare to look at her.

"Only one at a time . . .''

She returned the pressure, and he could feel the strength in her long fingers. As strongly as he had pressed, she had answered.

Jimjoy turned toward her, and found her turning into him, her eyes looking into his. He found his hands touching her cheeks, drawing her face toward him, even as her hands found his shoulders.

Outside, the darkness dropped through the fog like foam from the fast-breaking night.

In time their lips dropped away from each other, and they stood, wrapped in each other, unwilling to let go, holding to the moment.

"I'm still filthy . . . and tired . . ."

Her breath tickled his ear.

"Do you want a shower?"

"Not a joint shower . . . not yet. Remember, I hardly know you." But there was laughter in her voice.

"I hardly know me."

"We'll get to know you together . . . slowly . . . Jimjoy."

"That's the first time you've ever used my name."

"I don't believe in easy familiarity."

"I've noticed," he whispered dryly.

She laughed again, softly, and he marveled at the hint of bells in her voice.

"Well, it's about time you two got that over with," announced a voice from the foyer.

They turned, not quite letting go of each other.

Meryl was grinning with every tooth in her mouth showing. "Now, maybe you can concentrate on planning the revolution."

"That may be hard," noted Jimjoy to Thelina, "since you'll be here and I'll be on Thalos."

"Security has to inspect *all* installations periodically. I'm overdue for Thalos."

He wrapped both arms around her, bear-hug fashion, and she reciprocated.

"Good thing for us lesser mortals that you two confine your affections to each other. A hug like that would break anybody else's ribs," Meryl remarked from the landing as she headed up to her room.

"I have to go . . . the shuttle . . ."

"I know . . . but . . . I do inspect, Professor, and don't forget it."

"How could I? How could I?"

. . . XXIX . . .

Jimjoy glanced around the rough-hewn rock room, then at the group of twenty-plus fourth-year students and apprentices packed inside it. When the asteroid base had been built, it had not been designed for large meeting rooms.

Part of their training would consist of using new equipment to enlarge the quarters and facilities on Thalos, since the Institute would need additional off-planet facilities—hopefully for a long time to come.

In the meantime, the room was already getting uncomfortably warm, increasing the odor of oil and recycled air.

"You all know why you're here, I presume . . ." His tone was not quite overtly ironic.

Mera Lilkovie, in the third row, nodded.

"So why doesn't someone tell me?"

"Because Accord is about to rebel against the Empire . . ."

". . . we want to be free . . ."

Jimjoy waited until the words had died down.

"All of what you say is true, in a way, but no one yet has wanted to tell you the rest of what's going on . . . and I don't, either. But you deserve it, and anyone who doesn't want to stay on this team *after* I explain doesn't have to. But you *will* spend six weeks on one of the asteroid stations. And you'll understand that, too, after the explanation."

A few frowns crossed faces in the back.

"It's very simple. Without a new Prime, there's no real authority at the Institute, and no one wants to take chances. If we wait until that's sorted out, Accord will be under military oc-

cupation with a military reeducation team in place. I've seen
military reeducation." He paused. "How many of you have . . .
seen the debriefing on what happened on New Kansaw?"

This time nearly the entire room nodded.

"New Kansaw is the third system which has been 'reeducated'
in the past decade. Unless we do something, Accord will be
next."

"But . . ."

"How . . ."

". . . against the resources of the Empire . . ."

Once more he waited until the murmurs had died down.

"You were all approached because you are troublemakers of
a particular sort. You prefer action. You tend not to take anyone's
word for anything. You're going to have to take mine—since
we're going to succeed.

"Without a fleet, without a large standing military force, we
will quietly become independent and probably free a large number of other Imperial colonies or dependencies as well." Jimjoy
managed to keep a straight face.

"Wait a stan, Professor. Just how do you propose this miracle?"

"By doing the impossible. First, we will take over Accord
orbit control and operate it as if it were still Imperially controlled—except for some obvious gaps in information we will
not pass along. Second, we will undertake certain steps to ensure that the Empire cannot mount a full-scale military attack
against Accord."

". . . right . . ."

". . . so obvious . . . and so wrong . . ."

This time the muttering went on for a while.

Finally, Jimjoy stood up straight. *"TEN-HUTTTTTTTTT!!!!"*
The sound reverberated through the chamber, stilling it,
though none of the students and apprentices physically responded to the ancient command.

"Thank you. The Institute does not believe in either exagger-
ation or hyperbole. I am here to train you to help accomplish
both tasks. Successful completion of this course entails advancement to journeyman status in applied ecologic management tactics—a new field for the Institute, but the privileges and status
are just as valid and real for all the newness.

"As the old saying goes, that is the good news. The bad news
is that half of you will be engaged in extremely hazardous ef-

forts, and about thirty percent of you may not live to see advancement to Senior Fellow status. Of course, if enough of you don't undertake this effort with me, we'll all be dead, exiled beyond the Rift, or on the mushroom farms.''

He looked over the group—quite silent as the implications of what he had said penetrated. "I realize fully that I have given you insufficient information for an informed decision. Any more information for anyone not committed to the effort will cost lives of those who are.

"I can only stress that I am personally completely committed and that I'm not associated with losing ventures.'' He paused and glanced across the open and young faces. "Some of you may know I almost didn't survive several of my ventures and that Accord is my home by choice, not birth. Some of you will die. I wish there were another way. Neither I nor the other Institute fellows associated with this effort can see one.

"This is not a lark, and it is just the beginning of a long struggle. Those of you who choose to join the team will go down in history—one way or the other. You have until tomorrow to make your decision.''

Then he turned and walked out. His steps echoed off the stone and into the silence.

. . . XXX . . .

"*Roosveldt,* closure is green. Delta vee on the curve. Commence backburst."

"Stet, OpCon. Commencing backburst."

Jimjoy moistened his lips, listening. He glanced over at Arnault, watching the youngster check the small tank he carried for at least the fourth time in as many minutes. Lined up behind Arnault, the rest of the squad waited, each Ecolitan carrying some apparatus vital to the operation—a tank, laser welders, or cutters. Everyone carried stunners. The only weapons intended to cause death were the knives in Jimjoy's belt.

"*Roosveldt,* delta vee excessive. Increase backburst. Increase backburst."

"OpCon, increasing backburst."

Jimjoy tapped Arnault on the shoulder. Arnault nodded and tapped the next Ecolitan apprentice.

Jimjoy wanted to shake his head. Mounting an operation mainly with apprentices was crazy, but they had to start somewhere, and the handful of Senior Fellows who would have been helpful were too valuable to risk.

"*Roosveldt,* increase backburst. INCREASE BACKBURST . . ."

WHHHHHHSsssssssttt . . .

The steering jets kicked in with nearly full power with less than fifty meters remaining between the Accord transport and the orbit control station.

"*Roosveldt* . . . delta vee on curve . . ."

Clung . . .

At the sound of the locks matching, the modified cargo hatch slid open a mere meter. Jimjoy was the first out, riding a beefed-up broomstick, with Arnault and Keswen right behind him.

"OpCon, *Roosveldt*. We are setting out a maintenance party. Need to check the steering jets. Too much lag between control and response."

"Stet, *Roosveldt*. Maintenance party cleared. Next time, find out before you try to lock . . . if you wouldn't mind."

"Sorry about that, OpCon. We poor colonials have to make do."

"Don't take it out on us hapless Imperial functionaries."

Jimjoy aimed the broomstick toward the fusactor umbilical, touching the squirter controls, first to steady his heading and then to ease the speed up.

Glancing back, he could see that the last two Ecolitans, the two behind Arnault, were straying too far from the station hull. He motioned once. Nothing. "Hades." Touching the squirter, he slowed just enough to let Arnault ease up beside him.

Tap.

Arnault looked over. Jimjoy motioned again, gesturing for the two broomstick riders behind Arnault to move closer to the hull plates. This time Arnault nodded and dropped back to pass the word. The two offenders closed with the station, and all four broomsticks glided along in the shadows.

"OpCon, interrogative time between call for backburst and response."

"You don't know?"

"Come off it, Hensley. I know what our instruments show. When I called increased backburst, that's what the tape shows . . ."

"Hades . . . wait—we'll see if there's a visual . . ."

The *Roosveldt* was locked in on delta three, the closest main lock to the southern tip of orbit control. Five needleboats lay dead, shrouded, in a hundred-kay semicircle around the control station. The only ships locked in at the station belonged to Accord.

So far, so good. Jimjoy gave a hand signal and flared the squirters to slow the broomstick.

The umbilical to the fusactor was less than fifty meters away.

After another set of hand signals, Jimjoy brought the broomstick to a halt, suspended at a wide black band that separated the station junction plug from the silvery gray of the umbilical.

As Jimjoy took the tools and began to remove the collar, Arnault eased the tank into position while Keswen set up the laser.

Marcer took control of the broomsticks and watched the nearby locks.

"*Roosveldt—*"

EEEEeeeeeiiiii . . .

The commscrambler crew had managed to get their equipment installed and operating, which meant that the station crew had no internal/external transmission capability—except for torps.

Now, if the ventilation crew had managed as well . . .

Jimjoy grinned and chin-toggled down the helmet's receiver volume as he pulled the collar away from the plug, carefully tethering it. He would need it later, once the station was theirs.

He put the thought aside as Keswen moved the laser into position.

Four quick slices and the heavy bolts were severed. The laser was also out of power.

Jimjoy eased himself up to the connecting points and began the business of manually separating the connectors, making sure that he touched nothing except each connector.

Eeeeeeee . . . The scrambled sound of the jammer died away as the station lost all power except for the reserves. He would have liked to maintain scrambling longer, but his team needed communications, and the mass of a self-powered jammer would have been difficult to handle for his crash-trained crew.

Jimjoy toggled up the comm volume. "Interrogative status project green." Back on the broomstick, he guided himself toward the Accordan ship.

"Project green is go. Project green is go."

Jimjoy nodded at the sound of Paralt's voice.

"*Roosveldt*, are you crazy? This is an Imperial station."

The ship did not answer.

"*Roosveldt*, answer me!"

"OpCon, this is Commander Black. The *Roosveldt* is not responsible for this effort. We are."

"Who the hades are you?"

Jimjoy did not answer, instead checking behind him and motioning Arnault and Keswen closer to the station hull plates. Hensley, assuming he was the senior officer in OpCon, still had two operating lasers, two torp ports, and twenty-four hours of emergency power.

"Commander Black, energy concentration in beta three. Energy concentration in beta three."

Jimjoy sighed and pulled the red bloc from his equipment belt, thumbing the release.

One hundred keys out, five needleboats powered up, screens searching for the commtorp the station was about to launch.

"You friggin' Fuards . . ."

"We're—"

"SILENCE!" boomed Jimjoy, cutting off the incautious rebuttal of some outraged Ecolitan. Right now they were better off if the station thought that it was the victim of a Fuard sabotage effort.

"Captain Green," continued Jimjoy, back to a normal voice, "status of nutcracker." His feet touched the personnel lock still beside the ship lock. One Ecolitan looked him over, stunner lowering in recognition of his identity.

Jimjoy thumbed the entry stud, and the light began to blink.

"Commander Black, nutcracker is beta green."

"Stet."

Inside the lock another apprentice, too close, looked him over. Jimjoy made a mental note. Too many people where they couldn't do any good. Then he entered the station, heading toward the armored and self-contained operations center.

So far as he could see, only green-suited Ecolitans were moving. In the main corridor he stepped over two unconscious figures—one male, one female.

"Commander Black, green team, station is secure except delta five, and OpCon."

"Status delta five?" Jimjoy concentrated. Delta five? Electronics shop? Of course, the clean rooms probably had self-contained atmospheres.

"Delta five blocked, with power cut. Two holdouts, without suits."

"Drill it. Use the cutter from red team with a power adaptor, and punch a half-dozen holes in the side bulkheads."

"Stet, Commander Black."

Jimjoy stopped at the heavy metal emergency doors to the Operations Center. Four young green-team members turned as one to look at him.

"Slate?"

Even as paralt handed him the square of plastic and the stylus, Jimjoy was jotting a question he didn't want OpCon hearing, since he was certain that the OIC had already put the automatic frequency band monitors into full operation.

"Welds on torp ports three/five?"

Paralt shrugged, then took the slate back. "Blue team. Reported start."

"Blue team, Commander Black. Interrogative status. AFFIRMATIVE OR NEGATIVE ONLY."

"Prime affirmative. Secondary negative this time."

EEEEEEEEEEEEEEEEEEEEEEEEEEEEEEEEEEEEEEEEEeeeee-eeee . . .

Jimjoy winced at the white noise jolted through his helmet receiver. Some had realized that the communications benefited the invaders more than the invaded.

After chin-toggling down the helmet communicator volume, he wrote on the slate: "Send messenger. Report when all torp ports sealed."

Paralt read it and nodded, handing the slate to the Ecolitan next to him. With a start, as her helmet turned toward him, Jimjoy realized the messenger was Mera.

He took the slate back. "Casualties?" he wrote.

"One—Nerat. Sliced own suit. Blew," was the reply.

Jimjoy shook his head. Carelessness was the greatest enemy. Wiping the slate, he jotted out the next steps for Paralt:

"Swivel joint—plan 1. Force gas through line one. Min. 140."

Paralt shrugged as though questioning.

Jimjoy scrawled below his command: "OpCon hold out forever. Bring up main cutters after torp ports. Have to cut through. Reconnect direct supercon line from fusactor to laser. Ten hours!!!"

Taking a station was so damned much harder than destroying it. He hoped they had ten hours without an Imperial ship arriving unannounced, although he had planned on that possibility. Even a courier would require three-plus hours to make it from system jump entry to Accord orbit control.

He gestured to the young Ecolitan, signifying he was leaving. Next he had to gather the red team back and install a direct power line from the fusactor to the laser cutters needed to open the Operations Center. All that getting the gas into Operations Control would do would reduce the possibility that someone else got killed.

In the meantime, he needed to ensure that the blue team was securing the station and removing all the Imperial personnel.

With another sigh, he stepped up the pace toward the lock,

chin-toggling down yet another notch the noise generated by the
OpCon signal converter.

So . . . no one took an Imperial station?

He grinned as he walked on. The grin faded as he thought
about the next steps—including how to handle the first Imperial
ship that docked and knew the station crew, or wanted to wander
around.

Taking the station wasn't the biggest problem—keeping it
might be.

... XXXI ...

"Of those who claim the Empire is necessary for survival, ask for whose survival—ours or the Empire's.

"Of those who assert that Imperial unity is necessary to prevent rebellions and wars, ask why the number of wars and rebellions remains constant century after century—even as the Empire has grown mightier and mightier.

"Of those who declare that the Empire is necessary for the wise allocation of resources, ask how allocation is possible when the cost of transport between systems makes it infeasible for all but the most precious of goods.

"Of those who fear aliens hidden in the stars, ask why the Empire has enslaved those few found with less effort than ruling us.

"Of those claiming peace as the reason for Empire, ask why the Empire maintains the mightiest fleets and forces of all time.

"Of those who claim the Empire promotes free movement of peoples, ask why the Empire conquers and enslaves those who would leave peacefully."

Query I
Manifesto series
Circa 3640 O.E.E.

. . . XXXII . . .

He glanced toward the small room's privacy lock, a small brass device on the narrow and golden plastic door. The Ecolitans hated plastic, but carrying wood to an off-planet station just wasn't practical—not to Thalos, and especially not to one of the smaller outspace research stations.

"What are you thinking about?" She lay next to him on the narrow bunk, her left hand massaging his too-tight shoulders, her strong fingers working across his bare skin.

"You." He wanted to stretch. At the same time, he did not want to move away from the silkiness of her skin against his. With her beside him, the gray moon-rock walls seemed immaterial. They could have been back on Accord.

"Besides that . . ."

"You . . . yesterday . . . when you got here . . . and my heart . . . and I couldn't say anything." He edged closer to her, drawing in the scent of trilia.

"You've come a long way. But besides me . . . what are you thinking? There's a corner of your mind somewhere else." Her hand stopped, then traced a line from his shoulder to the back of his neck.

Jimjoy shivered, not saying anything, not really wanting to speak.

Thelina's hand rested lightly on his right shoulder.

Finally he stretched, shrugging his shoulders but letting himself drop back against her, hoping she would nibble his ear, or something equally pleasant. "What else is there as important as you?"

"You *are* planning a revolution . . . when you're not thinking licentious thoughts." The warmth of her words tingled his neck.

He took a breath. "Try not to think about it sometimes. We're asking a lot . . . maybe far too much . . . trying to outtrain the Impies without enough time."

Her hands kneaded the muscles at the base of his neck. "They did well with orbit control."

"Not bad. But that was close to home. We had all the advantages, and we knew everyone's habits and schedules. We still lost one person and had three other casualties. That's a lot . . . under the circumstances." He leaned back against her, savoring the feel of her skin, her uncovered breasts against his back.

"You're too tight. Roll over." She pushed him away as he started to pull toward her, to move between her long legs. "The other way—onto your stomach."

He sighed, louder than necessary, then took another breath, trying to relax with her warm legs straddling his, trying to enjoy her fingers probing and releasing the tightness in his lower back.

"You worry . . . about the SysCon expeditions?"

"Be a damned fool not to. Somewhere . . . someone . . . taken precautions . . . don't know what they are . . . pickups . . . problem . . ."

"What about the more experienced ones?"

"Geoff? Analitta? Kerin?" He grunted and stopped talking as her hands dropped to the backs of his legs.

"If you don't keep talking, I won't keep massaging."

"And then . . . ?" He made the question as suggestive as possible.

"I'll leave and inspect something else. This was *supposed* to be an inspection tour . . . Professor." She leaned down and kissed his neck.

He shivered as her breasts brushed his bare back.

"The experienced ones . . ." she prompted.

"The way you do that . . . experience . . ." he gasped.

"That's not what we were talking about." Her laugh was gentle. "What happened?"

". . . made them . . . draw straws . . . couldn't risk them all . . . tried to persuade Kerin and Geoff not to go . . . small children . . . turned me down . . ."

"You're going to let them?"

He sighed again, withdrawing from the pleasure of her hands at her question. "Couldn't stop them. They made a scene. I rigged it the best I could, but they insisted—Geoff and Kerin did. Yelled about how I couldn't do everything dangerous. Palmed Kerin's straw—don't tell her! Geoff grabbed before I could do anything. Insisted I needed some experience on the Fonderal mission, since it was the last one.''

''Too many observers?'' She leaned away from him, her back erect, moving beside his thighs, balancing on the narrow space between his legs and the edge of the bunk.

Jimjoy nodded, half turning toward her, feeling his eyes widen as he saw her body. ''Too much observation for me . . .'' His hands were greedy as he reached for her.

Thelina only put out her hands to his shoulders to break her fall toward him, and only for an instant before she drew his face and lips to hers.

. . . XXXIII . . .

To the right—that was what the map in his head said. But a map wasn't like *knowing* it. The broad-shouldered man in the counterfeit uniform needed to place the next charge by the connector lines servicing the recycling system.

The corridor was dim, especially for someone accustomed to field work planetside, and no short-term intensive training would change that. Gray steel and plastics of all shades, the corridor smelled of oil, sweat, and ozone.

His boots clicked faintly on the hard plastic underfoot, plastic that had lost its resilience years earlier. Only the minute fluctuations of his weight told him that his time was getting short.

How had anyone done it? Especially single-handedly.

He picked up the pace, then slowed as an officer emerged from the corridor junction in front of him.

"You! Technician! Your badge isn't current."

"Sir?"

"You don't belong on this level." The officer had a stunner in his hands, aimed squarely at him. "Move, *Technician.*"

The blocky man shrugged. "What can I say, sir? These new rigs . . . this new badge, that new badge . . . what difference does it make?"

"Your section chief will think it does. So will you after a week in confinement." The officer gestured with the hand not holding the stunner, which remained trained squarely on the technician. "Past me and up the lift."

"There's no lift that way, sir." He knew that from the drills, as well as from the hidden challenge tests. "Do you want me to take the right branch or go back?'' He kept moving slowly ahead, but as though he were still trying to follow the impossible instructions and avoid the stunner.

How much time? The Imperials were getting edgy, too security-conscious.

"That's right." The officer gestured again. "Who's your section chief?"

Thud.

Thrummm.

The stocky man blocked a scream—his own—at the line of pain searing the edge of his shoulder. The Imperial officer lay in the intersection of the two lower-level corridors, his neck at a disjointed angle.

He scooped up the stunner from the gray plastic floor tiles with his good right hand, trying to flex the fingers of his left as he did so.

Time! So little left. He forced himself into the junction, checking both directions. Momentarily clear. Only the next charge was critical before he could break off and meet the rest of the team. He began to trot, fast enough to cover the remaining few hundred meters quickly, slowly enough that he might not seem too out of place. Total secrecy was out anyway. And the badge business had to be a reaction to Haversol.

Whhhp . . . thewwwp . . . whhhp . . .

At the next junction he slowed, bringing the stunner up.

Thrum.

Another officer toppled. The blocky man jumped the body, landing awkwardly and off-balance, mainly on his right foot.

One more turn, and the proper piping/angle configuration appeared. A quick glance over his shoulder told him that the corridor remained clear—for the moment. He laid down the stunner. One, two, three flat cards went into place. He pressed a small cube on the outermost and nicked the corner off, taking longer than he should because of the shaking in the fingers of his left hand.

After retrieving the stunner, he turned and scanned the main corridor. Still clear. He could make the fingers on his left hand work, but their control wasn't going to be very good for fine work for a while. He picked up his steps until he reached the next junction, where he slowed, easing the stunner up at the sound of boots, and holding back from the intersection.

A technician eased into the intersection, holding a stunner, but checking the far side first.

Thrummm.

Thud.

The real technician dropped into a heap without another sound, except for the muffled *clunk* of his weapon hitting the tiles.

Beyond the junction, to the right, lay the maintenance lock that was his immediate goal. He slapped the glowing green stud, which blinked amber as the inner door opened.

Three suits. He checked the air supplies and took the center one, belatedly remembering to touch the panel to close the lock behind him, violating two safety precautions simultaneously. After setting aside his equipment pouch and tool belt and extracting the remaining explosive cards, he fumbled forth the all-plastic arrow gun and set it aside also. With the quick motions he had practiced so often on Thalos, he donned the suit, double-checking each connection. Finally he secured the suit and adjusted the equipment belt and retrieved the cards and tool pouch. Two of the cards he placed against the thinnest plating on the inner wall of the station, nicking the detonator cube.

Both broomsticks came out of their bulkhead brackets. He touched the red stud, which flashed. An alarm began to howl, although the hissing and sound loss told him that the lock pressure was dropping. As the outer-door iris widened, he slipped two more cards and a detonator into the plate interstices.

The suddenness of stepping from the low grav of the lock into null-grav off the hull plates brought his stomach up into his throat. He swallowed, wondering how much time remained. Again he remembered the procedures and chin-toggled the helmet communicator.

He tethered one broomstick to his belt and brought the other broomstick to him and himself to it, awkwardly settling into the seat. Then he touched the squirters.

"OpCon—emergency! Intruder, level three delta. Casualties."

Time? How much longer? Three delta? Who had that been? He corrected his drift to remain within elbow length of the station hull plates. Who?

You, he answered.

"ExOps, interrogative exterior maintenance this time."

"OpCon, that's a negative."

"Open lock, four delta."

"That's our bandit. Squad beta on target."

He glanced over his shoulder, seeing nothing but the regular exterior station lights and continuing to guide the broomstick toward the fusactor tether. He touched the arrow gun at his belt.

". . . friggin' Fuards . . . their asses . . ."

"Silence on the net. Silence on the net."

"OpCon . . . power . . . inter . . . say . . . surges . . . interrogative . . ."

A faint smile crossed the suited man's lips as he curved around the remaining quarter of the station's southern end—only to catch sight of two figures in marauder suits broomsticking toward the fusactor.

Marauder suits meant trouble. While he edged his own stick deeper into the hull shadows, he followed the Marines toward his and their destination. His left hand still trembling within the suit gauntlet, he left the arrow gun hooked to his belt. Against armor, he had to be closer, much closer.

"OpCon on emergency power. All hands! All hands! SysCon red omega. Red omega!"

Hades. This would be the last SysCon taken from within. *If* they could take it. Time? How much? He gave another touch to the squirters, closing more quickly on the Marines before him.

"Bandits on the southland! Bandits on the southland, OpCon."

"Stet. Omega measures. Omega measures."

The blocky man in the maintenance suit fumbled with the arrow pistol. Before him, one of the marauder suits balanced a laser rifle. Unless he stopped the pair, they would stop Niklos and Keswen, and none of them would make it to the pickup. Unless they took out the station, the modified needleboat wouldn't be able to make the pickup.

Another squirt, and he could see the distance narrow. Almost close enough. He raised the pistol, squeezed the wide trigger.

The first shot missed. At least nothing happened, and the plastic missile continued unseen into the darkness. He steadied himself and squeezed again.

"Frig—"

"Beta under fire."

One marauder broomstick veered. Stick and figure split and bounced separately and slowly against the station hull. The laser and power pack proceeded on a gradually diverging course, tumbling end over end toward the SysCon fusactor.

The other broomstick and its rider turned.

''Idiot,'' murmured the man with the arrow pistol as he squeezed the trigger again.

No sound—but the second Marine jerked as the plastic explosive blew open the front of his suit.

Tasting sudden bile in his throat, the survivor guided himself past the faint mist and tumbling body and toward the fusactor tether, where he could make out two figures.

He retrieved the green light/reflector square from the tool pouch, attached it to his shoulder, adjusted the position, and touched the stud to illuminate the light badge. He didn't need his own team turning an arrow gun on him. The two others triggered their badges, the green lights winking from their shoulders as they continued to work on the base of the fusactor tether.

That they were targeting separation meant real problems.

''ExOps, OpCon. Interrogative status squad beta.''

''Negative status. Negative status. Have dispatched follow-up squads.''

He touched the controls for the broomstick's forward squirters, coming to a near dead stop by the others. He gestured, not wanting to use the helmet comm.

Keswen gave him a quick series of motions, indicating a lock problem and the need to cut off power to the station.

The solo Ecolitan nodded and gestured toward the lock.

Keswen shrugged and returned to working on the connectors.

The single man touched the controls on the squirter, easing himself toward the bulbous end of the fusactor module, where he found that the standard entrance control plates had been replaced with an armored key and combination plate.

For a long moment he studied the arrangement, reflecting that the changes did not extend from the plate area itself, which indicated the possibility that the underlying circuitry had not been replaced. With a half shrug, he went to the carryall pocket in the maintenance suit.

Two squares, one cube, to begin with. He placed all three, nicked the cube, and climbed far enough around the bulb not to get punctured by the shrapnel from the explosion. The plates seemed to twist ever so slightly just before he put his feet down.

He waited until he felt the slightest shudder in the plates under his boots.

''Bandits! Detached the southland. Detached the southland.''

''Friggers! Blast . . .''

At least twenty broomsticks aimed toward the bottom end of the fusactor tether as he scrambled for the lock.

Forcing himself not to hurry, and ignoring the dampness on his forehead, he carefully picked away the remaining shards of plastic and plate to uncover the exposed circuit lines. There were three, each of which he pulled from a shattered circuit bloc. He trimmed the ends to expose bare metal.

He touched the black and red together. Nothing. The red and green. Nothing. Finally, the black and the green. The outer fusactor lock irised, jerkily. He staggered inside, dropping to one knee on his return to artificial gravity. On his feet, he slapped the interior controls to close the outer lock behind him. The inner lock door had no security combination, just a standard plate, which he pressed.

He wasn't supposed to be the one working the fusactor. That was Keswen, but Keswen was at the tether, and if—but Keswen wasn't going to make it in time. He glanced over the standard control board arrangement, trying to recall the backup briefings at the Institute and, later, on Thalos.

The bottle controls were in the third panel . . . was it from the right? They roughly matched the control layout. So he should count from the left. He stepped around the locked control board. Among the tools in his pouch was a long-bladed screwdriver. Two quick twists and the panel dropped off, bouncing off his suit boot.

His forehead was sweaty and clammy all at once, and he wanted to wipe it, but the only option he had wearing a suit was to press his forehead against the helmet pad.

"Ha—" He hadn't even considered that the fusactor was pressurized, but it had to be. Off came the helmet and the gloves. After wiping his forehead and taking several deep breaths of the stale power-section air, he began methodically to check the connections. A series of increasing magnetic bottle constrictions— that was the goal—each one building up the residual force within the bottle.

Three-quarters of the blocs uncovered were useless, clearly serving other functions. Attaching the program probe to one bloc, he pulsed it, leaning back to watch the power boards. There was a flicker on the output monitor. He pulsed it again. A larger flicker, a brief output drop before the return to normal. But the field size remained constant.

"Hades . . . never said it would be this hard or take so

long . . .'' Outside, he knew, the Marines were wearing down Keswen and Niklos. Against twenty what could they do?

He tried another bloc. Nothing. And another. Still no reaction. A fourth. The field strength monitor edged down.

He took a deep breath before looking around the control room. Fine—except he hadn't the faintest idea of how to program the parameters.

His stomach felt like lead.

"Carill . . . don't want to do this . . ."

Clank.

He hadn't locked the outer lock door.

Clung.

After scrambling over and around the control board, he threw himself into the lock and began to twist the manual locks into place.

Clang . . . hummmm . . . buzzz . . .

"Hades . . ."

The Marines were outside. He was inside, and unless . . . His heart was as cold as his guts as he walked back to the panel and the power probe.

Don't think about it. Don't think about Carill. Don't think about Shera . . . Jorje . . .

Pulse bloc two. Adjust.

Pulse bloc four. Constrict the field.

Pulse . . .

Constrict . . .

Pulse . . .

Constrict . . .

... XXXIV ...

Dear Mort:

I'll have to be quicker than I planned. First comes the good news. I was selected below zone for Admiral, and that means a boost to the Planning Staff. I'm looking forward to it, or think I am. With the situation out in your sector, I may not be as enthusiastic once I've moved and been briefed, although it's likely to be another month or so at the earliest.

There's more of the bad news. The FC has definitely been scrubbed. We did put the CX out for review, costing, and tech evaluation. We didn't lose totally, because a lot of the better features of the FC are incorporated in the CX, plus we've got the high-speed jump entry-exit thing licked—at least in theory. That ought to help a lot, *if* the Senate will approve it. The problem is we'd still be six, seven years away from deployment. What are we—you especially—supposed to do in the meantime?

With all the Fuard efforts, some of the "colonies" that really aren't colonies are trying to get actual independent-member status. Because of the higher imposts for colonies, the Senate hasn't wanted to grant them actual independent status. The honorable Senators finally did act, though. They passed a law making it so punitive for any colony that they have to rebel.

So a bunch have already started making noises—or worse. Worst is Accord—you know the place—combination free enterprise/ecological nut system out on the Parthanian Rift. The idiots took over their own orbit control station. No problem—except that there have been a few more Haversol-type "incidents" out there, and there's no convenient repowering for a full battle group. The Fuards have been really rattling their sabers. Anyway, you can figure out the logistics of that one! None of the politicos understand why you can't just dispatch a battle cruiser with a planetbuster. They also haven't figured out how you get that far without SysCons to repower—or, if we actually succeeded, how you collect revenues from assorted dust and debris.

The Social Dems, N'Trosia's boys and girls, are screaming about our procurement budget again. They want to put the credits into programs "socially" more valuable. They claim all our spending hasn't stopped the colony unrest or the Fuards. Forget about the difficulty of handling either one with inadequate and obsolete equipment. The worst part is that all of the rhetoric's bound to have an impact. How can it not when he's the Chairman of the Defense Committee?

I've got to get back to the work screens, trying to get caught up before I go over to Planning. Sorry about the bitching to you, but you always were a good listener. I'll try to keep you posted. My best to all four of you.

Blaine

. . . XXXV . . .

The thin man in the pale green laboratory coat looked up at the two visitors. His mouth twitched as he glanced from one to the other, from the man—two meters tall, silver-haired, bronze-skinned, and with green eyes that seemed to cut like a scalpel—to the woman, perhaps one hundred and eighty-five centimeters, just as silver-haired and bronze-skinned, with eyes as cold as the snows of Southbreak.

"Professor Stilsen, Ecolitans Whaler and Andruz. From the Institute. Ecolitan Andruz heads field training, and Ecolitan Whaler is in charge of applied ecologic management tactics." The young man in field greens inclined his head, then stepped back and closed the door.

"Field training and tactics . . . seem a far field from micro-genetic management," offered Stilsen, looking at the hard copy beside his console.

"Not so far as you might imagine, Doctor," offered Jimjoy. He gestured at the console and the hard copy. "Even though I understand a little about your work, I still found it hard not to expect a traditional laboratory setting."

"I'm sure you have a great deal to do, Ecolitan."

"And you'd like to know why we're here." Jimjoy laughed not caring if the laugh was false. "Fair enough." He glanced toward the small table and four chairs in the corner. Papers dribbled from an untidy stack in the center of the table. "Do you mind if we have a seat? While it won't take too long, we can't be quite that brief."

Thelina smiled, and her eyes warmed momentarily.

"I understand. I apologize for the disarray. My colleagues kindly refer to it as creative chaos. Would you like anything to drink?"

"No, thank you," answered Thelina in a low voice.

"No, thank you," added Jimjoy. He pulled out a chair for Thelina.

She raised her eyebrows, and her eyes raked over him.

"Simple courtesy," he said softly.

Stilsen swept the papers which threatened to drift from the stack and onto the brown-and-orange braided rug into a separate pile. Then he pulled out a chair for himself, the one closest to his console. He glanced at the image on his console screen, almost regretfully, and sighed. "How may I help you?"

Thelina glanced at Jimjoy.

He pulled his chin. "According to your last quarterly report, you have demonstrated some considerable success in bacterial 'parasitism' . . . and I'd be interested in learning how applicable that technology is."

"Applicable? Rather an odd choice of words, Ecolitan Whaler."

Jimjoy looked at Stilsen, levelly, directly.

The Professor looked away almost immediately. Then he coughed and cleared his throat. "I have to assume you are referring to my success in slowing down bacterial reproduction patterns by decreasing the internal tolerance to self-generated toxins and waste products."

"I did read about that . . . but I was more interested in the other ones. About replication of parasitic borer characteristics in a wide range of pests . . . and I was also interested in your references to spread vector distribution."

"I was afraid of that."

A faint smile crossed Thelina's lips at the scientist's response.

"Ethical concerns, doctor?"

"Partly, and partly . . ." Stilsen shrugged.

Jimjoy swallowed. "What do you know about Accord's current situation vis-à-vis the Empire?"

Stilsen smiled almost apologetically. "More than I would like, Ecolitan. Even with the careful management of news on both sides, it is clear that some sort of hostilities are imminent."

"Hostilities have already broken out, Doctor. We have been forced to take over Accord orbit control and quarantine all Imperial Forces in the system. The Empire is gathering a task group and a reeducation team to deploy here.''

"I don't see how I can help . . . not in that time frame.''

"I think we can buy some more time.'' Jimjoy shrugged. "But we need to deliver a message to the Empire that we can destroy the ecology on any planet we choose.''

"We're not in that class, Ecolitan.'' Stilsen's voice was cold.

"If we're not, Doctor, or if we can't get there hades-fired quick, then you and I and most of Accord will be dead before the end of next year.''

The scientist glanced down at a brownish-black spot on the orange section of the braided rug. "Are you the new centurions, then?''

Thelina looked baffled.

Jimjoy shook his head slowly. "No. We cannot compel anything. Came to request your help. But to keep the Empire from totally annihilating us, we need to demonstrate that we can destroy a planetary ecology. We could build a planetbuster. That won't work. Everyone *knows* that poor little Accord couldn't build the fleets to deliver enough of them to matter.

"Ecological war is another thing. People believe that a handful of little bugs can multiply and divide and destroy an entire food chain, whether it's true or not. They will believe that Accord can do that—whether we can or not.''

Stilsen shook his head. "I don't think you understand. There are at least four of us who can do what you want. I'd rather do it willingly.''

"Why?'' asked Thelina.

"Because there are good ways and bad ways to get there. Some ways would leave a planet destroyed forever. Others will have just as devastating short-term impacts, but relatively insignificant long-term environmental effects—besides mass starvation.'' His last words dropped like acid rain.

"Do you have an alternative?'' asked Jimjoy quietly.

"Do you?''

"I'd try to build that planetbuster and destroy Alphane.''

"You mean it.'' Stilsen's voice was matter-of-fact, unquestioning. He turned to Thelina. "Could he do it? Personally?''

"Yes. He's already done worse—at least in some ways.''

Stilsen's pale complexion grew paler as he glanced from one Ecolitan to the other. "And if I go to the Prime?''

"You know as well as I do, Doctor. Harlinn will dither, call three committee meetings, and put it out for study. The study completion date will be considerably after our demise under the Fourth Battle Group—or whatever they call the Fleet reeducation team. There is absolutely no pressure I can bring upon you to help us out. At any time, you can call a halt to this . . . starting right now.'' Jimjoy stood up. "I appreciate your patience. After you have a chance to think it over, one of us will be in touch with you.''

Thelina rose. "Thank you, Doctor. This puts you in an impossible position, I realize. Too many evils in history have been justified in the name of survival. Perhaps this would be one of them.''

Jimjoy added, "You don't know whether we are trying to preserve something unique against an implacable opponent or whether we are trying to bring down a great civilization for personal gain or vengeance.''

Stilsen stood up. "I don't know whether any end justifies such means.''

Jimjoy handed him a folder. "Before you decide, you might read through these. Then check with some sources you trust to see how true the stories are. We'll be in touch.''

"I'm sure you will be. I'm sure you will be.'' Stilsen inclined his head. "And now . . .''

"Good day, Professor.''

"Good day.''

The door closed with a firm click.

The two Ecolitans walked unmolested down the corridor and out through the research station doors. The station rested in a meadow. The meadow, clearly artificial with its green T-type grasses and flower beds beside the building, was surrounded by the darker native conifers, with a scattering of corran trees.

The Institute flitter waited on a section of the narrow stone-paved road that arrowed for a break in the trees.

Jimjoy pre-flighted the flitter, more to ensure lack of tampering than for concern that the aircraft had become less airworthy in the short time they had spent with the research station staff.

"What do you think?'' asked Thelina as she watched him strap in.

"What do I think? Why ask me? You understand people far better than I do.'' He clicked the straps in place and began the checklist. "What do you think?''

"He wants to help, but he won't, not unless the Institute encourages him."

Jimjoy nodded as he continued the checklist. "We've avoided Harlinn as long as possible. Probably can't be avoided any longer. Won't be pretty."

"Ha!" Thelina's laugh was short and sarcastic. "When you say that . . ."

"Hold on." The whine of the turbines through the open side windows cut off the rest of her comments. "Close the side ports. We'll need to plan strategy."

Though she frowned as she strained to hear his words, Thelina nodded.

. . . XXXVI . . .

"You asked for the meeting, Ecolitan Whaler," said Harlinn, acting as Prime.

Jimjoy reflected. Trying to express what he had in mind would be hard. "I did." He looked around the office. Thelina would listen. So would Kerin Sommerlee. The history philosophy types were out, as were the pure scientists. He wished he knew Althelm better—the economist could be the key. "It's time to put all the cubes on the screen. All of you know some of the pieces. First, most of you should know that the tactics group has taken over the control and actual operations of Accord orbit control. Some may have wondered why an Imperial Battle Group hasn't tried to take it back.

"Unless we act together they will. Right now they can't. The tactics group has managed to destroy two more Imperial Sys-Cons—"

"SysCons?" asked someone from the corner.

"Imperial System Control Stations—fleet repowering and restaging bases, usually placed in a stable orbit around an outer planet gas giant." Jimjoy cleared his throat and continued. "Anyway, we've destroyed the two along the Arm. After the accident at Haversol, that means the Impies can't attack us with a full fleet unless they replace the SysCons. Right now they can't commit the resources, not so long as their problems with the Fuards continue. But they can gradually replace those stations, or slowly shift resources toward us. And that they will do, until they've built a fleet out here." He looked around the Prime's office—he still thought of it as Sam's.

"Are you telling us that you've single-handedly declared war on the Empire on behalf of Accord—whether we and the Institute like it or not?" Harlinn's face had become paler with each moment.

"I could say I've just speeded the process. After all, the Empire already has doubled the imposts and declared that it will control every bit of research the Institute will ever do. That's just for starters." Jimjoy held up his hand to still the mumbling. "But I won't insult your intelligence.

"Yes. For all practical purposes, I declared war on the Empire. No mealymouthed apology will stop the Imperial Forces. Only good strategy and applied force. You can help me, or you can wait for the citybusters and the reeducation teams. Those are your options." Jimjoy waited for the outburst.

"What!"

"Madman . . ."

"Sam was a fool . . ."

"Wait . . ."

". . . historical inevitability . . ."

". . . give him a dose of his own medicine . . ."

". . . hire mercenaries, and this is the result . . ."

"WAIT A MOMENT!" Kerin Sommerlee's voice cut through the incipient arguments, and the grumbles died down as faces turned toward her. "Arguing over the past won't solve anything. Even executing Ecolitan Whaler wouldn't solve anything, and personally, I'd have to ask who would bell the cat. So we might as well hear what else he has to say. Then we can decide." She turned to Jimjoy. "Before we hear anything else, what were the results of your attacks? No one here seems to know. You indicated success. How much success?" Her face was pale also, and once again Jimjoy wanted to hold her and tell her that everything would be all right. But he couldn't lie.

"You should know that the destruction of the Haversol SysCon was total, along with three or four ships. Accord suffered one slight casualty, but the Ecolitan involved recovered and is back on duty. The Cubera mission involved a three-person team, two of whom were wounded. One will require complete visual reconstruction from laser burns. The Cubera station was totaled. Five Imperial ships were also destroyed." Jimjoy paused, hoping Kerin would not push.

"You mentioned another mission?" Finally, Althelm asked a question.

One look from Kerin to Althelm indicated that both wanted it on the table. Jimjoy had not told anyone but Thelina of the morning's report from the *Jaybank*.

He took a deep breath, conscious that Kerin was intent upon him. "The recovery needleboat for the Fonderal mission reported back just before this meeting. I do not have all the details of exactly what happened. The mission was successful in destroying the Fonderal SysCon."

"What about the team?" Kerin's words were evenly spaced.

"I'm sorry. The team did not make its rendezvous. The station fusactor approximated a very small nova. Six Imperial ships were destroyed. The *Jaybank* lost all screens and barely made it back. That was one reason for the delay."

Jimjoy met Kerin's gaze, watching for the tears he knew she was holding.

"Thank you, Professor Whaler. Is it fair to say that your missions have, with four Accord deaths and three other casualties, cost the Empire close to twenty ships, military control in three systems, four if you count Accord, and killed close to two thousand I.S.S. personnel?"

"That's a fair approximation."

The silence was absolute. The group in the Prime's office looked from face to face, anywhere but at the tall bronze man with the silver hair.

Jimjoy cleared his throat. "It's like this. If you want freedom, then you want it more than anything else. That cuts two ways. You all understand that you can't destroy freedom on Accord to fight the Empire. That way, you lose before you begin. That's why I didn't try to coopt the decision-making process or position the Institute for a coup. I just gathered enough people and resources to force the issue while there was still time.

"Second part is harder. If freedom is important, then anything else is secondary. *Anything*—that means your life, your family, your children, politeness, decency, and restraint. The question the Institute faces is simple. How much are you willing to give up for freedom?"

He held up a hand, as if to forestall a second set of objections, although no one seemed ready to raise any—yet. They were still in shock. "I'm not saying freedom at all costs. Some costs are too high. But we need to pare away the unnecessary restraints on our actions. We're in a war, whether you want to call it that or not. Can we afford to say, as the philosophy types have been insisting, that we must restrict our attacks to purely military targets?

"We'll all be dead, and Accord will be a large pile of dust orbiting a G2 sun, if we follow that course. If we kill off the population of Imperial planets, the same thing will happen."

"So you're saying we can't win?"

"I never said anything of the sort. In war, all targets are potentially military targets. What stops the other side from exterminating your civilians and innocents is the fear that you might do the same. You don't have to strike at noncombatants, but it helps to have the capability."

"We don't have enough weapons to hit military targets . . ."

"What's a weapon?" asked Jimjoy.

"Needleboats, tacheads, lasers—you know better than I do."

Jimjoy nodded. "You're right. I do. What about fusion power plants, hands and feet, rivers, meteors, rocks, sand, and forest fires?" He could see Thelina purse her lips. "What about disease, plague, and pestilence? Crop failures? Drought? Aren't all these potential weapons?"

Harlinn waved away the words. "Against the Empire?"

Jimjoy stood, trying to bite back the words. "A weapon is something you use to damage your enemy. I'll take an effective nuclear 'accident' any day over an outmanned needleboat. A series of crop failures over outnumbered recruits. The collapse of economically viable markets and the reduction in imposts at a time when the Empire is facing challenges from both the Fuards and the Matriarchy."

"I take it you are also willing to consider purely economic means?" asked Althelm.

"No. Pure economic means never work in this sort of situation by themselves. They can give greater weight to military and biological weapons."

Althem merely nodded.

"I've given you the current situation. Do you think the Empire will accept any surrender offer without prostrating us? Without wiping out Harmony and the Institute to the last man, woman, and child—unless we give them no choice?"

"You haven't given *us* much choice."

"You never had much choice," countered Jimjoy. "If you thought you did, you were living in a dream world. To face the Fuards, the Empire has to change its entire internal political and social structure—*or* find other sources of knowledge, technology, and cannon fodder. Unless Accord and the brighter outsystems fight, the Empire will find increased exploitation far, far easier.''

"So you made the choice for us." Harlinn's color had gone from white to red. "You single-handedly decided we would face down the Empire."

"No." The iron in Jimjoy's voice stilled the room. "The idea was Sam Hall's. That's why the Empire murdered him. And Gavin Thorson. That's why you were proposed as acting Prime . . . you couldn't decide to cross the room without a committee. I'm not a politician. I've talked to most of you personally, and nothing happened.

"The Planetary Council has met and dithered, and dithered and met. In the past three years, six outsystems have been brutalized by Imperial reeducation teams. At least three members of the Institute have been targeted by Imperial agents, and two Imperial Special Operative teams have been assigned to report on and/or disrupt Institute operations. One former fellow was an Imperial agent reporting directly to the I.S.S. Special Operative section.''

Jimjoy gave a theatrical shrug. "What do you want? Individually engraved invitations to a reeducation camp?" He made his way toward the door as the figures in green stepped aside from him. "It's your decision. If you decide the Institute will support the independence effort, then I suggest you select someone to act as coordinator. In the meantime, I'm going after some volunteers who understand their lives and future are at stake.''

The silence lasted well after he was outside the Administration building.

... XXXVII ...

The Admiral pursed his lips as he reread the screen for the second time, although his memory was good enough that he could remember the salient points without any reinforcement.

After taking a sip of water, he replaced the glass on the replica wooden desk with which all admirals were furnished. He stood. His long steps carried him into the open space between the desk, with its concealed console, and the empty briefing table.

First, the loss of Haversol SysCon. The loss of Cubera SysCon. The loss of Fonderal SysCon. Haversol *could* have been an accident, or more probably the work of a terrorist or small group. Three in a row meant organization, like something the Fuards would cook up. Then, of all things, across in Sector Four, the destruction of Sligo SysCon with an asteroid barrage.

Now, a report from his last agent on Accord that the first three SysCon destructions had been engineered by some unknown professor, with an equally unknown background, and a small "tactics" team.

The Admiral rubbed his forehead. Either the agent was lying . . . how could one small group from an obscure if brilliant ecological college possibly have the materials and expertise to destroy three stations, capture an orbit control installation without a warning going out, and annihilate fifteen-odd ships, including two cruisers? Especially without the knowledge or support of the college head or the Planetary Council?

His steps carried him back in front of the desk. He stopped and took another sip from the glass. His headache was definitely returning.

The comparator didn't help either, insisting that the closest match to the methodology was that of Imperial Special Operatives. Great help there—the death of every single operative over the past decade had resulted in a body and a complete DNA match. The Service was very thorough in ensuring its dead operatives were indeed dead.

He glanced at the holo of the Academy at Alphane. The view that overlooked his desk was the view of the Spire, its facets glittering in the gold-white light of noon.

Some days he just wanted to go back there and teach, make it all sound so simple, instead of trying to figure out what information meant what and why.

He took another sip from the glass.

How could anybody be building another team of Special Operatives? Especially in a nutty place like Accord? A system supposedly in revolt, and yet the Planetary Council had yet to decide what to do. He shook his head again, wincing at the stab of pain across his forehead.

Jimjoy took another deep breath, looking up at the five steps to the front deck. The unseasonable warmth of the day, combined with the moist odor of decaying needles and leaves, made him think of the spring that was not yet due, not until the suffering of a winter not begun had been endured. Weak but warm sunlight beat through the patchy clouds. Part of his walk had been chilled by their shadows.

On each side of the stairs, at the top, was a carved bird—a ferrahawk on the right and a jaymar on the left. Geoff's handiwork. The jaymar was golden, with black feathers of a different wood. The ferrahawk was clearly black oak, almost glittering in the midmorning light.

He swallowed, trying to force down the lump in his throat. Hades, why hadn't he taken the Fonderal mission himself? Or the negotiations off Tinhorn? Or let someone else come here? But after the meeting with Harlinn, he had practically run here. He couldn't let anyone else bring the news.

Finally, he started up the stairs.

Peering at him through the window on the stair landing was a small dark head. Shera and Jorje, wasn't it? The boy had to be the younger, then, the one with the serious expression watching the stranger climb the steps to the front deck. A stranger who should not have been a stranger, and who regretted again never having taken Geoff's invitations to stop by.

He paused by the wooden jaymar, taken by the delicate sturdiness of the carving. On some planets, the single bird would have been worth a month's earnings of an advocate or a systems engineer. Here—it was there because a man had loved to create beauty.

Jimjoy swallowed again and stepped up to the door. On the wooden plate was a hand-carved scroll: *Geoffrey & Carill Aspan.*

He hadn't known they had shared names in a time when that was the exception, not the rule. But he kept finding out there was a lot he didn't know. He raised his hand to the knocker beneath the carving.

Thrappp . . . thrappp . . .

The door opened. A dark-haired girl, broad-shouldered, with blue eyes, whose head reached perhaps the middle of his chest, held the door.

"Good morning, Professor Whaler."

"Good morning, Shera."

A tentative smile played around her mouth. "How did you know my name?"

"Your father told me." Before she could ask, he added, "Is your mother in? I'd like to talk with her."

"Who is it, dear?" a woman's husky voice called from the landing.

Jimjoy could see that the house's internal arrangement was similar to his, except that it seemed to have a larger upstairs— probably three bedrooms.

"It's Professor Whaler, mother!"

"I'll be right down. Show him in, and then come up here. I have an errand for you and Jorje."

"Mother!"

Jimjoy almost smiled.

"Please, Shera. I need your help."

The girl turned back to Jimjoy. "Would you come in, Professor?"

"Thank you, Shera. How old are you?"

"Ten standard." She held the door more widely and stepped back.

Jimjoy nodded, visually measuring the girl. She would be a tall girl, and she was already striking. Geoff was proud of them— had been proud of them. He moistened his lips and swallowed.

He stepped inside. A mirror with a hand-carved light oak frame hung over a small table. His face, somber and cold, stared back at him from the center of the oval glass.

"Professor?" Carill Aspan had black hair past her shoulders, loosely bound with a red band at the base of her neck, skin darker than Jimjoy's bronzed complexion, and brown eyes. A hint of tears hovered in her eyes. Almost as tall as Thelina, she wore a faded green tunic and trousers. Her feet were bare.

"Jimjoy Whaler . . ." he didn't know what to call her. "Carill" sounded too informal.

"Carill Aspan."

For a moment, neither moved.

"Did you have an errand you were going to send Shera and Jorje on?"

"Oh . . . I forgot." Her eyes said she had forgotten nothing. "Shera? Jorje?" As she spoke, she walked into the living area and pulled a slip of paper from the simple secretary that stood against the wall. Writing quickly, she jotted down several sentences and folded the paper over.

"Yes, mother? Jorje's still on the landing."

"I need both of you to take this to Cerla. Jorje!"

"Coming . . ."

Jimjoy and Carill stood in the space between the foyer and the living room, waiting as Jorje took one slow step after another down the wooden stairs.

Shera glared up at her brother even as she struggled with a light jacket. "Come on."

"Rather not."

"Jorje . . . please?"

"I'm coming." His last step took him to the main floor, where his mother extended a dark blue jacket. He did not protest as she eased him into it. Neither did he help, with arms as limp as overcooked pasta.

"Would you both take this to Cerla? If she's not home, ask Treil or Gera if they know when she will be back." Carill glanced from Jorje, who remained under her arm, to Shera. "Do you understand?"

"Yes, mother. We take the letter to Cerla. If she's not there, we check with the neighbors to see when she will be back. Then we come tell you. What if Cerla's home?"

"Then you come back with her. All right?" Carill had her hands clasped tightly together.

"All right. We won't be long." Shera extended her hand to Jorje. "Come on, slowpoke."

Jorje looked back at his mother, dark eyes almost liquid, before his sister opened the door and tugged his arm.

Carill looked at her son. "Go on, Jorje. I'll be here when you get back."

The boy slowly transferred his eyes from his mother to the floor.

"Come on."

Jimjoy kept his face relaxed, wanting somehow to hold both children, feeling like his silence lied to them both, as he and Carill watched them march down the steps.

Jorje glanced back once, twice, three times, until the walk took them out of the open door's direct line of sight.

Click. Carill shut the door. "Shall we go into the main room?"

Jimjoy nodded.

"Would you like any liftea? Geoff said . . ."

"No thank you. Not right now."

She stood, then waved vaguely. "Sit anywhere you like."

He waited for her to take a chair. Not surprisingly, she sat in one of the wooden armchairs, perched on the edge. Jimjoy took the one across from her.

"It's about . . . Geoff . . ."

"Yes. The recovery boat arrived this morning—"

"No . . ."

"Geoff did what he had to . . . but they didn't make it back." The words felt like lead in his mouth. "I'd asked him not to volunteer . . ."

"He told me." The tears seeped from her eyes. "He was afraid he wouldn't come back. He left a letter . . . told me not to blame you . . . if it happened."

Jimjoy felt his own eyes sting. Geoff had never mentioned it, not that he would have. "He didn't tell me. He wouldn't have."

"No . . . he wouldn't."

"I'm sorry. It's not enough . . . nothing is . . ."

"If it weren't for Geoff, I could hate you, Professor."

"If it's easier that way," he offered.

"We talked about it." She sniffed, pulling a faded handkerchief from somewhere, blotting her cheeks. "You talk, but you never think . . . it's always someone else . . ."

He nodded, hoping she would keep talking, wishing he had brought someone else, someone whose warmth would have eased the pain. His eyes burned.

". . . Geoff . . . he didn't want to go . . . he said he had to . . . that too many people would die if the missions failed . . . was he right . . . did it make any difference? Don't lie to me."

Jimjoy swallowed. "He was right. His mission succeeded. He brought us the time to hold off the Empire." He hated the pompous sound of his last words. "He gave up everything just to give us hope . . . just hope." He swallowed again, his mouth dry.

"You liked Geoff."

Jimjoy nodded, not having the words.

"He liked you, respected you . . . one reason why he went . . ."

Her words were like knives, even though she meant them as a kindness to him. A kindness to him? His eyes focused on the floor, picking out the lines of the planks.

"Professor . . . ?"

He looked up at Carill's tear-streaked face, knowing his own looked as streaked.

"Thank you."

"For what?" He wanted to bite out the words. For what? For killing your lover, your husband, and the father of your children? For destroying the one man who might have been my friend? For leaving Shera and Jorje fatherless? Instead, he repeated the words more gently. "For what?"

"For caring. For being the one to tell me . . . and for hurting."

Jimjoy shook his head. "I didn't want to come."

She wiped her eyes again. "But you did. Geoff said . . . if anything happened . . . you would . . . saw you on the steps . . . I knew . . ." She put her face in her hands.

Jimjoy stood up and walked the three steps toward Carill. Each step felt like he was moving in high gravity through syrup. Finally, he stood behind the chair and put both hands on her shoulders.

Neither said anything as a shadow from the overhead clouds darkened the deck behind Jimjoy, cutting the light that had poured into the room. Nor did either say a word as the small cloud released the sun and the light resumed.

Thrap!

"Mom! We're back. Cerla was home."

"Carill?" asked a woman's voice.

Jimjoy straightened and walked toward the doorway, toward the red-haired and petite woman in a blue blouse and old-fashioned skirt, toward Shera and, hiding behind his sister, Jorje.

Swallowing, Jimjoy stopped short of Cerla. Carill was almost step for step with him, although he had not heard her leave the chair.

"This is Professor Whaler . . . Geoff's friend. Cerla Mc-Winter . . . she's an old friend of mine."

Cerla's blue eyes raked over Jimjoy, took in his face, and looked to Carill. "I told Brice I'd be staying here tonight."

"Thank you."

Jimjoy felt out of place, invisible in a private communion occurring around him. He glanced at Jorje, saw the coldness, the stony expression.

"Jorje . . . ?"

The boy looked at the floor.

Jimjoy knelt until his eyes were level with the dark brown ones. Shera stepped aside. "Your father asked if I would be your friend."

"Daddy's not ever coming back."

"No, he's not. But before he left, he asked—"

Without a word, Jorje turned and began to run—out through the front door, down the steps.

"Jorje!"

Jimjoy stood, then sprinted after the child, just trying to keep him in sight. As he ran he felt like pounding his own head. Why couldn't he have said something softer? More appropriate?

By the time he took the stairs two at a time and vaulted the corner flower box, he had caught up enough to see Jorje take the path toward the gardens.

Jimjoy slowed his steps, attempting to keep them light.

The sky darkened again, and a gust of wind ruffled his hair. Ahead, the path narrowed and twisted through a saplar grove, where the tangled and leafless branches twisted back on one another.

Sciff . . . sciff . . . sciff, sciff, sciff . . . Only the sound of the boy's shoes and Jimjoy's boots on the gravel path filled the grove.

Scifff . . . scifff . . . scifff . . .

Jorje ignored the polished oylwood jungle gym and plodded past the bedded-down flower gardens toward the soccer field.

Scifff . . . scifff . . .

Jorje circled the south end of the field and took the path that led upward into the preserve. Underfoot the gravel became clay and wood chips, and both sets of steps, cushioned by the dampness, subsided into near silence.

Halfway to the gazebo that overlooked the south end of the Institute, Jimjoy slowed his steps to match the boy's tiredness.

Jorje continued to plod upward, one step at a time.

Jimjoy followed, also one step at a time, trying to give the boy as much space as possible, but not wanting to lose sight of him.

At the top, Jorje slumped to the ground, not at the gazebo, but leaning against a railing post at the overlook. He did not look back, but down at the Institute.

Jimjoy waited at the edge of the clearing, at the top of the path.

The clouds began to thicken, and the wind to rise.

Jorje did not move, slumped, watching sightlessly.

Jimjoy shifted position but stayed, letting the boy keep his space, checking the weather, wondering about the coming chill that would signify the end of the brief spring interlude in winter, hoping the entire Institute wasn't out looking for the two of them.

As the wind began to whine, Jorje straightened up, but did not leave his post.

Jimjoy waited.

As the sky turned darker gray, Jorje stood and turned. He walked straight for the path where Jimjoy stood.

The boy's steps took him to the tall Ecolitan. He looked up at Jimjoy and then down the path.

The two of them walked back down toward the Institute, not hand in hand, but side by side.

. . . XXXIX . . .

Jorje watched silently from the landing as the tall Ecolitan walked down the steps and into the afternoon mist that heralded the reappearance of winter.

Jimjoy had not looked back.

Overhead, the clouds from the southwest continued to thicken. A touch of frosty rain brushed his face, and his breath steamed in the quick-chilling air.

His steps lengthened as he headed toward Thelina's quarters. After the less-than-satisfactory meeting with Harlinn, and his effort to break the news of Geoff's death to Carill, he needed . . . something.

Thelina was not likely to be too sympathetic, nor was Meryl.

A figure appeared from the mist, ghostlike, heading toward him.

"Professor Whaler," called Althelm. Bundled in a heavy green parka and a green stocking cap, with only his unbearded face uncovered, he stopped.

"Yes," answered Jimjoy neutrally.

"You were rather convincing, if a trifle brutal." A trace of Althelm's thin white hair protruded from beneath the cap.

"Wasn't trying to be brutal, just to lay out the facts. I've—" He caught himself and stopped, trying to rephrase the words that would have indicated too much about his past. "I've seen enough of Imperial responses to know that the Empire isn't interested in sweet reason or freedom—only in tax levies and self-preservation."

Althelm shrugged, a gesture that incorporated a shiver. "You are doubtless correct, but that can be a hard truth to face. I would like to continue, but unless you are from Sierra or White Mountain, you should already be a block of ice, and my entrophy is carrying me too quickly in that direction—bad physics, I know, but pardon my excesses. We economists are known for our inaccuracies with hard numbers. In any case, my best wishes, Professor.'' He inclined his head, stepped around Jimjoy, and disappeared into the mist.

Jimjoy shook his head, realizing that even he felt a bit of chill, wearing only a set of medium-weight greens. He debated heading home first, but decided against the detour, since Thelina's and Meryl's was on his way in any case.

The steps to Thelina's front deck looked even more forbidding than those to Geoff's home had.

After a deep breath, he took the stairs two steps at a time, then paused. His hand reached to knock on the door.

''It's about time.'' Thelina's eyes took in the greens, the lack of a jacket, the dusting of ice on his hair and shoulders. ''Where have you been?'' she asked quietly. Like him, she had on the greens she had worn at the meeting.

''Telling Carill about Geoff.''

''You look like it.'' She stepped back and held the door open. ''Would you like something warm?''

He nodded. ''Liftea?''

''The kettle was just on. It shouldn't take long. Something to eat?''

''Anything light—I can get it,'' he protested.

''Just sit down, and take the couch. You hate the armchairs.''

Jimjoy eased onto the couch, taking a quick look through the closed sliding glass door at the light snow beginning to fall across the deck.

''Here's the liftea. I hoped that would be where you were. How did it go?'' She perched on the edge of one of the chairs.

Jimjoy did not answer, instead taking a sip from the dark, heavy mug, then looking again at the light snow outside.

Thelina waited, not quite tapping her toes in impatience.

Finally he shrugged, took another sip of the tea. ''Didn't want to walk up those steps. Didn't want to tell her that I'd killed Geoff.''

''Is that the way you really feel?''

''Not that I killed him, but that he'd be alive if he hadn't been my friend. Wasn't a friend to him. He was to me.'' Jimjoy took another sip of the liftea, welcoming the scalding taste. "One afternoon, almost a year ago, he came over, told me he recognized me. Just wanted me to know. We talked. Or he talked. And he asked me why I hadn't told you how I felt about you. If he hadn't asked, I never would have told you. So, in a way, I owe loving you to Geoff, too."

The snow outside began to swirl, although Jimjoy could only see the flakes closest to the window as the twilight dropped into darkness.

"Let me get you something to eat. You're as pale as that snow outside." Thelina hopped to her feet and headed for the small kitchen.

Jimjoy sipped from the mug and looked at the snow, not seeing it.

"Here you are." Thelina resumed her perch on the chair. "It's simple, and not up to your standards, but . . ."

"Thank you."

On a small tray were a stack of crackers, two types of sliced cheese, a sliced pearapple, and three thick slices of meat. He nibbled at a pearapple.

"How is Carill?"

"She's all right. A friend, somebody named Cerla, is staying with her."

"How are you?"

Jimjoy wanted to talk about Jorje, about the boy's reaction, his running away. But he couldn't. He took a cracker instead, put a cheese slice on it, and ate both in a single bite. Then he ate another.

"Guess I'm all right. Easier when I didn't have to worry about people." He folded one of the beefalo slices and began to chew, gesturing at the plate for Thelina to help herself.

"No, thank you. We ate earlier." In response to his unspoken question, she added, "Meryl went over to the Tielers for the evening."

Another period of silence followed, and Jimjoy took the second slice of beefalo, chewing it methodically. He followed with cheese, then finished off the pearapple.

"I worry about Shera and Jorje."

"You were there a long time."

"Jorje ran away, all the way to the top of the nature lookout. I followed . . . tried to give him space. Just waited for him. Took a while."

Thelina shook her head slowly but said nothing, balancing a mug of something on her knee.

"He didn't say anything . . . just ran out the door and kept running."

"You followed him?"

"Enough to make sure he was all right, that somebody cared." He looked at the snow, already beginning to taper off, before taking the last sip of tea.

"You knew. . . . Do you wish someone had followed you?"

He shrugged. "Little late for that now."

For a time they sat there, not speaking. The snowfall had stopped by the time Jimjoy shifted his weight, swallowed, and looked up.

"Just the beginning," he mused. "Hardly taken any real casualties . . . and they're all scared."

"Aren't you?"

Jimjoy smiled wryly and briefly. "I know what's coming. Just don't know what to do. Except I need to get to Thalos and start building up what space capability we can. Get me out of sight and get that job started. You and Meryl can do whatever has to be done here. Far better that I could right now."

Thelina set her mug on the table beside the half-eaten plate of food she had prepared. Then she moved to the couch, settling herself on Jimjoy's left, not quite touching him.

"You don't have to go tonight, do you?" Her tone was lighter.

"No." His hand found hers, but he only squeezed it, and let his shoulder rest against hers, trying to draw in her warmth, wondering if she could lift the chill inside.

. . . XL . . .

"Fine. We've got hulls for another fifteen needleboats. We've got drives and basic screen units. And no controls and no jump units." Jimjoy looked at Mera, then at the console blinking back at him.

The small office, with two consoles side by side and its single ventilator and rough-melted gray mineral walls, smelled of ozone, oil, and stale Ecolitans.

The apprentice who had just recently been a fourth-year student looked back at the Ecolitan professor. "Not bad, considering how little time we've had."

"Right," he snorted. "Except that without the micros for the screens and the grav-field controls, all we have is well-designed junk. There's still no response from the Institute. If we had just two lousy chip bloc machines . . ."

Jimjoy stood up and glared at the console, as if it were the nonresponsive Institute. He shrugged. "Going over to the magic shop."

"When will you be back?"

"Whenever . . . whenever."

"Don't forget that fax cube."

"Oh—thanks." Jimjoy picked up the cube he had made for Jorje. For the past day it had rested on the console because he had kept forgetting to send it.

"Do you think Jason can do it?"

"I can hope." He shrugged again, then lowered his head to clear the hatch, easing it shut behind him.

His boots echoed in the empty corridor, the sound bouncing

from the melted rock beneath to the melted borehole walls and back again. This latest addition to Thalos station had not been developed with long-term comfort in mind, but with cobbled-together equipment as a manufacturing/staging/facility.

While some of the Impies had probably learned the Institute had hidden facilities off Accord, trying to locate and neutralize them without an in-system base would require more resources than they could afford, not to mention better intelligence. Not even Harlinn knew exactly where the new facility was located.

Jimjoy looked back over his shoulder. Mera had not left his/their office.

At irregular intervals, hatchlocks punctuated the corridor. Jimjoy entered the third hatch on the right, south of his office. Inside, before a small console from which ran a handful of silvery cables, sat a youngster with short, nearly stubbly black hair. He did not look up from the console, which displayed a three-dimensional circuit bloc design.

Jimjoy watched as the bloc was rotated on the screen, broken apart, and reconfigured. Finally, he coughed.

"Oh—Professor!"

"Jason." Jimjoy inclined his head. "Any luck?"

"Yes and no. I think I can adapt standard fax transceivers and an obscure design probe, plus other assorted junk, into a screen controller . . . or a reasonable facsimile thereof."

"But we only have enough of that stuff for one or two boats?"

"Maybe three—if the shop doesn't make any fabrication errors."

"Forget that."

Jason nodded slowly.

"What about grav-field and jump units?"

"Do we need grav-fields on all the boats?"

Jimjoy pursed his lips. "Probably not. But that means heavier hulls and more reliance on the screens."

"We can design around that."

"The jump units?"

"That's the hardest. I can build one from the subcomponents, but I don't know enough and we don't have the documentation to redesign from other stuff."

"I was afraid of that. Who makes them?"

"Veletar, Osmux . . ."

"That's Imperial?"

"Yeah."

"Where do Halston and the Fuards get theirs?"

Jason shrugged.

"*If* I can ever get the grounders to answer, I'll see what we can find out. Can you rebuild faulty units?"

"If the two central blocs are intact. Those you don't play with."

"Maybe we can find a good scrap merchant . . ." Jimjoy took a deep breath, let it out slowly. "Thanks, Jason. Go ahead and cannibalize anything extra to get two of the new boats semioperational."

"What about Ecolitan Imri?"

"I'll talk to Imri." Jimjoy repressed another sigh. The mining/research station commander was not going to be too happy. Then again, she'd be less than happy if an Imperial fleet were to plow through the system.

He shrugged as he bent over again and left Jason in front of his screen, designing another way to accomplish the impossible.

. . . XLI . . .

The tall man eased the laser into position, readjusting the settings.

Hssstttt . . .

Nodding, he eased the laser into the next position, resetting the equipment, wishing he could shake his head, but not daring to. The basic equipment was good, but precision microcontrollers would have made the job easier—much easier. The Institute had never considered Thalos as a mainline production facility, only as a source of those few raw materials not easily available on Accord—and mainly for orbital or outsystem use.

All the controls and microblocs had been produced planetside or imported. Now the imports weren't possible, and microengineering equipment was scarce, even for the few independents that dared circumvent the Imperial embargo.

Hsssssttt . . .

He continued the laborious process until the two sections were welded together. After carrying the assembly to the storage area, he began the equally laborious process of storing and racking the laser and the welding heads. The morning shift would be arriving shortly and one more unit would help—some, at least.

With a last look at the equipment, he slipped on the more formal green tunic he would need for the rest of the morning.

He shrugged as he eased out through the crude lock into the main section of Thalos Base.

"Good morning, Professor."

He looked up sheepishly at Mera. "Good morning, Mera."

"A little midnight welding? Along with the twilight electronics? Or the lunchtime power systems?"

"Not midnight, just early morning. They needed a little help."

She shook her head, then turned and left him standing there. Mera did not argue, but left her position clear, quite clear, without ever raising her voice.

He took a deep breath and let his feet carry him toward the mess. His stomach growled, reminding him that he had not eaten since . . . had it been the afternoon before?

If they only had micros, or chipbuilders, or— But why not ask for an entire fleet? The needleboats would be fine for delivering biologicals, if they got the biologicals, if they could build the boats. If . . . if . . . if . . . He shook his head angrily.

He'd sent two messengers to Thelina, and still no answer. No answer at all, but he couldn't leave yet, not until the standard defenses were functioning and the station had managed to damp all EDI detectable radiation.

He slowed as he approached the mess, his steps dropping to a mere quickstep. His stomach added another sound effect to the echo of his boots.

"Morning, Professor," called a voice. Gilman, about to become an apprentice and another member of the needleboat framing crew, waved as he headed back in the direction from which Jimjoy had come.

"Good morning, Gilman."

This time he pulled at his chin, then ducked to step into the messroom. Most tables were empty this early.

On the heat counter were various hydroponics. No synthetics. The Institute did not supply synthetics. You ate real food of some sort. Better real dried kelp than tasty synthetic beef.

Jimjoy chose real and dry muffins with a large dollop of pearapple preserves, a slice of cheese that seemed more holes than cheese, and an empty mug. Carrying the mug to the beverage table, he filled it with old-fashioned tea, a variety even more bitter than liftea, and scooped in enough sugar to rouse departed dieticians from graves parsecs away.

He sat at the end of an unoccupied table.

"Good morning, Professor."

His mouth full, Jimjoy only nodded to the stocky man who eased himself into a chair to Jimjoy's right.

"How is your needleboat project coming?"

Jimjoy took a sip of the tea, so bitter that even a mug saturated with sugar could not remove the edge. "Well as expected."

"Do you really think needleboats can defend us against a fleet?"

"We can build needleboats. Can't build cruisers. No one's selling any these days, not that I know of." The muffin crunched as he bit into it and sprayed crumbs over the green cloth covering the table.

"Do you think the Impies will attack Thalos or Accord first?"

Jimjoy shrugged as he devoured the second dry muffin.

"They say you were once an Impie. Is that true?"

Jimjoy stuffed the hole-filled cheese into his mouth, wishing Thelina would send the equipment he wanted, and wishing Imri's deputy would stop making a practice of quizzing him at meals. "Yes. I've also been a Fuard, a Halstani, a true-believer, and a Swartician."

"A Swartician? Where . . ."

"On Swartis, of course." Jimjoy almost smiled. As far as he knew, there was no Swartis system. He stood. "Have a good day, Ecolitan Ferbel."

Now all he had to do was figure out how to get hold of three dozen jump units. Too bad you couldn't fit people in torps. . . .

He dashed toward Jason and the magic shop. The micros had to be the same, and that was what they needed, not all the power and hardware connections. At least that was what he hoped, but Jason would know, and three dozen torps, or even ten dozen, shouldn't be impossible to find. Obsolete ones might do as well, might even allow them to develop new torps.

. . . XLII . . .

"Go ahead, Ecolitan." The shuttle copilot, doubling as disembarking officer, nodded.

Raw damp air gusted into the shuttle, and the copilot edged toward the protection of the corridor to the control area as she continued to watch the handful of passengers—virtually all Ecolitans—line up to file out. The single exception was a woman nearly two meters tall, wearing the beige and blue of the Halstani diplomatic corps. She stood halfway into the control area, talking to the shuttle pilot.

Jimjoy stepped onto the landing stage. He had carefully avoided the Halstani diplomat, and his tactics team had not volunteered his role, other than as an Institute instructor. Jimjoy's hands were empty as he glanced across the white ferrocrete—almost grayish in the winter light—before heading down the half a dozen wide steps from the shuttle.

Thelina—why hadn't he heard from her? Before he had left for Thalos, she said she would let him know when he should return planetside. That had been nearly three tendays earlier, and he'd heard nothing. He pulled at his chin, continuing to study the port area as he reached the bottom of the shuttle steps.

Roughly thirty meters in front of the port terminal, a single figure paced slowly back and forth on the pavement. Beyond the terminal waited several groundcars painted green, and a sole commercial taxi.

Two flitters with Institute insignia rested on the ferrocrete. One was for Jimjoy, but he did not head directly toward either, but toward the terminal and the Ecolitan in greens. Even with the Empire's blockade on Imperially based traffic, there should have been more activity.

The man in greens turned toward Jimjoy.

Jimjoy took in the deliberately slow steps, caught sight of the face, took a step left, then dived into a roll right, pulling the knife from his belt.

. . . *hsssstttt* . . .

Thrummm . . . thrummm . . .

Whunnk . . . thud . . .

EEEEEEEEEEEeeeeeeeeeeeeeeeeeeeeeee . . . The shuttle's siren began to scream.

Jimjoy covered the remaining open space between him and the nearest flitter in a zigzagging and irregular sprint, ignoring the woman in greens with the knife in her chest and the stunner by her outstretched hand. A woman dressed deliberately like a man.

The flitter pilot already had the turbines turning by the time Jimjoy threw himself through the crew hatch.

"Lift it!" Jimjoy cranked the crew door shut from a prone position. Had someone already gotten to Thelina?

"Yes, ser. Lifting!"

Jimjoy finished cranking the crew door as the rotors began their regular *thwop, thwop*. Then he eased up into the space between the pilot and copilot.

The pilot, a chunky black woman with "Iananillis" stenciled on her flight suit, lifted the flitter, asking without looking at him, "What next?"

Jimjoy glanced at the copilot, a thin, sallow-faced younger man with limp black hair. His name patch was blank, but Jimjoy noted the partly unsealed flap of the right thigh pocket.

"Field unit three?" he asked Iananillis, suspecting the worst.

"Yes, ser. Do you have a destination?"

"The Institute will be fine . . . for now." He looked at the copilot. "Jimjoy Whaler, Tactics." He had raised his voice almost to a shout to override the sound of the turbines and to penetrate their flight helmets.

Both a knife and a stunner were in his hands, so quickly that neither pilot had seen them appear.

"Set it down! There!"

Iananillis looked at Jimjoy, then at the other pilot, her hand tightening around the throttles.

Crack!

Her face paled as she looked at her suddenly limp hand, wrist fractured from the unbladed edge of the knife.

"Don't try it." He doubted that either heard his words, but both respected the weapons. Either that or the look on his face. His head nodded toward the pad at the end of the shuttleport. "There! Now!"

Iananillis glanced at her copilot, who gingerly took the controls and began a slow flare into the pad.

Jimjoy grinned. In the other's place, he would have done exactly the same.

Thwop . . . thwop, thwop, thwop . . .

As the flitter settled onto its gear, Jimjoy's hands touched the harness locks. "Out . . . leave the helmets . . ."

The unnamed copilot left holding his ear. Jimjoy had been rougher than necessary in insisting that his helmet remain with the flitter.

Before the two had cleared the rotor path, Jimjoy had the pilot's helmet in place, although it was tighter than he would have liked, even with two of the shim pads quickly sliced out. Harness in place, he torqued up the turbines.

"Greenpax one, terminus. What is your destination?"

"Terminus, one here. Lifting for Diaplann."

"Understand Diaplann."

"Stet."

Jimjoy kept the flitter low, below two hundred meters, and well clear of the shuttleport, noting as he circled south that both the former pilots of his flitter were running toward the terminal and waving at the second flitter.

Diaplann was southwest of Harmony. Although Jimjoy did not intend to go there, he eased the flitter into a southwesterly course and began a transition into full thrust and rotor retraction.

As the turbine whine increased and the forest-green flitter screamed over the southwest highway, he began to cross-check the course line for the Institute against the rising hills beneath him. Harmony sat farther north of the mountains than did the Institute, even though they were at roughly the same latitude, because the range curved gently south about fifty kays east of the Institute.

Once he got beyond the first hills, his course line would change.

He shook his head, automatically increasing altitude to maintain his ground clearance. Seeing Sabatini in greens at the shuttleport, dressed as a journeyman and carrying a stunner, was a good indication that Harlinn had made a decision, a very unofficial decision. The flitter pilots had just confirmed that. Earlier in the year, Thelina, Meryl, and Geoff—he winced at recalling Geoff—had begun to shift personnel in the field training divisions, partly on skills and partly on loyalties.

None of them would have sent a pilot from field unit three. Unfortunately, that and Sabatini's presence meant Harlinn had his own organization.

Jimjoy smiled faintly. Nothing like a civil war within a revolution. He wondered if all revolutions were this messy.

"Greenpax one, Greenpax one, this is Harmony control, Harmony control. Request your course line and elevation."

"Hades!" He dropped the flitter's nose and inched up the throttles, leveling out less than fifty meters above the conifers on the rugged hillsides below. Still another ten kays before the first plateau lines.

"Greenpax one, this is Harmony control. Request your location. Request your location."

He eased the flitter even lower, not that Harmony control had ground-to-air missiles. He'd checked that out earlier. But he didn't know who controlled Harmony control at the moment.

In fact, stupid as it sounded upon reflection, he didn't know who controlled what. Accord was so libertarian—so disorganized—that once you got beyond basic principles of liberty, it was difficult to get more than a small group to agree on any specifics. Any good revolutionary was going to have to sell his or her wares under basic principles and avoid discussing specifics, or be discussing specifics still when the first Imperial fleet arrived.

Underneath the flitter flashed a narrow road. The conifers began to thin, showing reddish sandstone as the hills steepened. Beyond the tabletop mesa covered with native gold grass and scattered ferril thorns, conifers, and bare red sand, the ground dipped into the transverse interrange valley. The valley stretched northwest, eventually paralleling the Grand Highway, to a point twenty kays short of the Institute. Without detailed satellite coverage, which Accord didn't possess, he would be virtually invisible to Harmony control for that part of the trip. They might guess, but they wouldn't *know*.

"Harmony control, terminus. Do you have a location on Greenpax one?"

"That is a negative, terminus. Negative."

"Thank you, Harmony control."

Jimjoy smiled behind the dark plastic face shield of the too-tight helmet. That seemed to answer one question. The controller at the shuttleport was on his side, getting Harmony control to indicate they had no idea where he was headed. Either that . . . He shook his head. The possible mind games weren't worth the effort. He'd know when he got to the Institute.

In the meantime, he continued to scan instruments, airspace, and the ground beneath, looking for any sign of unfriendliness. At his speed and altitude, his greatest danger was impaling himself and the flitter on some terrain feature—like a rock spire— that he didn't see.

The high clouds would have helped against satellite detection, but without a concentrated down-array, that wasn't a problem either. That left other aircraft and pilot error as his two biggest threats. In his state of mind, pilot error was the biggest threat.

Already he could see the end of the valley ahead. The first time he had made the trip to the Institute, it had been by ground-car. Now he was traveling as fast as he could push the flitter, and the distance seemed minimal.

His fingers toggled the receiver through the major frequencies.

Nothing but static, and he left the frequency selector on control as he raised the nose and began the climb back over the front-range hills.

". . . control . . . location . . . one . . ."

". . . negative . . ."

He frowned. Someone was still looking for him.

Ahead, he could make out the hills behind the Institute, but not the buildings. He crossed the Grand Highway and dropped the nose. For a number of reasons, a high-speed approach was advisable.

The flitter screamed in over the south side of the Institute at less than two hundred meters. Abreast of the lake, Jimjoy flipped it ninety degrees to the ground, dropped full spoilers, cut the turbines, and brought the stick nearly into his lap, watching the airspeed bleed off.

As it dropped below two hundred kays, he punched the rotor deployment and eased the flitter upright, nose high, to bleed off more speed.

Thwop . . . thwop, thwop, thwop . . .

With the aircraft under full rotor control, he brought the flitter back around into the wind, scanning the space before the Administration building. At least a squad in field greens was deployed around the building. Two figures stood at the end of the walk to the circle drive. One, the shorter, waved a projectile rifle, indicating he should land.

The other, light-haired—was it silver-haired?—raised a hand. Jimjoy took a deeper breath and began his flare, easing the flitter into the open grass in the middle of the circle. At least Thelina was there, even if she didn't seem wildly enthusiastic about his arrival.

Even as the skids eased onto the grass, his fingers began the steps to shut down the flitter. Then he noticed that one of the Ecolitans—the one who had waved him in for a landing—had her weapon trained on him.

He raised both hands for a moment, then continued his shutdown.

Thelina stood outside the rotor wash, shaking her head sadly. Two Ecolitans, wearing field two patches and carrying the projectile rifles they were not supposed to have, were behind her. Neither was watching Thelina. One left her rifle loosely trained on the flitter. The other scanned the area around the Administration building.

As he shut down the turbines and continued through the checklist, bringing the rotors to a full stop, he noted the other Ecolitans in field greens scanning the area. He took off the helmet slowly, feeling his ears tingle. As he set it on the console, he rubbed his temples briefly with his right hand, then opened the cockpit.

The Ecolitan who had focused her rifle on him had now lowered it slightly.

Thelina waited for him to walk to her, not even lifting a hand, although he thought he saw a brief smile.

He wanted to put his arms around her, but she was waiting for him to get close enough to hear, and her body posture was formal—almost stiff.

"Congratulations, hotshot." While her words were sarcastic, her tone was soft, almost sad. "You precipitated another crisis, just by refusing to take the right precautions and then waiting too long."

"Waiting too long?" Jimjoy was puzzled.

"I sent you a message . . ."

Jimjoy was shaking his head.

"You didn't get it?"

"No. That's why I took the first shuttle I could. I expected something; you told me you'd be in touch. I didn't tell anyone . . . that's why, when that flitter team zeroed in on me and was from field three . . . and Sabatini was the clincher."

"Field three? Sabatini? What happened at the port? What did you really do? Harlinn tried to lock us up. Didn't use enough force—"

Her posture wasn't stiff, he realized. "How badly are you hurt?"

"I'll be all right."

"Let's see Hyrsa. You can tell me on the way."

The dark-haired woman who had watched him nodded at his remark. "I'll get a groundcar, Professor."

"I'll be fine," protested Thelina.

"Are things under control?" he asked.

"Yes. Kerin's squad took over comm, and that boy Elias—Elias Elting, the one you carried to the infirmary that night—he literally pulled Harlinn from his flitter, along with some very interesting files.

"His partner, Mariabeth, made copies and circulated them to everyone, immediately. That quieted the few who were actively resisting."

A groundcar purred up, stopping well clear of the grounded flitter.

"Is there anyone here who can get that flitter to maintenance?" asked Jimjoy loudly.

"Yes, ser. I can." The voice came from the other Ecolitan who had been guarding Thelina. "Ytrell Maynard, journeyman forest spotter."

"You have it, Ytrell. And thanks." Jimjoy nodded toward the groundcar, offering his arm to Thelina.

"Thank you, but no. It doesn't hurt as much if I walk alone . . . carefully. Probably just a cracked rib. I remember the last set, and this isn't that bad."

"Who?" asked Jimjoy. "Harlinn doesn't have it in him."

"Talbot, loyal to the Prime to the end." She started to shake her head, then pressed her lips together and stopped.

Jimjoy glanced at the other Ecolitan, who had continued to scan the area as the three had walked to the groundcar, finally catching her eye. "She took Harlinn's staff alone?"

"Yes, Professor. We were spread thin."

Jimjoy looked over at the groundcar driver. "You know the driver?"

"Yes—Altehy. She's fine. Helped Kerin with comm."

Jimjoy held open the groundcar door, again extended an arm for Thelina.

"Thanks . . ."

He hurried around the forest-green car and entered from the other side. "Medical one—do we know who's on duty?"

"Most of the senior staff," answered Thelina. "This wasn't without some casualties, unlike some operations."

Altehy eased the groundcar back and turned it to avoid the flitter, where the journeyman spotter was pre-flighting the turbine inlets.

"All right," began Jimjoy.

"You first."

He shrugged. "When I didn't hear from you, I set up Mera and Jerrite with instructions—"

"Jerrite?"

"We're also a little thin. You have Kerin, and . . . Geoff . . . Anyway, I set them up with a series of contingencies, including some pretty detailed plans. That was one thing that delayed me. Then I took a needleboat to orbit control, and I spent some time with them—with some more operating plans and procedures for handling various types of incoming traffic and ship classes. Like no direct locks for anything big enough to carry a squad of storm troops."

"You *have* been busy."

"Details, details. Much easier to *do* something than organize it."

"You've learned that?" Her tone was dry, although her posture was stiff.

Again he wanted to hold her, to tell her he would protect her, even as he realized that he was having trouble protecting himself. "Thelina . . ." His voice was low.

"Yes?"

"Please take care of yourself. Please."

Surprisingly, she just turned her head toward him.

He bent over and brushed her lips with his. "You mean too much to me." For a moment his vision blurred. He shook his head and swallowed, then took her hand, which was reaching for his, and held it, gingerly, afraid that the slightest pressure would cause her to tense the muscles over her injured ribs.

"Thank you for saying it," she whispered back.

"I care."

"I know." After a pause, her voice went from a whisper to a normal tone. "About the rest of your trip?"

Jimjoy did not release Thelina's hand, but cleared his throat. "Took the first shuttle possible down after I briefed Derrin. Did you know there was a Halstani diplomat coming in from orbit control? Transshipped on one of the independent traders."

"You get her name?"

"Something like Mariel. Didn't get too close. A little nervous about Halston," he reminded her.

"They wouldn't recognize you now."

He shrugged. "Anyway, I didn't get too close. Stepped out of the shuttle. Two flitters waiting, and then Sabatini, disguised as a man, just waiting."

"And? You commandeered the wrong flitter?"

"Sabatini tried to take me, and then I commandeered the wrong flitter."

"Dead or unconscious?"

"Probably dead. Had to use a throwing knife."

"Professor, Leader Andruz . . . Medical one," interrupted Altehy.

Jimjoy bolted from the groundcar, scanning the area around medical one, but, again, seeing only a light guard force from a field team, field team one this time.

He held the door and offered an arm. Thelina used both arm and doorframe to ease herself into a standing position.

Two Ecolitans with rifles stood by the entrance.

"Professor, Team Leader . . ."

"The Team Leader has some ribs that need looking at," volunteered Jimjoy.

Thelina grimaced at the explanation, but said nothing as they entered.

Jimjoy punched the button for the lift. Climbing stairs was hades on sore ribs.

"So . . . after you chose the wrong flitter? Did you impose murder and mayhem again?" Thelina glanced from the student Ecolitan at the information desk to Jimjoy and back to the lift door, which was opening.

"No. Broke one wrist, ordered them out. Iananillis, I think, and someone I didn't know. Then I told Harmony control I was heading for Diaplann. I did until I crossed the range, then took the valley parallel to the Highway.''

They stepped into the empty lift, and Jimjoy punched the square panel for the second floor.

"Now, quickly, what happened here?"

"There's not much to tell. Harlinn started trying to isolate us. He must have had a few we didn't know about to have gotten my message to you. I thought Daniella was a safe bet.''

"She might have been. Has anyone seen her?"

"Oh—I thought she was with you.''

"Could be another casualty of Harlinn's. You and Meryl started organizing, and Harlinn sent some troops from field three to round you up?"

"Sort of."

The lift door had already opened, and Jimjoy, out of habit, scanned the area. Dr. Hyrsa was talking to one of the medical technicians.

"Thelina! Are you all right?"

"No. She's not," answered Jimjoy.

"Let's get a look at you." The doctor's voice was no-nonsense.

Jimjoy followed as the physician led Thelina down the right-hand corridor.

"Professor? I'm not sure . . ."

"For the moment, I'm staying."

The doctor looked at Thelina, who smiled faintly.

"I wouldn't try to make him leave . . . yet."

"Oh, I wouldn't have guessed it from the way you two abused each other."

"Times change," said Jimjoy.

"So do people," added Thelina.

He could only shrug, as the doctor pressed a stud beside a closed door. Jimjoy stepped around the two and looked inside from a crouch. The examining room was empty.

"We are secure here, Professor," commented Dr. Hyrsa.

"I worry."

Both women exchanged glances.

Jimjoy smiled sheepishly. "All right. I'll wait outside."

Thelina looked at him. "I'll be fine. I'm not made of glass."

"I know." He stepped outside, again checking the corridor.

He ought to be checking in with Meryl, who was probably in Harlinn's office by now, running the entire Institute. But Thelina and Meryl and Kerin had done well without him. Better than he could have done. He shrugged again and leaned against the wall, waiting to hear from the doctor and hoping that Thelina's ribs were only bruised and not worse.

"Professor?"

He looked up, recognizing the copper-headed nurse. "Verea. How are you?"

"Are you all right? You looked worried."

"Oh . . . I'm fine. Nervous, but fine. Thel—Ecolitan Andruz is being checked over by Dr. Hyrsa. Bruised ribs, I hope." Seeing the look on the nurse's face, he continued. "Instead of cracked or broken ribs, I meant."

"Andruz? Oh, she's the one!"

"What was she doing? Being a hero?"

Verea ignored his soft sarcasm. "They say she personally disabled Harlinn's entire personal guard, including Talbot."

Jimjoy raised his eyebrows. Talbot was bigger than he was, and in good shape. While Jimjoy *thought* he could have taken Talbot, Thelina was giving away at least ten centimeters and thirty kilos. "She's good," he admitted, "but I hope the price wasn't too high."

"So do we, Professor. So do we." She started to leave, then paused. "But it's nice to see you have a soft spot somewhere."

Jimjoy frowned. What had he done to Verea?"

Click.

He turned toward the sound, so quickly that he found Dr. Hyrsa taking a step backward. "How is she?"

"Better than she has any right to be. Mostly bruises. She has a partial hairline fracture on one rib. How she got that . . ." The doctor shook her head. "She will be *very* sore for a while."

"Will she be staying here?"

"Not as long as she is careful. Right now we're a little overbooked, thanks to your revolution, Professor."

Jimjoy pulled at his chin, which felt stubbly. Why was it his revolution? "All right if I wait?"

"It's likely to be a while. We're fitting her with an inflatable support splint. Also getting some painkillers and supportive regenerative capsules. You could wait downstairs . . ."

Since the doctor's suggestion wasn't totally suggestive, Jimjoy nodded. "Thank you. Will you tell her?"

"I'll make sure she knows." Dr. Hyrsa turned back toward another room, presumably toward another injured Ecolitan.

Jimjoy started for the stairs, wondering just how many people had been hurt in the takeover of the Institute. As he opened the doorway to the upper landing, his mouth opened.

Stacked on the landing was a suspense cart, with three coff-wombs, the portable equipment humming. The chill from the coffinlike enclosures radiated from the cart.

"Excuse me, ser, but please keep away from the equipment." An orderly, or the equivalent, straightened up from adjusting something. She wore a stunner. "Pardon me, Professor. I didn't recognize you. What are you doing here?"

"Checking on the casualties," Jimjoy responded, hating himself for the partial lie, but not retracting it.

The woman nodded. "We did all right, considering that bastard Harlinn had a hidden armory. These are ours. Dr. Hyrsa thinks they'll make it, if they can hang on until there's a free operating room."

"All of you did the impossible," Jimjoy temporized.

"Just following your example, Professor. Take care." She returned to monitoring the equipment and the vital signs of the coffwombs' occupants.

Jimjoy started down the stairs, again wondering what in hades Thelina had been doing, and feeling guilty that he had been so concerned about her relatively minor injuries, and, as he thought about it, even more guilty that he had been exposed to so little of the danger. Clearly, a lot of young Ecolitans had suffered much worse.

He stepped through the doors on the main floor.

"Professor Whaler! Professor Whaler!" The speaker was a youngster in greens, so fresh-faced he had to have been a first-year student.

"Here!" Jimjoy called unnecessarily, since the young man was already making a beeline for him, thrusting an envelope forward.

The impromptu waiting area was not filled, but several younger Ecolitans, wearing splints, bandages, or vacant looks, turned to view Jimjoy. The faces of at least half carried a degree of respect that verged on awe.

Jimjoy took refuge in the envelope, which had written upon it "Professor James Joyson Whaler II."

Inside was a single sheet of paper.

Please come to the Prime's office as soon as possible (after you've reassured yourself about Thelina). Remember, you are this revolution's hero. So don't disclaim it.

Meryl Laubon

Jimjoy swallowed and refolded the paper into the envelope, then turned to the youngster. "Do you have a groundcar?"

"Yes, Professor."

"Good. I need to head back to the Admin building. Can you take me, and then return to pick up Leader Andruz and bring her after the doctors are finished with her." At the alarm in the youth's eyes, he added, "She's fine." Or mostly fine, he thought.

Act like a hero . . . remember? He stopped at the door and turned to the faces that had followed his progress. "Today represents a giant step toward freedom and self-determination. All of you have proved what can be done." He paused, then added in a lower tone, "But remember, this is only the first step on our way back to the stars—our stars."

Since he couldn't think of anything else to say, he didn't, but let his eyes cover the dozen or so wounded before he turned.

He had to remember not to walk through the student Ecolitan in his preoccupation to reach the groundcar and Meryl.

... XLIII ...

20 Trius 3647
Lansdale Station

Dear Blaine:

Why me? Last thing I need is an incident with a brand-spanking-new Fuardian S.D. Mucker was out to crumple *Halley*'s fields, no question about it. Flaunted his superiority. Just wanted us to know how good he was.

Two to one I get an inquiry or a reprimand. N'Trosia and his let's-not-make-trouble attitude. If I'd even had an "obsolete" FC under me, the outcome would have been different. But you do what you can.

Speaking of that—what's the status of the CX? We really could use something like that out here, as if I hadn't already made that clear enough. Poor old *Halley* isn't up to the rough stuff. We lost most of the converter, strained the whole front-frame structure.

More rumors again. I know you can't comment, but thought you might like to know what's circulating. My techs say a six-month extension is planned for duty in Sectors Five and Nine. One for the crews on the Rift and one for us. Speaking of the Rift, I haven't heard anything new, and that's always a bad sign. Between the ecologs and the Fuards and the damned and honorable Senate, I.S.S. is hurting.

I'll have my time in by the end of this tour, even if I'm not extended. Helen wants me to put in my papers, and I'm going to have to think about it. There's no reason to stay in if OpSec flashes a black one on the dossier for this.

Sorry for the complaints, but I have the feeling you're the only one back there listening. Jock still talks about going to the Academy, and I'm not really sure how I feel about that. Helen sends her love.

Mort

. . . XLIV . . .

Meryl wasn't in the Prime's office, but in the one next to it, the one that Gavin Thorson had occupied. The sliding window was ajar, with a definite chill from the outside filling the office. She was juggling her attention between two screens and a stack of notes. Her hair was mussed and oily, and a smudge of grease across her left cheek resembled a bruise. Her eyes took in Jimjoy.

"She's fine—relatively. One slightly cracked rib, being splinted," Jimjoy responded to Meryl's raised eyebrows.

"That's what she thought. That wasn't what I was about to ask."

Jimjoy shrugged. "Sorry. I got your message. Don't think I've fouled up too much, except for the incident at Harmony, but that was unavoidable."

"It probably was," responded Meryl. Her tone failed to agree with her words.

"Look," said Jimjoy, trying to keep his words even, "your messenger didn't reach me. I'm trying to develop space-based system defenses with no input from planetside. None. I sent two of my own messages—"

"Who?"

"Kermin Alitro and Jose Delgado."

"We got them, and that's why Daniella was sent back."

"I told Thelina. She never got there. Either to orbit control or to Thalos." He looked around the room, taking in the two standard all-wooden armchairs, the cluttered console top, and the two mugs half filled with cafe. Then he looked down at the blond woman.

Meryl looked up from the consoles at Jimjoy. "You men aren't worth a damn at patience, or at balancing personal concerns. You came down here either because you didn't have any confidence in us or because you hadn't heard from Thelina."

Jimjoy flushed, knowing exactly what she was talking about and not wanting to admit it. "You didn't even have a revolution before I got here."

"We didn't need one until you got here."

A gust of wind from the slightly ajar window threatened some of the papers. Meryl leaned forward and slapped them back into place.

Jimjoy glared at her. "You don't really believe that. You'd already be dead or in a reeducation camp. And you know it. If you want me to admit I was worried about Thelina . . . I admit it. But I kept asking for expertise and key supplies. I got no expertise and no supplies, and not one explanation.

"I needed micros for the ships we're building. I needed to know whether we had any progress on the biologicals. You can't design and build delivery systems without knowing the biological parameters.

"I needed more pilot trainees. I got neither trainees nor reasons." His voice was rising in intensity and volume, despite his resolve to keep it quiet. "Patience is *not* a virtue when there's no time."

"So you got your revolution, Professor, and there are at least one hundred unnecessary casualties. If we'd had two more tendays, we'd have had none." Meryl looked right through him.

Jimjoy ignored the steps behind him.

"Do we control Accord?"

"No," answered another tired voice. Thelina stepped around him. "We control the Institute, plus all the planetside field stations, plus the shuttleport. You control—I presume—all the off-planet facilities."

Jimjoy shrugged. "Then we need to take Harmony."

Meryl looked at Thelina. Thelina looked at Meryl. Both looked at Jimjoy, waiting.

A faint odor of hospital or disinfectant or both wafted from Thelina.

Jimjoy wrinkled his nose, trying to repress a sneeze, before going on. "You don't take cities. You put a supervisor in the police office and a coordinator in every media outlet. You suggest certain news stories, and you make sure the police continue to enforce civil laws. You disband the Planetary Council and call for new elections immediately—with the stipulation that since the Empire has repudiated and embargoed us, the Council will function as the civil authority. The Planetary Governor gets shipped back to the Empire."

"What if someone revolts?"

"Not many will. Liquidate their property and use the proceeds to pay for damages and their transportation to an Imperial system. Let them keep the balance. Anyone who wants to can leave—provided they can find transportation. If the word gets out, and it will, half the high-priced independents will show up looking for passengers."

"It might work," admitted Thelina.

"I doubt it," argued Meryl.

"Give it a try," suggested Jimjoy.

"Fine," snapped Meryl, "but who signs the documents? Who acts for the Institute with Harlinn a hopeless vegetable?"

"You," suggested Jimjoy.

"Not even Accord is ready for a female Prime."

"Then call yourself something like the acting Deputy Prime, pending formal selections. That will get them used to the idea. If they don't buy it, it gives us time to come up with someone else."

Thelina edged over to one of the wooden chairs, wincing as she lowered herself into a sitting position. Jimjoy stepped toward her, but she gave the slightest of head-shakes to wave him off.

Jimjoy and Meryl waited for her to sit down.

"And you? What do we do with you?" demanded Meryl.

"Me?" Jimjoy paused and took the other chair, the one closest to Meryl and her console. "You answer my questions, send me what supplies and the experts you can, and the bodies to crew what I'm building."

"What exactly are you building?"

"Mostly beefed-up needleboats. You had the hidden production facility on Thalos. We've about tripled its capacity. We're trying to design for the biologicals' delivery. And we're working on smart rocks, even big dumb rocks—anything that can disrupt an Imperial squadron.''

Meryl rolled her eyes. Thelina grinned momentarily as she watched her friend.

"How soon can we persuade you to get back to smart rocks?" asked Meryl.

He looked toward Thelina. "As soon as—"

"You can't wait that long. No pressure on the ribs for at least a couple of tendays."

"—we can make some plans and I've had a chance to fully discuss a few things," he amended, wanting to throw up his hands. "We still have to take over Harmony and put together at least a shell of an official government. That way, it will give the Halstanis and the Fuards the ability to communicate openly, at least on the pretext of investigating to see if we are a truly independent system. And it will make it that much harder on the Empire to keep calling it a rebellion or a civil war. That won't change the I.S.S. plan now, but the longer we can exist as an independent force, the sooner it might cross their minds that they'll have to deal with us."

"You talk about taking over government as if it were easy."

Jimjoy sighed, then leaned forward to pat down a stack of papers that threatened to lift off the flat surface with another gust of wind. He glanced over at Thelina. She shivered slightly, wincing as she did.

Jimjoy stood and walked around the console and past Thelina.

Clunk. Jimjoy winced at the sound, realizing he had used far more force than necessary. He turned and headed back to the uncomfortable and uncushioned wooden chair.

"The room smelled of Thorson's mints," observed Meryl.

"We'll survive." Jimjoy looked from her to Thelina, who mouthed, "Thank you."

"Besides," he added, "this way you won't have to chase hard copy all over the room."

"Always pragmatic."

"Harmony," insisted Jimjoy.

Meryl shrugged. "All right. How would you implement your ideas?"

Jimjoy pulled the chair closer and restacked the papers on the edge of the desk to get a clear spot.

Thelina sighed, very softly. Her eyes went from her friend to her lover and back again.

Meryl cleared one console screen, coughed softly, and met Jimjoy's eyes unblinkingly.

Jimjoy smiled wryly. It would be a long afternoon.

. . . XLV . . .

Jimjoy glanced over his shoulder, through the clear glass of the window to the pair of flitters waiting on the grass in Government Square. A squad of Ecolitans in full field gear, including projectile rifles, cordoned off the flitters, technically a poor defense position. But the squad's mission was not to defend, but to state the Institute's power. The second squad, the unseen one, was there to protect the men and women in plain sight.

Then there was the third squad, the grim-faced men and women who controlled the corners of the theaterlike Council room.

Jimjoy took a last look at the scene outside before heading down the steps from the landing to the heavy wooden double doors into the Council chamber.

One of the heavyset planetary guards glared as Jimjoy approached. The guard glanced at the tall Ecolitan, then at the armed Ecolitans, before letting his eyes drop toward his now-empty holster.

Taking over the chamber had been simple. Jimjoy and his three squads had arrived well before dawn, opened the building, and quietly disarmed everyone who arrived for the meeting. Then the flitters had been landed in the square.

Jerold caught sight of Jimjoy, stopped riffling through his notes, and waited for the Ecolitan to reach the smaller podium serving the elected delegates when they wished to bring an issue before the Council.

A series of murmurs swept over the nearly full gallery as the two hundred or so spectators caught sight of Jimjoy. Of the other eight members of the Council, five were present—four men and a woman. The woman, Charlotta deHihns, also watched from her carved dark wooden Council chair as Jimjoy approached. Only one of the men did, the white-haired Sylva Redark. The other three refused to look up as Jerold stepped to his podium.

Tap . . . tap, tap, tap . . .

"The Planetary Council will come to order. The purpose of the meeting is to discuss possible Council action in response to the Imperial embargo of the entire Accord system." Jerold paused, moistened his lips, coughed gently, and finally cleared his throat. "The Institute of Ecological Studies, less formally known as the Ecolitan Institute, has petitioned the Council for action. Therefore, the first speaker will be the representative of the Institute, Senior Fellow and full Professor of Applied Ecologic Management, James Joyson Whaler the Second. You have the floor, Professor Whaler."

Jimjoy stepped up to the podium, looked at the Council members in their chairs on the dais slightly above him, and swallowed. With his back to the gallery, he hoped his Ecolitans had been effective in removing weapons from the spectators and the few media in the gallery above. "Members of the Council, citizens of Accord. Today we face a decision. Should those of us who live in colony systems, those of us who have left the ecological disasters of overpopulation, overindustrialization, and mindless mechanization—should we continue to pay for the sins of an Empire that has repudiated us? Should we surrender our freedom of thought to the Imperial reeducation teams? Should we surrender our schools, our customs, and our personal freedom in the hope that, by some miracle, those few who do survive the Empire's tender mercies *may* see their grandchildren gain a fraction of the freedom and prosperity we now possess?

"The Institute cannot guarantee victory—only a chance at freedom and self-determination. The Institute cannot guarantee comfort or prosperity—only the chance to make our own future. The Institute cannot promise that any success will come easily—only a fighting chance for that success.

"The first step in that effort is to declare that we are free of the Empire's heavy hand. For this Council to freely step down, to declare that it will hold free and open public elections for delegates, and that those delegates will select the next Council. In the interim, the Council will express to the Empire our determination to remain free and will continue to minister to the needs of Accord.

"The Institute proposes no major changes in our way of life—except that the Institute will undertake with all of its resources the defense of the system. In return for that defense, the Council will provide reimbursement for those expenses it and the newly elected delegates deem reasonable.

"The Institute will accept and train volunteers, but not anyone coerced into volunteering. The Institute will work to guarantee the physical safety of any individual who wishes to leave Accord permanently until that individual is embarked upon a neutral vessel.

"Our recommendation is spelled out in detail in the document presented to the Council and released to the people and the news media." Jimjoy paused. "I respectfully request that the Council unanimously adopt the proposal."

Jerold stepped to the Council podium. "As acting Chairman, I bring the proposition to the Council and recommend its adoption. Is there a request for debate?"

The five remaining Council members exchanged glances. Charlotta deHihns, with a faintly amused smile, gave a minuscule and negative shake of her head.

Jimjoy waited. According to the script, nothing should happen, but scripts were no guarantee, even with three squads of armed Ecolitans to view the play.

"The Council will consider the proposal. All in favor, signify by voting in the affirmative. All opposed, in the negative."

Six green lights flashed on the voting board.

"The ayes have it. The proposal is adopted as presented."

"Mr. Chairman!" added Jimjoy. "I request that the Council set the date for elections as 20 Quintus."

"The proposal on behalf of the delegates is that elections be set for 20 Quintus. Is there any debate?" Jerold's forehead was damp and shiny.

Again, according to the script, there was no request for debate.

"There is no request for debate. The question is on the proposal to set elections for delegates on 20 Quintus. All in favor, signify by voting in the affirmative. All opposed, in the negative."

Six green lights flashed.

"Mr. Chairman, on behalf of the delegates and the free people of Accord, the Institute thanks you."

As Jimjoy spoke, Jerold produced a white handkerchief and wiped his forehead, then shook it as if to fold it. "There being no other business—"

At the flash of white, Jimjoy dropped from the podium.

Crack!

Thrum! Thrum!

As a single Ecolitan lifted a limp figure from the center of the media gallery, three others watched the crowd, weapons leveled. Two others pointedly turned their weapons on the Council.

"Traitor . . ." hissed one voice.

"Impie swine . . ."

"Served them right . . ."

Jimjoy stepped up to the delegates' podium again before the audience could fully recover. "Mr. Chairman, now that the Council has accepted the proposal and recessed, and you have declared your intention to leave Accord, I strongly suggest you accompany us to the Institute. Under no other circumstances will we be able to guarantee your safety.

"On behalf of the delegates, I declare the Council in recess until its replacements can be elected by the new delegates." He turned and walked out, not looking back, praying that his troops could keep him from being gunned down.

Once through the double doors, he turned right and sprinted down three steps and through a single door to the de facto command post.

There, Elias half stood as he burst in. "Professor! You all right?"

"Fine. This time they missed. Amateurs. Hades, a white flag yet. Can you alert the relocation team to get ready immediately? We'll see some Impie symps at the Institute within hours. Use the old transient quarters." Jimjoy took a deep breath. "Have you heard anything from the Halstani independents?"

"The latest word is that the *Blass* is en route. Ready to take up to three hundred. Nothing else. Meryl says that the planetary police will cooperate. They don't like us much, but they like the thought of either Impie reeducation teams or chaos even worse."

"That figures." Jimjoy pulled at his chin, aware that the gesture still wasn't perfectly natural.

. . . XLVI . . .

"We just can't do that kind of pilot project here, Professor," Stilsen added slowly. "We just can't. The risks are too high." He took a sip from the steaming mug of cafe.

Jimjoy tried not to wrinkle his nose at the odor. Unlike most I.S.S. officers, or former officers, he disliked cafe. "I thought you did most of the design work on the computer."

"We do. That takes most of the time, and, these days, we can predict with better than ninety percent accuracy that we'll get what we designed." Stilsen set the mug back on the edge of the table.

"But?" Although Jimjoy didn't see exactly where the genetic engineer was going, he had a good idea.

"You want biohazards. I understand the need. But what good does it do you if it escapes here? The idea, as I understand it," continued the scientist in a drier tone, "is to inflict damage on the Empire, not on Accord."

Jimjoy laughed softly. "Point well taken, Doctor."

"That means some other place."

Jimjoy pulled at his chin. "What sort of environment do you need?"

Stilsen looked from the blank console to the orange-and-brown rug, then at the wall. "Really . . . nowhere is suitable. . . ."

Jimjoy understood. Stilsen was agoraphobic, spacephobic, or both. "I'm not sure we're talking about the same need. A production or test facility doesn't need someone of your caliber. Besides, we can't have you isolated—"

"Isolated?" Stilsen's thin face expressed puzzlement.

Jimjoy shrugged. "Sorry. Thought it was obvious. We need to build several isolated, full-grav, asteroid-type outposts—only two- and three-person stations where you do the testing and production. If something goes, you lose one station and three people, not a town or a continent."

Stilsen looked down again. "I can't ask anyone to do what I wouldn't do."

Jimjoy took a deep breath, almost sighing. "I don't think you understand, Doctor. The odds for survival are probably better on one of those stations than here on Accord, particularly if the Empire ever figures out what you're doing." His eyes caught those of the genetic engineer. "If your design and preliminary work are as good as you think, the people on those stations will be fine. Besides, you're going to pay your own price, and we both know it."

Stilsen's smile was brief. "Odd you should say that. I was thinking that about you."

"Me?" protested Jimjoy. "I'm just doing what has to be done."

"Sometimes . . . sometimes that's the hardest thing of all."

Jimjoy pulled at his chin, then glanced at the closed door. "The Institute can probably supply some of the production station personnel."

"Anyone but Kordel Pesano."

Jimjoy frowned. The name was vaguely familiar, but he couldn't place it. "Why? Who is she?"

"He. He's a refugee from some Imperial colony, just recently, the past year or two. He is a first-class plant geneticist and molecular level engineer. I would recommend that he become my backup, assuming he is willing. Since he is at the Institute, would that really be a problem? Also, I was told he suffered space trauma, and going back into space so soon might not be wise."

Kordel . . . space trauma? That Kordel?

"I see the name is familiar."

"Sorry. At first it just didn't register." Jimjoy tried to keep his face moderately concerned. He'd been the one to rescue Kordel from the fall of New Kansaw, and the one who had given Kordel space trauma. Luren—the other refugee—was in field training, insisting she would be a needleboat pilot. With her determination, she might, even though she was a shade old for it.

Jimjoy almost laughed as the irony touched him. Late? Here

he was, probably a decade older than Luren, starting a third career.

"You find something amusing?" Stilsen's voice was suddenly chilly.

"Only my own limitations, Doctor. Only my own failings."

"Professor Whaler, you are a strange man. I saw your address to the delegates. You manipulate people, and yet you act as if you do not want to. You are a leader who has appeared from nowhere, with rumors of a bloody past, yet you have obvious concern and compassion." Stilsen shrugged and picked up his mug. "At a time when we need a leader, you arrive. Very strange."

Jimjoy cleared his throat. "I can have the first stations within the next three tendays. Can you have the personnel ready? If you can get me the specs and the type of equipment you need, I'll also get to work on that."

Stilsen laughed softly. "You can't work miracles that easily, Professor. All this is custom-designed." His arm swept around the office, gesturing more to the entire research station beyond the office walls.

"Tell me what raw materials and components you need to duplicate it, and we'll start there."

"You'll have a first list tomorrow."

Jimjoy stood up. "Thank you, Doctor."

"I won't thank you, since there really isn't much choice, is there?"

Jimjoy met the genetic engineer's gray eyes. "No. There isn't."

A whitened "L" from the air, the marine research station overlooked a near-circular bay carved from the solid cliff line that divided sea and land.

Thwop . . . thwop, thwop, thwop . . . thwop, thwop . . . The sound of the rotors echoed through the half-open flitter window.

Even with the side windows open and the airflow from the flitter's descent, the heat and humidity had glued Jimjoy to the seat cushions. Below, the sea was nearly glassy in the midday sun. Jimjoy flipped up the helmet's dark lens, squinting against the flood of light just long enough to wipe his steaming forehead with the back of his flight suit's sleeve. Then the lens came down.

"Equat Control, this is Greenpax four, commencing approach at marine two." He lifted the nose to flare off more airspeed.

"Stet, Greenpax four. Please advise on departure."

"Control, will do."

He lined up the flitter for touchdown on the pad farthest from the cliff edge. With the high-density altitude at the equatorial latitude, he at least wanted some ground cushion for lift-off. Half aware of the empty seat next to him, he wondered what Thelina was up to. Then he frowned. With Meryl and Thelina effectively running the Institute, anything was possible.

He brought his attention back to the flitter, noting that the turbine EGTs were almost into the amber. After lowering the nose fractionally and easing back on the throttles, he let the airspeed rise another ten kays. The area around the bleached concrete pad was vacant. Even the tattered, fluorescent green wind sock hung limply in the glaring midday heat.

As the flitter dropped toward touchdown, Jimjoy flared sharply, kicked in the turbines, and lowered the flitter onto its skids—all in a near-continuous maneuver to avoid any air-taxiing in the high-density altitude. The wind sock bounced in the rotor wash, shaking the thin wooden pole on which it was mounted.

Jimjoy cut the turbines and began the shutdown checklist.

Thwop . . . thwop . . . thwop . . .

As the rotors slowed, a head peered from the nearest building— the first one Jimjoy had seen on Accord that was climate-controlled. Waves of heat reflected off the bleached white concrete—no plas-tarmac at remote outposts.

After securing the rotors and the turbines, Jimjoy removed his helmet and unstrapped, stretching and peeling his damp flight suit from the pilot's seat cushions. His back was soaked from the humidity, and his forehead was dripping again. As he stepped out onto the concrete, he felt the heat roll up from the hard whiteness underfoot.

"Professor Whaler?" called a young man standing on the golden grass next to the landing pad.

Jimjoy nodded and turned toward him.

"Alvy Norton. I'm the junior marine biologist here, so I get sent out in the midday sun." He wore sandals and shorts and a short-sleeved tunic, both items of clothing of an open-weave green fabric bleached to an off-white.

"I see why you recommended an *early* morning arrival."

"It gets warm," answered the marine biologist. "Unless you've been here, it's hard to understand just how warm. Let's get you inside. You're not dressed for this."

"No," agreed Jimjoy. White Mountain—even at the equator on the hottest of summer days—got nowhere near as warm. In recent years, only New Kansaw, with its dusty plains and ash wastelands, came close. "I've seen worse, but not on friendly terms. This is friendly territory, isn't it?"

"Usually. Unless you're here to cut Dr. Narlian's budget." The marine biologist grinned briefly, then turned toward the door from which he had earlier watched Jimjoy land.

"That wasn't exactly what I had in mind. I wanted to ask about some potential applications of the station's research." By the time the two men had covered the fifteen meters or so separating them from the doorway, Jimjoy felt drenched, and the sweat was beginning to pour down his face. "Whew!"

"It is a little more comfortable inside, but not exactly temperate either," warned Norton as he eased open the door.

Jimjoy stepped inside the station, aware of two things. First, the station temperature was a good ten degrees cooler. And second, the corridor in which he drooped was still as hot as a warm summer day on White Mountain. Initially, the interior seemed dimly lit, but after a moment of adjustment he realized the wide polarized glass windows on the right let in a surprising amount of light.

"You see what I meant."

"I do," agreed Jimjoy, looking around as he followed the biologist along the corridor, which stretched the entire length of the structure. He wiped his forehead with his sleeve again, more to keep the sweat out of his eyes than in any real hope of stemming the flow.

The corridor walls were of local stone plastered over with a light green cement or stucco, the floor of polished gray stone. As they turned a corner at the end of the building, Jimjoy paused to look out at the glassy sea. A narrow ramp, not visible from the air, cut down through the rock and presumably toward the beach below, although Jimjoy could not see the end of the ramp.

"Dr. Narlian's office is this way."

"Oh . . . yes. I was just admiring the view."

"You really can't see all that much from here. If you have time later, and if you are interested, I could show you the cliff observation stations." Alvy Norton looked from Jimjoy toward the open doorway at the end of the corridor five meters ahead, then back at the senior Ecolitan. "Professor . . ."

Jimjoy pulled himself away from his study of the ramp wall cuts. "Sorry." He followed the sandy-haired junior biologist into the office ahead.

Norton cleared his throat, looked respectfully at the petite woman seated between a pair of console screens, and announced, "Dr. Narlian, this is Professor Whaler. From the Institute."

The office contained the two consoles, a conference table with two chairs on one side and a single chair on the other, a pair of old-fashioned filing cabinets, and what appeared to be a drafting board. A worn dark green rug covered most of the floor, with perhaps ten centimeters of stone exposed between the rug and the green stuccoed walls.

When Arlyn Narlian stood up, Jimjoy realized exactly how petite she was, since she barely would have reached the middle of his chest. Her face was elfin in shape, with olive-shaded and unlined skin. Her short hair was as much silver as black. The black eyes were sharper than the narrow and aquiline nose.

"Greetings, Professor. Have a seat." She nodded toward the pair of wooden armchairs—which looked even more uncomfortable than the ones Jimjoy had experienced at the Institute. "Thank you, Alvy." The doctor's voice was controlled, yet almost musical.

The junior biologist closed the door on his departure.

Jimjoy moved next to one of the chairs but did not sit down, waiting for the doctor to reseat herself or move.

Arlyn Narlian did neither, instead surveyed the taller Ecolitan. Finally, she spoke again. "What weapon do you want from me?"

Jimjoy smiled. "You've obviously thought it out. What makes sense?"

"Good." She smiled in return. "At least you're more than a mere figurehead for that pair at the Institute. Your address to the Council actually said something, besides giving people someone to rally behind." She pulled out the single chair on her side of the table. "Sit down."

Jimjoy followed her example, and the two ended up facing each other.

"You upset Stilsen. He's still shakes when he thinks about it."

Arlyn's hands rested on the table, which, Jimjoy realized, was wider and lower than normal, clearly modified for the doctor's needs. His legs did not quite feel cramped, but they would if he remained for any length of time.

Jimjoy shrugged. "I couldn't expect any less."

"Why did you start with him?"

"As opposed to you?" Jimjoy met the hard dark eyes. "Most Imperial planets get their food supplies from land-based cultivation. Wanted a temporary impact, not total ecological destruction."

She nodded. "What about New Providence?"

"Good example, but there's only one."

"So why are you here?"

"I could be wrong. And you might have a better idea."

"I like you, Whaler. You don't play games. You know what you want, and you'll admit you aren't infallible. And you're actually pretty good-looking."

Jimjoy managed to avoid swallowing at the last remark.

"I'm direct in *everything*, Whaler."

"I see." He managed a laugh.

"Are you committed?"

"Yes. It's hard enough to be honest in just one relationship."

"Fair enough." She looked like she actually might sigh before the near-wistful expression vanished. "I have a list of potential ideas which might help on a range of planets within the Empire. Basically, they're fresh water breaks in the food chain. You're right about the ocean link."

The doctor leaned back and retrieved three pages of hard copy, which she then slid across the polished surface of the wide gray-oak table.

Jimjoy scanned the list, which categorized each biohazard by target planet, the probable degree of success, the timetable, and any restrictions on delivery/application. "Most of these look good. A couple we can't deliver under the parameters you've listed." He inclined his head. "I'm impressed. Very impressed, especially considering I did not explicitly state my reasons or ask for assistance in advance."

He considered asking her what she wanted, then deferred. He knew what she wanted—the remarks about Stilsen had told him. "I can't promise immediate control of the research programs, but I can obtain immediate independence from current research department budget constraints. Obviously, if our efforts are successful, the Institute will have to be completely reorganized."

"Can you promise that?"

Jimjoy laughed. "In writing? No. But if you can produce what you have listed here, and especially if you can get Stilsen to act . . . . Do you want to take a real chance?"

"Try me." Even though her hands remained on the table, her voice still musical, a touch of intensity edged her words.

"How about running the outspace research production facilities?"

"Fine. Send me the details, and I'll be there."

"They're not complete yet, but be at the Institute a tenday from now." He pushed back the chair. "Thank you."

"My pleasure, Whaler. My pleasure." Arlyn Narlian stood

as he did. "I'm sure Alvy would be more than pleased to show you around."

"I'd be pleased to see it as long as I don't spend too much time outside."

"That shouldn't be a problem. And now . . ."

"I understand. You'll be receiving a package shortly."

Tap.

"Come on in." The doctor addressed the door.

The nervous smile of Alvy Norton filled the space between door and frame. "Yes, Doctor?"

"Professor Whaler would like a *short* and cool tour . . ."

"No problem, Doctor. It would be my pleasure."

Jimjoy inclined his head to her. "Thank you again."

"Thank *you*, Professor. I look forward to working with you."

Jimjoy turned and followed the junior marine biologist.

. . . XLVIII . . .

"Checklist complete," Jimjoy muttered. Although the cockpit was empty, he tried not to cut corners. Sloppy pilots ended up dead pilots. Slowly, he released the harnesses and pulled off the helmet, still damp from the bath he had taken in the equatorial humidity of Dr. Narlian's marine research station.

As he cracked the cockpit door, sliding it open, a gust of wind fluttered the sleeves of his flight suit. For an instant, the chill was welcome. Then, as his breath turned white in the late afternoon air, he reached for the leather flight jacket, carrying it out of the flitter. He stood on the grass next to the aircraft, shrugging the jacket on over the thin flight suit.

"Professor?"

Two Ecolitans were headed toward him—Fervan, head of flitter maintenance, and Eddings Davis, who had inherited Gavin Thorson's duties.

"Professor?" said Davis again.

Jimjoy turned and nodded. He didn't feel like talking.

"We have a problem with the sym—the refugees . . ."

"Can't say I'm surprised. Excuse me for a moment." He turned to Fervan.

"How was she?" asked the stocky white-haired man.

"Smooth most of the way. Turbines tended to overheat more than the specs on approach, but they admitted at Equat that it was as hot as it ever is—more than ninety-five percent relative humidity. No wind. Might have been the conditions. DRI worked fine on Harmony. Couldn't pick up the Equat beacon until the last one hundred kays. Might be beacon placement." He paused, coughed. "Then again, maybe the crystals for some of the freq subs are off."

"We'll look at them both. Any problem with rotor vibration?"

"No. Smooth there. Blade path seemed sharp, none of that flutter like on the last flight."

"Thanks, Professor. Appreciate your taking this one."

"No problem."

Fervan waved to a woman in a green parka who was steering an electotrac toward the flitter.

In turn, Jimjoy touched Eddings' arm, nodding toward the path that led to the transients' quarters and away from the maintenance line and its ramp into the underhill hangar.

"What's the trouble?"

"Some of the refugees have been here nearly three tendays—"

Jimjoy raised his eyebrows. "That's a problem? They're warm, fed, safe, and there's medical care."

"Professor, do you know who most of them are?"

Jimjoy could guess, unfortunately, after Jerold's assassination attempt. "Probably rich Imperials, second children's children . . . scared that they won't make it on their own, with enough money to live anywhere."

"Right."

Jimjoy sighed. "The poor can't and won't leave. They figure it will be worse anywhere else, and they're probably right." He shrugged as he continued toward the old transient quarters, waiting for the rotund Eddings to explain. The wind whined softly, tugging at his uncovered head.

Eddings hunched further into his jacket.

"I still don't know the problem."

Eddings did not answer.

At the top of the low hill separating the disguised flight line from the rest of the Institute, Jimjoy stopped, glancing back to the west, where the white-gold sun hung suspended in the winter haze just above the mountains. For several moments he just looked.

"All right, what is it?"

"Credits," blurted Eddings. "They're scared. They can't get to orbit control. They're afraid the Empire will blot out the whole planet any day. Not enough independent transports are ignoring the Imperial boycott . . . bribes . . ."

Jimjoy pulled at his chin. "Are our people taking bribes?"

"Mostly . . . no. Thelina gathered them all together a couple days ago, right after you left. She said that anyone who took a bribe would go with the refugees and their money."

Jimjoy frowned, then nodded. "Now they're getting nasty? Have they tried the hostage routine?"

"Not yet, but some of them are thinking about it."

"So . . . who's stirring this up? Jerold?"

"No. He's gone. Remember, Meryl Laubon threw the real troublemakers on that Halstani transport. That's another problem. The ones left feel slighted."

"Hades!" Jimjoy wrinkled his nose as they approached the end of the transients' quarters. A pair of third-year students, armed with stunners—permanently locked on nonlethal, Jimjoy knew—and wrapped in winter parkas, stood by the low brick gateway.

"Professor."

"Any problems?" He addressed the woman who had addressed him. Her companion, a young man half a head shorter, watched the double doors at the end of the two-story timbered building.

"No, ser."

Jimjoy wrinkled his nose again. "What in hades is that smell?"

Eddings looked at the ground, then at the waist-high brick wall. The woman student guard looked at Eddings, then at Jimjoy. The man kept watching the double doors.

Finally Eddings spoke. "It's the building . . . ser . . ."

"Don't tell me they can't be bothered to clean up!"

"Not exactly. It's neat, but there are a lot of people . . ."

"Damnation!" Jimjoy straightened up. "You!" He pointed to the woman, who was at least as tall as Thelina. "Come with me. Eddings, get a load of mops, sponges, clean-up supplies, and stack them right outside those doors there. In the next twenty minutes. Understand?"

"But . . . they won't . . . already suggested . . ."

"I'm not suggesting this time." Jimjoy turned to the student. "Let's go." Ignoring the young man, who had shaken his head, he marched straight to the double doors, ripped the right one open, and stepped through.

Even through the first door, the smell was sour. Inside the second door, the odor was rank, not of unwashed bodies, but of mildew, urine, and sewage. The hallway was dusty, but nowhere wet, and along the thirty meters before the doors and stairs at the middle of the building were gathered small handfuls of well-dressed, if wrinkled-looking, individuals, some in the latest Imperial styles.

He stopped by the first group, three men close to his own age, all slender, tanned, and hollow-eyed.

"If you're here to fix the plumbing, it's the first door to the right," offered a blond man.

Ripppppppp . . .

Without thought Jimjoy lifted the smaller man straight off the floor by his imported silk tunic, bringing him right up to eye level. "*You* are the one who will clean the sanitary and shower facilities. Every one of you. When this place is clean again—*then* I'll see about sending in a plumber."

He dropped the stunned man in a heap, turning to the second man, dark-haired and olive-skinned.

"Don't touch me, peon."

Snap!

Thunk . . .

The olive-skinned man looked stupidly at his broken wrist, then at the pieces of the plastic knife on the stone floor.

The student guard glanced around, bringing her stunner to the ready, as the others in the hallway turned toward the four men.

"You are here because the Institute offered to protect your miserable lives. The Institute is providing food, shelter, and medical care. Every student or staff member here cleans up after himself or herself. You're no different from us. Cleaning supplies are being delivered to that door." Jimjoy pointed to the double doors through which he had come. "If you don't want to end up back on the streets of Harmony—or worse—I suggest you get to work."

Jimjoy looked at the third man, nearly as tall as he was.

The redhead looked back. "Who are you? What right—"

"Whaler, James Joyson. I represent the Institute—"

Thud.

Clunk.

Jimjoy shook his head, looking down at the unconscious man and the miniature stunner. The three should have tried to jump him at once. He glanced around, reached down, and scooped up the weapon, slipping it into his flight-suit pocket. "Come on." He headed toward the next group, an older man and three women.

"Whaler, your name is. When do we get off this planet?" demanded the man with the thinning brown hair and double chin.

"When a ship comes that will take you. After you clean up this mess."

"We didn't make that mess," protested one of the women.

Jimjoy glanced at her, reevaluated his judgment of her age, and replied to the teenager. "It doesn't matter who did. I just want it cleaned up. Period. Do you understand?" His eyes raked the group.

No one would look back at him.

The next group was more submissive. "Yes . . . so sorry . . . we'll talk to the others about . . . form a committee . . ."

"Just get it cleaned up. How you do it is your responsibility."

Jimjoy kept moving, putting out the word, more curtly with each group, aware of the fatigue of three long days piling up. He still hadn't had a chance to talk to Thelina. He shook his head as he neared the building's center doors.

A little girl peered at him from an open door, as if she wanted to say something. For some reason, she reminded him of Jorje, despite the long braided hair and the green velvet jacket and matching trousers.

He stopped and knelt down.

"Yes, young lady?" He tried to keep his voice low.

She said nothing, glancing back into the room. A woman stood behind her, and the girl's hand twined into her mother's trousers—also green velvet.

Jimjoy waited, ignoring the student guard's impatience and continuing glances up and down the corridor at the muttering groups of refugees.

The girl looked down.

"Go ahead, honey," prompted a low, almost sultry voice.

Jimjoy's eyes flickered toward the mother, who looked only at the top of her daughter's head.

"Mr. Ecolitan, why do we have to go? Rustee couldn't come.

I love Rustee. Mommy said you wouldn't let him come. Is that true? You made me leave Rustee?'' Tears seeped from the dark-haired girl's eyes.

Jimjoy glanced from the girl to the slim woman whose trousers the girl clutched with her left hand, a woman whose features matched the girl's.

"Rustee is her pet gerosel."

Gerosel? Offhand, Jimjoy wasn't aware of the species, but there wasn't room for pets. That he knew. Not when so few ships ignored the embargo.

"Can I take Rustee?"

"No . . . I'm sorry . . . you can't take Rustee."

"I hate you! Go away!" She burst into another round of sobs.

Jimjoy straightened, trying not to swallow, catching the same dark look from the mother as from the daughter. He nodded to the mother curtly and turned. "Let's go."

A couple looked up from an embrace under the stairwell as Jimjoy burst through the first doors. They seemed to shrink away from him, but he ignored both and pushed open the doors to the fresh air.

"Hades . . . not made for this . . . drek."

"Ser?"

"Sorry you had to go through that. Should have let them stew in their own messes." He glanced around, then turned his steps toward the end of the building through which he had entered, studying each window as he passed. Some were ajar, but they all seemed in working order.

The single male guard took a deep breath as Jimjoy and the woman returned.

"Professor, Ecolitan Davis told me that the cleaning supplies would be here as soon as he could round them up."

"Fine." Jimjoy pulled at his chin. What else did the refugees need?

He pursed his lips. All the little girl knew was that she had to leave her pet behind because one Jimjoy Whaler said no. The adults—they got better than they deserved. But the children? And these were probably the luckiest ones.

"Can you two handle it?" he asked.

"Yes, ser," the pair chorused.

"Good." His voice softened. "Take care."

As he walked away, he could hear the woman begin to tell about the trip through the refugee quarters. He closed the top seam on the flight jacket.

The sun poised itself on the edge of the western mountains, and Jimjoy listened to the rising wail of the wind as he headed toward Thelina's office.

. . . XLIX . . .

Jimjoy poked his head into the small office to the left of the
now-empty Prime's office. Unlike Meryl's office, Thelina's did
not connect directly to the Prime's. From the right-hand office,
Meryl acted as Deputy Prime. Even though the Institute never
had such a function, no one questioned either the title or Meryl.
Not since Jimjoy's actions with the Council.

Jimjoy's incipient smile faded. Thelina was out.

Instead, Kerin Sommerlee was sitting there, the faint late-late
afternoon winter sunlight pooling on her and the left side of the
desk/console. Like Thelina, she had cut her blond hair short.
She was using the console, her fingers awkwardly tapping at the
keyboard studs.

"Oh . . ."

She looked up. "Professor . . ."

"Jimjoy."

She shook her head. "I don't know as any of us—Thelina
excepted—will ever think of you that way."

"Guess I'll never be accepted—"

"I didn't say that, Professor." Her tone was tart, as was her
expression.

"I know. No time for self-pity. Where is she? Thelina, I
mean."

"She didn't tell you?"

Jimjoy swallowed. The look on Kerin's face told him that
Thelina was up to something less than perfectly safe. And after
the mess with the refugees . . . "Where . . . is . . . she?"

"She said you'd know, that you'd agreed on certain duties . . ." Kerin moistened her lips.

"And she asked you to stand in for her?"

"I agreed to. It had to be someone that field three and Harmony civic would listen to."

Jimjoy nodded. "Did she say where she was headed?"

Kerin grinned ruefully. "She said to tell anyone who asked to check with you or Meryl."

"When did she leave?"

"Yesterday morning."

Jimjoy nodded again. Her reluctance to come with him to deal with the scientists made a lot more sense. She still didn't fully trust him. He sighed. "Anything else I ought to know?"

"Not really. There are a lot of details . . . police units all over the planet are faxing in reports about possible Impie agents. Althelm has taken over trying to locate that micromanufacturing equipment you need . . . has a lead from an independent out of Gersil. It's likely to cost the equivalent of—I don't know what . . . the number is enormous."

"*If* it meets Jason's specs, and *if* they can deliver within two tendays, pay whatever it takes."

"It's that important?"

"It's that important. You might check with Meryl on how to negotiate on it. She's far better than I'd be."

Kerin shrugged. "We have a few merchant types around here."

"I understand. You handle it."

She almost grinned.

"I'm going over to see Meryl."

Kerin nodded, took a deep breath, and looked back at the console, avoiding his eyes.

He pulled at his chin, wondering exactly what sort of danger Thelina had taken on. Then he shrugged and turned, slipping out into the corridor and walking the ten or so meters toward Meryl's office. Currently, with Harlinn's permanent indisposition, the Prime's office served as a conference room and a neutral meeting ground.

Meryl's door was closed.

Thrap!

"Yes?"

"Jimjoy . . . mind if I come in?"

"You will anyway."

He opened the door and eased inside. Meryl glanced up from a stack of hard copy and a screen surrounded with amber flashing studs. Her window was firmly closed, and she wore a dark green pullover sweater.

"Where is she?"

Meryl provided him with a nervous smile, which vanished almost simultaneously with the sunlight. Symbolic or not, the sun had finally dropped behind the mountains. Now the trees on the hillside had turned even grayer.

"I understand you've been busy laying down the law for our poor, depressed Imperial refugees."

Jimjoy sighed. "If getting them to understand that the Institute doesn't provide maid and valet service and that they'd hades fired well better act like responsible adults—yes—but some people, like the Empire, don't understand anything but force."

"That you can deliver."

He took another deep breath. "When necessary . . . I suppose . . . The children bothered me. They don't understand. Guess I didn't, either." He straightened. "Where's Thelina?"

"She didn't tell you?"

Jimjoy sighed. "She's up to something dangerous, and she's not about to tell me."

"You think she should?" Meryl seemed to be wrestling with her hands.

"Yes."

"Why? You didn't tell her about your suicide attack on the Haversol station. She found out about that from Dr. Hyrsa, when no one was sure whether you'd even live."

"But . . ." Jimjoy could almost feel the woman's words physically piercing him. He glanced over his shoulder, as if hoping Thelina might appear. Then he looked back at Meryl, who sat in the straight-backed chair, the hard copy piled across most of the flat spaces around the console.

Had Thelina really taken it that way? "Wait—she wasn't even talking to me at that point!"

"That doesn't mean she didn't care, or wouldn't have liked a little notice. You effectively declared war on the Empire. As you have told more than a few people with pride."

Jimjoy winced at the coolness of her last words.

"You have trouble treating her as an equal," continued Meryl. "Yet she's saved your life at least twice. All the professed love in the world won't be enough unless you really change."

"Change?" Jimjoy looked at Meryl. "I wanted to know where she was, and you talk about my needing to change. Change more?"

The slender blond woman stacked the small pile of paper on the console and stood up. "Would you like some tea? If I have to explain this, I need something warm. My throat's sore. There's a kettle set up in Sam's office." She shrugged. "Sorry. I still think of it as his."

"Suppose I do, too." Jimjoy also shrugged. Meryl was going to take her time, for whatever reason. Was she stalling to keep him from stopping Thelina?

"No, I'm not stalling. She's well off Accord. So relax, if you can."

Women! Besides reading minds, they were always suggesting that he consider something else. That was why he had left White Mountain. Or was it? "Liftea would be fine, if you have it."

"Either old-fashioned tea or liftea. Sam didn't like cafe."

"Liftea." He followed her toward the Prime's office and watched as she turned on the gas on the single burner.

Outside, the light dimmed further, leaving the Institute in darkness, with scattered lights appearing in the twilight. Meryl touched a plate and the soft ceiling lights came on in the almost stark office, empty now of most of the books and all the memorabilia. The table that had served Sam as a desk was bare except for a crystal paperweight with the green Imperial seal caught within it and an empty wooden tray that had contained papers.

Clink. Meryl took two cups from the shelf and set them beside the burner. "Did you expect to find Thelina dutifully waiting for you?"

Jimjoy swallowed, looking away from Meryl's directness to the dark outline of the upper hills. "Not dutifully. Surprised that she hadn't even told me."

"I asked you before, but you didn't answer. Did you tell her about your Haversol operation?"

"No. She would have stopped me."

Meryl snorted. "How? How could anyone really have stopped you? You had Sam's backing. You could have told her as you were leaving. Why didn't you?"

Jimjoy frowned. Unfortunately, Meryl's question made sense. Why hadn't he wanted to tell Thelina? He did not meet Meryl's eyes, instead focused on the crystal paperweight with the symbol of the Institute within it.

"When you put it that way . . . I'm not certain." He looked at the blond woman. "What do you think?"

"Do you really want to know?"

"No." He forced a short laugh. "But I'd better."

Meryl favored him with the faintest of smiles, then glanced at the wisp of steam beginning to escape the kettle. "It's only what I think—"

"Which is usually pretty close to target," interrupted Jimjoy.

"—but you try to avoid any advance approval, particularly from women. Sam's death really hurt that way. He wasn't a threat to you. You know Thelina, Kerin, and I have to run the Institute right now, and subconsciously you're back working for women—for your mother or your sisters. You chose it this time. It wasn't an accident of birth. And it's tearing you up—"

"Wait a minute. I went to Haversol *before* Sam's death."

"You still didn't want to get female approval." Meryl sighed, then turned off the burner and poured the boiling water into the green porcelain teapot. "It should steep for a bit," she added in almost an aside. "Why do you think we've tried not even to suggest your role, except when you ask?"

"Trying to tiptoe around the frail masculine ego?"

"You said that," noted Meryl tartly. "You have no reason for a frail ego. You've accomplished miracles—even if some have been miracles of destruction and escape. The problem is that you don't like yourself, deep inside."

"So what does that have to do with my not telling Thelina and her not telling me?"

"She doesn't trust men, and you don't trust women. If you don't trust her enough to tell her, how can she trust you?"

Jimjoy pulled at his chin once more. "You're saying that I have to trust her before she'll trust me?"

Meryl said nothing, instead poured the tea into the two cups. "Would you like sugar?"

"Did she tell you not to tell me?"

"Would you like sugar?"

Jimjoy sighed. "Yes, please. Two, please." He felt like tapping his fingers on Sam's desk, cursing feminine logic, and walking out. Instead, he looked at one of the hard wooden chairs, then took the heavy cup from Meryl and walked toward the middle chair. Despite the darkness outside, the flight jacket felt warm, too warm for his being inside.

Meryl stood beside the empty Prime's desk-table, cradling her cream-and-green cup in both hands, letting the steam drift into her face, as if warming herself, despite the heavy sweater she wore.

"Why don't you sit down?" he suggested. "At least for a moment."

Meryl nodded before easing herself into the chair nearest the desk.

Jimjoy sipped the liftea, too hot for more than sips. "What about trust?"

"What about it?"

"You said—"

"What I said was perfectly clear. You have to trust Thelina."

"She doesn't have to trust me?"

Meryl looked up from the cup she still held in both hands. "She has. She recommended the Institute accept you. She offered her whole career as hostage to developing your Special Operatives. She risked her life against Harlinn's bodyguards. She gave herself to you—even with her background. What else do you want? Don't you see? She had to do something without telling you, if only to deliver a message."

Again Jimjoy was forced to look from the intensity in the woman's eyes. What else did he want? What did he want? His eyes flicked from the floor to the window and the growing blackness of the western horizon, then back to Meryl. "Trust is a shared orbit?"

"I could almost hate your mother—and your father." Meryl took a deep sip from the cup, then brushed a wisp of blond hair back with her left hand.

Jimjoy didn't ask why. He knew. "Where is she? I know, based on the way I handled Haversol, you have every right to make me wait until she returns." If she returns, he thought to himself. "But I would like to know."

"She's in the New Avalon system, trying to negotiate an arrangement with Tinhorn."

Jimjoy winced. "An arrangement?"

"She thought she could use some former chips as a lever to suggest it was in the Fuards' best interests to let Accord salvage some old destroyers—minus weaponry, of course."

"Do they know who she is?"

"No. She has the history as an Institute operative to operate on her own."

"But the former chips?"

"She got someone to call them in for her. And that's all she told me."

Jimjoy pulled at his chin, then took a long swallow of tea, almost welcoming the burning it etched down the back of his throat. "So we wait?"

"No. You keep doing what needs to be done. Just like she did, just like I'm doing."

His eyes refocused on Meryl, her words recalling that she had been Thelina's friend and confidant far longer than Jimjoy had known Thelina. He swallowed. "Sorry . . . hadn't thought about it. Stupid, but I hadn't. Is there anything I can do?"

Meryl finished her cup of tea, then stood. "No. But understanding late is better than not understanding at all, Professor."

"I wonder." He stood. "The cups? Anywhere to wash them?"

"Thanks for the offer, but I can handle one extra cup. I would have had the tea anyway. Just leave it here for now."

"You sure?"

"Yes." She poured a second cupful from the teapot. "This goes back to the office." Then she set her own cup down and reached for his.

Jimjoy handed it to her. "Thank you."

She nodded as she set his cup beside the kettle. "What's next for you? More persuasion on the research establishment?"

"Dr. Narlian may do that for me."

"She could . . . but be careful."

"I see you've met the doctor."

"It only takes once." Meryl shook her head slowly. "What else?"

"Work with Analitta and Gersin to see if we can complete the off-planet research production post-designs."

"You aren't actually doing design work?"

Jimjoy smiled briefly. "They're better at that than I am. A whole lot better. Just give them the power and size parameters and the requirements. Plus pep talks. Then I'll try to find some more leads on bioweapons. And hope a lot . . . and try to trust."

"Thelina should be fine." Meryl lifted the teacup and started back toward the doorway to her office.

Jimjoy followed, not necessarily agreeing. The Fuards weren't trustworthy, but right now there was nothing at all he could do. Except trust—and he didn't like the feeling. "Let me know."

"You may see her first." Meryl's look seemed momentarily wistful as she set her cup next to her screen, where several more lights were now flashing, two of them changing from amber to red.

"Then we'll let you know."

Meryl took a deep breath and settled herself behind the console, looking back up at Jimjoy as he stood there. "Please do."

He nodded, not knowing what else he could trust himself to say, repressing a sudden shiver inside the heavy jacket that suddenly failed to warm him.

... L ...

8 Quat 3647
New Augusta

Dear Mort:

Urgency does happen—sometimes. I took your faxes and record to Graylin (Fleet Development), and he agreed to fight if N'Trosia pushed for a black flash on your dossier, but it won't come to that. N'Trosia doesn't want the incident to be brought to light, other than as an unfortunate and unavoidable accident for which no one was to blame, not with his talk about the Fuards being reasonable people and with the Declaration of Secession from Accord hitting the tunnels. So it looks like you're clear.

The manpower and operations costs for Sector Five (Accord) hit the Defense Committee, and they nearly hemorrhaged. N'Trosia was screaming, right in the hearing room, about the mismanagement of diplomacy by the I.S.S. He demanded to know how we thought we could conduct diplomacy with warships and no compassion. Then he told Fleet Admiral Helising that the Accord Secession was the direct result of the I.S.S.'s preoccupation with weapons of death and destruction.

Anyway, the long and short of it was that they scrapped the CX, at least for now, and compromised on more spare parts and limited retrofits for the Attack Corvettes. From what you said and from what I'd gathered, I wanted my new boss, the head of Plans and Programming, Admiral Edwin Yersin, to point out the problems. He declined, not because he didn't agree, but because N'Trosia had the votes. So it goes.

I wish I could offer more hope from the capital, but now it comes out that we've already lost a bunch of ships to the eco-freaks. They call themselves the Coordinate of Accord, and they're dignifying their little rebellion with the catchy title of the Ecologic Secession. Between N'Trosia's compassion, limited budgets, and a few missing SysCons, any application of massive force—trust you know what I mean—is currently out of the question. Then, the asteroid miners out of Sligo are trying the same thing. There our supply lines are clearer, and something might happen. But who really knows these days?

The Fuards are complaining about the three-system bulge again, you know, out your way, and where that will lead is anybody's guess.

I heard from Sandy again, last month. She left a delay cube for me, said she was on her way to Accord. Latest trend, of course, is to be fashionably ecological, but she, once more, will take it to extremes.

I shouldn't ramble on, but sometimes you just wonder . . . Enough is enough. Give my love to Helen and the kids.

Blaine

. . . LI . . .

The boulevard was almost deserted in the midafternoon freezing drizzle, a few hardy individuals in waterproof parkas slosh-
ing through the few centimeters of puddled slush that covered
the precisely cut gray stone sidewalks.

An occasional groundcar whined to or from Government
Square, hissing across and through the combination of ice and
rain that covered the roadway.

Jimjoy, his parka collar turned up, paused to look at the display in Waltar's, then smiled.

"Think Spring!" proclaimed the graceful script in the window. There, for all Accord to see, underneath an open umbrella,
was a copy of the formal picnic set he and Jurdin Waltar had
designed. As he studied it, he realized that Jurdin had simplified
the set and improved the design in several minor ways, allowing
the final backpack design to be even more compact.

On a whim, he pushed open the door.

Cling. A gentle bell rang as he stepped inside.

"May I help you, ser?" asked a young man, a youngster still
of school age, with slicked-back black hair and a fresh-scrubbed
and clean-shaven face.

"Is Jurdin in?"

"No, ser. He's out at the workshop. He said he wouldn't be
back until late. Is there anything I can help you with? Or Dor-
thea? She's in back."

Jimjoy shook his head. "No, thank you. I just wanted to compliment him on the picnic set in the window. You could tell him
I stopped by, if you would."

"Ser? You are . . . ?"

"Oh, sorry. Just tell him Jimjoy Whaler, and the picnic set."

"Whaler . . . yes, ser! I didn't recognize you. That was some talk you gave, ser. Are you going to run for Council? My whole family thinks you should."

"Run for Council? No, that should be somebody like Jurdin. I wouldn't make a good Council member."

"You aren't going to run?" The boy's tone was almost hurt.

Jimjoy smiled gently. "Young man, politicians have to make people happy. Spent my life doing things that made people unhappy, telling them things they didn't want to hear. Somebody has to but people would be unhappy hearing from me all the time. Better I stay with the Institute."

"You could still be an Ecolitan, Professor."

"No, I don't think so. Ecolitans should stay out of politics. All we did was make sure that the people get to choose their own politicians. We're idealists, most of us, and idealists make poor politicians." He shrugged. "I appreciate your support. Just make sure you choose an honest Council."

"Are you sure you won't run?"

"I'm sure. I may not even be planetside for the election. How could I be a Council member when I'm not here?"

Cling. The bell signaled the arrival of a figure in a hooded coat.

"Do you have any snigglers?"

Jimjoy nodded at the youngster. "Just tell Jurdin I was here."

"Yes, ser." All seriousness, the boy turned to the woman who had arrived. "Yes, sher. We have two, four, and eight meters. They're racked in the third aisle at the end . . ."

Jimjoy stepped out into the rain, heading uphill to Daniella's. With the intricate silvered spiral over the door, the stop stood out from the others.

Whsssstttt . . . splatttt . . .

Slush from a passing groundcar sprayed on the stone centimeters from Jimjoy's boots as he pulled open the heavy wooden door. Inside stood a single, heavy display case, unattended, as it had been the last time he had come.

Jimjoy swallowed, then stepped up to the case. No one was at the jeweler's bench, but he could see Daniella's broad back through the open door to the supply room.

"Daniella?"

"Be there in just a moment." Her head, covered with a thatch of thick and short gray-streaked brown hair, did not move.

Jimjoy waited.

"All right—oh, Professor! I think you'll be pleased." The near-elfin voice failed to match the solid and muscular body to which it was attached.

Jimjoy smiled back at the jeweler. "You're the one who looks pleased."

"I am. You will be, too." She went to the heavy metal case, more like an antique safe, and, after easing out a metal shelf, extracted a small box. "Here you are." Daniella laid out a soft black cloth, then, after opening the box, laid the ring on the cloth.

Jimjoy nodded, trying to keep the grin from his face. Thelina would have thought he was totally insane.

The ring was simple—two green diamonds, large enough to be noticed, not large enough to be called rocks, set in a platinum silvered to the shade Jimjoy had specified. The two stones flowed into each other, yet remained separate.

"I had to modify that design, Professor, just a touch. Here . . ." She pointed. "And there. Otherwise, a hard knock at the wrong angle and you could lose the stone."

"That's fine. Looks better that way, anyway."

"Thought so myself."

"You're the expert."

"Mind if I use the idea again?"

"Could you wait a while?"

Daniella grinned, wide white teeth sparkling. "You want her to know how special it is?"

Jimjoy nodded. "Spacer . . ."

Daniella shook her head. "Got to watch those women spacers, Professor."

"That's what she'd say about me." Jimjoy handed over a stack of notes, the total nearly depleting the funds remaining from his few Imperial assets.

"Thank you." Daniella carefully replaced the ring in the hand-carved black wooden box and handed it to him.

"Thank *you.*" He nodded and slipped the box into an inside pocket of the parka, making sure it was securely sealed before stepping back into the wind and freezing rain outside the jeweler's.

His steps were quick and light as he made his way toward the port to catch the afternoon shuttle back to orbit control.

Jimjoy scanned the controls, checking the EDIs and the far-screens yet another time. Theoretically, they were not in Imperial space, but the last thing they needed was for an Impie ship to see the distinct energy signatures of the *Roosveldt* and the *Causto* three sectors away from the Rift.

He looked at the representative screen again, wishing Broward would hurry in closing with the *Causto*. He hated to ask, even with tight beam laser comm. His fingers drummed on the edge of the finger control panel.

Mera Lilkovie grimaced as she looked pointedly at his left hand.

"All right. All right. Just wish Broward would move that tub."

She shrugged, as if to ask whether impatience would speed the transport.

Jimjoy watched the *Roosveldt*'s image cross the dashed green of the congruency perimeter on the representational screen.

Cling. His eyes flashed to the farscreen, noting the EDI entry. The system was supposedly uninhabited, like the one for which they were heading, and the presence of another ship was a definite warning—either military or an independent.

His fingers scripted the inquiry, even as he watched the *Roosveldt* close up to his ship.

"Incoming ship is Imperial scout. Probability ninety-five percent," the screen answered.

Jimjoy touched the laser comm stud. "Bellwar one, interrogative jump to salvage one. Interrogative jump."

From the copilot's couch, Mera Lilkovie again glanced at him and his finger tapping.

He kept his eyes on the screens. He also ignored Athos and Swersa in their crew seats. The incoming scout was too far away to track the two Accord ships, and near positive identification limits—possibly just on a border recon run. But the coincidence bothered him.

"Black control, one ready."

"Jump at my mark." He paused. "Now . . . MARK!" As soon as he saw the shimmer on the screen, he pressed the jump control, hoping he had not waited too long.

The blackness of the jump was as instantaneously endless as ever before the *Causto* dropped out at the edge of the target system—containing only three gas giants and two undeveloped rock balls.

Cling.

Jimjoy pointed the *Roosveldt*, well behind the beefed-up needleboat, then scanned the entire system.

One brightly pulsing blue dot and four fainter dots appeared at the orbit line of the fifth planet, right where they were supposed to be.

2214 Universal—leaving nearly two standard hours until the rendezvous target time. That the Fuards were already there indicated how successful Thelina had been, or how badly they wanted the Empire overextended on the Rift.

"Bellwar one, interrogative estimated closure."

As he waited for Broward's response, Jimjoy tried to keep a frown from his face. Having allies, hidden or otherwise, like the Fuards was not his preference. Bad as the Empire was, the Fuards were worse. But without the Fuards, the Empire would already be down on Accord. He pursed his lips and took another deep breath.

He hadn't liked the Fuards. He hadn't liked Thelina's negotiating the "salvage" arrangement with them, and he still didn't. They were perfectly capable of potting both the *Roosveldt* and the *Causto*—and not even worrying about it. But they wouldn't have offered four obsolescent ships as bait. For the fledgling Coordinate of Accord, one or two military ships would have provided plenty of bait.

"Black control, estimate closure in point two five stans." Broward's voice was as gravelly as usual.

Jimjoy had offered to let the senior civilian captain take the lead in the operation, but Broward had declined, politely, insisting that military operations be run by military types.

Jimjoy had not pressed, and neither had mentioned the exchange again.

"Stet. Changing course to destination line. Maintaining current inbound vee until closure."

"Understand current vee, new course direct to destination."

"Affirmative."

"Stet, black control. Estimate closure in point two stans."

Jimjoy nodded and continued to scan the screens, hoping they would remain empty. If anyone else showed, the Fuards were capable of anything. While they clearly wanted to provide the ships, the transfer location and method were designed to keep the ships' origin as quiet as possible for as long as possible.

"System clear, except for target," announced Athos from the small console tucked into the space behind Mera. Swersa, behind Jimjoy, coughed but said nothing. She was there to bring back the oversized needleboat.

"Let's hope it stays that way," muttered Jimjoy.

"It's Fuardian territory, Professor," offered Mera.

"Nominally, but you'll note it sits on a big area of uninhabitable systems with Halstani and Imperial systems nearby. They want us out of here in one jump. Even want to be able to claim we strayed here."

Cling.

Jimjoy checked the screens. A faint line of dashed blue ran from the bright blue dot—an outgoing message torp, probably reporting to Fuard HQ the arrival of the great Coordinate armada, reflected Jimjoy. He shrugged his shoulders, trying to release the tension.

"Black control, estimate closure in point one."

"Stet."

Still no traces of Impies or Halstanis, but Jimjoy kept scanning the screens, watching, and hoping they stayed clear. And, for Mera's sake, trying not to tap his fingers too much.

Finally, the Accord transport crossed the dashed green line on the representational screen.

"Bellwar one reporting closure."

"Stet, accelerating at point five this time."

"Accelerating at point five."

Swersa coughed softly behind Jimjoy. Mera glanced from the pilot to the *Roosveldt*'s second pilot. Athos said nothing.

Not quite three-quarters of a standard hour later, screens still clear, except for the two Accord ships and the five blips that represented the Fuard contingent, Jimjoy began deceleration.

"Commencing decel at point five five this time."

"Understand commencing decel at point five five."

"That's affirmative," responded Jimjoy.

"Killing inbound jump carryover?" asked Mera.

Jimjoy nodded. His eyes burned slightly, probably from too much concentration on the screens. But neither the *Causto* nor the *Roosveldt* carried any offensive weapons, and flight would be their only defense should an unfriendly armed vessel appear.

He sighed and began another wait, watching as he waited, again hoping that the system would stay clear. He could see Athos stretching out, but Mera continued to track the screens as the two Accord ships crept toward their rendezvous off the fifth planet.

After yet another interval, the screens indicated lock-on of the Fuard cruiser's EDI trace.

"Confirmation matches Fuard light cruiser parameters with a probability of ninety-five percent," the console scripted.

"Bellwar one, decel at point two."

"Black control, decel at point two this time." Broward's voice seemed even more filled with gravel than usual.

"Stet." Jimjoy fingered the comm controls, setting standard Fuard frequencies. Then he tapped in the message—all burst-sent copy.

"Green are the orchards of Jericho, and yet the walls have tumbled."

The receiving screen lit almost immediately.

"Loud are the trumpets in the name of righteousness and the host of the mighty."

Jimjoy nodded and tapped in the plain-language message. "Standing by for salvage operations."

This time, there was no immediate answer.

Mera looked at Jimjoy, who concentrated on the screens.

He sighed. All four faint dots vanished from the representational screen, leaving only a blue dotted ghost for each. "Screens down on the salvage ships. Probably disembarking crew."

As if to confirm his observation, a small blue dot separated from the bright dot that was a cruiser and merged with the first ghost dot on the representational screen.

"Bellwar one, close to standoff point."

"Following your lead, black control."

"Stet."

All three Ecolitans and Swersa watched as the shuttle moved from ghost dot to ghost dot and finally back to the cruiser.

The comm screen flashed again. "Hulks cleared for salvage. Past owner disavows any responsibility."

Jimjoy added his own follow-up. "Approaching this time for salvage."

"Cleared to approach."

Jimjoy coughed softly, then triggered auditory communications with the *Roosveldt*. "Bellwar one, cleared for approach to salvage operations this time."

"Black control, following your lead."

"Stet."

The Fuard cruiser remained stationary, hanging off the four destroyer hulls, its heavy screens pulsing at full power, as the *Causto* and the *Roosveldt* eased to within broomstick distance of the "salvage."

Jimjoy's fingers darted across the board, checking and cross-checking to ensure that the *Causto* was stationary with respect to the four hulls, particularly the nearest hull.

"Bellwar one. Commencing salvage."

"Stet, control. Let me know when you're ready for support crews."

"Will do."

Jimjoy unstrapped. "Swersa. She's yours."

"Thanks, Professor." The muscular second pilot of the *Roosveldt* had unstrapped and was stretching in place. "You do nice jumps. Better than Broward."

Jimjoy laughed softly. "His are safer."

"Could be. Could be."

The Ecolitan professor glanced at the other two Ecolitans. "Ready? Let's suit up and get moving. Sooner we clear those hulls and get out of here, the happier we'll all be." He led the way to the needleboat's lock.

After a time, three broomsticks glided up to the nearest of the four obsolescent destroyers hanging in the darkness off the fifth planet of a gas giant system that had only a catalog number. Unlike the light-absorbing composite plates of Imperial ships, the destroyer's hull was a softer, almost silvery dark gray. From a distance the color was as invisible as the darker plates of Imperial ships, but closer, it made broomstick navigation easier.

Behind the trio of broomsticks rested two ships—the bulbous
Accord transport and the needleboat from which the broomsticks
had come. Beyond the ''salvage'' loomed a dark, sleeker shape
with the silvery hull and faint crimson screen shimmer of a Fuardian cruiser nearly three times the size of the Accord transport.

Jimjoy wanted to pull at his chin or shake his head. He still
wished he had been able to see Thelina and to discover how she
had engineered the ship transfer. But all he had received was a
brief message outlining the details of the pickup and the cryptic notation that she was working on ''Phase II.'' Whatever
Phase II was, even Meryl didn't know.

Clung . . .

The lead broomstick touched the plates, and Jimjoy flicked
the squirters to kill any recoil.

''How do we get inside?'' asked Athos.

''Manually.'' As Jimjoy suspected, the electronics to the main
lock had been stripped away. After tethering his broomstick to
a recessed ring, he slid back a cover plate covering a small wheel
and began to crank. The crank turned easily, indicating that it
had been used frequently.

The slab air-lock door eased open, revealing a lock wide
enough to take all three figures. Even though the ship was in
stand-down condition, without grav-fields, the three Ecolitans
entered the lock oriented feet-to-deck.

All the equipment brackets on the lock walls were empty.
Mera opened the emergency locker—to find it empty as well.

Once inside, Jimjoy twisted the inside crank to reverse the
process. Although the interior wheel also turned easily, by the
time he had finished, his forehead was damp and his arm muscles were tight. ''Whew . . . little unplanned exercise . . .''

''No electronics?'' asked Athos.

Mera had asked nothing so far, instead concentrating on the
engineering details of the unfamiliar structure.

''Probably as little as possible. We'll have to do manual course
and accel/decel calculations and inputs.'' He turned toward the
inner lock, thumbing a heavy button to flood the lock with ship's
air.

. . . hhhhsssssssss . . .

A faint buildup of frost covered all three suits.

''Damn . . .''

''No dehumidifiers,'' stated Mera flatly.

''Probably inoperative. Have to fix that.'' Jimjoy checked the gauge he'd brought along with his tool pouch. "Pressure's a touch low, but steady." The inner lock controls—a heavy switch—were in place. He toggled the switch and waited as the inner door opened. The corridor was empty, as empty as the lock had been. Any movable equipment not essential to ship operations had been removed.

As the three floated in the corridor, Jimjoy toggled the inside lock controls, then, after the lock had reseated, began to crack his helmet seal. "Stale, but all right." He took off the helmet, but did not rack it or set it aside, instead fastening it to his shoulder strap. Not that he expected the ship's hull to fail, but without the added protection of screens, he preferred to have the helmet close.

The two others followed his example.

Hand over hand, Jimjoy edged himself toward the control section without looking to see whether Mera or Athos followed.

With the screens off, the control room was a steel-walled box, irregular gaps showing in the control board itself and in the equipment bulkhead behind the second row of consoles. Two control couches—pilot and copilot—faced the board. Behind the control couches were three smaller consoles, each with a couch.

"How big a crew?" asked Athos.

"Eight or nine, depending on the mission." He leaned over the board and tapped two studs in sequence. "Thirty percent. Not too bad, if the others are like that. Might not even use all the surplus from the *Roosveldt*." Pulling himself into the rough approximation of a sitting position—as well as possible in null-gee without actually strapping in—he began to run through the analysis programs, nodding or shaking his head as the outputs appeared on the small screen on the board itself.

He ignored the look that passed between Mera and Athos as they noted his familiarity with the controls. The older Fuard systems clearly didn't allow the flexibility of detailed split screens, instead tracking outputs to predetermined screens. "Rigid and idiot-proof . . ." he mumbled.

Mera and Athos exchanged looks a second time before Mera began to try to puzzle out the board in front of the copilot's couch.

Abruptly, Jimjoy tapped several controls and sat up. "It works. For now, at least. Let's see what it looks like below." He eased around Mera and pulled himself back into the central fore-aft corridor.

Floating just off the plastic-coated metal desk in the destroyer's stale air to inspect the hatch to the lower deck, Jimjoy used the suit's belt light to supplement the dim emergency lights. Around the squarish hatch were heavy scratch marks in the dark purple plastic finish. The hatch itself was a single piece of metal which slid into a recess under the deck, unlike the irised double hatches of Imperial ships.

He nodded. The Fuards used steel, probably asteroid-smelted, and far less composite and plastic than Imperial ships.

"What do you think?" asked Mera and Athos nearly simultaneously.

"Don't know. Let's see." He used the manual control wheel to crank open the hatch on a solid steel ladder leading to the deck below, and the drives, and screen, grav-field, and jump generators. Then he pulled himself into the narrow space at the foot of the ladder between the equipment.

Every single unit was at least a third again as big as the comparable Imperial equipment.

He shook his head ruefully, but he couldn't keep a smile from his lips. With all that power . . . But that led to the next question. He disconnected the light from the equipment belt and focused it on the thin line of silver that ran from the converter to the jump generator. He repeated the tracing process with the screen generator and the grav-field equipment.

"No cross-connects," he murmured. Not that he had expected anything else. The Fuards were known for their straightforward, brute-force, energy-intensive approach.

"Cross-connects?" asked Mera.

"Not the time for an explanation, but I needed to see these to make sure. Power flows run straight from the converter to each separate system. Probably has a tiered logic in the converter distributor . . . drives, jump accumulator, screens, and grav-fields. Logic system is based on normal loads. Ship is overpowered, but the logic fields act as a governor. No reason we couldn't cross-connect and shunt power from screens or grav-fields to drives."

Athos, floating down the ladder, shook his head. "You've lost me, ser."

Jimjoy finished his inspection and clipped the light to his belt. "Just a matter of expectations. Change the performance envelope of the ship . . . probably have to make it automatic . . .

most of our pilots couldn't handle it without more training time than we have, but it could throw off the Impies."

Mera nodded. "What's the standard deviation on a fire control system?"

"Depends on distance. Call it an average of less than five percent max on a deep-space solution."

"So a variation in acceleration/deceleration . . ."

"Right."

"You two," muttered Athos. "It's like an abbreviated code." He shoved himself back to the main deck of the former Fuard destroyer.

"How long will it take?" asked Mera.

Jimjoy shrugged and turned back toward the ladder, waiting for Mera to head up. "First we've got to get these home— looks like they'll make the jumps. But we'll do it in full suits. Screens are generally first to go. Once we're at Orbit Dark, we'll need to check out all the equipment, see what needs to be replaced. Then, if we have time, you can start on the modifications."

"Hold it. Can't we fix some things here?"

Jimjoy snorted. "Terms of transfer were *immediate* removal. The Fuards don't want anyone to prove that they're supporting a revolution that just *happens* to keep Imperial Forces tied up half a quadrant away from the Empire/Fuard border systems."

Mera sighed. "Nothing—"

"I know. Nothing we get into is simple. We did get four ships, and they're better than I'd really hoped for. Even if it will take some work."

"How much work?"

"Depends. First on the checkout of the existing gear. After that, mostly on how much supercon line we need and whether you can round up enough and if we have someone who can change the converter logic without blowing the entire system."

"Me? You keep saying 'me,' " observed Mera, her voice rising slightly. "I'm not even officially even a graduate."

"You will be. Who else? Thelina says I can't do everything. I'll give you a written set of performance requirements, and you'll have to figure out how all four ships can meet them. In the meantime, you're going to learn how to pilot this on the way back. Now . . . up you go."

Mera gave herself a gentle shove with her suit boot and drifted up along the ladder and through the hatch.

Jimjoy followed, slowing at the opening between the decks, then pulling himself to a stop in order to crank the hatch closed.

''Three more to go. Then we'll have to crank out the course lines, jump points, and get the hades out of here.'' He headed for the main lock, not mentioning once again that he would feel happier, much happier, outside of Fuard-controlled space.

. . . LIII . . .

The thin blond-and-silver-haired Admiral looked at his younger counterpart. "Hewitt, are you telling me that we can't win against those eco-freaks no matter how much money you get?"

"No." The dark-haired Admiral smiled easily. "I'm saying N'Trosia can't afford to give me the funding, or the time, it will take."

"And you think Intelligence can persuade him otherwise?"

"Not necessarily. I just thought you ought to have a full understanding of the situation. I came across an interesting report, two or three years old, from one of your Special Operatives . . ."

"Yes?"

". . . on Accord. I thought you might have a continuing interest in the situation." The younger Admiral smiled again, sitting comfortably in the leather-padded armchair.

"I can't say that I recall that report."

"You probably have so many it's hard to keep track. This one was by a Major Wright. I tried to track him down, but your office indicated he was a casualty of his last assignment."

"Major Wright? Can't say the name rings a bell."

"That's odd. He was the one who handled the Halston HUMBLEPIE operation. I would have thought—"

"Hewitt, what do you want, really?" The older Admiral counterfeited a sigh and leaned forward in his swivel.

"Me? There's nothing I could possibly ask for. No amount of resources will really undo the damage in Sector Five. Most of that seems to have been caused by some group at least as effective as your Special Operatives, I might note. I can't plan actions in areas that have no support or operating SysCons. Hades, I can't even recommend them as a good return.

"If the first report by Major Wright—I did mention that there were two that showed up in my files, didn't I?—if that first report is correct, those eco-nuts could create a great deal of ecological damage on Imperial planets."

The older Admiral nodded, still smiling. "I don't recall another report by a Major Wright, but supposing there were such a report, I'd be interested in what it had to do with Fleet Development."

The younger Admiral shrugged. "As I was saying, the Senate can't commit adequate resources for Sector Five, no matter what. Sector Nine is another question—a purely military one, which is appropriate for military solutions."

"You don't think that the Accord example won't cause problems throughout the Empire? What about the Sligo revolt?"

"Sligo is in Sector Four. Those hard-rock types have always been malcontents. If you want to make an example, do it there."

"You would support such an example?"

"Me? I'm just a very junior member of the staff command. I was only making an observation."

"And do you have any other observations, Hewitt?"

"I'd be very surprised if the late and unremembered Major Wright is as deceased as the files say."

"That's an odd observation."

"Perhaps. Leslie was the Comm Officer at Missou Base on New Kansaw. Call it slightly personal."

"I see. You'd question a complete dead body with a total DNA match?"

"Only where Accord is concerned, but there's really nothing that can be done there. Might as well leave the Rift alone. That might not have happened if the Service had better equipment, if we hadn't been forced to rely too much on Intelligence operations, if we could have built the FC or the CX—but I ramble too much. . . . It is too bad that the Honorable Chairman of the Galaxy's most prestigious Committee continues to try to run all aspects of military policy. One of these days, who knows, he might even start in on Intelligence operations, revealing another set of sordid details." The younger Admiral laughed. "It's so enjoyable testifying before him and that know-everything young staff of his. Just hope you never get that pleasure."

"You do have some interesting ideas, Hewitt. Have you

thought about retiring and writing them down? It might be a fascinating exercise in fiction.''

"Hardly. I have shared them with a few highly placed friends, but . . . what can I say? Our best bet would be if the Senator took up some hazardous sport like skim-gliding on Sierra, but he's far too devoted to his job. The only thing that would stop him would be a sudden stroke or an accident. Hardly likely these days, though it does happen.''

The older Admiral nodded. "Interesting speculation, but you still haven't told me the reason for your visit.''

"No real reason. I was over here and thought I'd stop in. Wondered if you had any thoughts on how we could concentrate on Sector Nine and our friends the Fuards. That's what we ought to be doing. Then they'd have to come to economic terms with the Matriarchy. If we'd done that to begin with, Accord wouldn't have dared . . . but I'm rambling again. What's done is done.'' He stood up slowly, as if requesting permission to depart.

"Well, Hewitt, you do have some intriguing thoughts, and someday you might think about writing them down.''

"There's too much to do, right now . . .''

"That's true.'' The older Admiral stood. "I appreciate your stopping by. Give my best to the Chairman the next time you see him.''

"Oh, I'll leave that to you. Our hearings are over, for a while anyway.'' He turned to go, then paused as if to add something, then stopped. He looked back. "Have a good evening.''

"You, too.''

. . . LIV . . .

Jimjoy tightened the straps holding him into the control couch in the weightlessness of the Ecolitan-designed and Thalos-built needleboat. He mentally reviewed the checklist, cataloging the items, occasionally stumbling at the not-quite-familiar order.

"You can start the checklist, Luren." He glanced over at his temporary copilot.

While the needleboat's overall design was an improvement, for the Institute's needs, on standard I.S.S. configurations, the new checklist took a little extra time for someone trained on the older design.

Luren did not have that problem, since she had been trained on the new Institute design.

Jimjoy watched as she began.

Her once-long curling brown hair had been trimmed nearly as short as Thelina's, and, according to Kerin Sommerlee, she had a near-natural aptitude for the martial arts and hand-to-hand. Her piloting skills were adequate, but not nearly so natural. Her determination was the compensating factor. Jimjoy had watched her spend her limited free time helping build the new boats with Jason and his team, as if by knowing every structural and engineering detail she could increase her skills.

Jimjoy pulled at his chin, glancing from the boards to the representational screens, still wishing he were doing the piloting.

"Converter . . . stand by . . ."

"Screens . . . up . . ."

Her motions were deliberate and practiced, not yet automatic.

Jimjoy's eyes surveyed the cabin, where no essential item was beyond the pilot's reach. The forward display screen showed mostly the black of space, sprinkled with the white scattered stars of the Arm, contrasting with the formless dark of the Rift. In the right-hand corner of the screen lurked an indistinct gray object, PAA #32, the asteroid his team had just finished converting into a two-person biohazard research/production station.

"Checklist complete, ser." Luren did not look at him, but continued to scan the controls and screens.

Jimjoy's fingers touched the small square of controls beneath his left hand. "VerComm, Jaymar two, departing Bold Harbor three this time."

With the time lag, he didn't expect an answer, but VerComm needed to know he was en route to the last station setup. Mera and Jason had already left with the big transport, the lasers, and the remaining fusactor.

Behind him would come the *Roosveldt*, trundling in the supplies and the equipment required by Drs. Stilsen and Narlian.

Jimjoy smiled as he recalled the meeting between the two.

"Stilsen, we don't need all that junk. This isn't research; it's war. We *know* what to produce. After we win, then you put in for all the goodies, when everyone's grateful—or, in our case, scared stiff." That was how Arlyn Narlian had attacked the cautious Dr. Stilsen.

He looked over at his copilot, still wondering if he should have switched the rotation. "It's all yours, Luren. Get us over to Bold Harbor four."

"Yes, ser."

He watched as her fingers flicked easily across the simplified board.

Waiting until the faint pressure pushed them back into the couches—this particular boat had yet to be fitted with grav-fields—he scanned the readouts on the board.

Then he triggered three studs. "Simulated emergency. Simulated emergency. Your decel is scheduled in three minutes."

Jimjoy had blocked the transfer of power from the converter to the drives.

Luren froze the board, then began to unstrap.

Jimjoy smiled. "What do you plan to do?"

"Unless an instructor freezes power, the only thing that will produce that blockage is either a converter malfunction or a short supercon line. There's no way to tell the difference without looking."

"Strap back in. How would you tell the difference?" Jimjoy unfroze the board. His actions had really been a trick to see if she would have tried to do *something*. Sometimes the best course was to do nothing, at least until you knew what to do. Luren had been right. Under the circumstances, she could have done nothing from the controls.

"I'd check the supercon line first, ser. Then the plug end from the converter . . ."

Jimjoy nodded. He still had another five requirements on which to test Luren.

"The board's open. Without any net increase in total power output or time of arrival, change our approach vector by at least ninety degrees. Don't hurry it. You have plenty of time." He kept his voice even, wishing in some ways he didn't have to double as check pilot, but he needed to know the new pilots' capabilities, and the Institute was short on top-flight pilots, even after co-opting off-duty time from the Accord line people, like Swersa and even Broward.

He leaned back, pretending to relax, wondering if he looked as much at ease as he tried to project, watching and hoping Luren would be able to figure it out. Then he could drop the next one on her.

He almost pulled at his chin. Instead he cleared his throat and glanced at the representational screen, glad that the only EDI traces on the system board belonged to Accord. How long that would last was another question.

. . . LV . . .

The Admiral frowned as he read through the report, still wondering how Graylin had come up with Major Wright. His head was beginning to throb again, and he reached for the glass of water, sliding out the small console drawer containing the capsules.

Water and capsules ingested, he turned back to the screen, again skimming through the information.

"Whaler, James Joyson, II . . . no known record outside of limited data bases prior to 3645 E.A. . . . Professor at Ecolitan Institute . . . applied ecologic management tactics . . . expert in field tactics . . . reported as besting system champion in hand-to-hand (open) . . . unexplained absences . . . reported as 'brilliant' instructor . . . inspires great loyalty . . ."

The Admiral rubbed his temples, then tried to massage out the tightness between his shoulders with his right hand before jumping to the last lines of the report.

". . . comparison between Wright, Jimjoy Earle, Major (Deceased) and Whaler, James Joyson, II . . . inconclusive. Physical parameters at limits of surgical alteration possibilities, even given assumptions of Accord biosurgery . . . psyprofile comparison indicates seventy-five percent congruency . . . equivalent to clone or identical twin raised in differing environment . . ."

He shook his head. What good would it do him, assuming he could spare the operatives, if Accord could clone the man again? Especially if he weren't even Wright? What if they had debriefed Wright, taken tissue samples, and cloned him—then murdered him on Timor II? With their technology . . .

He rubbed his temples again, hoping the capsules would take effect, waiting for the news bulletins.

. . . LVI . . .

Jimjoy watched as the suited junior Ecolitan realigned the drilling laser to follow the fracture line on the screen. Then Jimjoy shifted his study overhead, trying to pick out one of the needleboats orbiting the asteroid.

He'd gotten the idea from the reports on the way the Sligo miners had taken out Sligo SysCon. The concept was relatively simple, although the mathematics and the hardware for the remotes had proved beyond his pilot-oriented abilities. He would have turned to Jason again, but Jason was working too many hours trying to refurbish the destroyers and complete and upgrade the needleboats.

After several complaints, Meryl had finally drafted Orin Nussbaum, one of the senior specialists in mathematical constructs and analytics. Orin wouldn't dirty his hands with assemblies or with the tedious programming. So he instructed the brighter students, some of whom looked like they might learn enough for Orin to return to Harmony.

That would be fine with Jimjoy. Not a day passed when he was on Thalos that Orin didn't corner him. The food was boring. The maintenance staff preempted his latest modeling run with a power failure. The student Ecolitans were too interested in big yields instead of proper dispersion.

Even thinking about it, though Nussbaum was eighteen million kays away, started a faint throbbing in Jimjoy's temples. With Thelina somewhere unknown, he had enough to worry about. The thought of her still tackling another unnamed mission she hadn't even shared with Meryl twisted his guts whenever he let himself think about it. Damned near four tendays since he and the *Roosveldt* had "salvaged" the Fuard destroyers, and no one had heard from Thelina.

He moistened his lips, conscious of the sour smell of the suit, a smell that he was enduring more and more these days. The work grew faster than the trained hands. He took a deep breath.

"Professor, team one has the drive borehole complete. They want clearance to bring in the installation group."

"Stet. I'm on my way." He began to pick-bounce his way across the mostly nickel-iron asteroid—a little more than a kay in diameter, but located—for the next three standard years at least—along entry corridor two toward Accord.

"Jeryl, careful with the laser."

"Yes, Professor."

A greenish light blinked overhead, a periodic signal that the space tug was still standing by, waiting to bring in the simplified fusactor and drive unit.

"Professor, team two has an anomaly."

"Hold on the boring until after I check team one. Until I get there, split the remotes and take team one's over to their staging area."

"Stet."

In the center of a laser-melted circular space twenty meters across stood a laser boring rig and two suited figures, looking toward him.

"Meets all the specs, Professor. Five nines."

Jimjoy repressed a sigh and studied the readouts on the borer and on the tripod. The anchor holes for the drive unit met the five nines required, and the nickel iron underfoot was vapor-melted more than level enough for installation.

He nodded, then realized the motion was inconclusive within the suit. "Site one is ready for installation." He switched frequencies.

"Perch two, site one is ready for hardware. Triggering beacon this time."

"Perch two here. Understand site one is ready for hardware." Analitta's voice was crisp, cool.

"That's affirmative. Haylin standing by with anchors."

"Coming in this time."

"Stet."

Jimjoy turned toward the man in the yellowish suit, toggled

back to the working frequency. "Haylin, you've got the anchors."

"Yes, ser."

"Just follow Ecolitan Derski's directions. And answer her questions, if she has any."

"Yes, ser. You're going to team two?"

Jimjoy bobbed his head. "Some problem there. You can still call me if you need me."

"Yes, ser."

Jimjoy turned back toward the other borehole, where he had left Jeryl. "Team three, interrogative status of borehole."

"Depth at point two five. Hardness within point zero zero five."

"Stet. En route team two this time. Report when you bottom out."

"Will do."

Jimjoy picked his way out of the depression where Haylin had prepared the site for drive installation and toward the other borehold, and where Mariabeth had reported an anomaly. Ahead, he could see the thin pole with a green pinlight, presumably still attached to the drilling laser.

"Team three?"

"Holding as requested."

Mariabeth, in another dirty yellow suit, was standing by the flat plastic screen connected to the laser unit.

"What's the problem?"

"Looks like some sort of drastic density change, ser. Drops off from the standard nickel-iron density . . ."

Jimjoy frowned. If the damned planetoid had an unbalanced core, the whole project was shot. The fragmentation had to follow a programmable dispersion. Otherwise . . . He shook his head.

"Have you been able to determine how far that extends?"

"It's not too bad horizontally—not much more than five meters." She touched the display controls. "See . . . it's like a soft rock tube at an angle."

Jimjoy frowned again. It didn't look too bad, but . . . He glanced around and toggled the frequency shift. "Perch two, interrogative link with VerComm."

"That's affirmative."

"Tell Nussie that we're sending him a geology mass problem. Need a placement recalculation based on real-life geology.

Somebody missed an interior spike. Should have a complete data profile within point five. And, Analitta, tell him this takes top priority of *his* time. No students. Him."

"Yes, ser."

Jimjoy switched back to common. "Mariabeth, you heard that?"

"Yes, ser."

He smiled. He thought she had switched frequencies with him. "You understand the data needs?"

"Yes, ser."

He touched her suit's shoulder. "Take care of it. Bring me a cube as soon as you can. I'll be on Perch two, trying to calculate what borehole latitude we have in terms of the physical limits and geology."

He took another deep breath and began to pick his way back to where the tug was approaching to off-load the fusactor and drives. Trying to develop smart and destructive rocks could be frustrating as hades, between Orin Nussbaum and unscanned geology.

. . . LVII . . .

The suited figure rechecked the laser rig, the anchors, and the readouts on the condensers. Purity still well above ninety percent.

EEEEEEEEEEEEEEEEEEEeeeeeeeeeeeeeeeeeeeeeeeeee . . .

The scream of white noise from the helmet receivers stunned her, and she had to jerk her chin twice to toggle the volume off. Her hand grasped one of the anchor struts as she stood on the asteroid surface, wobbling and shivering from the intensity of the sound.

Finally, she shook her head, and with careful quick steps headed back toward the tug, scanning the star-studded sky. Overhead, she could see Ballarney, the gas giant, like a dull red ball the apparent size of her gloved fist.

Nothing in the Belt skies seemed different. She shook her head again, then concentrated on reaching her tug.

Once inside the *Jeralee*, the thin miner only cracked her helmet before moving forward and slumping into the tug's control couch. She flicked the board activation stud and watched as the three functioning screens lit up.

Her left hand, the one that would have showed a map of scars and welts had it not remained gloved, clenched and unclenched as she waited for the old equipment to come on-line.

Clung.

Her gloved fingertips carefully punched out a query.

Hmmmmmmmmmmmmm.

Again she waited.

Her eyes widened as she took in the EDI indications on the

representational screen, mouthing the numbers. ". . . thirteen, fourteen, fifteen, sixteen of the mothers . . ."

As she watched, the old system laboriously scripted the parameters.

"EDI traces match Imperial warship configurations. Three cruisers, twelve corvettes, three scouts. EDI shifts indicate course for Sligo."

"Hades!" She pursed her lips.

Finally, she tapped the comm stud.

"All Belters! All Belters! Impie fleet en route Sligo. Impie fleet en route Sligo. Pass the word."

She slapped off the comm stud, not really wanting to be the target of an Impie homing torp, shaking her head again.

Then she sighed and closed the helmet, preparing to head back out to shut down the equipment. Sligo wouldn't be needing the metal, and she would need every erg of power she had. It would have to last for a long time. A very long time.

. . . LVIII . . .

Jimjoy reached for the door to the closet that served as his stateroom/sleeping quarters when he was on Thalos. The gray plastic door set in gray rock, opening from a gray rock tunnel, depressed him. At least it did at those times when he wasn't too exhausted to care.

The corridor was empty, not surprising in midmorning, but the asteroid reconfiguration work didn't exactly require rigid adherence to a planetside schedule.

He opened the door slowly and stepped through, loosening the helmet from the shoulder straps as he did so and setting it on the shelf, also carved from the rock. Then came the suit gauntlets. Finally, he began to strip off the armored maintenance suit, all too aware of how rank he smelled, even to himself.

Only the faint hiss of the station ventilators and the muted clicking of the suit connectors broke the silence.

Glancing over at the narrow bunk, Jimjoy noticed a white oblong on the green blanket. His eyes widened and his hands dropped from the suit connectors. In two quick steps he had the envelope in hand.

"James Joyson Whaler II," read the scripted black ink.

A sigh of relief escaped him. He'd tried to avoid thinking about where she had been and what she had been doing. He shook his head and pushed the thoughts away, concentrating instead on the envelope.

Jimjoy smiled wryly, knowing the handwriting had to be Thelina's, although he had only seen the crisp note she had left him in the hospital—the one suggesting he had better hades-fired become a decent ecologic scholar if he intended to join the Institute. His fingers seemed to fumble over themselves as he eased open the lightly sealed flap of the faintly greenish linen envelope.

A second envelope rested inside the first with the single name ''Jimjoy'' written upon it. From the unsealed inside envelope he eased out the formal card.

> The honor of your presence is requested at an indoor luncheon for two at 1315 H.S.T. on the fourteenth of Sixtus at the look-in on Thalos Station (Alpha Three-D). Refreshments will be provided. Suitable attire is suggested.
>
> Thelina Xtara Andruz
> S.F.I.

As he read the card, then reread it, his smile grew broader.

After a moment he frowned, letting his hand with the card drop. Why now? The time to have replied to his formal luncheon invitation would have been months earlier, before they had become so intimate. Was she trying to tell him something?

He pursed his lips, then lifted the card again, rereading each word, finding nothing beyond the words themselves.

Finally he set it on the shelf, propped up by both envelopes, and continued to unsuit. He glanced at his wrist. Only 1043 H.S.T. That gave him time to get ready and still dash off the fax message for Jorje that he had promised himself he would send.

As for Thelina . . . he was glad he had taken care of a few advance preparations of his own.

Still . . . He pulled at his chin momentarily before racking the heavy suit on the wall brackets.

. . . LIX . . .

Alpha three delta, on the station's top level, was the end of the Ecolitan station farthest from the tactics/manufacturing section added by Jimjoy's team.

Jimjoy checked the time. 1313 H.S.T. Thelina had not kept him waiting, but had arrived on the minute, and he intended to return the favor. In his pocket rested the package he had brought from Harmony for her.

As he turned into the number-three corridor, he passed through a simulated wooden archway. His eyebrows lifted. Underfoot, the laser-melted stone was covered with green carpet. Thin synthetic carpet, but carpet nonetheless.

The doorway to three delta was not the standard old-fashioned doorway, but a modern, heavy portal. Jimjoy frowned as he touched the entry stud.

Cling. The soft chime rang in the empty corridor.

Jimjoy glanced around, but the corridor remained empty. After the portal irised open, he stepped through into a small wood-paneled foyer. On the right was a small wooden table, on which rested a simple green porcelain dish. Above the table was a half-meter-square wall-hung mirror framed in dark wood. Directly before him was a solid wood doorway—closed.

He fingered the small black wooden box in his belt pouch again, then stepped up to the doorway. He turned the solid bronze lever and pushed. The door opened silently. As he stepped onto the heavy dark green and plush carpet, Jimjoy swallowed.

Overhead, through a clear crystal dome covering the entire ceiling, swam the dayside of Permana. Above the planet sparked

the lights of two thousand Arm stars. The combined lumines-
cence filled the room with a summer-evening twilight. Below
the planet simmered the darkness of the Rift.

By the single table in the center of the room stood Thelina,
wearing a single-piece dark green silken jumpsuit with a V neck.
A silver chain glinted on the bronzed skin below her neck. She
had let her hair grow, long enough to be swept back with combs
that matched the dress and to impart a softly regal appearance
to her face.

A single white candle burned in the center of the table, which
was covered with pale linen and set with silver, crystal, and
china.

In his clean working greens, the most formal clothing he had
on station, Jimjoy felt pedestrian—extraordinarily pedestrian.

After easing the door closed behind him, he inclined his head
to Thelina. "You look . . ." He shook his head. "It's . . . hades, I missed you . . ." The words seemed to catch in his throat.
He wanted to hold her tight, to crush her against him—to shake
her for going off where she might have gotten killed without
saying a word. Instead, he just stood there, looking at her in the
starlight under the crystal dome, watching the woman who
looked like an ancient goddess of the night.

"I'm glad you could make it, Professor." Her voice was light,
not sarcastic but not romantic, either.

He swallowed, glad he wasn't close enough for her to see how
hard it was for him, and nodded again. His eyes burned momentarily. It was as if she wanted to go back to when he had
started courting her. Didn't she know how much he cared? Or
did she care? He swallowed again. "The timing . . . was a bit
close, and I am afraid . . . I did not have the most appropriate attire. This . . ." He gestured down at his working greens.
". . . was the best available."

"I had wanted to respond to your luncheon invitation in kind,
but we never seemed to have the time on Accord. I'm sorry you
had so little notice, but I wanted to surprise you."

He took another slow and deep breath before stepping toward
her and the candlelit table. "You certainly did. No idea you were
here . . . or that this . . . was here." Up close, she looked even
more stunning, despite the darkness under her eyes.

"Would you like a seat, Professor?"

Jimjoy sighed softly. "Thank you." He took the seat and
watched as Thelina slipped into the chair across from him.

"I'm not about to try to match your abilities with cuisine. instead, I sought a little help. I hope you don't mind."

"No. Though you overestimate my abilities." He glanced around the space, easily the size of a conference room.

"Yes. It's normally a conference room for the station commander, but Imri let me borrow it."

With the starlight and the candle, Jimjoy found it hard to remember that it was midday, not evening. "Hard to remember that it's lunch." He glanced up at the silvery bulk of Permana.

"It could be evening, if you wish."

He finally was able to smile. "Suppose I do."

"Would you like some Hspall? Or something else?"

"Hspall is a little strong. I've been mostly awake for the past day and a half. Water until I have something to eat. What about you?"

"Two of us, then." Her hand reached for the crystal.

He lifted his glass to hers. "To your return, lady."

"To your efforts, Professor."

Clink. As they sipped, Jimjoy watched Thelina's face, noting for the first time the exhaustion in her eyes, the tension still in her body posture, as if she were for some reason on guard against him.

A doorway to Jimjoy's left opened, and a woman entered, carrying two plates.

"Salad," observed Thelina.

"Salud, perhaps?"

Thelina frowned.

"Sorry. Ancient pun, meaning greetings, health, something like that." He paused. "When did you get back?"

"Ten stans ago. With the *Vruss*—Halstani independent. I used your shuttle service from orbit control." She put down the glass, let both hands rest in her lap.

"Do they know who you are? Or were? The Halstanis?"

"They know who I am. I doubt they know who I was. That person is officially dead, like a certain Imperial Major. But you never know."

"Must have been quite a strain on you."

"How are the destroyers?"

"From what we can see, two of them can be beefed up almost to light cruisers. Jason thinks the Fuards don't really understand ship interconnectivity. The ships could make the difference."

"Will anything? Honestly?" Her voice was flat.

Jimjoy shrugged. "Thought this was supposed to be a relaxing time."

"Sorry. I'll try."

"Thelina . . . you don't have to force anything, or try anything . . ."

A faint smile crossed her lips. "Remind me of that in—say—five years."

Not catching the implications he knew were there, Jimjoy smiled in return, faintly. "We've diverted most of the needleboat crews to get all four back in shape. How did you manage it?"

"Negotiating was the easy part." Thelina took a bite of the salad. "Setting up the negotiations wasn't."

Jimjoy lifted his fork and speared a section of the crisp, almost purplish greenery.

Crunnchhh . . .

"It's priolet, very crunchy," noted Thelina with a smile. "It's also tart, but that should make it more appealing to you."

Ignoring the innuendo, he managed to swallow the first chunk of tangy greenery without further sounds like a rock-crusher, but used his knife to cut the remaining salad into smaller bits, following Thelina's example.

"How do you like it?"

"Taste is good, but it makes me feel like mining machinery. Who eats this? Hard-rock miners?"

"No. It's a delicacy in Parundia. Originally came from Cansab. No miner could possibly afford it."

Jimjoy pulled at his chin, then took another bite. The second tasted better than the first. "It does grow on you," he admitted.

"That's appropriate." For the first time, her voice held a touch of music.

He smiled, sneaking another glance at her as he finished off the salad, and realizing exactly how hungry he had been.

Thelina set her fork aside without quite finishing the salad, tilting her head to the side almost quizzically. She said nothing.

For a time neither did Jimjoy; he studied her face and tried not to look below the necklace that glittered on her skin. Something about the lunch . . . he couldn't quite finger it. He took a sip from the goblet instead, noting absently the seal of the Institute etched into the crystal. "Are you all right?"

Thelina shrugged. "It's always a strain, and I worry about what I'm going back to."

"Meryl and Kerin seem to have things pretty well in hand."

"I talked to Meryl on the tight-beam a while ago." She smiled again. "She said the same thing about you."

Jimjoy pulled at his chin, then sipped from the goblet. "I've managed, with a lot of help."

"Meryl said you were working on something new—called sharp stones?"

Jimjoy laughed. "Another pun. I got the idea from reading the Sligo reports."

Thelina shook her head. "Poor people. I suppose that is our fault."

"They've been looking for a reason to hit the Empire for years. They finally did, and that gave the Impies an easy way out." He took another sip from the glass. "In another four or five days we have to meet on that at the Institute, Meryl says. Figure out how to brief all the new delegates and Council members."

"Has the Empire made any demands?"

Jimjoy shook his head. "Just a general announcement regretting the necessity, but reminding all the colonies that the great and mighty Empire does indeed collect its debts—one way or another. Not phrased that bluntly."

"Of course. Let's talk about something else."

"All right. The view is lovely, and the stars are spectacular, though not as spectacular as you."

"That sounds a bit too practiced . . ."

"You've caught me out again, dear lady." He gave an exaggerated shrug. "What can I say?"

The woman who acted as the waitress appeared and removed the salad plates, returning immediately with two dinner plates.

Jimjoy did not recognize the entrée, except that it appeared to be some sort of fish, garnished with fruit. He glanced at Thelina.

"Go ahead." She laughed. "With your connoisseur's palate, you should like it."

"I might," he acknowledged, taking a small morsel of the fish that appeared almond-colored in the light from the stars and the solitary candle.

Thelina followed his example.

The taste was a lemon-electric shock, tempered with plum fire.

"Ansellin . . ." he murmured after savoring that single morsel. He looked at Thelina. "How . . ." The two fish on the table represented as much credit as . . .

"Don't worry. They were a gift from the past."

Jimjoy wondered who would make that kind of gift, either so casually or from such deep feeling. He put down his fork, his stomach suddenly churning, the corners of his eyes threatening to burn again.

Rather than look at Thelina, he studied the ansellin in the dim light, noting the uniform texture, the even color. In time he took another sip of water from the nearly empty goblet.

"Your family was from Anarra?"

Thelina nodded.

Jimjoy shivered. Anarra—most fanatical of the stronghold planets of the Matriarchy. Anarra—whose Eastern Sea was the sole provider of ansellin. Anarra—founding chapter of the Hands of the Mother. He shivered again.

"Don't you like it?"

Jimjoy wanted to let go of the tears he held in. Instead, he raised his eyes to the shadowed face across the table from him. "It's . . . Thelina, there aren't any words . . . never taste anything like it again."

"I doubt either one of us will."

Silently, Jimjoy took another morsel, trying to savor the lemon-electric tingle basted with plum fire, wondering again at the prices she had paid, wondering how he could ever have thought he had suffered.

Wordlessly, he put down the fork.

"You don't like it?"

He said nothing, afraid his voice would break, his fingers twisting around the bottom of the crystal goblet as he swallowed nothing, and swallowed again.

"The price . . . perhaps too high . . . too rich . . ."

Thelina's lips pursed, tightly. "It wasn't that kind of gift, Professor."

"I knew that, Thelina. That just made the price a whole lot higher."

Her lips relaxed, but her eyes never left his. "How would you know?"

He swallowed, concentrating on the technical reasons. "Spent some time in the Institute archives. Trying to find out more about the culture and background of a lady. In addition to everything else, ran across something called *The Anarra Complex*. Very detailed . . ." He took a deep breath.

This time, Thelina's eyes rested on her plate.

Jimjoy used the silence to regain his composure, trying not to think beyond the moment.

"Do you think it's accurate?"

"The tone was so understated, so clinical, so dispassionate. Yes, I'd say it was probably a living hades for anyone with sensitivity and intelligence." Like you, he wanted to add.

"You can't love someone because you pity them."

"Someone told me I had to get to know them, and that I couldn't possibly love without knowing them. I've tried, even when you haven't been around."

"You've shown more overt emotions, compassion, sympathy, understanding, even tears, in the last stan than the universe has seen for you in thirty-odd years. I do love you, in spite of myself, but please pardon me if I'm just a little skeptical of this gush of emotionalism."

Jimjoy shrugged. "Can't say I blame you. Can't even say I understand it myself." He used the linen napkin to blot his forehead, catching the remnants of his own tears under that cover. "All I know is that you've turned everything upside down. Until I saw you tonight—this afternoon, I mean—I didn't even realize it. Not fully," he amended, thinking of the black wooden box.

Thelina arched her eyebrows. "Do you want to explain?"

"No. I can't explain. In between each project, on each solo flight, before I collapse every night, I've been going over what's happened . . . I've wanted you, for you, not for Dr. Hyrsa's artistry, since the first time we talked in the formal garden more than two years ago. Yes, I know. You were only doing your duty. But I think I've just about reordered a section of the Galaxy because of you. Hades, neither Helen nor Jaqlin nor Terrisa had anything on you . . ."

"For me . . . you committed mass murders, insurrection, and plot genocide and rebellion? What an incredibly touching thought."

He shook his head, aware his thinking was muddy and his common sense nonexistent. "That's not what I meant. You know that." He finally eased out the black wooden box and slid it across the table. "Lost the words. Maybe this will say it better."

She looked at the box, then at him. "You should take it back. I'm not what you think."

"Neither am I. But it's yours. It couldn't be anyone else's." He lowered his ragged voice. "Go ahead. Open it."

She fumbled with the catch, then eased open the carved cover, looking with frozen eyes at the twin green diamonds of the ring.

Jimjoy waited.

"Do you expect me to fall into your arms in abject gratitude, longing for you after days of deprivation from your masculine charms?"

Jimjoy sighed, not looking away from her. "No. I expect that you will take your physically, spiritually, and intellectually exhausted body and mind and collapse somewhere and get some well-deserved rest. I intend to do the same. Then, say in about twenty-four stans from now, I hope you'll think about what I said, and why I gave you the ring." He looked across at the open box still sitting before Thelina. "Not an hour goes by that I don't think about you. Does that mean I love you? That I'll always love you?" He shrugged. "I don't know. I think I know. But you could be right. Perhaps all I want is your body, and the rest doesn't count. I don't think so."

He met her eyes, ignoring the tears seeping from his own. "Until tonight—this afternoon, whatever it is—I didn't understand. Maybe I still don't. Now . . . I know, I think. Call the ring a courtship ring, an engagement ring, a promise that I'll do my best never to stop courting you. How can I say I may have lost you by loving you too hard too soon . . ." He shook his head, finally standing up, ignoring the light-headedness that threatened his balance.

"You need me to love you without always physically wanting you. Until I saw you tonight—now, this afternoon, I mean—I didn't understand. For me, the two have always gone hand in hand. Right now they can't, not if I want a future with you. It's hard . . . hades-fired hard."

He reached down and across, squeezing her hand, then releasing it. "Thank you . . . for sharing, for telling me before it was too late . . . and for giving me another chance to love you."

Jimjoy straightened up. "Will I see you tomorrow? Or do you have to leave immediately?"

"Tomorrow." Her voice was a whisper.

He did not look back, but concentrated on putting one foot in front of the other as he made his way off Alpha three delta and back toward the much ruder, unfinished rock walls of the tactics section of Thalos Station.

... LX ...

New Augusta [14 Sixtus 3647] Seven black atmospheric fighters thundered over the Capitol. An honor guard of the Imperial Space Force stood watch as a black casket passed into the shuttle.

The shuttle lifted on the first stage of its mission to consign Emile Enrico N'Trosia to the flames of Sol, to the heart of the Empire he served, first as an Imperial officer, then as a Senator, and finally as Chairman of the Senate Defense Committee.

N'Trosia, always a partisan of an efficient military, was combative to the end, fighting off the effects of multiple brain aneurysms for weeks.

The Emperor proclaimed a day of official mourning. . . .

—*FaxStellar News*

. . . LXI . . .

Thrap! Thrap!

Jimjoy rolled over, then automatically found himself on his feet. He stared from a half crouch at the back of the gray plastic door, shaking his head mainly to clear the remnants of an unpleasant dream sequence in which Thelina rode a blue skimmer toward a thunderspout . . .

"Yes . . ." he croaked.

"May I come in?" asked Thelina from outside.

"Hold on." He grabbed for a thin robe he had never worn. Together with the shorts he slept in, the robe could help him pretend to be decent.

Despite his plea, the door opened about the moment he had stuffed his arms into the robe's sleeves.

Thelina, wearing a green shipsuit and carrying a small kit bag, eased the door shut and set down the bag. "Sleeping late, I see."

He rubbed his eyes. "Didn't get to sleep very early, or for very long. How about you?"

She rubbed her arm. "Imri didn't give me much choice. She said one of us two idiots needed the rest."

Jimjoy looked at her, not really knowing what to say, feeling grimy and disoriented.

She edged closer. "I'm sorry."

"For what? You were right. You've always been right."

"Not always. Not last night—or yesterday afternoon."

He wanted to hold her, but stood there, waiting, afraid to reach for her.

"I have to go, but . . . not like yesterday." She looked down. Finally, her green eyes met his. "Would you hold me? Just hold me?"

He nodded, his arms going around her as she stepped into them.

As he held her, she began to cry, softly, as if she refused to acknowledge it. His arms tightened around her, just a touch. At the same time, his composure dissolved with hers, though he did not shudder, but let his tears flow, knowing, this time at least, they were shared.

In time she cleared her throat. "I have to catch the shuttle."

"I know." He let go, let her step back.

"Jimjoy . . . it's hard for me, too . . . but don't stop . . ."

"Don't think I could." He swallowed.

She looked deliberately down at her left hand.

His eyes followed hers.

"It's beautiful. You designed it?"

He nodded.

Her hands brushed his cheeks before their lips touched.

"I do have to go."

"I know."

"I'm still scared . . . and it's not fair . . . but I am. I can't help it. Please keep understanding."

Jimjoy swallowed and drew her to him, trying to hold her tightly enough to reassure her, not tightly enough for their closeness to lead beyond reassurance, yet being all too aware of how little clothing lay between them.

"You have to go . . ." His voice was husky.

"Yes . . . oh, I really do . . ."

He shook his head as she grabbed for the kit bag, then almost smiled as she bestowed a quick kiss on him and opened the door. "Let me know when . . ."

"Next tenday . . . the delegates . . ."

He watched, a bemused look on his face, from halfway out his door as Thelina ran down the corridor toward a shuttle that would certainly have waited for her.

... LXII ...

Dear Blaine:

You were right about the impact on us. As you can see, I'm not at Lansdale, and who knows when I'll see Helen or the kids next. We're on what amounts to a permanent rotation, trying to guess about Tinhorn's next probe.

Will it do any good? Beats me. I'm just a skipper trying to keep the plates together. The Sligo mission froze a lot of my crew. Lucky I didn't have anyone with family there. Suppose it was necessary. After all, whoever it was did destroy a SysCon and a good thousand innocent individuals. Whether busting Sligo and the three million people on it will deter a system like Accord is another question. Those eco-freaks are nuts. You even said so.

Rumor mill—once again, the rumors are in advance of the official notifications—says that Accord has racked up more the twenty I.S.S. ships to date, not to mention three SysCons. No wonder we're stretched thin out here. There's another rumor that—somehow—the ecotypes managed to "salvage" a bunch of "obsolete" Fuard destroyers.

Hades! Bet those obsolete S.D.s pack twice the power of the *Halley.* And if Accord's as inventive as the rumors say, that spells big trouble in Sector Five. Not sure I wouldn't rather be facing the Fuards. At least, it's only rat and dragon, not declared war. So far.

Helen and the kids went to Sierra—officially home leave. But I feel better about that, especially after . . . anyway . . . See what you can do to get us *something.*

Mort

... LXIII ...

Jimjoy looked at the flat card, reading again what he had written.

> You have brought me light
> so bright that the sun dims,
> so true that the shadows of my past
> vanish into forgotten nightmares.
>
> You have brought me love,
> a flame so hot that suns retreat
> from its intensity,
> and so dangerous that death
> will not limit you.
>
> Most of all, you have given me
> back to myself, and I would do
> the same for you,
> in loving you.

The calligraphy was good, but he wished the words were better. The three words which summed up his feelings had been so overused for so long they would have been meaningless. He pulled at his chin and slipped the card into the envelope bearing her name.

He was due at the meeting to discuss what the Institute should say to the recently elected delegates and Council members. His recommendation was likely to be too blunt to be accepted.

Shrugging, he pocketed the envelope and stepped out the doorway into the early winter drizzle.

Glancing uphill and to the left, toward the other complex where Thelina and Meryl lived, he descended from the front deck slowly, deliberately. No one else moved in the morning chill. After clicking up the collar of his foul-weather jacket, he turned his steps toward the Administration building.

What else could he say to Thelina? What else could he do? A romantic he was not, nor was he someone who gloried in the company of people. He moistened his lips and took a deep breath, smiling faintly at the cloud of steam he exhaled.

As he reached the crest of the path, the one spot from where he could see both his quarters and the main Institute complex, he looked back again through the shifting drizzle. No one was out around the quarters complex.

Ahead, a scattering of student Ecolitans, all in forest-green foul-weather jackets, followed the walkways between the buildings. For all the crises, the normal life of the Institute continued for most.

"Good morning, Professor."

"Good morning," he responded to the youngster who dashed past him toward the teaching labs.

His steps carried him past the history/philosophy/tactics classrooms.

"Professor Whaler?"

He stopped, not recognizing the student, dark-haired, thin, male. "Yes." His voice was casual.

"Ser. . . . is there any possibility you will be teaching the theories course next term?"

Jimjoy shrugged. "I don't know. I probably won't teach that course until next fall, but that's . . . still up in the air."

"Oh. Really wanted to take it . . ."

"Professor Mardian is quite good, and he'll be handling it if I don't."

"He is good, but I've already had him for the basics course . . ."

Jimjoy smiled at the student. "I'd like to, but there are a few other . . . commitments."

"Were you really an Imperial agent, ser?"

Jimjoy forced a laugh. "Don't believe everything you hear."

The student looked away, almost as if embarrassed.

"Son, let's put it another way. If I had once been an Imperial agent, I'd probably be embarrassed about it and wouldn't want to talk about it. If I hadn't been one, I'd also have to deny it. And if I had been an agent for another government, I certainly wouldn't volunteer that. More important, what's past is past. You can't deny what you are or what you've done, but you don't have to be bound by it, either. What I do now is what's important."

"You believe that." It was a flat statement, almost unbelieving.

Jimjoy laughed softly. "Most of the time, at least."

"Thanks, Professor."

Jimjoy wiped the drizzle off his forehead and away from his eyes as he watched the youngster dash off. He nodded absently to several more students as he made his way to the Administration building.

Once inside the main doors, he shook his coat and tried to get most of the moisture out of his hair. He took the inside working stairs to the second floor, which allowed him to reach Thelina's office without passing by the main conference room across from the Prime's office.

Thelina's door was ajar. He stopped, listened. Silence.

He stepped up to the door, rapped softly, and slipped inside. As he had thought, the office was empty. In a quick motion, he took out the envelope and placed it on her chair. As he straightened up, a brownish-tinged and ragged-edged paper half under another sheet caught his eye. The paper shade screamed of out system origin.

The covering sheet was a brief notice of schedule changes, signed by Meryl. Scrawled across the upper left-hand corner were the words, "Thel—see any problem here? M."

Jimjoy glanced back at the door, feeling guilty, and eased the second sheet out from underneath. His eyes flicked through the fax copy, picking out the key phrases quickly.

"[Anarra, 20 Julia 3647] . . . untimely death of Matriarch K'trina Veluz . . . poisoned ansellin . . . traditional Bremudoes method of assassination . . . likely to shift foreign policy . . . successor in State Counselate . . . K'rin Forsos . . . considered a pragmatist . . ."

He slipped the copy back in place, replacing the covering sheet. No wonder orchestrating the diplomatic relations with Halston had been a strain on Thelina. He wondered what other extremes had been required.

Poisoned ansellin. He couldn't repress a shudder, thinking about their starlit luncheon/dinner.

Clunk. Through the half-open doorway he heard the conference room door close.

He eased out from behind the desk and from Thelina's office. The corridor was vacant, except for a figure walking along at the far end of the building. Jimjoy replaced the door in the ajar position in which he had found it, then turned and headed down the hall.

He could hear voices, some of them already heated, from ten meters away through the closed doors.

. . . LXIV . . .

"It's the beginning of the end," said Sergel Firion sadly. "Now that they've decided to break up planets, why even bother with this nonsense of telling our brand-new politicians that everything will be fine?"

Jimjoy frowned, pulling at his chin. After nearly a standard hour, no one had come up with an outline of the stand to take in briefing the new members of the reconstituted System Council, which replaced the old Planetary Council. Now Sergel was preaching doom and gloom. Jimjoy wondered if the entire leadership of the philosophy department had been owned by the I.S.S.

Meryl shifted her gaze from the head of the philosophy department to the former Special Operative. Thelina looked at Meryl, then back to Jimjoy.

The silence in the Prime's office dragged out.

Jimjoy glanced through the open door at the recently completed portrait of old Sam Hall, then back at Sergel. "No," he finally said slowly. "I'd say that we've won. Believing we've lost is exactly what the Empire hopes."

Sergel caught the eyes of Marlen Smyther, serving as his personal advisor.

Marlen straightened and cleared her throat before she began to speak. "This former . . . military officer . . . he claims that the loss of our strongest ally . . . the destruction of the entire planet of Sligo . . . constitutes a victory. Would you care to define a loss, ser?"

Sergel nodded.

Jimjoy looked from the almost smiling Marlen to the pensive Sergel. "A loss, sher," replied Jimjoy, refusing to give either Ecolitan any title, "would be surrendering when victory is possible."

Even Meryl looked puzzled. "Would you explain that in more detail?" Her tone was neutral.

Jimjoy shrugged. "Seems simple enough. They couldn't persuade Sligo to stay within the Empire. They didn't have the ability or the resources to attempt a conquest. So they had to destroy it. The Empire hopes that we'll give up, because they can't rule us. All they can do is destroy."

He looked around the room. What was so painfully obvious to him was clearly not obvious to anyone else—except Thelina, on whose face discomfort warred with amusement. "Let me try again. The Empire needs control. It needs the resources of other planets. The ecology of Old Earth has never fully recovered from the ecollapse, and Alphane cannot shoulder that burden alone, particularly with the population growth that it is experiencing now. Any prolonged conquest effort requires *more* resources, not less. The Empire doesn't have those resources, not to deal with more than a handful of planets. Someone in the High Command has obviously realized that and wants to send a message before anyone else realizes the Empire's vulnerabilities."

"You can't be serious . . ."

"Truly insane, Whaler . . . truly insane . . ."

The voices were low enough not to be easily identifiable, but Jimjoy marked the insanity comment as coming from Sergel. He shrugged again and stood, looking from one face to another.

"You asked for my opinion. It's just that—an opinion. However, I'm not the one who destroyed an entire planet. No one does that lightly. So why did the Empire do that, with all their fleets and Imperial Marines? It has to be an admission of weakness. They just told the Galaxy that there was no way they could reclaim Sligo and its resources.

"Either that, or the Empire is so rich and so powerful that a entire plant full of human life means nothing. Take your pick. The result's the same."

"I think I see what you mean." The speaker was Kerin Sommerlee. "Either we can win, or we can't live under that kind of Empire."

"Isn't that a rather presumptive conclusion?" Sergel's voice was pensive.

Jimjoy decided to ignore him, head of the philosophy department or not. At times like this, he wished the Institute would get its act together and agree on a permanent replacement for Sam Hall. So far everyone just seemed happy to accept the compromise he had suggested, with Meryl in effect running the Institute's day-to-day operations. "Either way, we have to fight, and we can. We can show that the Empire is both callous and weak and that we know it. Second, we can point out the obvious to the Halstanis and the Fuards—and then show we have the ability to destroy the ecology of both Old Earth and Alphane. If the Empire can't support its core population and can't conquer anyone else . . ."

"Absolutely insane . . . absolutely . . ."

"We're not savages . . ."

"They'd just destroy Accord . . . and then where would we be?"

Jimjoy waited for the exclamations to die down.

Then he sighed once. Loudly.

"Let's get this straight. First, you don't have any choice. Because we've already been identified as stirring up this secession movement, everyone in this room is dead if we don't win. So is most of Accord. We attack, or we die. That's your choice. Second, if you think things will get easier for those you leave behind if you do choose surrender . . . forget it. The Empire won't take assurances, but blood. Does anyone remember what happened on New Kansaw?"

He scanned the room. Thelina had shaken her head minutely at the New Kansaw reference. Most of the others were looking at the floor.

"So far, by destroying the key system control stations, by planting ideas and rumors, by indirect action, we've managed to avoid an obvious and direct response from the Empire. By obtaining diplomatic recognition, we've managed to retain some trade and obtain critical technology. Sligo was not known for subtlety, and they took a confrontational stance before they were ready to back it. They were also practically next door to the Fleet headquarters.

"That made it easy for the Service to send a message without overextending itself. Accord would be different, and don't think the Empire doesn't know it. What they're trying to do is to isolate us through force and fear, and if we play dead and let everyone else do it, we *are* dead.''

"That's fine in theory, Mr. Ecolitan Whaler," noted Marlen, "but we don't exactly have a fleet to put up against the Empire."

"We do have a fleet. We have the equivalent of one small fleet, or two without capital ships. That's more than most independents—not Halston, Tinhorn, New Avalon, of course. But we don't need more than one fleet. We need applied knowledge, applied psychology, and some applied mayhem and leverage. And some unique weapons. We have all that. All we need to do is apply it.''

"And you think the Empire will stand aside and give us that time?"

"That's about all they'll give us. They're still hoping we'll capitulate. If they made another move right now, with both Halston and the Fuards as jumpy as they are . . . it's too great a risk, especially as far out as we are. Their fleets could be blocked near the Rift.''

"So . . . they will be spending the next few tendays getting ready to move against us . . . and you're proposing we do the same?'' asked Sergel.

"We don't have a choice. We have some time. They won't expect an immediate reaction to Sligo, and they'll give us time to think about it. And we should make noises about thinking about it.''

"But what can we do, really do?" asked Kerin Sommerlee.

"Spread the faith . . . spread the ecological faith to new converts . . . while working like hades to stop the one fleet they might think about throwing at us.''

"The one fleet?" prompted Meryl.

"No one will admit it publicly, but they can't back down without some sort of armed confrontation. Otherwise everyone will be trying to rebel. Whatever the cost, we have to destroy that one fleet totally. If we do, then the Fuards will try to gobble up something like the three-system bulge, and the Halstanis will pressure the independents into changing their high-tech and info trade patterns.'' Jimjoy shrugged. "At that point, as far out on the Arm as we are, Accord suddenly becomes either ignored or a potential ally.''

"Ally? You've got to be crazy."

"I said potential. We still have more in common with the

Empire than the Fuards do, and the Empire needs a peaceful border with us to address them.''

Thelina nodded with a faint smile.

Tap, tap . . .

Meryl applied a wooden gavel, bringing the mutters around the room to low whispers or outright silence. ''We still need to agree on exactly what to tell the new delegates and Council members.''

Thelina stood up. ''If Professor Whaler is correct, and so far at least his analyses have been more accurate than those of, say, the philosophy department, then we have very little to say. We provide them with the outline just employed by Professor Whaler. If we can beat back the Empire, we gain great credit. If we don't, no one will be alive to care about it.''

The silence became absolute.

''Any questions?'' asked Meryl softly. ''Then the suggestion as proposed is adopted as Institute policy, and the meeting is closed.''

Jimjoy almost smiled as he caught the brief eye exchange between Thelina and Meryl, but he kept his face impassive.

''. . . can't believe it . . .'' muttered Marlen as she and Sergel left.

''. . . impressive . . .'' murmured another voice Jimjoy could not identify.

Meryl motioned to Jimjoy.

He made his way slowly to where she stood by the Prime's desk. ''Yes?''

''You're clearly elected to brief them. I've already scheduled it for tomorrow morning. Do you have any problem with that?''

''Same place as before?''

''Yes. The main Council chamber.''

He shrugged. ''Why me?''

''Who else will they believe? You told them there would be free elections, and there were. You can tell them about sweat, toil, and tears—or whatever you chose to call the coming disaster . . .''

''Tomorrow's fine. Then I'll have to get back to Thalos, unfortunately.''

''Why so soon?'' Meryl looked at Thelina, who had turned from a brief discussion with Althelm and was headed toward them.

''Because we need to stage a preemptive strike within the next two tendays. That's as soon as Arlyn will have the first load ready.''

Meryl frowned. ''Isn't that pushing it?''

''We have to strike and announce it first. Preferably to the whole Galaxy. Has to be done before they launch a fleet. Then, when we destroy their retaliatory strike, we're even. Otherwise they have to retaliate again.''

Meryl and Thelina both nodded. Then Thelina frowned.

''We'll discuss this later,'' Jimjoy added hastily. There was no way he wanted to discuss who was going to pilot the missions to either Alphane or Old Earth. Besides, he wanted Thelina to read the card he had left her, and to talk to her personally.

Thelina and Meryl both raised their eyebrows as they looked at him.

He shrugged. ''After I deal with the Council.''

''We will discuss it,'' said Thelina softly, but her voice was firm.

''I know. I know.''

Jimjoy added two split logs to the fire, noting that his supply
of split wood was getting down to near zero.

"What happens when you're never here . . ."

Outside, the freezing drizzle of the morning and afternoon had
changed into a freezing mist that drifted down in the twilight
almost like snow, swirled occasionally by the gusty winds out
of the north.

Should he have been more direct? Asked Thelina to have dinner directly?

He glanced at the kitchen. If he had to eat alone, it would be
rich and fattening. His eyes went to his wrist. 1643. Still early,
especially if she had work to do after the interruptions that were
bound to have followed the noontime meeting that had led to his
assignment to brief the Council.

He pulled at his chin. How unlike the Empire. A briefing
would have required a staff and days of preparation. Instead,
here he was, one former agent, part-time professor, and full-
time troublemaker, off to tell the unpleasant truth.

The Imperial conditioning persisted. Upstairs was the third
draft of his remarks, briefing, whatever it would be. A good
chunk of the afternoon had been devoted to that—except for the
time at the commissary to pick up the ingredients for dinner.

1645. Still no Thelina.

"Do you just expect her to read your card and show up? You're
nuts, Whaler," he told himself as he closed the woodstove.

WWWWhhhhhhhuuuuuuuu . . . The wind outside picked up,
threshing the icy crystals on the deck.

Moistening his lips, he walked back to the kitchen and checked the ingredients—standard chicken, lightlons, the herb pack. In the cold box were the chilled and lightly brandied fruits. The skillet was laid out.

"And so is your common sense. . . ."

1648. He glanced out the small garden window, then walked to the narrow slit window by the front door, peering through the glass into the darkening ice crystals and snow swirls.

Nothing. Not a soul outside.

With a sigh, he walked to the closet and pulled out his parka. He had hoped . . . but if the mountain refused to budge, he wasn't going to stand on pride.

He eased into the heavy coat, yanked on a pair of thin black gloves, and checked the time again. 1650. No Thelina.

According to her schedule, her last meeting had been at 1500. He rubbed his forehead and stepped to the door, easing it open.

A gust of wind nearly tore it from his fingers, and he clutched it, using his other hand to grab the lever and close it behind him.

Thud.

He started down the steps. Should he try the office—or home?

As he reached the bottom step, he glanced in the direction of the main Institute complex. No one in that direction. Then he looked toward the other quarters complex and began walking. Even if Thelina intended to see him, the odds were that she would go home and talk it over with Meryl, unless she were really angry. In that case— He winced and kept walking.

Although the temperature was not much below freezing, the wind and the dampness of the tiny crystals and flakes chilled as they whipped by his uncovered ear.

Jimjoy followed the path around the corner and stopped. Ahead was a woman headed his way. Then he resumed walking. Whoever she was, she was too small for Thelina, or even Meryl.

"Chilly afternoon, Professor, isn't it?"

"Oh . . . yes. In more ways than one, Cerla." He managed to remember the woman's name, the one who had helped Carill. "Take care."

"You, too."

Was he crazy to think anything could change?

Thud. A muffled door slam echoed down the hillside as he turned his steps up the rough stone path toward Thelina's.

He loved her, and he thought she loved him. But was love enough? Or was there too much in his past for her to accept?

He took another deep breath, blowing steam into the darkness. Another figure appeared on the path leading toward him.

A glint of silver . . . he found his steps quickening . . . then he was running, and damning himself for caring with every step.

For a long moment, he could see her standing there . . . stock-still.

His footsteps faltered . . . and he slowed.

Then, suddenly, she began to hurry toward him.

"Oooooffffff . . ."

She almost rebounded as his arms encircled her, and his left foot started to slide on the instantly treacherous grass beside the path.

Stumbling, he managed to plant both feet, holding on to Thelina as if he never wanted to let go.

". . . do want to keep my ribs . . ." she mumbled into his coat.

Jimjoy slowly eased his hold.

"Came to find you . . . worried . . ." His words were uneven, hesitant.

She drew back slightly, studying his face. "Why?"

He forced a grin. "Ask you to dinner."

"Serious?" She smiled briefly. "After the way I pushed you off?"

"Deserved it, especially after thinking about it. Why I . . ." He paused. Had she even gotten his note? "Did you ever get back to your office?"

"My office?"

Was she hiding a smile?

He nodded slowly. Had she read it? Was it too sentimental? Unrealistic? His stomach turned to ice, colder than the snow falling around them.

"I read your poem . . ."

"Not poetry," he protested. "Just how I feel . . ."

"Jimjoy . . . writing that took more courage than storming Haversol."

"It was hard."

"But you did it." Her gloved hand touched his cheek. "Did you mean it about dinner?"

He swallowed and nodded.

"Good. We need to talk—about us, not revolutions and institutes—and I could use a good meal." She eased out of his hug, somehow keeping his right hand in hers as they walked back toward his quarters.

The snow had shifted into a heavier fall. The footsteps he had left in the dusting that had already fallen were covered now.

"Any fallout from the meeting?" he asked, not wanting to deal with anything heavier yet.

"No. Everyone's relieved that you'll be the one facing the Council."

He squeezed her hand. She returned the pressure.

"Sort of unreal, like a white fantasy," he offered as they reached the steps to his front deck.

"If I weren't so cold, I'd stay out here and watch it with you."

Jimjoy took the hint and started up the stairs. "There is a fire going."

"Good."

The warmth billowed out the door as he opened it.

"You weren't exaggerating."

He closed the door, made sure the latch caught, and turned to help her out of her parka—except she had it off and was hanging it up.

"Sorry—just habit."

He shook his head. No matter what, Thelina would be independent.

"What were you thinking?"

"That I'm still not used to you being extraordinarily able, independent, and feminine."

She smoothed her hair unconsciously and stepped toward the stove. "Feels good."

"Would you like liftea, cafe?"

"Liftea, please."

He put on the kettle, wondering whether she would follow him or sit before the stove to get warm.

She stood at the end of the kitchen island, her back to the woodstove. "Why did you write me?"

"Because I love you. Because saying that isn't enough. Because . . . words don't come easily."

"You spoke well today. You were outstanding when you dissolved the old Council."

He set out the teapot and two large cups. "That's different. You know it's different. No sugar, right?"

"No sugar." Thelina flexed her shoulders.

He waited for the kettle to boil, not clear what else he could say.

"Did you mean what you wrote?"

He nodded, then answered, "Yes. Hard to write it down."

"Because you don't trust women?"

"Partly. Partly because I don't trust me."

"You don't want to love me?"

"Sometimes I think about that. Then I think about how empty everything seems. Sometimes I feel like I'm just going through the motions. You . . . you always seem so alive."

The kettle began to bubble. He lifted it and poured the boiling water into the teapot. Then he replaced the kettle and turned off the burner.

Clink. The heavy earthenware lid clattered as he placed it on the teapot.

"Jimjoy?"

He looked up from the cups and the teapot.

"Do we have to circle around everything?"

He looked back at the teapot.

"Do we?"

He took a deep breath. "When you want to talk about things, I always feel like you're ready to cut me down. Like there's something else I didn't understand, or something else I did wrong." He swallowed. "When we make love, I know you care, and I know you aren't ready to cut me apart."

He looked down at the counter, then lifted the teapot and began to pour into first one cup, then the other.

"Don't you see?" Thelina stepped around the island and stood almost behind him. "I need to talk to you. I need you to be able to hear my complaints, my fears, to make me feel special. When you want to love me without that, I feel used. I know that's not what you mean . . . now. But that's what it could become."

Jimjoy turned to face her, one cup in hand. He wanted to hold her, but that wasn't what she had in mind. "Let's sit down where you can get warm."

She took the cup, and he reached for his, following her to the other end of the room. He took one end of the couch, which, although upholstered, was neither soft nor cushiony. Nothing created by Accordans was soft or cushiony.

Thelina sat at the other end, leaving half a meter between them.

He shifted his weight, holding the cup in his left hand, to face her. She looked toward him, but crossed her left leg over her right, her body facing the stove. "You feel . . . used?" he asked.

"Not always. Sometimes I feel like all you want is a body. I feel what I want and feel doesn't count, and that everything will be all right so long as we make love. And it won't be."

Jimjoy swallowed. "That's not . . . Maybe in a way, though, it is how I feel . . . because words—women's words—have hurt so much."

She transferred the teacup from her left hand to her right. The fingers of her left hand squeezed his free hand gently, warmly, but only momentarily. "We can work this out."

"How?" He sipped from the cup, not looking at her. "If every time I want you without hours of conversation you feel used. . . ?"

"It's not every time. It's the pattern." She uncrossed her legs and set the cup on the low table. "That's why your note was so important. For you especially. Why your coming to find me was important. I knew you wanted me to come to you. I just couldn't."

"Uncouugh . . ." Jimjoy almost choked on the tea. *"Uuuchhhhuffff . . ."* He cleared his throat before setting his own cup down and turning to face her. "Wait a moment. I heard your door open and saw you coming toward me."

Thelina smiled, almost sadly. "I couldn't wait any longer. Wrong or not, I was going to come to you."

He wanted to reach for her. Instead, he said, "I thought you should come, but I couldn't wait either. I kept looking at the time, and looking outside, and looking at the time."

"Jimjoy. . . ?"

"Dinner can wait."

This time he did move toward her. She met him, her hands reaching for him, her lips wordless, but warm.

Outside, the snow continued to fall.

... LXVI ...

Jimjoy looked around the small, squarish room, which he had stopped to see again. Why, he couldn't say. The last time he had been here was after he had told the previous Council to resign. The stone walls of what had once been a lower-level storeroom were damp, exuding a chill. Almost expecting Elias to be manning the command post that had long since been removed, he glanced down at the briefing papers, then folded them in half.

He couldn't read from a prepared text. He just hoped what he had planned would come out right.

With a shrug, he opened the door, carrying the folded papers in his right hand, and stepped out onto the staircase that led upward toward the speakers' foyer outside the main Council chamber. The public foyer was on the other side of the building.

At the top of the stairs waited two guards, dressed in the maroon of the planetary police. The foyer, a good ten meters deep and fifteen wide, was empty except for the three of them.

"Professor Whaler?" asked the taller police officer, a woman.

Jimjoy nodded.

"If you would care to wait—either here or . . ."

"Here is fine." Jimjoy sat down in one of the dark-wood armless chairs standing by the closed double doors to the Council chamber. He didn't really know what to do with the briefing papers, so he finally folded them in half again and tucked them into an inside tunic pocket.

"It may be a few minutes."

He nodded. All deliberative governmental bodies ran late, and even Accord's fledgling Council had apparently succumbed to the virus of rhetorical delay within the first tendays of its founding. He hoped he could keep his own efforts brief.

Both guards kept glancing at him, but whenever he looked in their direction, they were studiously surveying some other part of the speakers' foyer.

After a time, he stood up again and walked over to the largest portrait on the wall, roughly life-sized and full-length, framed in gilded wood and covered with lightly tinted permaglass.

"Ross Beigner deHihns, Chairman of the First Planetary Council of Accord, 3421–3438."

With the perfect blond hair, blue eyes, straight nose, firm lips, lightly tanned skin, the first Planetary Council Chairman looked just like the young man whose family had purchased a planet on which he could test his ecological ideas. Jimjoy smiled. If his readings between the lines of the histories were correct, that was what had happened. Next to the first Chairman's portrait was the portrait of the third Chairman, an even tighter-lipped and white-haired Ross Beigner deHihns III, 3454–3456.

There was no portrait of the second Chairman. Jimjoy frowned, trying to remember.

Click.

"Professor Whaler?"

He looked up to see one of the double doors open. Another police guard held the door. "The Council would appreciate having your briefing, ser."

Jimjoy nodded, stood, and walked through the door—and almost halted.

The spectator gallery was overflowing, as was the media section. The section reserved for delegates had more bodies than there could have been delegates elected in the past two elections.

Jimjoy moistened his lips and forced himself to continue an even pace to the speakers' podium. As he stepped up to the podium itself, he noted that the entire row of pinlights was lit and bright green. He swallowed. Every media outlet possible was here to record what he said, including the Fuard and Halstani outlets.

Instead of shaking his head, he cleared his throat softly and swallowed, then surveyed the galleries, the delegates, and finally the Council.

"Council members, delegates, and honored guests . . . you have asked the Ecolitan Institute of Accord for a public briefing on the status of the Institute's efforts in supporting and enhancing the efforts of the Council in obtaining true independence from the United Confederation of Independent Worlds.'' He paused. ''Still . . . an Empire by any other name is still an Empire.''

A light murmur of amusement rippled from the spectator gallery.

''Our current situation is critical. That is no surprise to any of you. Working together, we have made great steps toward standing alone. The Coordinate of Accord has obtained diplomatic recognition from the Matriarchy of Halston, the Fuardian Conglomerate, and the Independent Principalities of New Avalon. We have signed trade agreements with Halston, and with several of the non-Imperial independent systems.

''In this effort, the Institute has been able to assemble, through salvage, purchase, and construction, a space force equivalent to two Imperial fleets without the largest capital ships. . . .

''To date, Accord forces under the direction of the Institute have taken control of all space and off-planet facilities within the Accord system. . . . We have also neutralized the Imperial system control stations—military staging points—in all three Arm systems with direct jump access to Accord. . . .

''Our research efforts into biological processes have indicated the possibility that certain biologicals can be used, if necessary, as weapons. While the Institute regrets the necessity, we are prepared to use such weapons to guarantee our survival. We admit that the threat or the limited use of such weapons is blackmail. But the Empire's decision to destroy the entire planet of Sligo was an attempt to blackmail all colony planets into remaining hostages for Imperial plunder. . . .''

Jimjoy tried not to hurry, but still to cover clearly the points he felt needed to be made.

''There is no possibility that the Empire will surrender Accord without at least one attempt to destroy Accord itself. There is no possibility of surrender, unless all leadership and independence are forfeited for the next several generations. . . .''

Even without looking, Jimjoy could sense the stiffening when he declared ''no possibility of surrender.'' Even the more independent Accord politicians were still politicians, looking for the possibility of compromise.

''In short, ladies and gentlemen, we cannot compromise; we cannot surrender. The Institute believes we can win a military victory sufficient to earn peace, but we cannot buy the peace, nor can we negotiate except through victory. We must earn victory, and no victory can be earned except through blood. Some children will be left without mothers or fathers. Some parents will be left without children.

"The alternative is a reeducation team, slavery for all Accord, and children without futures, without parents, and without hope.

"Regardless of the Council's decision, the Institute will oppose the Empire, holding to the ideals for which it was founded and by which it lives."

Jimjoy nodded to the Council, knowing his presentation had been too brief, probably too emotional, and not exactly what anyone had wanted to hear. "Thank you, members of the Council, ladies and gentlemen. If you have any questions, I will be happy to answer them to the best of my ability."

For a long moment there was silence throughout the chamber. Then the murmurs began, first as whispers, then as normal conversation.

Jimjoy stood at the podium, ignoring the Council and trying to gauge the reaction of the spectators and the delegates.

"Professor Whaler," began Clarenz Hedricht, the newly elected Chairman, "one aspect of your closing remarks troubled me greatly. You said, if I recall correctly, that the Institute will continue to oppose the Empire, regardless of what the Council decided. What if the council decides that the only hope of survival is an agreement of some sort with the United Confederation of Independent Worlds? Would the Institute make that agreement meaningless by continuing to fight?"

Jimjoy caught the nods from some of the new Council members, most of whom he did not know.

"Mr. Chairman, I appreciate your concern that the Institute not undermine the elected role of the Council. First and foremost, however, the Institute believes in freedom and self-determination. Therefore, I can assure you that the Institute will stand behind any Council decision which leads to that freedom for all people in the Coordinate." Jimjoy wanted to wipe his forehead. Instead, he waited for the follow-up he knew would come.

"Professor, you seem to be indicating that the Council is free to exercise its will only so long as it does not consider what the Institute views as surrender. That may be fine for those of you without families or ties to lands forged through centuries, but such fanaticism may be too high a price for those of us less . . . idealistic."

Jimjoy nodded at Hedricht. "The Institute is not composed of soldiers, nor of cast-steel fanatics. Most of the Senior Fellows have families and children. Most have come from generations of Accordans. Some of them have already died in this struggle and left children. Others know they will die. No one wants to wake up in the morning thinking it could happen to them.'' He paused, moistened his lips, then continued. ''But the Empire—and it is an Empire—will not accept a settlement other than total capitulation. Not unless it is forced to. The Institute must force the Empire to settle on our terms. Nothing else will ensure your survival.''

''Are you saying the Institute will fight, even if we order you not to?''

''Mr. Chairman, the Institute made possible the first totally free elections ever held in this system. Since I am not the Prime Ecolitan, I cannot definitively declare that the Institute would ignore such an unwise request.'' He looked squarely at the Chairman. ''But from what I know, I think it is fair to say that the vast majority of Ecolitans would reject such a request. And so would most thinking Accordans—''

''Professor!''

Jimjoy ignored the Chairman. ''You have asked me the same question three times, and each time you have asked it, it becomes clearer that your interest is not the freedom of those who elected you, but the power of the Council. The Institute is based on ideals, and stands apart from politics. As idealists, we will do what must be done. So long as I stand, no Ecolitan will enter politics. So long as I stand, power will serve principles, rather than principles serving power.'' He paused again, then looked at the Chairman and asked in a lower voice, ''Are there any questions of *fact*?''

''Professor?'' The speaker was a heavyset man at the far right end of the Council table. ''Meyter Nagurso, Parundia sector. Can you provide any support for your contention that the Institute can in fact force the Empire to terms?''

''We have so far been able to nullify the Empire's ability to project a fleet into our system. We have regained sufficient trade to offset the Imperial embargo's effect on high-tech micros, and we have developed the fourth largest space force in the area surrounding the Empire. We are currently developing additional weapons and are completing an in-depth system defense network. Nothing is certain. But if we can withstand a first Imperial attack, further pressures by other united systems along the Imperial borders are likely to provide a considerable incentive for the Empire to grant us independence without further hostilities.

We may be required to demonstrate our ability to carry war to the Empire, and the Institute has developed such a capacity. I will not expand upon that at this time.''

''Thank you.''

''Professor, how long before you expect an armed response by . . .''

''Ecolitan Whaler, is it true you have built a large fleet of obsolete needleboats . . .''

Jimjoy answered the remaining questions one by one, providing detail where he wished and avoiding it where possible.

Tap, tap, TAP.

Finally, Clarenz Hedricht stood at the Council table. ''Professor Whaler has been most patient, most unusually candid. The Council appreciates your willingness to brief us, Professor. Thank you.''

''Thank you, Mr. Chairman.'' Jimjoy stepped down from the podium and walked down the aisle in near silence, wondering as he did so how much damage he had created. He kept his head high, even as he asked himself what else he could have done.

Once outside the chamber, he did not wait for the murmurs or the private condemnations that might occur. Instead, he nodded at the two police officers, and with a polite ''Thank you,'' left through the lower-level door, heading for the flitter waiting for him on the green.

Jimjoy gave the pilot, Huft Kursman, the signal to light-off the flitter as soon as he crossed the first stone walkway. Kursman responded with a thumbs-up and the whine of the starter.

Jimjoy stretched his steps, but did not run. As he climbed into the copilot's seat, he looked at Kursman. ''Lift off as soon as she's ready.''

''Stet, Professor. A little too much truth for them, ser?''

Jimjoy shrugged as he pulled on the helmet. ''Didn't stay to find out.''

Thwop . . . thwop, thwop . . . thwop, thwop, thwop . . .

As the rotors came up to speed, several media types, fax rigs slung over shoulders, hurried around the corner of the stone structure.

With a wry smile hidden behind the dark visor of the helmet, Jimjoy waved to the lenses as the flitter lifted.

. . . LXVII . . .

"Did you have to be quite that blunt?" Meryl's normally composed face was slightly flushed. Whether the additional color came from the viral infection she was fighting off or from anger was another question.

Jimjoy sat down in the chair, taken aback at the intensity of the first words she had addressed to him as he walked into her office. He thought about answering, then shrugged. "What would you have had me say? That a negotiated settlement was possible? That we all will live happily ever after without any sweat, toil, or tears? That everyone of us has laid his or her life on the line so that another generation of irresponsible politicians can bargain away the gains bought by those lives?"

He shook his head, then fixed her with his eyes. "I meant what I said. No Ecolitan is going to mess with politics, except over my dead body. The Institute will never bow to the politicians. We made them to serve the people, and they damned well are going to serve the people. Not the other way around."

This time Meryl sat back. "You feel rather strongly." Her raspy voice was barely above a whisper.

"I do. I'm not a figurehead. I never will be." He looked out the window into the high and hazy winter clouds.

"So what do I do when half of those politicians are calling for your head?"

Jimjoy grinned. "Tell them the same thing, except with the finesse that you have. Tell them that the Institute stands for freedom first and foremost, and above partisan politics. We intend to remain that way, thank you. Do you want us to remove our protection of all your children and advise the Empire that Accord no longer has an armed forces?''

Meryl smiled crookedly, then blew her nose. ''What if they agree?''

''They won't. They're not stupid. They just want to control the power behind the power. And we can't let them—ever.''

''I wish I had your confidence.''

''Meryl, I don't know how to manipulate people. This morning showed that I don't. But I know power and structures. Trust me on this one.''

She took a sip of water, then whispered back, ''Do we have any choice?''

''Not really.''

''I didn't think so. Neither did Thel.'' Another sip of water followed.

''Where is she?''

''You're changing the subject. You always do when subjects get unpleasant.''

Jimjoy laughed ruefully. ''You're right. But where is she?''

''Visiting Dr. Hyrsa.''

Jimjoy's stomach turned. ''Now what?''

''Not for herself. Your comments about deaths and casualties got us thinking. We really need to build up a more dispersed emergency health care system. What happens if the battle of Accord vaporizes the Institute? She went to talk to Erica about that.''

Jimjoy pulled at his chin. Still so many details unresolved, unplanned for, and less and less time remaining.

''You look worried.''

He nodded slowly.

''Well, don't tell anyone. If nothing else, your confidence has been beamed all over the planet. After that performance, the Empire will probably want your head—again.'' The acting Deputy Prime Ecolitan coughed twice, then took out another tissue.

''What else is new?''

''They'll take a planet to get it this time.''

Jimjoy's stomach twisted slightly, even though he nodded again. ''We'll have to see that they don't get it.'' He stood up. ''See you later.''

Meryl only nodded in return, transferring her attention back to the screen and its priority lights, still clutching yet another tissue in her left hand.

. . . LXVIII . . .

2 Oct 3647
New Augusta

Dear Mort:

Wish I had been more timely in responding, but, as you know, all hades has broken loose. First, N'Trosia died of those aneurysms, and the media had a field day speculating about the probability of natural occurrences. Then the Halstanis recognized the Coordinate of Accord, and the Fuards did the same.

For whatever reason, the Fuards have notified us that they have junked the Treaty of New Bristol—officially this time—and are required to develop adequate self-defense capabilities, independent of the Empire. So Hemmelman, N'Trosia's successor, has "requested" the Planning Staff to brief the Committee in depth on the implications for the I.S.S. and has asked Intelligence to provide an assessment of probable Fuard actions.

Hemmelman seems more open to fleet modernization and agreed to our request to reopen the CX question—next year. What we'll do in the meantime, I don't know. It's no secret that we'll be hard pressed if anything else comes up, particularly if it's a goodly distance from Sector Five.

Scary thing about Accord is that their war leader, or whatever he's called, has thought rings around the tactics staff, even Intelligence. Showed up from nowhere. Did they just make him with their biotech? Who knows? Wish we had some like that. Then we might never have gotten into this mess.

Glad to hear that Helen and the kids had a chance to take home leave and trust they will be able to enjoy it for a while . . . a good, long while.

If anything definite occurs, I'll let you know. Hang in there.

Blaine

. . . LXIX . . .

"There's another reason why you can't afford to be a hero."
Thelina looked pale under her bronzed complexion.

"I'm not trying to be a hero."

"You're not? Then why did you try and hide this mission?
Like the one that took out the Haversol System Control? Why
have you put off discussing it for the past tenday?" She glanced
across the deck into the late fall afternoon.

Jimjoy followed her glance, wondering where the year had
gone. The sky was a crisp blue, cloudless, and the sun hung
over the western mountains. With all the time he had spent on
Thalos, it seemed as though he had been in some sort of suspended animation so far as the seasons at the Institute went.

He sighed softly. "I didn't want you to worry."

"Going off in the middle of the afternoon to get yourself killed
isn't going to make me worry?" She twisted in the hard chair.

"Let's stop arguing." He straightened. "You said you had a
reason. Not an emotional reaction, but a reason." He paused.
"And why haven't you come to see me? It's no harder for you
to get to Thalos than for me to get here."

Her green eyes met his green eyes. "Sometimes, even though
you try so hard . . . sometimes . . ."

He sighed again. "Sometimes—sometimes what?"

"Sometimes you are so predictably male and dense."

His guts twisted, like they had at the formal under-the-stars
luncheon, and he found himself moistening his lips, squeezing
them together, then moistening them again. He swallowed. "That
bad?"

"You can't help it, not yet. Not when you see the truth and don't want to face it." Thelina turned even paler. "Excuse me . . . just a—"

She was gone toward the facilities.

Jimjoy looked after her then out through the open slider, swallowing as the breeze ruffled his hair. Despite the unseasonable warmth, the air held a hint of chill. His stomach churned, though not nearly so badly as he imagined Thelina's was doing.

He understood now, but was it better to be understanding or dense? Most times he would have said understanding, but he still had to go. What was worse was that he might have to do it again, when the Empire returned the favor.

Standing up from the uncomfortable chair, he paced over toward the deck, half listening for Thelina's return.

With the slightest of whispers of boot leather on polished wood, he turned and hurried toward her. Taking her hands before she could draw them from him, he met her eyes.

"Do you want to tell me? Or me to tell you?"

She looked down.

"You . . . we're going to have a child. Is that so bad?"

Thelina's eyes charged his. "You said 'we.' Will it be 'we' if I'm left like Carill, like Kerin? How many times can you go out there and come back?"

"Who else is there? It won't work if we can't deliver it to Earth itself. And let them know we can."

There was a long silence.

"Why didn't you train anyone else?"

"I've been training all year. So has Analitta. So has Imri. So has Broward."

Her hands squeezed his. "Don't you understand? I refuse to be a single parent so that you can be a hero."

He sighed. "Don't *you* understand? I don't want to be a hero. But I have to act like one. That's my only chance of getting back." He remembered what Kerin had said to him nearly a year earlier, about his having no hostages to fate. No hostages to fate?

"I did want to ask one question," he added, knowing he was changing the subject, and knowing he was being extraordinarily unwise. "How . . . ?"

"I lied. Just like you did. For a good reason."

"A good reason?" He bit off the retort he almost made.

"Would you listen?" Her voice was as gentle as he had ever heard it.

He shrugged. "I have been listening. I've been listening to you for two years. You're usually right." Except about military tactics, he thought.

"I love you. I love you, not the hero image that isn't you. I want you to want to come back."

He looked down. There it was . . . what he'd been looking for through three lifetimes, what he had refused to admit he wanted. And he'd set it up so that he had to risk losing it, because everything rested on his being able to deliver one ship full of the deadliest biohazards ever developed to the most heavily guarded planet in the human Galaxy.

"I . . want . . . you. Have to . . . come . . . back . . ." He shook his head.

This time, Thelina, pale and trembling, drew him to her.

. . . LXX . . .

"Why you?" she had asked.

Who else had there been? A year of training wasn't enough. His own ten-plus years might not be enough.

She had sighed and turned and looked out into the woods behind the deck.

Now he was in the best of the Accord couriers, a ship stripped of everything but minimal screens, overgeneratored, overpowered, and underprotected. A ship carrying two hundred minitorps filled with the nastiest of self-reproducing biohazards possible, and two thousand shells filled with the hardiest versions of the nasties. All because . . . because . . . why? Because he had to strike the heart of the Empire before the Empire struck Accord? That was what he had told the Council, and Meryl, and Thelina. Now he wasn't exactly sure of that any longer. Or was that because he really didn't want to be in the courier, screaming down from above the ecliptic on Old Earth?

He forced himself to concentrate on the audio channel, flicking from one frequency to another.

"Satcom five . . . EDI register Hammerlock one . . ."

"Belter three . . . ETA is five plus . . . five plus . . ."

With a frown, he keyed in the Imperial tactical frequencies, hoping that the comm guard this close to Old Earth was more lax than in the Arm and toward the Rift.

He could smell his own sweat. That and an odor of fear. His fear.

"Artac . . . monitor three, inbound . . . sitmo . . ."

"Clearance amber three . . ."

"Stet . . . monitor three . . ."

In some ways, coming to understand Thelina, and himself, had just made things worse. He was thinking about the future, and thinking about the future could be fatal when he needed to concentrate on the present. He wiped his forehead and tried another band.

. . . scccrtitisss . . .

With a tight grin, he touched the on-board scrambler and entered a code-breaking program.

. . . sccctrtttscchhh . . .

He tried a second. And a third.

. . . tresascrrtttsss . . .

It took another thirty minutes and most of the descrambler program before he got something intelligible.

"Ellie five taccon, Turtle three. EDI scans normal. Continuing this time."

"Stet, Turtle three."

"Turtle four, this is taccon. Interrogative scans. Interrogative scans."

"Ellie five, Turtle four. Scans negative."

The Impies could have used tight-beam lasers, but lasers were limited by speed-of-light considerations, unlike standing jump wave. The compromise was usually scrambled standing wave.

Jimjoy listened as he wiped his forehead and studied the readouts on the board in front of him. The *Greenpeace* was damped tight, coasting at an angle to the system plane, like an anomalous piece of cosmic junk, emitting no radiation except a minimal amount of heat.

His chances—not exactly good—depended on the accuracy of his initial course plot and on his ability to use the earth's atmospheric shield. The reentry course had been designed to let the ship coast at high speed until it intersected the normal out-system shipping points serving the L-5 nexus. But no courier carried equipment sophisticated to plot and set that precise a course from a third of a system away with only one of two bursts of energy. The idea was that he would be able to make an adjustment or two near the shipping levels without creating immediate attention.

He could have done the job by setting a real cometary orbit and letting the ship drift into position. The problem with that was he would have died of old age before the courier reached Old Earth, and Accord would have long since lost.

The compromise was a ship with no radiation leaks, no outside energy expenditures, sprayed with nonreflective and energy-absorbing coatings, but traveling at high speed. All he had to do was make one or two course changes, swing around Old Earth, and launch a mere two hundred minitorps, followed by two thousand shells which would light up every satellite detection system possessed by New Augusta.

Of course, there was the small problem of getting the ship back above the ecliptic before the Imperial Forces could react.

He checked the readouts again, then the screens. Old Earth was showing a disk, as was the moon. So far, so good.

Strange, to look at them from above. The techs had initially protested his determination to rely on sampler densities and an average of precalculated values to determine jump and entry points as far in-system as possible.

Thelina had worried right along with them. "What if you're wrong?"

"A little bit won't matter. A lot and I'm dead. Nothing else will work."

"Will this?"

He had shrugged. There hadn't been much choice, not after the stinks he'd made. Besides, of all the Ecolitans, only Broward and Analitta had experience equivalent to his. And Broward wasn't at ease in small ships.

There was a risk in everything. He had awakened with cold sweats, thinking that Thelina had fallen back into the Hands of the Mother on her Halston mission. Now, with the diplomatic recognition from Halston, followed by Tinhorn, Accord was receiving more independent shipping, and access to the high-tech designs and critical microblocs necessary to complete outfitting the needleboats. Thelina had made it all possible, but he still had nightmares.

Wiping his forehead again, he waited, listening.

The courier's velocity was too high to be natural, even for the oddest cometary, but before he was detected, he hoped to make the last course change to set his final-approach angle.

"Ellie five, Turtle two. Negative on scans."

The courier pilot checked his own passive EDI readouts. The spread of the outer orbital picket was wide enough. Not a real detection line at all—but a mere precaution. The real detection arrays, the ships he had bypassed by his angular approach, were farther outsystem and concentrated on the possible standard approach corridors. An above-ecliptic approach like Jimjoy's was neither practical nor advisable in most circumstances. Since the calculation of jump points was problematical at best, nonstandard approaches would, over time, destroy a lot of ships.

Jimjoy wiped his forehead again to keep the sweat from his eyes. The control area temperature was normal, about fifteen degrees centigrade, but it seemed hotter, and the moisture endless.

He laughed, abruptly, and unstrapped, heading for the small fresher unit. Last chance he might have to relieve himself before he discovered whether he was a lucky fool or a dead idiot. As he left the controls, he twisted the audio up to full volume, then half pulled, half floated toward the fresher. The grav-field generators had been pulled to allow for beefing up the drives and more converter power.

"Turtle three, Ellie taccon. Interrogative screens."

"Ellie five . . . negative this time."

"Turtle three, we have enhanced negative optical at plus five. Coordinates follow. Plus five point four three. Sector red. One eight three relative. Direct feed to your taccomp."

"Stet, Ellie. Receiving feed. No EDI from sector red. Plus ten to negative ten. Interrogative negative optical."

"Negative optical—no radiation, no emissions. Detected from crossing other optical sources."

"Stet, Ellie."

"Turtle three. Understand no EDI."

"That's affirmative. Negative on EDI this time."

Jimjoy took a deep swallow of metallic-tasting water before heading back to the controls. His mouth was dry even after he drank. He listened while he strapped back in and readjusted the audio. They had him. But did they know it?

He wiped his forehead again, glanced at the elapsed time clock, and took a deep breath. The next few hours would be long.

With a sigh, he began recalculating his options. If . . . if the Impies decided he was the space junk he looked like, in another hour he might be able to pull off a quick burst to adjust course.

"Ellie taccon, three here. Negative on EDI. Negative on RAD. Negative on enhanced optic."

"Stet. Request you continue monitoring area. Probably essjay."

"Stet. Will continue periodic sweeps."

Jimjoy let out his breath, wiped his forehead. He was temporarily safe, until he had to make a course correction. He began to plot out the alternatives available for the spacing and timing of the second correction, displaying them on the navigation plot. He shook his head as he studied the courses.

No matter which one he took, the gee forces required would be close to his tolerances . . . and the ship's.

"Turtle four, Ellie taccon. Request sweep in sector green, two seven three relative, negative point three."

"Stet, Ellie five. Sweeping this time. Initial negative on EDI or enhanced optical."

Jimjoy wiped his forehead with the back of his nearly soaked sleeve, studying the course options again.

"Turtle three, Ellie taccon, interrogative status of essjay."

"Three here. Status is constant. No EDI, no optical on heat, conforms to hard cometary profile."

"Ellie taccon, Turtle four. Have reading at two six nine relative, sector green, coordinates to your taccomp."

"Stet, four. Stand by."

"Standing by."

Jimjoy moistened his lips. The Impies were jumpy. Too jumpy. He looked at the options, selecting one, the one holding off the course change until the last possible moment. Then he ran the inquiry through the plot computer.

"Probability of success exceeds point nine eight."

He winced. Someday, those two-percent chances would turn on him. Still, the representation screen showed him "above" and fractionally inside the orbit line of the Imperial ship that seemed to be Turtle three. Every minute counted now, because a torp would be on a stern chase, rather than a closing vector.

"Turtle three, this is Ellie taccon. Interrogative peacekeeper status."

Jimjoy's stomach twisted. His fingers reached for the controls, plugging in the contingency course he had hoped not to use.

"Ellie five, three here. Status is green at point eight. Interrogative status check."

"Stand by, three."

Jimjoy watched as his own screen sketched out the near-suicide course line. The basic idea was simple enough—full power straight at Earth. Full decel just before hitting the edge of the extended radiation belts, and then using the planet to sling the *Greenpeace* at right angles to the ecliptic, distorting the mag-

fields and hopefully messing up communications and detection
long enough for Jimjoy to reach low-density space and jump.

"Turtle four, Ellie taccon. Interrogative peacekeeper status."

"Ellie five, status is green at point nine."

"Turtle three and Turtle four, stand by for peacekeeper release."

Jimjoy squinted, touched the control to bring the variable
stepped acceleration program up from standby. Finger poised,
he watched the representation screen. He had needed another
twenty standard minutes, and he wasn't going to get them.

". . . sssssss . . ."

Jabbing the acceleration controls, he keyed in the variability.
The abrupt frequency shift told him enough

". . . oooo*ffff* . . ." The sudden power surge drove him back
into his couch.

On the screen three blue dashed lines flicked from the picket
ship closest to him toward his position.

Jimjoy blanked the screen receptors, moistening his lips. For
a moment he hung weightless as the courier dropped its acceleration to zero and changed course line. Then he was jammed
back into the couch even more forcefully. Each course led to
Earth, not always directly, with ever-increasing speed.

His fingers called up the scrambler program and the frequency
hunter. He might as well try to find out what they were up to as
the courier scrambled sideways at an acceleration well outside
the standard Imperial profile.

". . . sccctttcchhhh . . ."

Using the fingertip controls, he tried one of the earlier programs.

". . . sctttccchhh . . ."

And another.

". . . sctttchhhh . . ."

Then he punched out the analysis. He had to squint against
the acceleration to try to read the figures. The pattern seemed
logical, and he tried another combination. Just then, the acceleration stopped. His stomach lurched upward in the weightlessness.

EEEEEEEEEEEEEEEEEEEEEeeeeeeeeeeeee . . .

He felt that the courier ought to be shaking, even as he knew
tacheads in space didn't create atmospheric effects.

EEEEEEEEEEEEEEEEEEEEEEEeeeeeeeeeeee . . .

The courier was programmed to halt all acceleration at tachead detonation, as if to indicate to the Impies their efforts had been successful.

EEEEEEEEEEEEEeeeeeeeeeeeee . . .

One glance at the representational screen told him that either Turtle three had incredibly poor tracking or the courier had been extraordinarily effective in evading the three-torp spread. His fingers dropped the evasion system into standby and called up a course line recalculation.

He pulled at his chin as he noted the courier course and speed. Course was fine—directly at the northern hemisphere of Old Earth. Speed was well above the minimum necessary to turn both Jimjoy and the *Greenpeace* into the finest of interstellar dust.

He noted the resumption of audio lock as he began to refigure power outputs, trying to determine the range of escape options.

". . . status . . ."

"Ellie five, EDI traces lost at time of detonation. Scans reveal no EDI, no optical, and no enhanced heat."

"Stet, three. Continuing cross-optical scans in sector orange this time. Interrogative remaining peacekeeper status."

"Status is green, at point five."

". . . mothers . . ." mumbled Jimjoy, his mouth dry again. L-5 control would come up with another enhanced optical scan in roughly five standard minutes, cross-check it within another five, and have another spread blown out, probably with all five remaining tacheads.

He called up the course line projections, marking his own position in ten minutes, and asked the plot computer to provide options for evasion, still toward Old Earth.

"Turtle four, interrogative status of essjay target."

"Ellie five, four here. Negative on EDI at any point. Dust dispersion indicates standard comet profile."

"Stet, four. Continue scanning this time.

"Turtle three, interrogative sector orange."

"Negative on EDI or optical."

"Stand by for peacekeeper release. EDI traces prior to detonation indicate Charlie Alpha courier."

Jimjoy wiped his forehead, wishing the duty officer on the L-5 control station were not quite so persistent, and checked the course line and the preprogrammed evasion pattern—with a healthy decel built in after the initial turn.

Approximately two minutes before detection. He swallowed, letting his fingers reach for the evasion kick-in.

Knowing he was probably too early, he jabbed the stud.

"Three. Coordinates . . . release. MARK!!!"

Jimjoy released his breath just as it was knocked out of him by the courier's quick acceleration.

Before he had recovered he was thrown against the straps by an even more brutal decel kick.

EEEEEEEEEEEEEeeeeeeeeeeee . . .

EEEEEEEEEEeeeeee . . .

EEEEEEEEEEE . . .

The screams of the three tacheads battered his ears, while another attack of weightlessness assaulted his guts.

Blinking, he scanned the screen, noting that the corvette's torps had been almost as wide of the mark as on the first salvo.

"Turtle three, interrogative status. Interrogative status."

"Negative EDI. Negative optical."

"Interrogative peacekeeper status."

"Status is green at point two."

"Stet. Standby.

"Turtle four, interrogative time to omega three."

"Ellie five, four here. Estimate point two five to omega three. Point two five."

"Four, stand by."

After scanning his own screen, Jimjoy could see the L-5 operations coordinator's problem. Turtle three was nearly out of torp range, and would have to leave station to chase a small courier-sized ship that could be a decoy. Turtle four could cover, but only by leaving an even larger uncovered area, and it would be another ten minutes before the enhanced optics would sort out to discover whether the target still existed.

Jimjoy smiled. One set of problems passed. The smile faded as he contemplated the courier's power levels—less than seventy percent, with the bulk of the power requirements yet to come.

He shook his head before he began fiddling with the comm freq hunter. L-5 was surely trying to talk to either Lunar Control or inner orbit control.

". . . sccctttcchhhh . . ."

After a time, he managed to lock in with the correct scrambler keys, the ones Accord was not supposed to have, courtesy of the *D'Armetier.*

". . . recommend patrollers along upper green, inbound two eight zero, dispersion . . ."

". . . this is absolute interdict. Say again, absolute interdict . . ."

Not that the decision to vaporize him was any surprise. He had one surprise of his own left—his decel pattern. Or lack of pattern.

He took a swallow of warm water from the squeeze bottle and replaced it in the holder, watching the time run down and the distance decrease.

"Hawkstrike one, Lunie Prime, charlie inbound on roger three. Roger three."

"Understand roger three. Negative EDI, negative optical, negative lock. Negative on laser focus."

"Stet, one. Coordinate feed follows."

Jimjoy watched the screen and listened, knowing he could do nothing else, suspecting they wanted him to move, to provide a burst of energy for them to lock in on.

Not yet.

"Prime, one here. Coordinates accepted. Negative on EDI lock. Negative optical."

Jimjoy could hope. The *Greenpeace* was aimed nearly straight at the patroller. With no radiation and no optical parallax . . .

He wiped his forehead. Just another minute or two and the *Greenpeace* would be silently whipping by the patroller, perhaps as close as thirty kays, and as effectively as distant as half a system away.

". . . bastard's here somewhere . . ."

"Silence on the net."

Jimjoy almost grinned. Too close in without energy sources for locks, and they were blind . . . and once he hit Earth's magfield . . . if he hit it.

"Hawkstrike one, charlie should be three zero zero, immediate local. Immediate local."

"Prime. One here. Negative on indicators."

Jimjoy waited, fingers ready to trigger the final inbound evasion.

"Prime, Hawkstrike three. Parallax indicates charlie is absolute orange, coordinates follow."

"All units fire on mark . . ."

Jimjoy slapped the control activation, watched his vision tunnel into darkness with the sudden acceleration, then expand, then drop away again.

". . . MARK!!!!"

EEEEEEEEEEeeeeeeeeeeeeeeee . . .

Clunk.

Jimjoy didn't like the last sound, but the board indicators showed nothing as the *Greenpeace* plunged toward Old Earth's upper atmosphere.

". . . absolute orange at two five . . ."

". . . beams on charlie . . ."

Three lights flashed red as the lasers of the nearest patroller locked on the courier.

Jimjoy flicked up the screens to avoid being fried.

"EDI on two five."

"What in hades is it?"

". . . almost in the mag-field. Interrogative laser punch."

"Trying lock-on . . ."

Jimjoy flicked another evasion macro.

". . . lost . . . lock-on . . . reacquiring this time . . ."

His neck ached. His stomach muscles were knotted; his forehead was clammy; his mouth was dry.

Another check of the decel parameters. He kicked in another acceleration jolt, then cut the power. . . . waiting.

Amber on the nose. . . . amber on the lower hull . . . amber on leading edges . . .

"Charlie's inside the mag-field, touching oscar . . ."

The stress lines climbed.

He jammed the drives to full decel, letting the courier drop further toward lower orbit, out of the patrollers' reaches, assuming the atmosphere didn't ablate what was left of the hull.

Jimjoy could feel the heat leaching through the hull, could feel the strain placed on the supercon lines, on each and every system, without checking the rows of red-and-amber status lights flashing on across the board.

His fingers flicked three studs.

". . . torp sequence one . . . complete . . ."

He forced himself to wait, mentally counting for a minimal separation, before triggering the second sequence.

. . . eeeeee . . . eeeeeee . . . eeeeeee . . .

The wave receivers were deaf and blind once the courier was so far within a planetary mag-field. Jimjoy grinned grimly. The Impies certainly couldn't shoot now, not when the traces of the upper atmosphere and the mag-field made torps impossible. He was too high for missiles, and particle beams weren't allowed inside lunar orbit.

So all he had to do was survive the drop orbit and pick an exit course—blind where the Impies weren't lined up to pot him.

The course was set. No real choice there.

He triggered the second torp drop, then added the first hazard shell drop.

". . . torp sequence two . . . complete . . ."

Most of the warning lights had dropped off the red and into the amber—except for the hull thickness/integrity warning. Would he have a hull left?

He noted the deviation from the lead to the exit course and attempted an adjustment. The courier slewed, then straightened.

". . . torp sequence three . . . complete . . ."

The next round of hazard shells followed.

By now, as close to the upper atmosphere as the courier was, the only workable instruments were the laser plotter and the internal systems.

". . . torp sequence four . . . complete . . ."

He checked the energy reserves. What reserves? If his exit course weren't perfect . . . He pushed away the thought and concentrated on the next drop.

". . . torp sequence five . . ."

The process seemed to telescope. Scan, calculate, release torps, release shells. Scan, calculate, release torps, release shells . . . and start all over again.

". . . torp sequence ten . . . complete . . . hazard shell drop away . . ."

He shook his head, aware that he and his shipsuit were dripping and that every metal surface was pouring heat at him. Another head-shake and he called up the exit profile, then punched the red stud.

. . . *eeeeeeEEEEEEEeeeeeeeeee* . . .

The interference began to drop almost immediately as the courier plunged skyward through the magnetic south pole.

Twenty percent, nineteen percent, eighteen percent—Jimjoy cut the acceleration, feeling his exhausted stomach flip-flop again.

". . . interrogative . . . intercept . . ."

"Ellie five, Hawkstrike two, that is negative. Bogey's outbound beyond Hawkstrike return envelope."

Jimjoy glanced at the representational screen, watching his own track sprinting away from Old Earth at nearly a right angle to the ecliptic.

Next time, next time, the Impies would be ready for the above/below the ecliptic approach. Which was fine with Jimjoy, because there wouldn't be a next time.

If either Narlian or Stilsen were correct, Old Earth was going to be far too busy trying to survive to worry about Accord. Still, he continued to watch the screen, wondering if any heroes were going to chase him into the uncertain dust densities below the ecliptic.

"Ellie five. Hawkstrike three, releasing this time."

Jimjoy held his breath as the nearest I.S.S. corvette released a full spread of tachead torps, watching as the blue dashed lines appeared nearer and nearer on the representational screen.

EEEEEEEEEEEEEeeeeeeeee . . .
EEEEEEEEEeeeeeeeeeee . . .
EEEEEEEEeeeeeeeeee . . .
EEEEEEEEEeeeee . . .
EEEEEEeeee . . .

When the earsplitting comm interference ceased, Jimjoy was still squinting. Then he laughed.

The disruptions from the tacheads had destroyed his residual EDI track, and the *Greenpeace* was outbound, shuttered and without EDI emission. By the time L-5 control could get clear enhanced opticals, he would have jumped.

No matter that he'd probably require either a tow or a power transfer before getting far in-system at Accord. That he could handle.

He began setting up the jump coordinates. His mouth was still dry, and he reeked of sweat and fear. But he could set a homeward jump.

. . . LXXI . . .

"Commander Black, Perch two. We have lock-on. Estimate rendezvous in point two."

"Stet, two. Glad to see you." Jimjoy eased back in the cushions of the control couch, waiting for the space tug. He had his all-too-clammy vac suit on, except for the helmet, which he had on his shoulder straps.

"Not so glad as we are to see you. Someone promised to make life very hard on us all if . . ." Analitta didn't finish her sentence.

"I understand."

"By the way, interrogative success probability."

"Packages were all delivered. How the garden grows depends on the package designers." Jimjoy's voice was ragged, he realized. "Their scarecrows were a bit shocked at the delivery service. More later."

He checked the representational screen again, confirming the closure of Analitta's tug, then switched to visual. He could see only a dull silvery blot representing the *Percheron*.

Cling. The alarm signaled the end of the power reserves. With the reserves went the screens—and the air pressure. He pulled on his helmet and plugged in the belt jack to the ship's comm system.

"Holy drek. . . . Commander . . . any atmosphere there at all? Hull looks like a cheese grater. I've seen Swiss cheese with fewer holes."

"I'm suited."

". . . least he can't breathe vacuum. . . ." Jimjoy smiled at the voice from the *Percheron*.

"Don't be too sure," commented Analitta to the unknown speaker. "Hold tight, Commander. Commencing lock-on this time."

"Understand lock-on. Be careful of my cheese grater."

"Stet."

The *Greenpeace* shuddered as the magnetic locks brought the ships together.

"Perch one, leave your crew aboard."

"Interrogative your last, Commander."

"I'm slow, Perch one. We don't have a confirmation that some of my packages aren't still hanging tight. I'm walking across. Have a decontamination crew for my suit. Same for me. Send an inquiry to Narlian requesting advice."

"Oh . . ."

"Yeah . . ."

Jimjoy shook his head as he eased himself from the lock. While it wasn't likely that *anything* could have survived his departure from Old Earth, Narlian and Stilsen had engineered their cargo to take extremes of temperature and pressure, or lack thereof. And the *Greenpeace* might be better off in a terminal solar orbit, with a sure sterilization.

His feet touched the tug's hull, and he took step after careful step toward the main lock.

"Commander . . . Professor . . . ?"

"The same."

"Just step into the little lock. We'll flood it with a decon gas. Once the lock's clear, leave the suit and your clothes there. Dr. Narlian says there's nothing that you personally could carry."

"Narlian . . . she was waiting?"

"Waiting? She's been pacing around Thalos Station for the last twelve hours, biting off any head that came in range."

Jimjoy closed the lock, wondering how soon he could see Thelina, glad at least that this time he was a live coward, a sneak poisoner, a thief, what have you, rather than a hero.

He didn't look, smell, or feel like a hero, not surrounded with purplish decon gas in the lock of an ungainly space tug after abandoning a courier he'd turned into shredded metal.

He waited for the lock to clear, to begin the trip back to Thalos Station and, more important, back to Accord.

. . . LXXII . . .

12 Novem 3647
On-station

Dear Blaine:

Now it's my turn to be late in responding, but, as you noted in your last, all hades has broken loose.

Right after we got the media reports on the attack or whatever it was on Old Earth, activities here went crazy. Is it true that *something* got loose inside the L-5 picket line, pulled a double orbit, and made a right-angle ecliptic exit off the south pole? But no one is saying what happened . . . if anything.

The attack has been all over the media, but not the results. We've seen more close calls in the last week than in the previous year. They seem to be probing everywhere.

We've had two converter replacements since my last. Neither the ship nor I nor the crew is up to this for much longer, but all rotations have stopped, and we've even had some transfers. The squadron lost two ships for "redeployment." They won't say where, but everyone knows.

The problem is we're going to pay for it, now and not next year or the year after.

Haven't heard from Helen, but that's not surprising, since not even much official stuff is reaching us right now.

Have to close if I want to get this off, but see if you can do anything—I'll even take old needleboats!

Mort

. . . LXXIII . . .

The Admiral with the silvered-gold hair swallowed the two capsules and rubbed his temples.

"You're taking them too often," he reminded himself in a low voice.

His fingers reached for the screen controls, then paused. After a moment, he shook his head and called back the draft report, searching for the section that had troubled him, flicking down the lines.

". . . as demonstrated by the rapid success of the mutated core borers, the anchovy virus, the high-speed wheat rust . . . Ecolitan Institute has established capability to disrupt if not destroy . . . food chains . . . on any Imperial planet . . .

". . . independent confirmation by . . . Herbridge University Biotech Center . . . indicates genetic engineering capability to wage antipersonnel campaign . . . Directorate's excesses would be mild by comparison . . .

". . . Intelligence unable to pinpoint Ecolitan production facilities . . ."

The Admiral winced and rubbed his temples again before continuing. The words before him were almost a jumble, though he knew them nearly by heart.

". . . Fuards massing in Sector Nine. . . . stepped up production of new S.D. class vessels . . . restriction in public travel in the area of the three-system bulge . . .

". . . Halstani announcement of closing the University of Teresa's High Science Center to Imperial scientists . . ."

He focused in on the key paragraphs.

"Based on these factors, the Intelligence Service concurs with the recommendations of the Planning Staff and Fleet Development Branch. Military action against Accord—even if successful—will result in even greater casualties to Imperial Forces, staging bases, and personnel. More important, given the rapid mobilization of Accord and the desperation of its leaders, no military action against Accord is likely to prove successful without at least a three-fleet action.

"In addition, the single large fleet-action limitation established by the Defense Committee makes it extraordinarily difficult to guarantee success and could further weaken Imperial Forces. Finally, to date, the Accord Coordinate has used only a single ship to deliver biological weapons targeted against food chains. In any prolonged conflict, this restraint would not be continued.

"Under such conditions, the Fuardian Conglomerate could consider acquiring disputed boundary territories of greater value, both economically and strategically, than the Accord system.

"Therefore, the Intelligence Service strongly recommends against overt military action against Accord."

The Admiral rubbed his forehead and looked over his final recommendation again. "Damn you, Hewitt . . ."

With a sigh, he tapped the stud releasing his hold on the recommendation, then touched the comm settings. "Darkman . . . put our recommendations in final . . . send a copy to Planning . . . and leak it to the usual sources."

"Yes, Admiral."

The Admiral did not respond. His temples were throbbing, and it would be another four hours before he could take any more of the green capsules.

"Damn you, Hewitt . . ."

. . . LXXIV . . .

Outside, on the bedroom deck, a light covering of snow swirled in the gray morning. The sliding door rattled in its frame.

Jimjoy sat on the edge of the bed, formal greens on, kit bag by the door.

"I know. You have to go." Thelina sat beside him, silver hair tousled, wearing a faded green sweatsuit.

Jimjoy looked down. "I shouldn't have come at all, but . . ." His hand gripped hers too tightly.

"You were here only one day."

He grinned. "It was a good day."

She punched his arm. "You're impossible."

"I know. Takes that to stand up to you."

"You're really impossible."

Shaking his head, he stood up, not letting go of her hand and lifting her to her feet as well, drawing her to him, bringing her lips to his.

"Mmm . . ."

Finally he let her speak, not that she was struggling that hard. "Jimjoy . . ."

He waited, her head on his shoulder, his eyes fixed on the shifting clouds, not wanting to let go of her.

"Don't be a hero . . . we need you."

"Try not to do anything stupid," he whispered.

She stepped back, forcing his arms from her, and met his eyes. "Listen to me, will you? We need you. Not just me. Not just our child. All of us need you. The only reason I have to let you go is that your little fleet needs you to protect us. But every one of them would lay down their lives for you. If it comes to that, let them!''

"But—''

"Listen to me, you big dumb hero!'' Tears began to form at the corners of her eyes. "You're what holds it all together. You *have* to come back. Don't forget it.''

For a time that seemed forever and all too short, the two of them clung to each other.

"You'd better go . . . or I won't let you.''

"Suppose so.'' He ignored the burning in his eyes, touched her lips with his a last time, and stepped back. Then he picked up the kit bag.

They went down the stairs side by side.

. . . LXXV . . .

"Break out in corridor two," announced the pilot, her low voice crisp.

"Stet." Jimjoy wished he, and not Analitta, were at the controls of the *Adams* instead of overseeing the operation. But he was the closest thing the Coordinate had to an admiral, and the last thing he needed was to worry about the details. That alone was enough to make him shiver.

"EDI registers multiple breakouts," continued Analitta.

Jimjoy's combat screen confirmed her announcement. Three reddish lights pulsed, followed by a second set of even more intense lights. He recognized the formation. "Green forces, plan Beta blue. Plan Beta blue."

"Interrogative timing, Commander."

"Move it. Now!"

As the faint whine of the overhauled drivers began to build, the reengineered and renamed *Adams* swept toward the preselected position behind Donagir, the largest satellite of the system's sixth planet. Jimjoy began keying instructions for the five torps waiting in the ex-Fuardian destroyer's message tubes.

"Gilman?" Jimjoy's voice did not rise. His fingers completed the instructions and sent them to the five torps. He swallowed as he continued to track the EDI traces on the screen.

"Yes, ser." The apprentice's voice wavered.

The representational screen showed the five green sparks streaking from the *Adams* toward five separate points surrounding corridor two.

"Send a message torp—regular torp—to Thalos control. Tell

Imri the Impies have sent a full-fleet battle group. Down corridor two." He rechecked the screen. Eighteen red dots paraded down entry corridor two in a general V shape, aimed straight at Accord. Three were scouts, from the EDI profiles, followed by twelve corvettes and three battle cruisers.

Destroying the three capital ships was imperative. If necessary, Accord could survive anything the corvettes could throw. They weren't big enough to carry planet-busters. "Tell her to use evacuation plan two. Evacuation plan two."

"Yes, ser. Evacuation plan two for Thalos Station."

Jimjoy concentrated on the screen, wishing he were closer, without the data lag, but knowing that the four destroyers had to be saved for a better shot at the cruisers. He wiped his forehead with the back of his hand, waiting.

"On course to control point beta, Commander."

"Stet."

The first two green blips dropped from in-system jumps nearly on top of the lead scout. A third blip did not appear.

Jimjoy pulled at his chin. One needleboat down to the dust buildup—despite jumping in from above the ecliptic. The two green dots, half the size and intensity of the scout, closed on the Imperial ship. Abruptly, one green dot flared and vanished. The remaining needleboat continued to close.

This time the red dot flared and disappeared. The needleboat jumped off the screen.

Three more green dots appeared abreast of the corvette at the tip of the right wing of the Imperial formation, one appearing almost on the Imperial ship.

Jimjoy nodded, wondering how really close the needleboat had been.

"Time to station twelve plus."

"Thanks, Analitta."

All three of the green dots on the screen flared, as did the corvette they had bracketed.

"Hades . . ." Jimjoy wiped his forehead.

Beside him, Gilman took a noisy and deep breath as he calculated vectors and closures.

"Enemy continues to accelerate, Commander," the apprentice said.

Jimjoy smiled. If the Imperial commander continued that tactic . . . He pulled at his chin. Nothing was certain.

The Imperial battle group edged inside the dotted blue arc on the screen that signified the orbit of Rachelcars—planet eight.

Three more needleboats flicked out of the ecliptic at another corvette on the Imperial formation's left wing. A second corvette seemed to crawl toward the ship under attack to bolster the defense.

One needleboat disappeared—without the flare of destruction. Then a corvette toward the middle of the Imperial formation flared and vanished. At the same time both remaining needleboats flared and disintegrated under the fire of the two wing corvettes.

"What happened?" asked Gilman.

"Our boy jumped into the formation. Blind suicide shot. Took a corvette."

The seven pilots and their needleboats, and their hard-won electronics, from the Accord forces had cost the Imperials two corvettes and a scout.

At that rate, calculated Jimjoy, use of all sixty-one needleboats would still leave the three battle cruisers and three or four corvettes—more than enough to deliver the planetbusters carried by the cruisers.

"Gilman, forget the vectors. Get on the scramblers and see if you can find out their tactical wave freqs. They may not be using them yet. I'd be using tight-beam lasers."

"On the scramblers, ser."

"Thanks."

Jimjoy wished he could do it himself, but trying to anticipate what the Imperial fleet did next was more important. The relatively tight formation indicated their knowledge that Accord had no capital ships to speak of.

On the screen another pair of green dots materialized, back on the right flank of the Imperial fleet, this time each releasing a pair of torps, torps which flashed heavy dotted lines on the screen toward the rear-guard corvette.

Jimjoy held his breath. Each of the special torps carried double tacheads and a few associated leftovers from obsolete technology—a modification of the old X-ray laser. Jason had thought it might work once or twice—at least until the corvettes overlapped screens.

The blue dotted lines converged on the corvette.

The Imperial ship did not so much flash as fade off the screen. Jimjoy exhaled.

A single needleboat appeared above the Imperial right wing, the bluish tint on the screen indicating relative elevation, only long enough to launch another pair of torps before jumping.

"Negative on standing wave frequencies, ser."

"Keep at it, Gilman. Try and find a carrier near the orange."

"Yes, ser."

Jimjoy's eyes watched the special torps, realizing that the needleboat pilot had launched one toward the lead battle cruiser, on an angle between the guard corvettes. He shook his head. The cruiser's screens should be able to take that punishment.

The first torp flashed into another corvette, which glimmered, flashed on and off, then faded from the screen.

"Estimate three plus to station, Commander."

"Stet." Jimjoy watched as the second torp flashed against the lead cruiser's screens. The cruiser remained on the screen, but the dot image shifted from red to amber.

"Hades!" Jimjoy's hands flicked across the message torp controls, then to the command control. "Greenpax blue, target bulldog lead. Wedge one. Wedge one. Mark! Target bulldog lead. Immediate target. Immediate target."

"Targeting bulldog lead this time. Targeting lead."

Jimjoy's fingers clenched, then tapped the edge of the tactical screen as he watched the Imperial cruiser's image flicker from red to amber and back, clearly struggling to maintain screen integrity. Two Imperial corvettes began to move forward from the area of the trailing battle cruiser, as if to ward off further attacks.

Six green dots appeared in a wedge above the uppermost corvette on the leading right edge. The green wedge angled toward the struggling cruiser.

"On station, ser."

"Stet."

The lead needleboat launched two standard torps toward the single corvette between the wedge and the cruiser, then flared into oblivion.

The two needleboats now in the lead launched torps—standard torps—toward the corvette, whose screens flicked red-amber but held.

The leftward needleboat disintegrated under the return torps from the corvette, while a trailing needleboat launched a single special torp toward the corvette.

Jimjoy watched, his fingers tight around the edge of the screen controls, as the pair of Imperial corvettes continued to move forward to intercept the Accord wedge.

Abruptly, the single corvette between the wedge and the ailing cruiser faded from the screen under the impact of the special torp, but not before knocking out the needleboat which had launched it.

The four remaining needleboats in the wedge kept accelerating toward the battle cruiser, whose screens continued to flicker.

"Locked on carrier wave, ser. No transmissions."

"Put it on audio, Gilman." Jimjoy's eyes were locked on the screen as he began to calculate. Assuming the Imperial fleet commander realized Accord's apparent desperation and the Impies' limitations shortly . . . The figures appeared on the second screen.

He stopped for a moment to watch as two more needleboats vanished under the concentrated forces from the cruiser and one of the approaching corvettes. Then the two trailing needleboats launched four special torps—all at the cruiser—and jumped.

Jimjoy hoped they made it out as he watched the torps converge on the cruiser. He pulled at his chin momentarily. So far, Accord had lost at least twelve needleboats, possibly three more to dust/jump destruction. If he had counted correctly, only a handful of the beefed-up special torps remained.

"*Sssssssssssss* . . ." The low hum of the Imperial standing wave frequency punctuated the sudden silence as Jimjoy and his crew watched the Imperial battle cruiser flare into sudden oblivion.

"Greenpax blue, stand by for red charlie. Stand by for red charlie." Jimjoy was calling off the pick-off attempts, knowing the Imperial commander had realized he could not afford the losses of a standard approach.

"Hammerstrike, Hammerstrike, this is Radian Mace. Commence Omega Delta. Commence Omega Delta."

Jimjoy nodded, watching as the Imperial Forces drew closer together and began to accelerate, shifting slightly toward Accord itself, crossing the faint dotted line on the screen that represented the orbit of Eyres, the gas giant seventh planet. Eyres itself was on the other side of the sun.

The close-in screen showed the battle group around him—three other destroyers and ten needleboats.

Shortly, it would be their turn.

"Commander, status check. Thirty-four needleboats operational, four destroyers."

Jimjoy winced. The dust had done more damage than the Impies. But the needleboats couldn't stand and fight. That left in-system jumps.

He checked the screens. "Commence red charlie. Commence red charlie."

The Coordinate squadron slipped from behind Donagir and into an intercept course with the Imperial fleet.

Jimjoy continued to calculate, measuring the vectors and comparing the possible errors.

Then he began to reset the last set of sharp-stone drive control programs.

"Commander, Accord forces, this is Radian Mace. This is Radian Mace. Request your surrender to lawful Imperial authority. Request your surrender to lawful Imperial authority."

Jimjoy sighed.

"Saying anything, Commander?" asked Analitta conversationally.

"Should I?"

"Tell them to do the anatomically impossible."

Jimjoy grinned. Only Analitta would paraphrase swearing and still have it sound worse than the vulgar original.

"Radian Mace, this is Greenpax black. Request your departure from Coordinate space. Request your immediate departure from Coordinate space."

"Greenpax, this is Radian Mace. Without immediate and unconditional surrender, no terms are possible. I say again. Without immediate and unconditional surrender, no terms are possible."

"Radian Mace, Greenpax black. Concur. Without *your* immediate and unconditional surrender, no terms are possible."

For several long minutes, the Imperial frequency remained silent.

"Did you mean that, Commander?" Gilman finally whispered.

Jimjoy continued to watch and listen. He had more than meant it. Unless Accord could totally annihilate the Imperial Forces, their victory would not be convincing enough to persuade the Fuards of the Empire's weakness and to allow the I.S.S. to recommend granting Accord's independence.

"Greenpax, this is Radian Mace. Your position is unacceptable. Accord remains an Imperial colony. Request your immediate and unconditional surrender.''

"Radian Mace. We regret your last. So will you.'' Jimjoy regretted the flipness of his last transmission even as he spoke it. He took a deep breath and triggered the drive control commands for the sharp stones, wondering what the Imperials would think when three EDI traces appeared, indicating ships larger than the largest Imperial battle cruisers.

The screens indicated less than five minutes before his small fleet reached torp range to strike at the main body of the Impie fleet.

Three needleboats bracketed the lead Impie scout. A coruscation of torps, screens, and energy concentrations flicked back and forth. The scout and two needleboats disappeared.

Two more needleboats engaged the remaining scout. One needleboat and the scout vanished.

"Red charlie one. Red charlie one.''

Three of the remaining needleboats and two destroyers—the *Dinvair* and the *Wett*—created a wedge aimed at the rightmost of the battle cruisers.

Between the small Accord formation and the battle cruiser were four corvettes. One of the corvettes launched a series of torps. The *Dinvair* flicked its screens outward momentarily to deflect three of the torps. A single needleboat, unable to shake the remaining torp, jumped.

Jimjoy shook his head. Too high a dust density.

The *Wett* countered with two special torps. Both bypassed the corvettes, but dissolved against the battle cruiser's pulsed screens.

Jimjoy eyed the representational screen. The three large EDI tracks continued to close.

The Imperial Forces edged closer, bringing together the interlocking screens necessary to resist the X-ray laser torps and to keep the needleboat jump tactics from picking off another corvette.

"Target purple. Target purple.''

One corvette lagged in joining the Imperial formation, and the Accord wedge curved away from the main body and toward the corvette.

A hail of torps, several short-range laser pulses, and the isolated corvette's screens failed. Then the corvette disintegrated.

So did one more needleboat.

"Green frank. Green frank," ordered Jimjoy.

The Accord forces eased into an in-system course—a rough wedge formation on each side and ahead of the advancing Imperials, whose force concentration made the needleboats almost useless.

Only the two battle cruisers and six corvettes remained, but so long as they remained in the tight-globed formation, nothing short of suicide jumps from the destroyers was likely to penetrate the interlocked screens.

Nothing conventional, corrected Jimjoy. He checked the massive EDI traces.

"Twelve standard minutes until avalanche one," he announced to his own crew, not daring to broadcast the timing to the Imperials.

One of the wing corvettes showed some acceleration away from the center.

"Greenpax blue, target straggler. Target straggler."

One of the needleboats darted closer and released a single torp. The corvette's screens took care of the weapon, but the Imperial ship eased back into the interlocking screen protection.

The Imperial formation eased across the imaginary orbit line of Reelee—planet six. Two EDI-seeking torps peeled away from the battle cruiser and toward Donagir, the moon behind which Jimjoy had staged the Accord forces. Jimjoy hoped the research personnel had evacuated the station proper.

"Commander, the Impies are accelerating."

"Stet. Understand acceleration." He rechecked the calculations.

He couldn't understand why the Impies remained in formation, not with what appeared to be three giant battle vessels sweeping in toward them.

"Maybe they don't believe their screens," he muttered.

"They think we're bluffing?" asked Analitta.

"Less than three minutes. Then it won't make any difference."

He triggered the command circuit. "Green charlie. Green Charlie. EXECUTE GREEN CHARLIE."

All the Accord ships split away from the Imperial fleet at flank acceleration.

On the representational screen, for a full minute the Imperial fleet continued down entry corridor two unopposed.

Coming outbound on the entry corridor were three massive

green EDI tracks, each track an iron-nickel asteroid propelled by a fusactor-powered drive system.

Slowly, the Imperial ships started to spread away from the battle cruisers.

Jimjoy wanted to scream at the Impie officers, to tell them to forget order, forget discipline, to get the hades away from the oncoming asteroids.

The Imperials still seemed to regard the asteroids as a mere obstacle, as three corvettes and one cruiser edged leftward and the other corvettes and cruiser edged rightward—just as if the asteroids were nothing besides heavy and unwieldy lumps of metal.

Jimjoy continued to calculate, his finger on the override.

The figures matched—one minute and thirty standard seconds before the automatic triggers.

Jimjoy jammed the override. "Full shutters! Full shutters!"

Just before the shutters activated, Jimjoy could see a handful of dashed torp lines leaving one of the Imperial battle cruisers—not toward the Accord forces, but in-system.

"Hades . . ." He wished he knew their targets, not that it mattered now. From the distance they had been launched, the torps couldn't affect an atmosphered planet. Thalos Station, and the outspace research facilities, were another matter. He doubted the Impies had data on any locations except Thalos. He wiped his forehead, hoping Imri had completed evacuations of the vulnerable sections of the station.

Inside the *Adams*, all the displays showing exterior inputs went blank.

The Commander of the forces of the Coordinate of Accord wiped his forehead.

Gilman looked over at Jimjoy, then looked away.

"Permission to unshutter, Commander."

"Wait one, Captain."

"Standing by."

Jimjoy refigured the energy paths. "Clear to unshutter, Captain."

"Shutters down."

The representational screen displayed hundreds of objects where the Imperial fleet had been. All but two were clearly fragments of the three asteroids that had carried citybusters in their centers.

The two remaining Imperial ships were both corvettes, both

apparently shielded by the bulk of one of the battle cruisers. The screens of one were in the amber. The other looked untouched on the screen.

"Imperial ships, this is Greenpax control. Request your immediate surrender. Request your immediate surrender."

Jimjoy noted that the *Fitzreld*'s screens were also amber, another casualty, and two more needleboats were missing.

If they could get the two corvettes, that would be some help in rebuilding. He triggered the transmission on the Imperial frequency again. "Imperial ships, this is Greenpax control. Request your immediate surrender."

"Greenpax control, this is *Suleden*. Dropping screens this time. Dropping screens this time. Would appreciate medical assistance."

Jimjoy noted the corvette with the ailing screens had dropped them into standby.

"Stet, *Suleden*. Please stand by."

The second corvette, which had still not responded, began to step up acceleration toward Accord. In the confusion following the asteroid bombardment the corvette had continued to track in-system of the Accord forces.

"Hades!"

He touched the command circuit. "Greenpax blue, you have local control. Accommodate *Suleden*. Swersa, join up to Greenpax control. Greenpax needles"—he looked at the remaining clear needleboat numbers—"two seven, two nine, and four four, join to Greenpax control."

Swersa, Broward's former copilot, had command of the *Wett*.

"Captain, let's see if we can catch that bastard." Jimjoy again wished he were at the controls. Instead, he concentrated on the screen. The corvette couldn't destroy Accord, but even corvette tacheads could do a great deal of damage to places like Thalos and Harmony.

"Stet, Commander." Analitta already had the *Adams* in pursuit of the unnamed Impie corvette.

"*Suleden*, medical assistance arriving via needleboat."

Jimjoy nodded. Broward, coerced away from the *Roosveldt*, had the mop-up in hand.

The corvette had dropped screens to half power—just enough to hold off a single needleboat—and channeled screen power into drive energy, almost reaching needleboat speed in a mad dash toward Accord.

"Commander, request permission to cross-connect."

"Granted, Captain."

The *Adams* did not immediately gain on the corvette, but the gap began to narrow fractionally.

Jimjoy began running vectors and speed options through the taccomp.

"Needle two seven, interrogative torp status."

"Status green at point five."

"Two nine, interrogative torp status."

"Status green at point seven."

"Four four, interrogative status."

"Status green at point two."

The last pilot's voice rang familiarly. Luren. Somehow, he was glad she didn't have the most torps left.

"Two nine, request intercept on charlie target. Coordinates follow." He touched the laser tight-beam control, letting the taccomp send the data package.

"Greenpax control, coordinates received. Proceeding."

"Why, Commander?" asked Gilman.

Jimjoy took a deep breath, not moving his eyes from the screen as the needleboat began to race away from the *Adams*. "Because we need to slow him down before he can drop a half-dozen tacheads all over Accord." He wiped his forehead again.

On the screen the needleboat edged slightly off a straight stern chase and continued accelerating. Jimjoy nodded. It would take most of the needle's power to complete the maneuver, but even an unsuccessful attack should delay the corvette.

"Accord orbit control, this is Greenpax control. Single bandit charlie inbound this time."

Orbit control had three needleboats for a last-ditch defense, but Jimjoy doubted they would be necessary. The corvette seemed intent on reaching Accord itself, not orbit control.

The representational screen showed orbit control's full screens flicking into place. What it did not show was any EDI traces on Thalos. Again Jimjoy hoped that Imri had completed evacuations to the outlying stations. While the screens would prevent actual physical penetration, they would not prevent damage from second shocks and ground movement.

"Greenpax control, understand single charlie inbound this time."

"That's affirmative. Coordinates two seventy relative, orange, plus point zero two."

"We have charlie on screen. Good luck, control."

Jimjoy and Analitta watched the screens. Behind them, Broward took over the *Suleden* and continued to gather the scattered Accord forces. Before them, Accord grew in the screens.

Needleboat two nine, after pulling abreast of, then in front of, the corvette, continued to move in-system, almost to within multiple planetary diameters of Accord, before beginning a tight turn.

The Imperial corvette edged away from the needleboat, as if for an angled pass.

Jimjoy swallowed hard, visualizing the corvette's strategy, and hit the command circuits.

"Orbit control. Launch needles on north hemi swing to intercept torps. Coordinates and intercept parameters follow." His fingers managed to catch up with his words, and the taccomp burned a string of figures.

As he spoke, five torps flashed from the still-turning corvette toward Accord.

"Greenpax control, orbit control. Launching this time. Coordinates received. Intercept probability point five to point seven."

"Understand point five. Do what you can." Jimjoy shifted to the out-front needle. "Two nine, shift target to torps."

"Already shifting."

While he spoke, two torps flickered from the needleboat toward the corvette's citybusters, followed by a third torp, and a fourth.

One needle torp intersected one of the Imperial torps. A quick flash appeared on the screen.

"Commander . . ."

Jimjoy, catching the tone in Analitta's voice, refocused on the corvette, which had continued to turn back toward the *Adams*.

". . . he's head to head . . ."

"Hades." Jimjoy's forehead felt suddenly damp. Whoever turned first was most vulnerable to torps. Too late a turn and a laser punch was certain. But the Imperial pilot wasn't about to turn.

"Two until impact."

A green dot accelerated from beside the *Adams*, burning toward the corvette.

"Keep the faith, Commander." Luren's voice.

Jimjoy stared momentarily, protesting that the needleboat
would break on the corvette's screens.

"Oh . . ."

All the screens went black.

Jimjoy looked down at the blank plot board, fighting back the
tears no one would understand, swallowing before looking up,
quickly wiping his forehead and cheeks with his sleeve as if to
wipe the sweat alone off his face.

"What—" Gilman broke off as he looked at Jimjoy.

"She . . . jump-shifted . . ." mumbled Analitta.

"Right through his screens," finished Jimjoy. "Yeah . . . all
that kinetic energy . . ."

"Brave frigging lady."

Jimjoy nodded, swallowed, and stared at the blank screens.

As the screens returned to normal, Jimjoy noted that Luren
had been accurate. Very accurate. Not even a single fragment
remained of either ship.

"Where to, Commander?" Analitta had left the *Adams* heading toward orbit control.

"Thalos Station. We need to put her back together. See what
help we can provide. Build more needleboats—just in case." He
looked into the depths of the representational screen. "Just in case."

"Greenpax control, this is orbit control. Looks like we only
got one of the four that got here."

Jimjoy didn't like the sound of the ops officer's voice.

"Interrogative targets."

"Precise coordinates unavailable. Impacts projected at Harmony, plus or minus five kays, unknown point on the equator,
and Parundia City, plus or minus ten kays."

"Interrogative impact force." Jimjoy's voice was tired. It
could have been worse, but Harmony . . .

"Impact in Harmony area, estimate forty kaytee. No estimates
for other targets."

"Stet. Greenpax control proceeding Thalos Station. Return
needles to Accord control."

"Understand needles to remain Accord orbit control."

"That's affirmative this time. Have them restock and stand
down."

"Stet, Greenpax control. Congratulations, Commander."

"Don't . . ." Jimjoy caught his tongue. "Orbit control?"

"Interrogative, Greenpax control."

"Just . . . keep the faith . . . keep the faith . . ."

. . . LXXVI . . .

The smoke lingered over the area ahead, bitter, oily, with a char to it even weeks after the firestorm. The tall man, wearing only his undress greens despite the chill of the short winter days, walked toward the security perimeter.

"Ser, you can't go there—ser! HALT!" The sentry, scarcely old enough to have finished secondary school, lifted the stunner rifle.

The silver-haired man stopped and turned, fixing his green eyes on the young civil guard. "I beg your pardon?"

"Ser—that is—" stammered the girl.

"I know. I know," answered the Ecolitan as he stepped closer. "I've been away." In a lower tone, he added, "For too long."

She stepped closer, close enough that for an instant the plumes of white they exhaled in the cold air touched.

The worn greens caught the sentry's eyes, as did the single gold-and-green triangle on the man's collar.

"Ser . . . I'm sorry." Her eyes flicked just away from meeting his, as if she were inspecting his shoulder. "I didn't recognize you."

"That's more than all right. I won't cross the perimeter. I'd just like a last look." He paused. "Why don't you come with me?"

She looked around, as if to see whether anyone were watching.

"I doubt if it matters now, young lady. The biologic teams start in first thing in the morning."

Jimjoy began to walk toward the iridescent red plastic strip—

held waist-high by a line of wooden stakes—that encircled the stricken area.

"Yes, ser." But she still looked back over her shoulder as she followed him. Behind them, uphill, was the abandoned Regency hotel. With a good section of central Harmony, it would be coming down in the days ahead.

The stone-paved street continued—rubble-strewn—beyond the thin warning line, marking the residual radiation barrier, down toward the dark, water-filled, unnatural lake that still steamed. Beyond the barrier, little was recognizable.

There had been mastercraft shops—places like Waltar's, where Jurdin had set out the picnic set developed from the one he had made for Jimjoy, or Daniella's, or Christina's, the little bakery he had always enjoyed. Now there was charred wood, if that, seared stone, and lingering radiation.

Farther down, at the blast center, where the old Government Square had been, was the unnatural lake whose murky waters steamed in the winter air.

Dr. Narlian declared she could decontaminate the whole place, and she probably would, Jimjoy reflected.

Beside him, the young sentry said nothing, looking nervously at the destruction, then behind them, then at the tall, silver-haired man with the green eyes that seemed black.

Jimjoy took a deep breath, still looking downhill at the ruins. Had he delayed on Thalos just on the excuse of rebuilding the Accord forces?

"Ser?"

"Yes, young lady?"

"Pardon me. . . . Are you . . . ?"

"For better or worse, Jimjoy Whaler—sometime Professor at the Institute—onetime Defense Commander of the Coordinate." He did not wait to see the possible distaste in her eyes and turned his glance back to the destruction he had failed to prevent. He should have developed an evacuation plan for Harmony. But he hadn't. He had only thought in terms of preventing the planet's destruction.

The odds said he had done well. Odds weren't towns. Odds weren't people. People like Jurdin Waltar, like Daniella, or Geoff Aspan, or Luren. Luren, whom he had saved once only to sacrifice again.

"Ser?"

He repressed a sigh, waiting for the inevitable question.
"Yes?"

"Thank you."

"For what?" He kept his voice soft. For what, young lady?
For losing over forty needleboats and their pilots? For provoking
a war that could have lasted forever and destroyed the most
promising culture produced yet?

"Just . . . for being there. For doing what had to be done."

Jimjoy turned to the youngster. "Aren't those just words?"

"No, ser. I heard you talk to the Council. I heard them talk
for hours afterward. They were afraid to say anything. They
were afraid to act. Sometimes, somebody has to act. . . . Sorry,
ser. I didn't mean . . ."

Jimjoy touched her shoulder gently. "You're right, and you're
wrong. Have to act, but it always costs more." He gestured
downhill. "They don't care, not when they're dead."

"Will you do it again—if the Empire comes?"

Jimjoy shrugged. "I could lie. I won't. I'll do it again, only
so no one else has to." Then he laughed. "Sounds so frigging
noble. I'm not."

He turned and walked back uphill.

"Ser?"

"I'm on duty. Good-bye."

"Good-bye . . . and thank you. . . . Again."

"For?"

"Like you said . . . for being here."

He began to walk toward the groundcar that would take him
to the shuttleport and to the flitter to the Institute.

. . . LXXVII . . .

28 Novem 3647
New Augusta

Dear Helen:

I wish I could be with you and the children now, or that I could have been the one to break the news. I've put this off longer than I should have, and I know that a medal—even the highest honor bestowed—is cold consolation for a man like Mort.

Mort was right, and he fought for what was right. He fought knowing he didn't have the best ship and knowing that he'd been betrayed in a lot of ways by the government he supported. Because he gave everything and more, I've done something that maybe you wouldn't like, and maybe you would. I don't know, but I couldn't take the thought that Mort faced down a pair of brand-new Fuardian cruisers for nothing.

You may have seen it already, but right after the report came in, I gathered up all the faxcubes Mort had sent me, and everything else I could lay my hands on, and with a little help I wheedled an appointment with the Privy Council. I laid everything out—Mort's tapes, the maintenance failures, Graylin's resignation (he resigned because they refused to listen on either the Accord fiasco or the failure to build adequate ships to deal with the Fuards), and some other matters. I told them what Mort's death meant. The Council took it to the Emperor. That was what led to his speech to the people. Even if he didn't get Mort's name right, it was important that Mort got the credit.

Some people are claiming I did it to get Graylin's job. I won't turn it down if it's offered. I don't think Mort would have wanted me to refuse. I didn't do it to get Mort a medal, and I didn't do it to get me a job. I did it because the problems won't go away by ignoring them. I did it because men and women like Mort need better ships.

We're going to get the CX. It's too late for these fights. The Fuards have the three-system bulge, and we'll have to accept some sort of terms from Accord. We don't have the ships or the technology. But we can when Jock or Cindi enters the Academy—if they choose to. That's up to them, but because they're children of a man who won the Emperor's Cross, their admission is automatic. Perhaps they'll reject the Service. I hope not, because we need them.

I wish I could offer more comfort, more warmth. You and Mort had so much, and I always looked at you two in awe. I've tried to do what I can, to give some meaning to what Mort had to do, and I hope you understand.

Blaine

. . . LXXVIII . . .

From the copilot's seat, Jimjoy took a deep breath, exhaling, trying to get the stench of burned wood, charred flesh, and death from his nostrils. He hated to think of the immediate aftermath of the attack. The situation on Thalos had been bad enough—with just secondary damage.

On Accord itself, the casualties had been the western half of Harmony, the equatorial marine research station, for whatever reason, and Parundia Town proper. The Institute had been spared.

Just from one corvette with a few remaining tacheads. He shuddered, thinking how little would have been left had battle cruisers gotten through.

A flash of light seared across the western horizon, visible even in the bright winter sun.

"Know what that was, Professor?" asked Kursman.

"Oh, that? Suspect it was either a large chunk of former spacecraft or a sharp-stone remnant."

"Sharp stone?" questioned the pilot.

Belatedly realizing he had never briefed the planetside Ecolitans on the details of the space defenses, Jimjoy shook his head slowly, then pulled at his chin. "A chunk of one of the asteroids we threw at the Imperial fleet."

"Oh . . ."

Still smelling death in his nostrils, despite the airflow through the cockpit, Jimjoy let the subject drop.

As the Institute appeared in the flitter's front windscreen,

Kursman eased the nose back, bleeding off airspeed, and began rotor deployment.

Thwop . . . thwop, thwop . . .

"Greenpax ops, Prime one, on final descent this time."

Jimjoy glanced at the final lineup, noting that Kursman was not lined up for the flitter area, but for the open grass opposite the main Administration building.

More unusual was the small crowd of Ecolitans gathered here.

He looked again, realizing that the crowd was not nearly so small, perhaps several hundred people—all in green.

He looked over at Kursman, but the pilot appeared intent on making the landing, and with the westward approach and the sun cascading across the dark helmet visor, Jimjoy could only make out a determined set to the young pilot's jaw.

Jimjoy shifted his glance to the instruments, relieved that Kursman was on target for a letter-perfect approach.

The last thing he wanted was a welcoming committee, especially after the carnage in Harmony and the destruction of Thalos topside. At least he'd had enough sense to order the evacuation to the outlying Thalos facilities. That had held down the casualties there. You couldn't evacuate an entire planet, but he should have thought of Harmony. He should have. It was the only real target on all Accord—except for the Institute.

Thwop, thwop, thwop. . . . The increasing volume of the rotors brought his attention back to the flitter and the waiting crowd. He had sent a message to Thelina, not to the entire Institute, hoping to see her first, to explain.

He pulled at his chin and straightened in the copilot's seat as Kursman executed a perfect flair and touchdown in the center of the grass patch before the Administration building.

"We're here, ser," Kursman turned to Jimjoy, a wide grin on his face, even before starting the shutdown checklist. "I'll get us shut down as quickly as possible."

Jimjoy nodded and looked beyond the rotor blade path at the crowd. He thought he saw Thelina, tall, silver hair swirled by the rotor wash, in the small subgroup closest to the flitter. He slowly pulled off his helmet.

Thwop, thwop . . . thwop . . . thwop . . . The rotors came to a halt.

"Shutdown complete, ser."

Jimjoy slid open his door and stepped out into the silence, glancing from one side of the crowd to the other, catching one set of eyes, then another. All of them were waiting. He almost shrugged, instead raised his hand in greeting, knowing there was nothing he could say. Nothing at all.

The silence persisted, except for a few whispers, as he started toward Thelina. With her were Meryl, Elias, Dr. Narlian, and a man he did not recognize at first. He thought, then remembered. Clarenz Hedricht, the Council Chairman. Obviously, he hadn't been in Harmony when the tachead hit.

The group stepped forward toward him.

Jimjoy focused on Thelina, whose face remained almost impassive, and whose tunic seemed too tight in front. She carried a small carved box.

Regardless of the crowd that began to curl around to see what was happening, Jimjoy wanted to run to her, to hold her.

Her eyes reached him, and she mouthed, ''No. Not now.''

The group of four stopped. Since it was clearly expected of him, he stopped, too. They couldn't be doing this, he thought. Not now.

"James Joyson Whaler." Meryl's voice was pitched to carry to the entire group. "You have put action above ceremony. Results above position. You have never spared yourself in following your principles. You have set an example for all future Ecolitans.

"Today, following that example of avoiding ceremony, of doing what should be done, we are gathered together. We declare that for your example, for providing leadership when all Accord needed leadership, for inspiring and motivating all people, and for bringing freedom to the entire Coordinate, the Institute's electors, the Ecolitans of Accord, officially recognize what has long been unofficially known.

"Welcome home, Prime Ecolitan Whaler."

Jimjoy did the only thing he could. He bowed his head momentarily to accept the tribute, then raised his face to Thelina and the crowd, letting the tears fall where they would as Thelina stepped forward and placed the single gold pin on his chest, a golden triangle within a green circle.

"Sam's?" he whispered.

She nodded.

His hands held her elbow to keep her from stepping back. "I'm no hero, and I came back, and I love you."

He could see the tears in her eyes, and instead of releasing Thelina, he pulled her to him, gently, not wanting to let go, feeling every curve of her against him, including the new one, the one that would be named Geoff or Luren.

A sigh seemed to come from the crowd.

"All right," whispered Meryl. "A little is understandable, but . . ."

Jimjoy tightened his grip on Thelina, then let go, linking her arm in his and turning to face the Ecolitans, his chosen people.

He raised his arm again and smiled, and began to walk with Thelina toward the future.

. . . EPILOGUE . . .

"Summary:

"Detailed psyprofile comparison between Wright, Jimjoy Earle, III, and Whaler, James Joyson, II:

"Initial physical parameter comparisons, based on updated analysis of Ecolitan Institute capabilities [see H-G, sec. 32], indicate a physiological congruency range of 73% - 94%.

"Psychological analyses, including statistical correlation of surface carriage indices, Mahaal-Pregud overlays, and Aaylward Socionormic Scores, indicate a congruency range below 45%, equivalent to environmental/genetic similarities or cultural congruency of point five on the Frin Scale.

"In numerous recorded observations, Whaler's actions— accepting the sacrifice of two other needleboats, entering a permanent marital contract, and displaying visible emotion— signifying a significantly less sociopathic and a more emotional personality than that of Major Wright . . .

"Conclusion:

"Despite conflicting evidence {see Appendices I–IV}, direct and indirect psychological evidence, DNA-matched physical remains, and an absolute match of implanted Imperial identification tags confirm the death of the following Imperial officer:

"Jimjoy Earle Wright III
Major, I.S.S./S.O./B-941 366."

—*Termination Records*
Vol. XL (3646–3648 I.E.)

GORDON R. DICKSON

MORE FROM GORDON R. DICKSON